Lincolnshire
COUNTY COUNCIL

Working for a better future

discover libraries
This book should be returned on or before the due date.

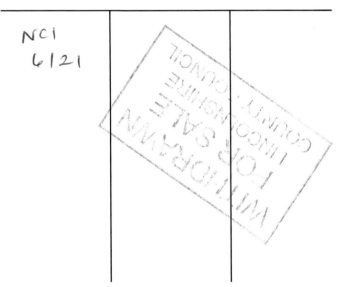

NCI
6121

To renew or order library books please telephone 01522 782010
or visit https://lincolnshirespydus.co.uk
You will require a Personal Identification Number
Ask any member of staff for this.
The above does not apply to Reader's Group Collection Stock.

EC. 199 (LIBS): RS/L5/19

just for fun

escape to new zealand book four

ROSALIND JAMES

ISBN: 0988761939
ISBN 13: 9780988761933

author's note

The Blues and the All Blacks are actual rugby teams. However, this is a work of fiction. Names, characters, places, and incidents are products of the author's imagination or are used fictitiously and are not to be construed as real. Any resemblance to actual events or persons, living or dead, is entirely coincidental.

table of contents

new zealand map

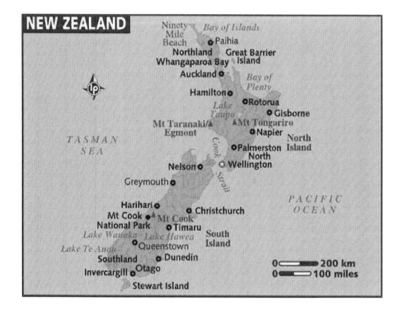

Note: A New Zealand glossary appears at the end of this book.

gobsmacked

♡

Nic Wilkinson wasn't looking to change his life. He just wanted to go home. Instead, he quit watching where he was going, stepped in a puddle, and swore. It had rained the night before, and this part of the field was still muddy. The hundred or so boys gathered for the last day of Rob Euliss's rugby camp weren't helping a bit. They'd churned up the grass good and proper this week, Nic saw with disgust as he felt the water squelch inside his shoe. This wasn't his idea of a fun way to spend a Sunday morning during a rare bye week. The kids were OK. He wasn't always too keen on the parents, though.

But Rob was a neighbor, and a mate. Anyway, when a legendary former All Black asked a favor, you didn't say no. So here he was, trying to avoid the rest of the muck around the edge of the enormous field that made up the North Harbour Rugby Club, and preparing to do his duty.

He squinted around the clusters of boys playing their final matches of the Easter-week camp under the watchful eyes of volunteer coaches and a sprinkling of dads who'd been pressed into service. He finally spotted the still-imposing figure of Rob, issuing impatient instructions to a hapless dad, and made his way toward the pair.

"Get them to stay onside," Rob was barking at the harassed-looking volunteer, intimidating the poor bloke with his trademark volcanic frown. "They know better."

Nic waited until the chastened dad took himself off, then offered, "Morning, Rob."

"Nico. You took your time," Rob grumbled. "I said ten."

"Sorry. Claudia wasn't rapt about my plan for the day. Where do you want me?" Nic could see a few of his Blues and All Black teammates, each surrounded by a little knot of starstruck boys, their parents hovering close. "I'll help out here, if you like."

"Don't want to meet the mums, eh. Don't blame you. Stay with me a minute, then. I'll find a spot to pop you into."

They fell silent, watching the boys in front of them play. "Second year?" Nic asked, watching as a pass fell uncaught at a small pair of feet.

"Yeh. Six," Rob answered briefly.

"That one's good," Nic remarked as a boy from the opposing team picked up the ball, made two defenders miss with his abrupt changes of direction, then passed the ball accurately behind him to a teammate who dove across the line for a try.

"Yeh. Got a boot on him, too. Can't use that in Rippa, of course. But he'll be making his mark in a few years," Rob said. "Hell of a kick."

"Some talent there," Nic agreed as the boy darted in, on defense now, and ripped an opposing player's flag from his belt. "Fast-twitch fibers, I reckon. Reminds me of someone. Somebody's kid?"

Rob looked at him oddly. "You. Who he reminds you of, I mean. Good pair of hands, reflexes. And a boot as well. They usually aren't much chop at this age, but he's different. Been watching you, I'd say. Got your moves. Even has a bit of a look of you. They're about done here. Stay here and you can see for yourself, when you do your meet and greet."

It was on them soon enough. The boys crowded around, offering up mud- and grass-stained backs for autographs. Nic signed jerseys with the Sharpie Rob wordlessly handed him, offered a bit of chat to the kids. The boy with the skills, he saw, hung back a bit, waiting for the crowd to thin, his eyes on Nic. A good-looking kid, straight dark blond hair getting a bit long over the forehead and at the back.

The boy came forward at last, turned his back. "Can you sign huge?" he asked. "I want yours to be the biggest."

"Can't turn that down, can I," Nic answered good-humoredly. "There. Straight across. Nobody'll miss that."

"Thanks." The boy stood aside as Nic signed the jersey of a boy with a comical, mobile face and a mop of wild red curls.

"I saw you hurt your leg last week," the blond boy offered as Nic finished. "Has it got any better? Will you be able to play in South Africa?"

"Not too bad," Nic assured him. "Bit of a crocked thigh, that's all. Be right as rain by Saturday." Which wasn't strictly true, but it was the kind of niggle you expected, midway through the season.

"Would you run, though, normally?" the boy asked hesitatingly. "When you have a bye like this, I mean? If you weren't injured? On your days off?"

"Yeh, I would," Nic answered.

"See, Graham. Told you," the blond boy said triumphantly to his redheaded friend. "Graham said you just rested. But I said you have to keep training, if you really want to be good."

"You're right," Nic said. "Plenty of blokes with talent. You have to have more than that, if you want to make it to Super level. Takes a fair bit of discipline. Do you do some training yourself, then? You're pretty good."

The boy flushed with embarrassed pride. "Yeh. I run before school, lots of days. With my mum. She likes to go too," he hurried on to explain. "Not because she has to take me."

"Good on ya. You've got a pretty fair boot, too, Rob tells me. What's your name?"

"Zack. Zack Martens."

"Good to meet you." Nic shook the offered hand. Manners, he saw. "And who's this?"

"Graham MacNeil," the redhead said, offering his own hand and turning a violent shade that clashed with his carroty hair.

"Well, Graham, your mate's right. Do all the running you can. You boys better get off and get some more signatures on those jerseys, though. Ben over there looks like he's about to pack it in."

"C'mon, Zack," Graham urged.

"Thank you for signing," Zack said politely. Dark brown eyes fringed with long, thick lashes looked shyly up at Nic's own before the boy turned to run off with his friend.

"Nice kid, that Zack," Nic told Rob a bit later from the middle of another group of kids.

"Got a nice mum, too," Rob said, nodding toward a group of parents on the sideline. "Quite pretty. Think she's single, too. Most of them don't show up without a dad, the last day."

"You old goat," Nic chided him. "Lucky I don't tell Rebecca."

"Still got a pair of eyes, haven't I," Rob countered. "That one there, see? Kind of blonde. The small one. Tell me I'm wrong."

Nic looked where Rob was gesturing. Suddenly his sodden feet seemed to be sending a chill straight through his entire body. He saw Zack again, excitedly showing off his newly collected autographs to the slim, graceful figure bending towards him. The honey-blonde hair was shorter now, but her curls still fell around her face in the way he remembered. She straightened, turned. And stood stock-still at the sight of him.

He wasn't more than twenty meters away, but she moved fast. With a quick word to Zack, she'd melted behind the group of parents and was lost in the taller crowd within moments.

Nic stood, gobsmacked. He recovered his wits as another group of boys crowded around him, signed jerseys and rugby balls mechanically, offered encouraging words, but kept an eye out all the while for that slight figure. He didn't see her again, though. And to his frustration, by the time he could look for her properly amidst the thinning crowd, she was gone.

♡

Rob was issuing more instructions to the volunteers who were helping to round up equipment. He turned, though, at a hand on his elbow. "Still here, mate?" he asked in surprise. "Thought you'd left with the rest of them."

"Need to ask you a question," Nic said. "I need to know something about that kid. Zack."

"Rightyo, then." Rob was surprised, but agreeable. "Hang on a tick while I finish up here. Or better yet, give us a hand."

Fifteen minutes later, he was packing file folders into a carrier bag inside the Rugby Club's office. "Now," he said, "what did you need? Are the Blues scouting them that young now?"

"Zack Martens." Nic brushed the joke aside. "You said he was six. When's his birthday?"

"Why? You planning on sending him a present? Too late, I reckon. He's one of the young ones. Just turned six, I think. That's what surprised me about the skills. They usually can't even offload worth a damn that young, let alone kick like that."

"His birthday," Nic insisted. "When is it?"

Rob sighed. "Hang on, then." He pulled a ring binder from the bag he'd been loading, found the sheet. "February fifteenth. Barely made it under the cutoff. Happy now?"

Nic felt his mouth go dry as he subtracted in his head, saw those dark eyes again, raised to his own. The way they turned down at the outer corners to give him a sleepy look, fringed by lashes his mum had always said were wasted on a boy.

"I need his mum's address," he told Rob.

"Mate. You know I can't give you that." Rob was puzzled now, and a bit alarmed as well. "What's this all about? Better not be something about you I don't know."

"Don't be bloody stupid," Nic said impatiently. "I need his mum's address. Emma's address. Because that's my son."

an unexpected visitor

♡

Emma pulled the parking brake with a jerk and pressed the button to unlock the doors. The ancient Nissan seemed to be running a little rough, she thought worriedly. She really couldn't afford a repair bill, not this month. But that bit of hesitation wasn't going to improve by itself, and she didn't need a breakdown on the Harbour Bridge.

"Can you grab a grocery bag, please?" she asked Zack. She didn't like having to stop again after picking him up from childcare, when they were both tired. But she hadn't realized he'd eaten the last of the bread until she'd gone to make his sandwich this morning. It seemed like he ate more all the time, and he was still only six.

She'd been too distracted yesterday to notice the state of her pantry, that was the truth of it. Had Nic got a good look at her? She didn't think so. It didn't matter anyway, she reminded herself firmly. He'd made his feelings clear a long time ago. He'd sure taken his time chatting to Zack, though. Her son and Graham had talked of little else during the drive home the day before. Nic hadn't realized who Zack was, obviously, or he wouldn't have bothered. Or, more likely, would have taken himself off in the opposite direction, as fast as those speedy legs could carry him.

She gathered her purse, gym bag, and the remaining groceries and finally stepped away from the car, shifting the heavy load and feeling the lumpy green fabric bags bang against her knees. Zack struggled along with his own backpack and bag as they climbed the steep driveway together in silence. Until Zack stopped dead at the sight of the tall, dark-haired figure perched on the steps leading to the main house.

"Nic." Emma stared at him stupidly, unable to process his presence. "What are you doing here?"

"Came to see you." None of his famous self-possessed good humor was visible as Nic rose to his feet. The well-formed mouth was grim, his expression set, and there was no humor in the dark eyes that stared into hers.

"Cool," Zack breathed. "D'you want to see our flat?"

"Yeh." Nic looked down at the boy, his face relaxing a bit. "Yeh, I do."

"Come on," Zack said. "I'll show you my room." He led the way around the side of the building on the concrete path, down the few utilitarian steps to the wooden door that was the entrance to their ground floor flat at the back of the house.

Emma followed behind, her mind racing, as man and boy stepped aside to allow her to unlock the door. Nic reached for the bags of shopping, and she surrendered them reluctantly. She didn't want to let him in, didn't understand why he had come, but she didn't know how to avoid it, either. And Zack wasn't helping.

"We can put the shopping down here," Zack said excitedly. It was only a few steps to the kitchen doorway, and inside to the small table where they ate. "Then I can show you my room."

"In a minute," Nic told him. "I need to talk to your mum first."

"You can have your bath, Zack," Emma decided. "I'll run it for you now. By the time you're done, Nic will be ready for his tour."

"Promise you won't leave first." Zack looked at Nic beseechingly.

"I won't leave," Nic assured him. "Come get me when you're clean."

"Wait here, then," Emma told Nic helplessly. "I'll be a few minutes."

♡

Nic was sitting on the small slipcovered couch in the tiny lounge, frowning absently at the painted coffee table, but stood as Emma reappeared from the little hallway that led to the bedrooms and bath.

"Come into the kitchen," she said warily. "Since you're here." She took a deep breath, tried to calm her racing heart, to still the anxiety that rushed through her, threatened to overwhelm her. Nic, in the flesh. The solid, *hard* flesh. Taking up way too much space in her flat.

"Do you want something to drink?" she asked as she waved him to a chair at the kitchen table. "I don't have much, I'm afraid. Water? Juice? Cup of tea?" She snapped her mouth shut on the words. Why was she trying to make him comfortable? Because she felt so uncomfortable herself, she supposed.

"Cup of tea, thanks."

She could feel his eyes on her as she pulled bread and milk from the grocery bags and moved to put them away. She was aware of a pang of embarrassment for the modesty of the little room. No dishwasher, just the ancient faucet over the dented stainless-steel sink. Nothing new or flash here. Nothing like the house he shared with his fiancée, which she'd seen profiled in the *Herald* only a couple months ago. How she'd envied that big, gleaming, modern kitchen—although she'd wondered if anybody had ever prepared a meal in it.

Well, whose fault was it that he had all that, and she had only this? She had nothing to be ashamed of, she reminded herself fiercely. She switched the electric jug on, then turned and leaned against the bench, her hands gripping the tiled edge behind her. "Why are you here, Nic? What's this all about?"

"What d'you think? I met Zack. Then I saw you, and I knew. He's mine. Isn't he?"

She stared at him. "Are you trying to pretend you didn't know? That this is the first you've heard of him? I'm going to ask you again. What's this all about?"

He shook his head as if trying to clear his ears. "What?" he asked in obvious confusion. "Of course I didn't know. How was I supposed to know? You didn't tell me."

She looked at him a moment longer, searching his face for the truth, then turned at the sound of the water boiling, busied herself fixing the cups. She really had become a Kiwi, she thought briefly. She was completely discombobulated, so she was making tea.

By the time she had turned around again, she had herself back under control. "I think we need to start over. Yes. He's your son. And I did tell you. But you didn't want anything to do with him. Are you trying to tell me that didn't happen? Because I can show you the letters. Refresh your memory."

"I think you'd better."

"Fix the tea, then."

She left the room abruptly, and he found the milk and sugar, prepared his own mug. He paused as he tried to remember what she took in hers. How could he have forgotten that, when he remembered so much? The way she'd looked that last morning, pulling herself up in the big bed, wrapping her arms around him to kiss him goodbye, her eyes huge and soft, mouth swollen from an early morning of lovemaking.

Her face was as pretty as ever, the broad forehead and cheekbones together with the pointed chin giving her the same adorable kitten look that had captivated him from the beginning. But there was a wariness about her now, as if the kitten had found the world to be a more hostile place than she'd expected. And none of the softness he remembered when she turned those big blue eyes on him.

He heard her talking to Zack, the sound of the water beginning to run from the tub before she came back to join him, a slim manila folder in her hand.

"We need more time to talk about this," he told her. "Could I take you somewhere?"

"I don't want to talk in front of Zack," she said.

"Can't he stay here for a bit? Or go outside and play, or something?"

She looked at him aghast. "He's *six*, Nic. What do you want me to do, send him down to the pub? I need to make dinner, anyway. Maybe we should talk about this another time." She pulled her hair back from her face in a tired gesture he'd never seen.

"How about if I go for a takeaway," he suggested. "Eat it with you, and we can talk once Zack goes to bed."

"All right," she agreed reluctantly. "I guess it's better to do it now. And I don't have enough to feed you, too."

Zack appeared in the kitchen doorway, dressed in a pair of faded All Black pajamas that drooped over his hands and feet. "You aren't leaving, are you?" he asked Nic anxiously when he saw him standing. "You said you'd come see my room."

"Just going for a takeaway," Nic assured him. "I'll see your room afterwards, I promise. Chinese OK?" he asked Emma.

"Fine," she answered distractedly. "Not too spicy for Zack, though," she added as an afterthought. "Chicken and vegetables. Something like that."

"See you both in half an hour, then," he promised.

He was afraid she wouldn't open the door to him on his return. He wondered what he was doing, planning on sitting down to dinner with her. He'd been so angry when he'd realized what she'd done, his first impulse had been to go straight to his lawyer. But in the end, he'd decided to talk to her first. Claudia hadn't seemed too fussed at his being out this evening, luckily. She had to work late as well, she'd told him. He wondered now why he hadn't told her about Zack. Well, he hadn't been sure the boy was his, had he?

Yes, he had, he admitted to himself. The birthday. Those eyes. And most of all, the way he'd moved. He'd known from the moment he'd seen him on the field, some flash of recognition. But he wanted to learn more before he discussed it with Claudia. She had a way of looking at you, so calm, so sure. He was so unsure himself just now, he wanted it straight in his own mind before he shared the news with her.

Emma had changed out of her work clothes during his absence, he saw when she opened the door. She was wearing some kind of lacy light blue pullover over a pair of worn, faded jeans that clung to her slim legs. With the makeup washed off, she looked more like the girl he remembered. Softer. Younger. And her feet were bare, narrow, the long toes with their nails painted pink. He felt his pulse give a kick in spite of himself when he saw the silver toe ring.

She had literally made his own toes curl, he remembered. He had a quick vision of how she'd looked, one afternoon when he'd come back to the *bure* after a swim. On her back, her head toward the foot of the bed, legs up against the wall, slim ankles crossed as she read a paperback. And that silver toe ring. She'd been wearing a little dress that had fallen down around her hips to reveal her bare legs. But she hadn't been wearing it for long. And she'd looked so good when he'd pulled it off, had shivered under his hand.

He forced his mind back to the present, smiled down at Zack. "Chicken and veggies, as promised. Beef, too. But I brought some potstickers as well, because they're my favorites."

"Mine too!" Zack said happily. "Potstickers are yum!"

"You have good taste, it's clear. Eating in the kitchen?" he asked, got a nod from Emma in return.

"Water OK?" Emma asked him as they sat down to eat, indicating the glass at his place.

"You don't have a beer, I suppose."

"Sorry."

"You used not to be averse to a beer, as I recall. Or the odd bottle of wine."

"Expensive," she said briefly.

"OK." He turned to Zack. "So tell me about your team. Playing Rippa, eh. They didn't have that when I was a kid."

"You tackled?" Zack asked, eyes wide.

"Yeh." Nic smiled. "We tackled. Think it's better now. Nine's soon enough to start getting bashed in the head."

"I guess," Zack said doubtfully. "I *want* to tackle, though. And I want to kick," he added fiercely. "I really want to kick."

"Rob said you had a boot," Nic agreed, spooning out another large serving of beef and vegies. Zack had a good appetite, he saw, but Emma ate as little as ever. Or maybe she was just nervous. She was certainly glancing anxiously between the two of them.

"I want to get better, though," Zack told him, oblivious to his mother's tension. "I want to kick like you. I want to play fullback, too. We only play seven on a side in Rippa, you know. I can't wait to be nine."

"It'll come soon enough," Nic said.

"That's what everyone says," Zack sighed.

"Maybe you'd like to practice some kicking with me," Nic suggested.

"Really?" Zack asked, eyes wide. "Would you help me?"

"Nic," Emma cautioned. "Wait."

She turned to her son. "We need to talk about it," she told Zack, "Nic and I. Let's make sure he really has time to help you before you start getting excited. Finish your dinner. If you want to show Nic your room before bedtime, you need to hustle up."

Zack gave her a chastened look, then dropped his eyes back to his plate, began to eat again.

Nic started to say something, stopped at a warning glance from Emma. He finished the rest of his own meal in a few more bites, looked across at the boy. "Ready, mate?"

"May I be excused, Mum?" Zack asked.

"Sure."

Zack carried his plate and glass carefully to the sink, stood on a small stepstool to place them inside. He turned back to Nic and said, "You need to clear your place. It's the rules."

"Zack," Emma protested. "Nic's a guest. He doesn't have to clear his place."

"No worries." Nic took his own dishes across and set them with Zack's. "I like to follow the rules. Let's go."

"Wait." Emma pulled Zack to her, rolled up his sleeves and pajama legs with a few deft moves. "Or you're going to trip over yourself."

"Got a bit of growing to do before you fit those," Nic remarked to the boy as they left the kitchen.

"Mum found them at the Op Shop," Zack explained. "They're a bit big, but they're my favorites. Mum's a champion Op Shopper. That's what she says. They were for my birthday. They're brilliant, aren't they? They're real, you know." He looked up at Nic anxiously. "Mum made me some, before. But these are the *real* ones. They would've been in the regular shop."

"That's important, eh." Nic tried to push away the thought of his son having to get his pajamas from the Op Shop, concentrating instead on the tiny bedroom Zack was proudly showing him now, a large All Black poster and flag dominating the wall space.

"This is you," Zack told him, pointing to Nic's figure amidst his teammates, all standing with arms folded, the players looking large and menacing against a dark background. The wall to which the poster was pinned was painted a rich, deep orange, a contrast to the blue of the rest of the room. It shouldn't have worked, but it did, imbuing the little room with personality and warmth.

"I have a Blues poster, too," Zack went on. "But it's behind the door. Because there was no room." He closed the bedroom door to show off the image. "You're on that, too. You're my favorite." He looked up at Nic beseechingly. "D'you really think you could help me kick? If Mum says yes?"

"Course I do. And I'll talk to your Mum about it. As long as she says yes, I'll help you."

"She doesn't want me to be disappointed," Zack explained, his face serious. "Because you're not my dad. Dads mean it when they say things to their own kids. But not to other kids. They get busy, and they forget. And it makes Mum sad."

Nic felt a lump form in his throat. "I won't forget," he promised. "I'll talk to her tonight."

Zack nodded. "D'you want to see my Legos? I don't have as many as Graham." He pulled out a robot from a three-tiered shelving unit consisting of orange-painted boards resting on brackets affixed to the blue wall. In addition to the few carefully assembled Lego figures, the shelves held an assortment of children's books. The simple assembly was the only furniture in the room other than the bed and a small dresser. No room for a desk anyway.

"I got money from Grandpa and Grandma for Christmas and my birthday, and I'm saving up for a big set," Zack was saying now. "A *Lord of the Rings* set. That's my favorite. D'you want to see, in the catalog?"

"Yeh. I do." Nic dropped to the floor beside the small, earnest figure, onto a round woven carpet in blue with touches of orange that covered the worn beige carpeting. He watched as Zack pulled a well-thumbed catalog off the shelf, opened it to a marked page.

"Helm's Deep, see?" Zack showed him.

"Have you seen the films, then?" Nic asked.

"Yeh. At Graham's. Mum was angry as. She said I was too young. But I wasn't scared. Well, maybe a *bit* scared. Of the troll. And the orcs. The orcs are scary. Specially that one, where the man puts his hand on his face? And he has those teeth?"

"He was very scary," Nic agreed solemnly. "This is an awesome set, though."

"Yeh," Zack breathed. "I can't wait till I get it. Graham says he'll help me put it together. But I want to do it myself. I think I can."

"I'm sure you can. And good on ya for saving up. Not easy."

"Yeh, nah," Zack sighed. "It's not. Because I always want lollies, too. But I'm saving," he repeated firmly. "Till I have enough. Because I want it more than anything."

Emma poked her head in the door. "Bedtime," she told Zack. "Come brush your teeth and go to the toilet, please. And say goodnight to Nic."

Zack got up from the floor obediently. Looked at Nic, shy again now. "Night," he said softly.

Nic stood himself, rested a hand briefly on the top of Zack's head. "Night, mate. And we'll make a plan once I'm back from Safa for that kicking lesson. I promise."

proof

♡

Nic was standing in the kitchen when Emma returned from putting Zack to bed. He'd been turning the canisters on the bench to examine them, but turned at the sound of her step. "You did these, eh."

"Yeah. That one's Zack."

"Got that." Each of the porcelain containers was painted as a castle tower, each tiny brick outlined neatly, the whole surrounded by sky and varying landscapes, as if each tower were being viewed from a different perspective. In the smallest, the tea container, a younger Zack seemed to be communing with a tui who sat on the ledge, its white throat feathers clearly visible against the glossy black, head tilted inquiringly, as a lizard crept around a vine on the other side of the window.

"Painted him in a jersey, I see," Nic commented.

Emma had to smile a bit in spite of her tension. Thinking about her son always did that to her. "He insisted. I said it wasn't very authentic. No All Blacks in medieval Europe, I said. But then, no castles in New Zealand either. So the whole thing's silly, really."

"Who are the others?" he asked.

"My dad." She touched the flour container, the bespectacled scribe gazing abstractly into the distance, scroll and quill pen in hand. "And my mum." On the sugar canister and clearly the castle's chatelaine, wimple framing a stern face, looking out over rolling green fields dotted with cows as if counting them.

"And my sister and me," she finished, touching the coffee container with two young girls peering out of their window, arms around each other.

"No prince," he remarked. "No maiden in the tower, either."

"Yeah. Well. I've kind of given up on the prince thing."

He looked at her searchingly. "Time for you to tell me about that."

"Right." She pulled the manila folder from where she'd stashed it on top of the fridge and sat down at the table, waved him to a chair, her tension, briefly dispelled, returning in full force. She considered moving to the more comfortable lounge, then dismissed the idea. It was disconcerting enough being in here with him, oddly intimate. She needed to keep this as businesslike as possible.

"You say you told me. But you didn't," he said. "I think you'd better start at the beginning, and explain." His face was closed again, the brief moment of softness over.

She rested a palm on the closed folder and spoke through a throat that tightened as she remembered. "You were going to ring me, if you recall. I waited. And waited. I couldn't believe it. I thought something had happened. Then I saw a story online, about the team, and I realized that something *had* happened, and what it was turned out to be pretty simple. You left, and you forgot me."

He shifted in his seat. "I was going to," he said lamely. "But there was so much to do, at first. And then time had gone by, and I felt bad, didn't know what to say. Then..." He shrugged helplessly. "I got caught up. And when I did think about it, I told myself you'd moved on, too."

She laughed, feeling the bitterness rise in her, a familiar tide. "Yeah, I moved on, all right. At least, my body did."

"But why didn't you get in touch?" he asked in exasperation. "Once you knew you were pregnant? And how the hell did it happen, anyway? You told me you were on the Pill, or I'd've been more careful."

"I forgot a couple," she admitted, flushing. "I wasn't too good at that kind of thing back then. And with everything that happened that week…I forgot, all right? I thought it wouldn't matter. Wishful thinking, it turned out. Anyway. When it did happen, once I knew, I tried to tell you. Over and over." She opened the folder at last and handed him a small stack of paper. The top sheet was a copy of an email addressed to the Bath team's publicist, asking the woman to have Nic get in touch with Emma urgently "on a personal matter."

"Please tell him it's important, or I wouldn't be contacting him," he read aloud. "Because of what happened in Fiji."

He looked up at her. "She didn't answer?"

"Look at the next sheet," Emma told him.

"Unfortunately, I can't help you with this," he read. "I'm sure you can see that the players have the right to their privacy, and if they choose not to share their personal contact information with others, that is their decision to make."

"She never even told me," he protested.

"So I sent a letter," Emma went on, ignoring him. She nodded to the stack he held. "You can read it."

He shifted the papers, found the covering note to the same woman, asking her to forward the enclosed letter.

He looked up again. "Two months after I left for England."

She didn't say anything, because the letter pretty much spoke for itself. She just sat, her tension increasing, and watched him read.

Nic,

I've figured out that our time together didn't matter to you after all. I guess you were just talking. But I need you to know that

I'm pregnant. And I could really use your help. Please write to me, or email me, or something.
Emma

Her contact information was all there, too, she knew. Even though he'd never answered.

"I never saw this," he told her.

She looked at him searchingly. "I don't know if that's true or not," she said slowly. "I don't know what to believe. I rang, after that. Several times. Left messages. When I finally got that woman to talk to me, she told me she was sorry, but she couldn't help me. I asked her if she'd given you the letter, and she just said, sorry. As if she'd told you, and you'd said…" She took a breath, went on. "I thought she might be sympathetic, being a woman, you know. But I guess not. It sounded like she'd heard it all before."

He handed back the stack of paper. "Why didn't you get a lawyer?" he demanded. "Somebody who wouldn't have given up till he'd bloody well tracked me down?"

"I asked," she told him, on the defensive now. "And they told me, if you were working overseas, it wasn't possible to pursue you for maintenance. There was no point, if you wouldn't cooperate. The laws don't…don't extend."

"What about when I came back, then?" he asked. "Zack couldn't even have been two then. And he's six now. Why didn't you try again then?"

"I did," she said, her voice heavy with remembered defeat and anger. "I did. I didn't kid myself that you wanted anything to do with him. But I sure could have used some help. So I tried again."

"And? I wasn't overseas then. So what happened?"

"Same thing," she shrugged. "Sorry. Sorry. Sorry. Protecting your privacy, they said. One guy even told me, 'Do you know how many women I hear this from? That a player is their kid's mystery dad? Sorry, love, can't help you. Find somebody else to pin this on.' I'll never forget that one. He made me feel like a whore."

Nic winced. "What about a lawyer, then? Why didn't you try harder?"

She knew he thought she was soft, but there was nothing at all soft in the blue eyes that looked steadily back at him. "I walked into the lawyer's office and told him my story. And he said, 'OK, you're telling me your baby's dad is an All Black now? And you want to get him to take a paternity test? Did you ever have an acknowledged relationship with him? Have a flat together? Anyone who knew you were his girlfriend? No? You slept together for a week, overseas? The courts are going to think that's awfully convenient. No judge in En Zed is going to order a paternity test on the basis of that. It's going to look like harassment of a sportsman, plain and simple. Not worth my time to pursue, and not worth your money to hire me. Save it for the kid.'"

She pulled out a piece of notebook paper, creased where it had been folded again and again, the last item in the folder. "I still remember, you see. I wrote down what he said. It seemed so final. My last try."

He stared down at the yellow lined paper, her neat writing filling the sheet. "I never knew," he said slowly. "You have to believe me, I never knew. Or I would've helped."

"It doesn't matter now, does it? It's all in the past. But when you say I didn't try…I tried, Nic. Over and over. Do you think I wanted Zack not to have anything?" she asked fiercely, her eyes bright with unshed tears. "I've done the best I can. But it kills me. He knows what we can't afford. He tries not to ask. But it kills me when he does ask, and I have to say no. And his feet grow, and he grows, and…"

She stopped, took a deep breath. "So, yeah. You left. And you left me holding the bag. And I'm still holding it."

♡

"So what do we do?" Nic asked after a long silence. "Now?"

"What do you mean, what do we do? I do what I've always done. Raise my son."

"Are you working, though?" He wasn't sure what to ask, what to say.

"Of course I'm working. What do you think?"

"Doing...the art? Something with that?"

She laughed, a quick sound, the bitterness coming through again. "Not exactly. I'm a CAD operator at Morrow & Associates. The engineers."

"OK. Uh...I guess we need a DNA test, right? And a court order?"

"Why?"

"Because I'm his *dad*. And I want him to know it, and to do what's right."

"No," she said immediately. "No. You're not telling him. Not now."

"I have a right," he insisted. "A right to support him, and to be there. To have him with me."

"A right you haven't exercised for more than six years," she flashed back.

"Because I didn't *know*. And now I do. A DNA test. Means all three of us need to be tested, I reckon. And then we go to court. I'll do it whether you cooperate or not," he threatened, his tone flat, eyes intense. "Better to do it this way. I won't tell him now, if you really think better not. But I want to get to know him, and for him to know me. And to pay what's right, so he doesn't have to live here." His quick glance took in the scarred tabletop, the faded old lino.

"This is Northcote," she said angrily. "He's going to a Tier 9 primary school. I'm spending half my salary for this place that you're looking at as if...as if you're seeing a cockroach."

He moved his hand impatiently as if he were literally brushing her objection aside. "We can do this the easy way, or we can do it the hard way. I don't want to get into a custody battle with you. I don't want to make Zack's life harder, or yours either. But I'll do that, if I have to. If you make me."

She leaned back, her face going pale. "You wouldn't do that."

"I don't want to," he said, shame overcoming the anger. "Come on, Emma. We'll do the DNA testing. I'll find out what I have to do to establish...establish paternity, I guess it is. And then we'll go from there."

"But you won't tell Zack," she said, searching his face. "When it's time, it needs to come from me."

"What does he think now?"

"I told him that his dad had to go away. He's young. He hasn't asked more than that yet. I hadn't decided what to say when he did start asking the tough questions."

"Now you don't have to decide. I won't tell him, for now. But I want to get started with this. I'll be in Cape Town this week, back quite late Sunday night. I could come Monday after school, my day off. Take him out and do a bit of practice."

"School holidays, still," she said slowly. "A couple hours. That's it."

"And the DNA test," he reminded her. "I'm off with the squad tomorrow. Bugger. We can do it next week, though. I'll set it up."

"I work all day," she protested. "I can't just take off."

"After five," he suggested. "I'll have training as well. I'll let you know."

"All right," she said reluctantly. "But, Nic. Don't start this unless you're sure. He's not something you can...try out, and see if you like it or not. If you get involved, you have to mean it. Kids aren't temporary. They're forever. We've got along without you so far, and we can keep doing it."

"I'm committing to it," he promised. "I already did, or I wouldn't be here now."

No warmth, only stern resolution in the face that looked up at his own. "If you desert him now, Nic. If you decide it doesn't fit into your image, or your lifestyle, or something. If you let him down, I'll make you sorry. I'll find a way, and I'll do it."

"What d'you take me for?" he asked, flushing with anger.

"I take you for somebody who's got a pretty sweet deal right now. A lot going for him. And who may not want to risk jeopardizing it."

He got up abruptly. "No point in this. I'll text you about the DNA testing, and about Monday. The footy. You can tell me where and when to collect Zack."

"Fine." She got up too, walked him to the front door. He heard it close behind him as he jogged up the concrete steps and left the two of them behind.

a few bumps

♡

Nic eased himself into the low-slung car in one quick movement and slammed the door. He took the turns automatically
that would lead him back to the opulent house in Narrow Neck.
His new house, that he'd been so proud of until tonight. So different from the dodgy little flat he'd just left. Emma's flat.

Emma. How could she look the same, but seem so different?
He could still remember the feel of her when she'd landed in his
lap, that first time.

He'd been leaning back in his aisle seat in the small jet,
headphones on and eyes closed, when he felt the lurch and sickening drop as the aircraft hit the air pocket. His eyes had snapped
open and his hands gone up automatically to catch the girl who
landed hard against him at the jolt, then lost her footing and fell,
sprawling, across his lap.

"Oh! Sorry," she squeaked, struggling to sit upright. He had
his arms around her now as the plane lurched again. The "Fasten
Seatbelt" sign came on with a *ding,* then the pilot's voice over
the intercom, asking passengers to return to their seats "just till
we've got through these few bumps."

Nic grabbed the girl close again and tugged his headphones
off as the plane took another lurch. He couldn't help but notice
how good she felt against him, the soft curves of her under the

thin white cotton sundress. Or the faintly floral scent of her honey-colored hair, the curls streaked with blonde. Or that she'd been crying.

"Think you'd better stay here a minute," he said, reluctantly lifting her off his lap and sliding into the empty window seat as the aircraft continued to bounce. "Till we're out of this." He saw her grab unsteadily for the armrest and reached out to fasten her seatbelt. "There," he said as he snapped the belt together around her, pulled it tight around the narrow waist. "Good as gold."

She reached with both hands to wipe the tears away. Turned to him, big blue eyes still swimming with tears. Her soft little mouth, with its strongly defined cupid's bow, trembled as she looked up at him.

"I've lost my shoe," she told him tragically.

He looked down, saw one slender foot in its high-heeled, slip-on sandal, the other bare. Leaned over to check under her seat, fish out the other shoe. He slid it onto her foot, noticing while he was down there how slim her ankles were, and how smooth and firm her bare legs looked in the short sundress.

"Bad flight?" he asked her after he'd reluctantly returned to his upright position and resecured his seatbelt. "Scared of the bumps?"

"No." She shook her head decisively, then kept shaking it. She was more than a bit drunk, he realized, as well as whatever else was wrong. And there was an accent. Something, he couldn't tell quite what. "But this was a mistake. I shouldn't have come. And I have to stay for a *week*." The round blue eyes were looking more tragic than ever, and her mouth drooped. She looked like a kitten who'd just got some very bad news.

"A week in Fiji, eh. That *is* sad. Wrong partner? Is that it?"

That started the tears again. "I'm on my honeymoon," she got out. "My honeymoon. Can you believe that? I'm on my honeymoon?"

"Uh...nah." Figured. "Hubby back there?"

"No. He's not here. He's not coming. We didn't get married. Because he wants Karen *Fuchs* instead," she said fiercely, her tears drying up at the thought. "But I'm prettier than Karen Fuchs. Don't you think I am?"

"Never met Karen," he pointed out. "But I'll bet you're prettier." She was prettier than just about anyone, he reckoned, even in her current state.

She nodded with certainty. "I don't have a pig nose, either."

"You've got a beautiful nose," he agreed solemnly. "Running a bit now, though." He fished in his seatback pocket for the serviette he'd stuck in there earlier. "Here."

"Thanks." She wiped her nose, sniffed, then turned those eyes on him again. "He says Karen understands his work, because she's getting her masters in engineering. That she can help him. They can sit around and solve equations together before bed," she said, her mouth getting firmer and losing the tremble. "In their matching pajamas."

"What are you? Eighteen, nineteen? Too young to get married anyway, aren't you?"

"I am *not,*" she said indignantly. "I'm twenty-one. And I have a degree."

"But not in engineering? Not up to Karen's standard, eh."

"In Fine Arts. Which isn't easy." She glared at him. "Just because it's not engineering, doesn't mean it's easy."

"No worries," he said hastily. "I'm not judging. Didn't finish Uni myself, so I'd be the last."

"Anyway," she said glumly. "I'm supposed to be married now. He said I should go on the honeymoon. Because the bookings are nonrefundable. Because he got a deal." She glared again. "Isn't that romantic? Nonrefundable?"

"Couldn't find someone else to go with you?" Nic hazarded.

"On my *honeymoon?*" she asked incredulously. "I was supposed to be with my *husband.* Look at my hair," she demanded. "Look!"

"Uh…something wrong with it? Looks good to me."

"It's *highlighted*. It took *hours*. Do you know what I've done this week? I had a facial, and a body scrub, and a wrap." She ticked the items off on her fingers. "And my hair. I had my brows and lashes done, and I had a manicure and a pedicure, and I had everything waxed. I got a *Brazilian* wax. And it *hurt*. For *nothing.*"

That got his attention. Every part of him. He'd bet it looked choice. And he'd like to see it.

"And Karen Fuchs doesn't shave her legs. Would you want to go to bed with somebody who didn't shave her legs? Or her armpits? Instead of me?"

"Nah," he answered honestly.

"You'd choose me, right?"

"Yeh. Yeh. I'd choose you," he agreed. In a heartbeat. Well, as long as she wasn't crying. Maybe. He wasn't sure even that would matter.

She gave a satisfied nod.

"So this bloke wasn't any real loss, then," Nic said. "Seeing as he was blind, and had no taste. And he's, what, an engineer?"

"An Assistant Professor of Sanitary Engineering," she said gloomily.

He had to laugh. "Sounds dead sexy. Too old for you, too."

"How old are you?" she demanded.

"Twenty-two," he grinned. "How old was—whoever he was?"

"David. Twenty-eight. That seemed like a good idea. I thought, OK, he's boring, maybe. But he's older, settled. Responsible. Good for me. And he's *safe*. Ha. What a joke *that* turned out to be."

"Why d'you want to be safe?" he asked with real surprise.

She looked surprised in her turn. "Doesn't everybody want to be safe?"

"I don't. I want to have every adventure there is. The more unsafe, the better."

"Then you're not an engineer," she said firmly.

He laughed again at that. "About as far from it as you could get, I reckon. I'm a rugby player."

"Are you really?" She stared at him in fascination. "How come you're going to Fiji? For a game?"

"Nah. Holiday. Off to England to play, in a week or so. Decided at the last minute to have a bit of a holiday in the Islands before I turn into a bloody Pom in the frozen north. No booking, refundable or otherwise. Just turning up and taking my chance."

"Better than me," she said glumly. "You might even find somebody to hang out with. What am I going to do, at a honeymoon resort by *myself?* Not that I know what I'd have been doing with David," she added in another burst of candor. "You're supposed to be getting shagged up, down, and sideways on your honeymoon, right?"

He choked a bit at that. "I've heard," he managed.

"Yeah," she said. "I've heard too. Oh, well." She sighed. "I brought books. It was never going to be that kind of honeymoon anyway."

"The more I hear," Nic offered, "the more I think you got off easy."

"You think?"

"Would he have packed books too?" he demanded.

"Yeah. He did. And some work. I saw. Before he told me, I mean. That I was going alone."

"Maybe you should take me with you instead," he suggested with a grin. "We could have a non-honeymoon, put some of that waxing to use. Because I didn't bring any work, or any books. And I'm fairly sure I could deliver on the up, down, and sideways bit. Give you everything you want."

That had been a hell of a week. Up, down, sideways, and then some. He felt a surge of heat at the memories that rushed back, still strong after all this time. No wonder, the way they'd played out in his head for years. His mind insisted on going there again for a few pleasurable minutes before he snapped it back to the present, took the final turn onto Seabreeze Road and up the sloping drive that led to the big house, sitting well back from the street. The lights were on, he saw. Claudia was home, then. He punched the button on the visor for the automatic garage door, pulled the car in and punched again to shut the door behind him. Then sat for a minute, gathering his wits.

Claudia was in the lounge, working on her laptop.

"Hi," he said, leaning over and giving her a kiss. "Long day?"

"Yeh." She frowned lightly. "Chinese food? Ugh, Nic. Awful."

"Sorry. What about you? Did you eat?"

"At the office. I'm assisting at that Fonterra meeting tomorrow. Heaps to do before that. How are you getting to the airport in the morning? I could give you a lift, but it'd have to be early."

"Nah. I'll drive, save you collecting me Sunday. It'll be late. Midnight."

She nodded, her attention already drifting back to the computer. He sat on the couch next to her. "Mind if I watch *Top Gear?*"

"Do you have to? It's not like you need a new car."

"It's not about a new car," he tried to explain. "I just want to relax for a bit. And they're funny."

"More like silly," she complained.

"Want me to watch upstairs, then?"

"Would you mind? I could move to the office, if you'd rather."

"Nah." He got up again. "I'll go."

"Before you do, we really do need to schedule a time to sit with my mum and go over the guest list."

"Do I need to be there for that? I gave you my list. Whatever you decide is good. Anyway, does it have to happen now? More than six months away."

"And we need to send Save the Date cards," she said in exasperation. "I told you. I'm not asking you to help decide on flowers, or the band, or anything else. You've hardly had to do a thing. All I'm asking for is one afternoon."

"Have to be Saturday week, and in the morning. I need the afternoon, before the game."

"Fine." She clicked again, typed in the appointment with her usual brisk efficiency. "I'll make that work. And send you a reminder, so you can calendar it."

He sat down again. "D'you ever want to chuck all this?" he asked her suddenly, causing her to look up from her laptop in surprise. "All the planning? The arrangements? I don't mean not get married," he said hurriedly at her shocked expression. "But maybe we should just…run off. Between the work, and doing this place up, and the wedding, don't you get a bit fed up?"

She stared at him. "Don't be ridiculous. We can't run off. We have a deal, remember? *Woman's World* might have something to say about that."

"Still sure you want to do that, though? Doesn't it feel a bit intrusive?"

"They're paying well for that intrusion," she reminded him. "It'll cover the cost of the wedding, *and* the honeymoon."

"We can afford it, though," he argued. "Do we really need this?"

"We discussed it. We agreed. Why not get it, since we can? It's just a few photos, for heaven's sake. You're on TV every week. What's the difference?"

"You don't think there's a difference? That's work. This should be the most private thing there is."

"Which we're sharing with four hundred people," she said. "It's not *that* private."

"OK," he said reluctantly. "Just wondered if you'd had any second thoughts."

"No. None."

"Well, it's your day. If this is what you want."

"It is," she said. "And no, I don't feel like running off. That's pretty impractical, Nic. We both have way too much on our plates to be thinking that way."

"I know we *can't*. Just wondering if you ever wanted to, that's all. Just talking, I guess."

Her eyes strayed back to the screen again. "Well, if that's all, I'm sorry, but I really do need to get this done before tomorrow. Maybe you could ring me from the hotel tomorrow night, once you get in. I'll be able to give you my full attention once I have this meeting behind me."

He considered telling her about Zack, but was overwhelmed with unaccustomed fatigue at the thought of the explanations, the discussion. She was right. It was late, she had a meeting tomorrow, and he was leaving in the morning. This wasn't the time.

He sat up in bed a half hour later, muted the advert interrupting *Top Gear.* Not that he was really watching anyway. He needed to go to sleep. Twelve hours on the plane tomorrow. He wished Claudia would come to bed. He would've liked the security of her body next to his. Even if she were still working on that bloody laptop.

He switched the TV off, turned out the bedside lamp, punched the pillow and tried to get comfortable. South Africa would be a relief, he decided. Time to focus on the footy for a bit, get his mind back on its usual disciplined track. Keep it from straying off to thoughts of Zack. And Emma.

dream girl

♡

Emma sat curled at one end of the couch, pulled the knitted afghan more closely around her, needing the comfort of its warmth. A single lamp on the end table provided a pool of light. She was knitting, of course. And, ostensibly, watching *Top Gear*, absently observing as a car made its skidding, precarious way around the track to the accompaniment of the usual caustic commentary.

After Nic had left, she'd closed the door behind him, then stood for a minute with her forehead pressed against the worn wood. Just when she thought she had a handle on things, life kept finding a way to throw her off-balance. And this time, she was afraid it had knocked her completely over the edge. She just hoped she could keep Zack from going with her.

The worst of it was that she couldn't really blame her situation on Nic. It was her own impulsive nature that was really at fault, and she knew it. Why had she had to meet him when she was at her most vulnerable? The first day of her non-honeymoon. The day after her non-wedding.

She hadn't thought about that day in a long time. But seeing Nic again brought the whole disastrous weekend back. Most women would have thought themselves unlucky to have been spectacularly dumped on their wedding day. Only she, Emma thought glumly, could have managed to be left twice in a single week by *two* men, each of whom she'd considered the love of her life. At one point or another, anyway. Just showed what kind of judgment she had.

"Emma," her mother had said sharply that morning nearly seven years earlier, as Lucy finished fixing the wreath in place over Emma's blonde-streaked hair. "Pay attention. You're off someplace else again. I asked if you were ready for the dress."

"She's entitled, Mom," Lucy said, coming to her younger sister's defense as she had so many times in their childhood. "It's her wedding day. She's *supposed* to be dreamy today."

Emma barely heard them. She stared into her own eyes in the mirror above her little dressing table, her face looking unfamiliar under the coating of mascara, eyeshadow, and foundation she rarely wore. "Are you sure I'm doing the right thing?" she asked slowly. "When you married Dad, Mom. Before, I mean. Did you have any...any doubts?"

"Of course not," her mother answered briskly, with the obvious impatience she so often showed her younger daughter. "Your father and I had a lot in common. Shared interests and backgrounds, academically and intellectually. You and David might not be as alike as we are, but he's good for you. He'll settle you down, keep you focused."

"Do I want to be settled down, though?" Emma asked her reflection.

"It's not too late to back out, if you're having second thoughts," Lucy said helpfully.

"Of course it is," her mother shot back. "It's cold feet, that's all. You're just being a little flighty, like always. David's perfect for you, Emma. He'll give you stability. Trust me."

"Shouldn't I feel more...excitement, though?" Emma asked. "Thrilled, or something?"

Lucy looked down at her sister thoughtfully as their mother moved to the closet for the simple dress she'd helped Emma choose. "No sparks, huh?"

"Well, not *no,*" Emma conceded. "But you know, not a burning flame or anything. He doesn't seem to feel like that either. I thought men were supposed to be more eager than that. More excited."

"That's a myth," her mother said, coming back with the ivory silk held carefully in her outstretched arms. "You'd think men were some kind of animals, the things people say. Anyway, that certainly isn't what carries a marriage through the years. It's the friendship that matters. That's what lasts."

The door to the bedroom opened, and the man in question stepped inside, closing it again behind him. All three women turned to look at him. He hadn't changed into his dark blue suit yet, Emma saw with surprise. Instead, he wore his usual khaki Dockers and blue button-down Oxford cloth shirt. And his usual white New Balance shoes. Emma felt a guilty flash of annoyance even through her puzzlement. She wished he'd take her hints and buy a pair of more fashionable shoes like the ones she kept pointing out to him. How was she supposed to get excited by somebody who clipped his phone to his belt, and flossed every single night, and wore those *shoes?* She felt a wave of actual revulsion. *Was* it just cold feet? Was this normal?

"David," Frances said in surprise. "Why are you here? I don't believe in that nonsense about bad luck, of course. But Emma needs to get ready, and you should be getting dressed yourself."

David, for once, ignored the wife of his department head. "I need to talk to you, Emma," he said instead. "Privately."

"Five minutes, then," Frances decided. "Come on, Lucy."

Lucy's observant glance shot from Emma to David, then back to Emma. "I can stay, if you want," she offered.

"No," Emma said, swinging herself around on the little stool so she faced the room. "David wants to talk to me alone." Icy fingers of dread were running down her back, even as her mind went blank. Something was about to happen.

Her sister nodded, gave David one final appraising glance as she left the room with their mother.

Emma watched the door shut behind them, then turned to look again at David. "What's going on?"

He sank onto the bed, put a hand on each knee, and exhaled in a long sigh. "I know how much this is going to hurt you. But I can't pretend anymore, and it wouldn't be fair to you to marry you, feeling the way I do."

"What way?" Those icy fingers were playing some kind of sonata now. "Are you *dumping* me? On our *wedding* day?"

"I just don't think we're compatible enough," he explained. "You have good values, and the right background. But there's something missing."

"I have good *values?*" she asked, staring at him. "That's it? That's been the attraction?"

"You're a nice person," he explained. "Not that steady, maybe. A little moody. But you have a good character. And that's important, in a partner. But I'm sorry. It isn't enough for me."

"My good character isn't enough," she said, fighting an absurd desire to laugh. Or cry. Or something. "It doesn't make up for...what?"

"For a real connection. I've realized I need somebody who understands my work, and can have a real discussion with me about it. Somebody who's intellectually compatible."

"You want to discuss your work more? Who with? Who is it that's going to have this real discussion with you?" Her breath was coming faster now, and she could feel the heat burning in her cheeks.

"Don't get excited," he cautioned.

"Don't get *excited?* Don't get *EXCITED?*" Her voice was rising. "Could you have maybe figured this out a week ago? A *day* ago? Instead of me sitting here in my slip, ready to put on my fu—my frigging *wedding dress?* So who is it? Who is it who understands you so well?" she demanded again.

"Nothing's happened," he hastened to say. "Nothing inappropriate."

"Oh, no. Nothing inappropriate," she said sarcastically. "You've just been having meaningful, *real discussions*. About your *work*."

"Yes!" he said in relief, misinterpreting her remarks as always. "She's been helping me with some numerical analysis, these past weeks, and something's grown up between us. It isn't fair to you to go ahead with this, feeling the way I do. I know it'll cause some trouble in the department, and I'm prepared to deal with that."

"Well, goody for you. How noble. So we're talking about Karen Fuchs here? *That's* your dream girl?"

"Nothing's happened, I said," he reminded her sharply. "There's been no inappropriate behavior."

"Don't worry," she said bitterly, getting up and going to the door. "I'm not going to sic my dad on you for having an affair with a student. I don't care. Just leave." Tears of humiliation burned in her eyes as she pushed the handle down, pulled the door toward her.

"I know this is a disappointment to you," he went on, standing up awkwardly. "And I'm sorry. But we both need to be sure. And I found, when it came down to it, that I just couldn't settle."

"*You* couldn't settle," she said, feeling the bubble of hysteria rising inside her. She felt like screaming, slammed her mouth shut on the impulse. She made a wide sweeping motion with her arm. "Here I thought *I* was settling. Wow. Get out."

"I was hoping you'd understand. That we could be civilized about this. Bury the hatchet, before I left," he said pleadingly, standing reluctantly as she continued to gesture at him.

"I'll bury it," she told him furiously. "Right in your head. *Out.*"

"Here." He held out an envelope she hadn't noticed. "The bookings. For the honeymoon. Take them."

"You want me to go on the *honeymoon?*" she asked, that bubble rising again. "Doesn't Karen want to go to Fiji? Show you her fine growth of body hair?"

"She has exams," he said guilelessly. "She can't go. And the tickets are nonrefundable. As it's the last minute. So you may as well take the trip." He held out the envelope again, then set it on the bed as she continued to glare at him, making no move to take it. "Well, I'll just…leave this for you, I guess," he said hastily, seeing her feet shift and her face redden even more. "Sorry about this. But I think it'll be for the best."

"Oh, I know it'll be for the best. I'm counting on that. Would you just *leave?*"

She watched him walk through the door at last, then gave in to temptation and slammed it after him. She hoped it made him jump. She pulled off her slip so she was standing in her wedding underwear—*wedding underwear*, she thought savagely. Maybe she should offer that to Karen too. Along with David. Wrapped up in a big red bow. White running shoes, khakis, dental floss, and all. Good luck with that.

She wrenched off the lacy white bra and thong, threw them across the room. They weren't even substantial enough to make it to the opposite wall, fluttering down before they'd got halfway. No chance, anyway. Karen would never be able to get into them.

So there she'd been. She hadn't been able to stand staying in her parents' house on what had been supposed to be her wedding night, facing their concern, with its clear undercurrent of disappointment in her failure to make her life work as neatly as theirs always seemed to. Their obvious opinion that, once again, she'd proven to be a failure. A screwup. She'd given up her room in the flat she'd shared in preparation for moving into David's sterile, modern flat in Newmarket ("so convenient to the University, and easy to keep clean"), and she hadn't been able to face the humiliation of going to stay with a friend.

In the end, she'd taken a taxi to the Heritage Hotel, booked into the room David had reserved for their wedding night, wanting to face the experience down and conquer it. She'd had an image of herself, strong and brave, moving on with her life. And had known that on some level, she was relieved. But all the same, to her frustrated bewilderment, she'd ended up crying most of the night, and on into the next day. Had got on the plane, still teary, sleepless, and fortified by a big glass of wine from an airport bar. Another two glasses on board, and she'd been more than ready to make a fool of herself with the irresistible package that had been Dominic Wilkinson at twenty-two.

He'd been so easygoing, so offhand, so effortlessly, casually attractive, in his shorts, T-shirt, and jandals. His arms around her, holding her so securely as she fell into his lap, his solid thighs underneath her. All that lean, hard muscle. And those eyes. The lazy tilt of them. The gleam in them, promising something she hadn't quite understood, but had recognized all the same.

But none of the hard edges, the toughness she'd seen in him tonight. Just...fun. That's what she'd thought, sitting next to him, looking at him while he made his cheeky proposal. He was like a big, beautiful present, being handed to her. She'd tried so hard to focus, to be serious, to do what was expected. And look how much good that had done her. Now here he was, looking like that, smiling like that, offering her this week out of her life. That nobody would ever, ever know about. Something just for her. Just for now. Just for fun.

something special

♡

"My legs are rubber," Lucy complained, wiping her face again with the towel and dropping onto a stool at the juice bar of the Les Mills gym. It was quiet this Saturday morning, all the young singles still recovering from their Friday night out. "You're killing me."

"Hey. You said you wanted to do this." Emma gave her own face a swipe. "It won't always feel so bad. I swear, I can see a difference in you already." She inspected her sister's taller, curvier figure. "Your arms look great. I can see the weight loss, but you're looking toned too. And it's only been, what? Five times?"

"Six," Lucy groaned. "But who's counting. I was so sore after the first time, I almost rang up on the Monday, pulled a sickie. But in the end, I couldn't imagine explaining to the head that I'd overdone it at Body Pump. How can you put that much weight on your bar, anyway? You're smaller than me. Where are you hiding the muscle?"

"It's just practice." Emma shrugged and took a sip of her own water. "And muscle doesn't have to be big and bulky, you know."

"Sure you don't want a smoothie?" Lucy asked as she saw Emma's eyes drift to her own slushy concoction.

"No. Too many kilojoules," Emma said firmly.

"Like you need to worry about that," Lucy scoffed. "You know I don't mind treating you. It's just a smoothie, for heaven's sake."

"No," Emma said again. "You've done enough for me. I don't like juice that much anyway, and water's the best hydration."

Lucy sighed. "You're too proud." She rubbed her thighs. "How did you do all those squats? Let's hope Tom doesn't think he's having sex tonight. My range of motion is going to be limited for days here."

"Luce. Shhh," Emma hissed, unable to stop a giggle from escaping her. "I swear. You'd better not talk like that in the classroom."

"No worries. Those kids're all so hormonally crazed, that'd send them right over the top," Lucy declared. "Fourteen-year-old boys. What was I thinking? I could've done something easy. Been a welder, or a lion tamer, or something."

Emma laughed again, then looked at her watch. "Twenty minutes before we have to leave, if we're going to catch the ferry. Be quiet and listen. I have to tell you something. And I don't want to force Tom into taking care of Zack for another half hour."

Lucy's gaze sharpened at the change in tone, and Emma could see the concern in the blue eyes that were so like her own. "He won't mind. You know they're sitting on the couch, watching some Saturday morning sports chat show. What is it? What's happened?"

Emma was grateful as always for her sister's easy understanding. They'd always been reasonably close, but after their parents had made the decision to emigrate to New Zealand when Lucy was barely into high school, necessity had forced an even tighter bond. And when she'd become pregnant...that's when Lucy had really come through.

"Nic," she said with a sigh. "I've been waiting all week to tell you. He showed up."

"*Nic?*" Lucy asked in astonishment. "What d'you mean, showed up? When? Where? After all this time?"

Emma told the story as quickly as she could. "So here he is," she finished. "Well, in Cape Town right now. But he wants to take Zack out on Monday. And we're meeting him for DNA testing on Wednesday."

"Wow," Lucy said soberly, her sore thighs forgotten. "He's serious, then. How could he not have known?"

"I've been asking myself that all week," Emma said in frustration. "But I don't see why he'd refuse to be involved all this time, and suddenly decide to start. So he must be telling the truth, don't you think?"

"I guess," Lucy said doubtfully. "Like you say. Hard to think why he'd go to the trouble, unless he really didn't know, before. What do you think about it all? How are you feeling?"

"Completely confused," Emma admitted. "Is it a good thing for Zack? Or not?"

"Depends whether Nic's going to follow through or not," Lucy said shrewdly. "Entirely. If yes, then yes. It's a *great* thing for Zack. If no..." She shook her head. "Then it's what I see every day. Better not to be involved at all."

"That's what I told Nic," Emma said with a worried sigh. "I hope he got it."

"And that's Zack," Lucy said. "How is it for you?"

"Me? How d'you mean?"

"Em." Lucy shot her little sister her best exasperated scowl. "This is me. Your labor coach. Remember whose name you yelled out? Not mine, despite the fact that I was the one going to those stupid classes with you, hauling around those big pillows like a fool. I know what a torch you've carried for him."

"That's all over," Emma said. "Six years gone."

"Are you sure?" Lucy pressed. "He hasn't got any worse-looking in that time."

"No, he hasn't. But he's engaged," Emma reminded her.

"When's the wedding again?"

"After the World Cup, I think. End of the All Blacks season." Emma tried to sound casual, as if she hadn't read every report, right from the start. She knew the date. November 25th.

"Long engagement," Lucy commented.

"A long time leading up to it, too. They've been together for years. But whatever." Emma caught herself. "Not my business."

"Who else's business would it be? She's going to be Zack's stepmother, you know," Lucy pointed out. "If he's serious about this, which it sounds like he is. You hadn't thought that through, had you?" she guessed. "But yeah. She's going to be in Zack's life. Which means she's going to be in yours."

Emma put her head in her hands, pushed back the sweat-soaked strands of hair, feeling the panic rise. "Too much. I've just got used to being on our own, without you. I thought I was handling things. Getting it together. And now this. I feel like I'm actually going crazy. Forgetting things. Losing my keys. Losing my mind. Yesterday, at work. Roger was talking to me about the drawings for the Emirates building, and I just...zoned out. Which you know gave him a thrill. He got to reprimand me for something real. What if I lose my job? What's going to happen to Zack then?"

"Roger's a jerk," Lucy replied automatically. "And you're doing fine. You're not going to lose your job. Of course it's disconcerting. But this could be a good thing, Em. Zack needs a dad."

Emma looked up at her older sister, her attention arrested. "Why? What? Is something wrong?"

"No," Lucy sighed. "It's just...it's kind of sad, how much he seems to look forward to his time with Tom, isn't it? I mean, Tom's a great guy, and I love him. But a couple hours with your aunt's partner, once a week...should that be the highlight?"

"He's so kind, though. He watches sport with him. And throws the footy with him too, some," Emma objected. "And you know how much that means to Zack."

"Yeah, and how great would that be, if Nic really did step up to the plate? A dad, and his favorite thing in the world, all wrapped up in one pretty terrific package?"

"I don't know." Emma got up and picked up her gym bag. "Come on. We're going to miss the ferry unless we leave now."

"What did he seem like?" Lucy asked curiously as they walked the few blocks to the Ferry Building. "Nic. The same?"

"No. Older. Harder," Emma said briefly.

"Hotter?" Lucy asked slyly.

"Luce. Quit it. He's *engaged.* And I wouldn't go there anyway. Not for a million dollars."

"Really?" Lucy looked surprised. "That's not the impression I got. I thought he was something special."

"He is. The most special thing there could be. But the price is too high."

♡

"Zack." Emma gave his shoulder a shake the following morning. "Time to get up, sweetie."

"Ummmm," he protested. "Wha?"

"If you want to watch the game," she told him, "it's on in fifteen minutes."

"Oh!" He sat up, and Emma smiled at the spikes of hair sticking up. He really needed a trim, much as he resisted. "I'm getting up."

"OK, then. I'll fix you a hot chocolate while you're in the bathroom. Brush your teeth," she reminded him as she left the room.

"Why do they play so early, Mum?" Zack asked once he was tucked up on the couch under the afghan, carefully holding the

Peter Rabbit mug she'd found in another Op Shop success years earlier. Peter was a bit faded now, but it was still her own favorite. It always reminded her of his three-year-old self, the sweet little boy she missed, even as she enjoyed watching him grow up.

"I explained, remember?" she told him. "It's time zones. It's not early, in South Africa. It's Saturday night."

"Oh. I forgot. D'you think they get confused? The Blues? D'you think Nic does?"

"I don't know. They're used to it, I suspect." Emma sank down next to Zack with her own mug of tea. It *was* too early, not yet six. She wanted to watch, though. Ironically, she'd become interested in the game when Zack had, after getting through her life first blithely ignoring rugby, then studiously avoiding it. Though she'd wished Zack didn't follow the Blues, once Nic had moved there from the Chiefs the previous year.

"There he is!" Zack cried, as the players came out of the tunnel. "He said his leg would come right, and it did! He's starting!" Zack had changed out of his pajamas despite the early hour, and was wearing his rugby camp jersey in honor of the occasion, with Nic's signature black and bold across the back. Emma knew, though, that under the afghan, he was still clutching Raffo, the flocked giraffe that, in odd preference to a more conventional stuffed animal, had always been his comfort object.

"It's going to be hard," Zack said with fierce concentration as the Stormers kicked off to the Blues, Nic fielding the high ball and returning it with a kick that was chased down by another Blues back, who was instantly tackled. "For Nic, I mean. Because all the South African teams kick heaps. And that means Nic has to catch heaps too."

"How come he sometimes kicks it away, and sometimes he runs with it?" Emma asked Zack an hour and a half later. She'd never watched Nic closely before. Had never wanted to. But this time, she'd found herself riveted. The game had been an intensely physical one, a battle of forwards so typical in matches against South African rivals. The Blues had come away with the narrowest of victories at 17 to 16, aided by two missed Stormers conversions. Zack had been on the edge of his seat during the entire second half, his usual close attention with a desperate edge now. He'd eaten the cereal she'd given only after it had turned to mush in his bowl, and the toast too had grown cold on his plate.

"He decides," Zack told her. "Which is better. But I'm not sure how. How does he know? I could ask him, d'you think? Tomorrow? If he really comes?" His hand went out for Raffo, Emma saw, and her heart lurched with fear for him. If Nic didn't keep his promise…

"You can ask him," she agreed. No point in trying to dampen his expectations. He'd only worry. Time enough to comfort him if Nic failed to appear.

Show up, Nic, she thought fiercely. *You said you would. Show up.*

the first time

♡

"Am I keeping you?" Roger asked sarcastically as he intercepted Emma's glance at the clock.

She flushed, turned her attention back to him. "Of course not. I want to finish that Emirates drawing before I leave tonight, that's all." *Was that pointed enough for you?*

"It would've been done already, if you'd been willing to cut your lunch hour short," Roger reminded her.

How had she ended up with the only supervisor in New Zealand with an American attitude toward her legally entitled work breaks? "I like to think that working out at lunch helps keep me productive during the afternoon," she said, doing her best to keep her voice level. "Do you have a problem with my performance?" She was startled at her own directness. She'd never challenged his jibes before, but she was so sick of his harassment.

She saw the flush rise to the scalp visible under his thinning hair, his lips hardening above the indeterminate chin. She'd only made him more hostile, she realized. Mistake.

"Just be sure you get all those drawings done this week," he warned her. "You've said you could do it."

"And I can." She'd better mend this fence, as much as she could. "They'll be done, I promise."

"Because I've been wondering if you value your job," he said meaningfully.

A bolt of pure fear shot through her, the anxiety making her feel physically ill even as her anger rose. "I value my job, Roger. In fact, I'd like to finish one of those drawings tonight. Before I leave." She glanced at the clock again.

"Good," he muttered, and took himself off at last. She turned back to her computer, trying to calm her racing pulse. However she felt about it, she needed this job. Not just the paycheck. The sickness benefit, and the holiday leave. She couldn't afford to lose it. Not now. Not ever.

She turned reluctantly again as she saw Ryan making his way towards her desk. Yet another interruption before she could even get the document open.

"Hi," she greeted him briskly. "What can I do for you?" Blond hair, carefully mussed. The close-fitting, casually untucked dress shirt atop slim trousers. The complete, casual young Kiwi professional.

"Just wanted to ask you how you're going with those bridge drawings," he said with a smile. He asked nicely, but when she thought about it, he was at least as demanding as any of the other engineers, asked about the status of his projects more than anybody else. Or maybe just came over to talk to her more than anybody else.

"Next on my list," she promised.

"Because I'm getting pushed on the internal deadline," he confided. "So if you could do it earlier, it'd help."

"I said next week, and it'll be next week." She heard the *ding* of a text from her mobile, tried not to glance at it on her desk. "3-D takes time. You know that. If you need them sooner, you'll have to talk to Roger. Maybe he can shift them to Sean. He has less on his plate than I do. Or Roger may even be willing to do them himself."

"Nah. I want you to do it. Don't want to have to give them back six times."

"Shh," she hissed, shooting a quick glance to her right. Roger was over talking to one of the engineers, and Sean had ducked out early, she saw with relief. She might not appreciate her colleague's work habits, but she didn't want to talk behind his back, either. "I'll do my best. But I've got quite a stack, and I take orders from Roger."

"Wish you took them from me." She glanced up at him, startled. Surely he couldn't have meant *that.* "How about coming out with us for a drink after work on Friday?" he asked. All right, he *had* meant that.

"Can't do it," she said. "Sorry." She enjoyed going out with the group sometimes, but the ongoing drama with Nic had her unsettled and faintly panicky. She wasn't going to feel like socializing this weekend, she knew. She just wanted to go home and be with Zack.

Ryan took himself off at last. Emma cast a quick glance around for Roger, then checked the text on her mobile. Nic.

Got Zack. Back around 6.

She set the phone back down, looked at the clock on her monitor. Four-thirty. She was leaving on the dot today. With luck, she'd be across the bridge and home by five-thirty. Time enough to change and be a bit more composed by the time he brought Zack home, be ready to meet him again. She took a deep breath and finally opened the document. She wouldn't have time to finish it tonight after all. She couldn't worry about that now, though.

Keep plugging away. Do what she had to do, right now. That was all she could do. All she'd ever been able to do.

♡

"Mum!" Zack burst in through the front door. "It was brilliant!" He kicked his shoes off impatiently, dropped his rugby boots next to them before struggling out of his jacket. Nic followed him in, grabbed the jacket and hung it on the brightly painted rack next to the door when Zack would have dropped it on the floor.

Emma reached out for a hug that, Nic saw, the boy was still willing to give his mother, at least here at home. Her eyes met Nic's as she looked over her son's head. How did she always look so soft? So...pettable? She was wearing another sweater, that was all, he told his troublesome libido. Another light, lacy one, prettily trimmed once again. A pale pink cardigan with pearly shell buttons, edged in cream, over a long stretchy top and leggings. She looked like an invitation to cuddle. Like the best blankie ever.

"Can Nic stay for dinner, Mum?" Zack asked excitedly, offering a welcome distraction from his wayward train of thought. "He could help me tell you all the things we did. We're having spaghetti!" he told Nic. "It's really good."

"Can't, mate. Sorry," Nic put in hastily at Emma's instinctive shake of the head. "But I'll have a glass of water, if one's on offer."

"Sit down," Emma told him. "Please."

Nic slipped off his own shoes before heading to the couch with Zack. "Cheers," he said as she came back from the kitchen to hand each of them a glass, then took her own seat in a small armchair next to the couch, the only other option the little room offered.

"You look tired," she said abruptly. "And bruised. Are you OK?"

"Just a bit confused on the sleep schedule, still," Nic admitted. "I took a wee pill on the flight home, but it never works that well."

"It's a long way, Mum," Zack put in. "South Africa's really far."

Nic took a long drink of the cold water, looked around for something to set the glass on. "Coaster?"

"Just put it down," Emma told him.

"Don't want to spoil this," he said, looking more closely at the coffee table. The simple rectangle had been transformed into a forest of ferns, with native birds peeping out from underneath fronds, perched in trees. The parson-throated tui making a meal of red fruit, the colorful, stumpy takahe on the forest floor, tiny fantails darting overhead.

"You can't," Emma assured him. "It's all enamels. Everything in this house is pretty indestructible."

"Did you find the ruru yet?" Zack asked him, leaning forward.

"Don't tell me," Nic said. "Let me look." Zack watched him eagerly as he searched and finally pointed triumphantly to a notch in a tree where the owl blended into the bark. "There."

"You did this too, eh," he asked Emma. "Nice."

"I did everything. That's my decorating theme. Things I made."

"I like it," he said. The warm colors of the lounge seemed to cocoon them. Two walls were a rich caramel, the others a warm yellow. She didn't even paint every wall in a room the same color, he realized. Well, at least in the kitchen it was all the same. Purple. He wondered what color her bedroom was. How it looked. And found himself wishing, against every better impulse, that he could see it.

"So did you kick?" she interrupted his thoughts to ask her son. "Did you get your practice?"

"Yeh." Zack's smile was enormous. "And Nic explained, what I told you. About when he kicks it back. So I can do it, when I'm nine. And I got better already, Mum! He said!"

"He needs better boots, though," Nic remarked. "Where'd you get those?"

"Trade Me. But they're Pumas," she hastened to add. "They don't have any holes or anything. And they're the right size."

"I know they're Pumas. But they're worn down."

"Go wash your hands, sweetie," she told Zack. "Bath can wait till after dinner."

"OK." He bounced up, still buoyed by the excitement of the afternoon. She watched him go, then turned back to Nic.

"Don't tell me what he needs in front of him," she said levelly. "He doesn't need to feel...deprived."

"He's not going to be deprived anymore," Nic said in frustration. "I'll buy him new boots."

"Don't promise him that," she said sharply. "It's too soon."

He didn't answer her directly. "Blood test Wednesday," he reminded her. "Five. D'you need me to collect him? Because I can."

"No. I'll meet you there."

He nodded, stood to leave as Zack came back into the room. "Got to go have my own tea. See you in a couple days, mate."

"Really?" Zack asked.

"I'm going to meet you and your mum. We're going to see a doctor," Nic told him. "All together." He looked across at Emma again.

"A doctor? I'm not ill. I don't have to get a jab, do I?" Zack asked in sudden alarm.

"Why? D'you mind jabs?"

"I hate them." Zack looked worried. "Mum. Do I have to get a jab? I just *got* them."

"A bit like that," Emma admitted.

"We'll do it together," Nic said. "I'll go first, and then you. It won't be so bad, I promise."

"Really?" Zack looked at him doubtfully.

"Word of honor. And then we'll have dinner, all together," Nic told him.

"We didn't talk about that," Emma protested.

"Hamburgers?" Zack asked, ignoring his mother.

"If you like. Hamburgers," Nic agreed.

revelation

♡

Nic took the drive back to Narrow Neck again, his mind still back in the cozy lounge. The flat might not be flash, but she'd made it into a home, he had to admit. And with all the money he and Claudia had spent, could he say that? He'd liked the sleek modernity in their decoration of the big house, the black leather couches and white walls, the recessed lighting and splashes of color that came from the modern paintings that hung here and there, the dark wood pieces and gleaming hardwood floors. He still liked it. But maybe it could use a bit of warming up. Something. Some...touches. He shook his head. He wouldn't have a clue how to do that. Maybe he could ask Claudia.

But first, he had to get this over with. He felt the fatigue overcoming him again at the thought. Maybe he could get some rest first. But no. If he were going to get blood tests with Zack and Emma on Wednesday, he needed to tell Claudia first. It was only fair. And it would be a long training session tomorrow, followed by an endorsement obligation with Cooper's. He had to turn up, do a video session at their new bakery. And then he'd be telling himself he was too tired again.

Harden up. Do it now. He pulled into the garage, walked through the connecting door into the house without wasting any more time thinking about it.

"Hello, darling. You've been awhile." Claudia came into the entryway where he was shedding shoes and jumper. "I was just about to eat without you."

"Sorry," he answered automatically. "What is there?"

"Steak," she said. "Rose marinated it, fixed a salad and some vegies, too. All we have to do is grill it."

"Give me a few minutes to take a shower, OK?"

"All right. But be quick, will you? I'll get the steak started."

The warm water helped revive him. She was opening a bottle of wine as he came downstairs again. "Want one?"

"Just a small one. Still a bit knackered from the time change. I'll fall asleep if I drink much and be rubbish tomorrow."

"Where did you get off to tonight, anyway?" she asked him as they finished their dinner. She'd just wound up a long work story, with the upshot that the long-sought, much-anticipated partnership looked to be within her grasp. They sat at the sleek dark wood table, eating from heavy, square white plates set on woven mats along with chunky cutlery and glassware. The modern furnishings gave a stylish effect to the greenhouse-style dining room that protruded from the back of the house, offering the feeling of eating in a forest of the native plantings that surrounded it on three sides. Artfully placed lights glowed amidst the fern trees, allowing them to appreciate the greenery even at night. This was his favorite part of the house. A good place to talk.

"Doing a bit of training with a kid," he said, setting his fork down and looking at Claudia. As flawless as always, her perfection matching the room. Dark hair falling in a straight, glossy curtain to just below her shoulders, makeup light but precise, defining her elegant features. Her beautiful figure was, as ever, casually chic in slim jeans and a deceptively simple heavy cotton shirt that hadn't, he thought suddenly, come from Trade Me or any Op Shop on the planet. He looked at her as if seeing her for the first time. The last time, before he changed everything.

She looked up at him, took another dainty bite of salad and chewed it carefully, then wiped her mouth. "What kid? Somebody's son?"

He took a deep breath. Prepared for it. "My son."

Her fork stayed in the air for a long moment as she stared across at him, before she set it down with deliberate care. "I think you'd better explain."

She was still calm, still collected, he saw. Irrationally, the quality he'd always admired in her now annoyed him. What on earth *would* rattle her?

He explained how he'd seen Zack at Rob's camp, then Emma. "I checked his birthday. And I knew," he finished. "And then I went to see her, and she admitted it."

"When was this?" she asked.

"Just before I left for Safa. Last Monday."

"And you saw them again tonight."

"Yeh. Took him out. He's really good. Burning to play."

She brushed that aside as the irrelevancy it was. "How do you know? That he's yours?"

"No proof yet," he admitted. "We're doing that on Wednesday. And then I'll make it official, do the legal things."

"So you *don't* really know," she pointed out. "What makes you think she's telling the truth? That she isn't just trying to trap you? So you slept with her. So what? Who knows who else she was sleeping with at the time, somebody like that?"

"I know. We were together. Trust me, there wasn't anybody else. It wasn't like that anyway. And why would she agree to the blood test, otherwise? Anyway, he looks like me. Got my eyes. When you see him, you'll know too. I don't need a test to be sure."

"But you're getting one. You have that much sense, at least. What does she expect? What's she looking for?"

"She's not looking for anything. She wasn't too keen on my being there at all."

"Right." She was clearly unconvinced. "She wasn't happy that a meal ticket fell at her feet. How do you know she didn't do the whole thing on purpose?"

"That was her strategic plan?" He was getting angry now. "She's a bloody bad schemer, then, isn't she? Took about seven years to pay off."

"So it didn't work out the way she was hoping. That doesn't mean she didn't plan it."

"This doesn't matter anyway," he said with exasperation. "He's here, and he's mine. He's in our life now, no matter how it started out."

"*Our* life? How? What is she expecting?" Claudia asked again.

"She's not expecting anything. I told you. What *I'm* expecting is that I'll pay the maintenance, and work out some kind of visitation."

"What kind of maintenance?" she asked in alarm. "What have you said to her? You shouldn't be having any kind of conversation like that. Let your lawyer handle it, with hers. What were you thinking?"

"She doesn't have a lawyer," he said impatiently. "Can't afford one, I'm sure. They're living in a tiny flat. It's not hard to suss out, anyway. There's a formula. I checked already."

"You checked. With Oliver?" she asked, referring to his attorney. "Well, thank goodness for that. What did he say?"

"About the money? There's a formula," he repeated. "Simple enough."

"How much money are we talking about?" she demanded.

"Fifteen hundred a month," he admitted. "That's the top bracket. If she has him all the time."

She drew in her breath with a hiss. "Not like we can't afford it," he pointed out.

"*Now* we can. What about when you're done playing, though? This is our time to lay down a foundation for the future. We've discussed that. Rugby isn't forever."

"He's part of the future too," Nic said angrily. "He's my *son,* Claud. Not some…some disaster. A collapsed roof or something."

"And what about our own children, when we have them? What are you taking away from them?"

He'd never seen this side of her before, not in their personal life. He'd known she could be ruthless at work—that was why that partnership was looking so promising—but whatever he'd expected when he told her, it wasn't this.

"I'll be as concerned for their welfare as I am for Zack's," he said, his own voice hardening. "And that's his name, by the way. Even though you didn't ask. Zack. Zachary, I guess. I don't even know," he realized. "I'll have to get the birth certificate sorted, too. So there isn't an empty space there."

"She must feel like Christmas has come early," she said sarcastically. "Already planning the big move, I'm sure. On our money."

"Nah. She hasn't said a word about it. Hasn't talked to me about money at all. We've hardly had a chance. Barely had a conversation. She doesn't even want me to tell him yet, not till we've got to know each other a bit. But yeh, I'd like them to move. The neighborhood's good enough, but the flat's pretty dodgy. I'm thinking some kind of settlement, for the back support. What I'd have been paying if I'd known."

"*What?* You have no legal obligation, Nic. Surely Oliver explained that. I've barely touched on family law myself, thank God, but even I know that. There's no obligation until maintenance is ordered. You'd better not have mentioned *that* to her. I'll ring Oliver tomorrow," she decided. "Find out what the process is, what our options are."

"No." He was firm, now. "I'll cope with Oliver. This is my responsibility. And it has nothing to do with what's legally ordered." He cut her off as she began to argue. "It has to do with getting them out of there, and into something better. He's wearing buggered rugby boots, and pajamas two sizes too big." He struggled to express the distress those pajamas had caused him. "He deserves better. They both do. Emma didn't ask for this."

"I think that's exactly what she asked for," Claudia said sharply. "If she dropped her drawers for you two seconds after meeting you."

He stared at her in shock. "And how long was it before we had sex? If you'd fallen pregnant, what would you have expected me to do?"

"That was different. We were dating. I wasn't some groupie."

"And neither was she. It wasn't like that." He was in dangerous territory, he knew, but he couldn't help coming to Emma's defense. "Anyway, it doesn't *matter*. What matters is that we're having the blood tests on Wednesday, so I won't be home to dinner. And I'm giving them tickets for the game on Saturday," he went on, wanting to get everything out there now, since it had all turned to custard anyway.

"Oh, no. You're not expecting me to get to know him. Or that…woman."

"Of course I am. They're both in our lives now, like it or not. Sooner or later, he'll be here. Every week, I hope, if I can make that work. And the only way to do that without a court battle is if we have a civil relationship with Emma. I need your help with this, Claud." He softened his voice, reached for her hand. "We're meant to be partners, aren't we? This is one of those times, one of those unexpected things that happens in life, that we need to get through together."

She held his hand, but he could sense the reluctance in her, the unmistakable pulling back. "I just don't know," she said slowly. "I'm not ready for this. She's not sitting in my section, is she?" she asked in sudden alarm.

"That's where all the seats are, that I get," he said, exasperated again. "You know that. It'll be a chance to get to meet them in a neutral setting. Think of it that way."

"No." She shook her head, the silky hair swaying. "Not yet. If they're coming on Saturday, I'm staying home."

"I'd like you to be there. For me, as well as for this."

"No," she repeated. "Not yet. Give me a chance to get used to this, Nic. I'll watch the game, here. But I'm not going to sit next to that…" She broke off, seeing the danger in his expression. "And be friendly, like this is some kind of normal social occasion. She won't want to meet me either."

"She's going to want to get to know the woman who'll be looking after Zack, while he's here," he pointed out. "And I'm sure she's none too comfortable with that idea, either. He's her world. That's plain to see."

"That'll mostly be Rose, surely," she objected.

"Not if it's at the weekend. Which'll be hard enough, with my playing schedule." He ran a hand over his face, rubbing his eyes, suddenly feeling alarmingly weary again. "I don't know. I don't have the answers yet. I only learnt all this myself a week ago. And I'm shattered from the game, and the journey," he admitted. "But I wanted to tell you now. Share it with you."

She nodded stiffly, got up and picked up both plates. "Let's go to bed, then."

That was it? Those were all her questions? She hadn't seemed the least bit concerned about the relationship he'd had with Emma. Was *any* woman really that secure? Her lack of fuss was rational, he supposed. The whole thing was in the past, after all. But it didn't seem…normal. And she had barely even mentioned Zack. Not as a child. A person. Well, he supposed it was good that she was focused on maintaining their own relationship.

But later, when he reached for her, she pushed his hand away. "Not tonight. I'm not feeling very close to you just now."

He sighed, rolled over, punched the pillow a few times. It had been a long week in the hotel. Too much work, and too much upheaval. He could've used the comfort of her body tonight. He might be able to convince her, with a little more effort. But he was suddenly too tired to make it.

jabs

♡

Nic was pacing up and down on the pavement in front of the doctor's office when Emma hurried up, holding Zack by the hand.

"I was afraid you weren't going to turn up," Nic said with obvious relief.

"Sorry. Work. Traffic. Collecting Zack…" She trailed off. She was always rushing, never seemed to be quite organized enough, to be able to get anywhere exactly when she was supposed to, the way other people did. Due to sheer fear, she usually made it on time to work, if only just.

He nodded. He wasn't going to berate her, she saw with relief. She felt like she couldn't handle another criticism today. She was nervous enough about this as it was. What would he say when he saw how much Zack hated needles? Not to mention whatever was going to happen next. Her life was careening out of control again, and she hated the sensation. She tightened her hold on her son's hand as Nic held the door to the clinic open for them.

"Mum," Zack complained. "You're squeezing too hard."

"Sorry." She loosened her grip and took a deep breath, trying to calm the nerves that had had her jumpy all day. It wasn't going to help Zack to see her anxious.

"Go sit and look at a magazine for a minute," she told him now. "Do you see the kids' area over there?"

"I want to stay with you." He was the one squeezing now at the familiar sight of a doctor's waiting room. She didn't try to convince him, just focused on giving the receptionist their details, once Nic had finished checking himself in.

"We'll pop you into a room straight away," the woman said. "Just be a sec."

"Cheers," Nic said gratefully.

"I never get that," Emma told him in a low voice as they moved to the line of chairs. "Seems like we wait forever, where we go."

He shrugged, but sure enough, a technician was calling them now. The sound of Nic's name had heads turning and curious looks cast in their direction, Emma saw, and she realized the reason for the quick processing. Well, whatever it took. Zack didn't need any excuse to get more nervous.

As she'd expected, Zack quailed at the sight of the chair with its attached armrest, the rows of test tubes. He was hanging back now, pulling at her hand.

"Who's going first?" the technician asked cheerfully.

"That'd be me," Nic said. He winked at Zack. "Come over here and sit by me, mate. Keep me company."

"I want Mum," Zack said, lip already trembling. He pressed closer to Emma, and she scooted the single hard chair closer to the one Nic had settled into and pulled Zack into her lap, bending her head to kiss the top of his, her arms going around him securely.

This was too hard, she thought in despair. All of this. For Zack, and for her.

♡

Zack's face went white when he saw the technician fit the needle to the test tube in a gloved hand. "It's jabs," he said in a reedy voice. "Isn't it?"

"Not too bad," Nic said encouragingly. "What I do is, I think about a footy problem. And before I know it, it's over." He looked into Zack's eyes, got the boy focused on him instead of the band the technician was putting around his arm, or the needle resting on the tray. "Just now, I'm thinking about that Rebels wing. Miller. Those quick moves he's got, inside the 22. How he moves his head just before he offloads. How I have to tackle if I'm going to get him."

"You think it, in your head?" Zack asked.

"Write it too," Nic said. "Got an exercise book, for when I watch the films, when I look at their form."

"But doesn't the coach tell you? He always tells us."

"The coaches aren't on the paddock with me, on the night," Nic explained, holding the cotton ball to the crook of his elbow and noting with satisfaction that Zack hadn't even watched the blood-drawing process.

"Your turn," he said as the woman finished applying the adhesive tape. He stood to let Zack take his place.

The boy shrank into his mother's arms. "It's a needle," he said, eyes welling. "I saw."

"Over in a sec," Nic promised. "Come sit here, mate, and let's see what you remember from Monday."

Unwilling to disappoint his hero, Zack disentangled himself reluctantly from Emma and climbed into the chair.

"Give us your arm," the technician coaxed. "And look at your dad there."

"He's not my dad," Zack corrected her.

"Sorry. Your mate, then," the woman said. She glanced at the printed order sheet, then looked at Nic in sudden speculation.

Nic squatted next to the chair, took Zack's other hand in his. He felt the cold little fingers trembling, saw the effort the boy was making to be brave in front of him. *Your dad.* He cleared his throat. "This is a quiz. Pay attention, now. When you get the high ball, near your own try line, what do you do?"

"Kick it away," Zack said. He jumped at the feeling of the tight tourniquet on his arm, and Nic tightened his hold on his hand, looked intently into the eyes, so like his own, raised to his.

"And why d'you do that? Why would you just give it straight back again?" Nic demanded as he saw the technician insert the needle, felt the boy jerk.

"Because," Zack said in a trembling voice. "Because you want to keep the play away from your territory."

"Well done," Nic congratulated him. "And what's important under the high ball?"

"Watch it," Zack said.

"Focus," Nic agreed. "And practice catching. Over and over. Want to do some of that, next time?"

"Yeh," Zack breathed. "Will you take me again?"

"Too right I will."

"And we're done," the technician said briskly. "Hold this cotton to your arm, like this." She demonstrated the pressure. Zack blinked in surprise, placed his fingers obediently over the white stuff.

The woman moved quickly to cover the spot with tape. "That's you done, then," she said. "Let's get your mum up here. This *is* your mum, isn't it?"

"Course it is. Don't be scared, Mum," Zack said encouragingly as he climbed down from the chair. "Just think about something nice. It doesn't really hurt."

Emma smiled down at her son as Nic shifted across to the chair she'd just vacated. He took Zack with him, did his best to keep him from focusing on the needle, or the blood filling the tube. Within minutes, they were on the other side of the door again, the two of them waiting as Nic paid the bill for all three tests.

"Thanks," Emma told him as they waited outside the toilets for Zack to make a suddenly urgent stop before the promised café visit. "It's being scared, and having it be over," she explained. "Why he had to go. I'm just glad he made it in time. But I wanted to say…" She looked away, then back at him, and he could see the effort it took her to say it, to thank him. "You did that really well. He does hate jabs. He's usually pretty brave, but he has a thing about needles."

"No worries. I know what diverts my own mind." He smiled down at her. "When I'm trying to forget something else. I reckon he may be the same."

"Rugby will do it," she agreed. "I think I'm going to duck in for a moment myself. Will you wait for Zack?"

"Course."

He'd been nervous too, Nic admitted to himself while he and Zack waited in their turn for Emma. Nervous that she wasn't going to turn up, that she'd changed her mind, that he really was going to have to get that court order. Whatever Claudia thought, he could see how torn Emma was by all this. He reminded himself never to underestimate how fiercely she would fight to protect her son.

salt and sand

♡

"We should leave for Mum's at about nine," Claudia told Nic on Saturday morning, moving briskly into the kitchen area where he sat lingering over his toast at the breakfast bar. "I said nine-thirty, as you wanted to do the morning."

She was ready to go, he saw. Already made-up, dressed in casual but snug crop pants that flattered her willowy, elegant figure.

"Done with this?" she asked, reaching for his plate.

He held onto it. "In a minute. Geez, Claud, you could at least let me finish first." He took another sip of tea, looked out the floor-to-ceiling windows at the terraced garden, the sun shining on the foliage in the large square planters set around the spacious patio area. "It's a gorgeous day out. Want to bunk off here, run away to the beach with me?"

"Mum's expecting us," she reminded him.

"Maybe we could do it tomorrow," he suggested.

"That won't work. You'll be lying on the couch half the day."

"Maybe she could come here and we could do it while I lie on the couch. Come on," he coaxed. "We could swim, fool around in the water. Find a quiet spot to get up to a bit of no good."

"You have a game tonight."

"And I need to relax, get right for that. Long Bay in the sunshine sounds perfect."

"It'll be full of people," she objected. "If I wanted to watch Polynesians play rugby, I'd be coming tonight, wouldn't I?"

She looked a little shamefaced at his obvious shock. "Sorry. It's been a long week. I'm getting a lot of pressure on the Fonterra deal. And all the wedding details..." She trailed off. "I need to get the guest list sorted. I need to tick this off the list, make some progress."

"If it's really Zack you're upset about, we should discuss it," he said. "We hardly got started, the other night."

"Nothing to discuss. Not till you get the results, and talk to Oliver again. Are you going to get ready to go? We need to leave in fifteen minutes." She motioned at him, and he heard the *click*. "Get a move on, Nic, or we'll be late."

"Did you just snap your fingers?" he asked incredulously.

Her defenses came up in a flash. "You're being so *slow.* Finish your toast and get dressed, please. We need to go."

"Don't snap your fingers at me," he said quietly. "And don't talk to me like I'm a kid. I know you aren't too happy with me just now, but I hate that. Both things. Please don't do them again."

♡

He was looking out a different window an hour later, but still wishing he were at the beach. Sitting in his future mother-in-law's painfully correct lounge, filled with the latest modern decorating trends, from the inevitable black leather couches to the completely transparent Plexiglas coffee table.

"I need at least eighteen more spots for clients," Claudia was saying. "I can't see any way to cut this down. Nic, do you really have to invite so many of your teammates?"

"Yes," he said.

"I understand you want your friends there," Elizabeth, Claudia's mother, said in a tone that was obviously meant to be soothing, but that set Nic's teeth on edge, as if he were a recalcitrant child who needed coaxing. "Maybe we could free up some spots if everyone didn't bring a partner."

"You want me to tell them they can't bring their *partners?*"

"Of course not," Claudia put in hastily. "Not if they're married, or have a real girlfriend. But does every twenty-two-year-old have to bring a date? I can understand inviting the senior players, anyway. But between the Blues, and the Chiefs, and the All Blacks..."

"They can bring whoever they want," Nic said. "I'm not going to quiz them on their bloody relationship status. I've played with some of those blokes for four years now. They're mates. Look. I gave you two hundred fifty spots. I only have a hundred fifty. Use your two-fifty however you want, but my teammates are invited. *With* any date they may want to bring. My list is sorted."

He looked out the window again. *Long Bay*, he thought with another inward sigh. He wouldn't go so far this afternoon, of course, wouldn't have time. He'd take an hour to walk the Narrow Neck shoreline, then sit with his exercise book, quietly visualize everything he planned to do tonight. He'd need the time anyway to put his mind right, after a couple hours of this. The beach would have been so much better. Especially if there'd been a bit of fun attached.

♡

The weekend chores could wait until tomorrow, Emma had decided. This would be a special night for Zack anyway, his first Blues game, so why not make the whole day fun? She hadn't had any trouble talking Zack into a trip to the beach, though she hadn't been able to round up any adult companionship.

"I've had enough kids for one week," Lucy had declared when Emma had invited her along during their ferry ride home from their early-morning gym class. "No offense, Em. You know I love my nephew. But I'm looking forward to some serious adult entertainment this afternoon."

"Told you the thigh soreness would get better," Emma said with a smile.

"Plus, Tom's loving the new me," Lucy said with satisfaction. "Nothing like a bit of honest appreciation to get the motor running."

"Not to mention the body confidence," Emma pointed out. "That's probably not hurting either."

"True. I'm definitely getting more comfortable with the lights on. And wearing what he likes, too." Lucy stretched out a leg in its spandex capris, pointed her toe. "Look, calf muscles. But *you* can't have any body confidence issues," she continued. "No excuse there. So what's the story with *your* love life?"

Emma turned to look at the wake disappearing behind them as the ferry sliced through the harbour toward Devonport. "My what? That fell overboard a ways back, I'm afraid."

"Why? You used to date a fair amount when you lived with me."

"I still do, some, but it isn't much. Having to get someone to mind Zack is part of it. But it seems like it's getting tougher anyway. How excited do you think most guys in their twenties are to go out with somebody who has a six-year-old? A lot of them have barely moved out of their own parents' houses. They're living in a flat with three other guys. Zack and I are way outside their comfort zone."

"What about older guys, then?"

"Yeah, they might be living in Grown-Up World. Though I mostly know engineers these days. Bad enough if he's going to be ten years older than me, I don't need him to be boring, too. I don't need somebody else who eats the same breakfast every morning, and thinks I'm flaky because my kitchen table isn't cleaned off."

"Lots of people eat the same breakfast every morning. I pretty much do."

"I like a little spontaneity. Sue me. David always had the same exact three spoonfuls of plain yoghurt on his muesli. And then he'd take this little knife and slice his banana in half. Half a banana, every day. I used to want to scream at him, just eat the whole frigging banana! Or, I don't know, get all wild and crazy and go for strawberries! I wanted to grab that banana and throw it right out the kitchen window."

"You had a *lot* of hostility there," Lucy commented. "Good thing he dumped you."

Emma laughed. "They sent me a birth announcement, can you believe it? They waited to have a baby until she finished her Ph.D. Of *course* they did. And who knows what they did to get it timed so perfectly. Born at the start of the summer holidays."

"I shudder to think," Lucy agreed.

They grinned at each other in perfect accord as they stood to exit the ferry, docking now. "Point taken," Lucy said. "No engineers. But maybe one of Tom's mates?"

"Like Mr. Sucktoes?" Emma asked, causing heads to turn in the boarding queue, and both sisters to burst out laughing.

"OK, the foot fetish was a surprise," Lucy conceded when they were free of the crowd and walking along the wooden wharf together. "What are the odds of that happening again, though? Isolated disaster. I'll make Tom vet them better for kinkiness next time."

"Well, *bad* kinkiness."

"Is there a good kind?" Lucy asked, staring at her sister.

Emma shrugged and smiled, waited till Lucy popped the lock on the car, then swung in with her gym bag.

"Don't answer that," Lucy decided. "TMI."

♡

So that was no Lucy on the beach trip. Graham's mum Stephanie was a washout, too.

"I think that cold of Heather's has turned into an ear infection," she'd sighed on the phone. "Looks like another fab Saturday in the doctor's office."

"Let me take Graham," Emma urged. "Then at least you'll only have the one."

"Thanks," Stephanie said. "I owe you."

"Nah. It all evens out."

Now she sat at a picnic table with her grid-lined sketchbook, working on a design and casting an occasional eye at the distant play structure where Zack and Graham were happily scrambling, climbing, and taking turns zipping down the long flying fox with the other kids. She found her attention straying as well to the group of young men playing an enthusiastic game of touch rugby in an open space nearby. It would be exciting to see Nic play at Eden Park tonight, she had to admit. Zack wasn't the only one looking forward to that performance.

Some of the guys here didn't look too bad with their shirts off, she decided. But none could hold a candle to Nic, the way he'd been in Fiji. Brown and hard-muscled, impressive even then. He'd added a few more kilos of power in the years since, she'd noticed. The shoulders and thighs might be a bit bulkier now. His arms, too. Her gaze became abstracted as her mind drifted to those powerful forearms, the bit of bicep showing beneath the hem of his T-shirt sleeves, all she'd really seen of him so far. She'd bet the rest of him still looked as good as ever, though.

She glanced across at the water, the long stretch of beach that gave Long Bay its name. Pity she hadn't been able to arrange some additional adult supervision. She'd have liked to have a real swim herself. Or something else, she thought as she felt the tug of desire. To be with Nic again, the way it had been.

They'd taken one of the resort's kayaks out one morning, had paddled to an isolated beach on the other side of the island, pulled the boat up high on the fine white sand and gone for a swim in the clear turquoise sea, diving down to look at shells, picking up live sand dollars where they lay humped just under the sandy bottom, then setting them gently down again. Nic made her laugh by kicking up into a handstand, then walking on his hands, strong brown legs waving in the air.

"Show-off," she chided as he shot back up to the surface in a spray of salt water.

"Race you," he said with a grin. "To the other side of the bay."

"You have to give me a head start," she objected. "You're too fast."

"OK. I'll count to twenty. Ready…steady…GO!"

She'd set off with her fastest crawl, putting all she had into it, knowing he'd beat her anyway, her heart thudding at the thought of him behind her, catching up.

She'd got more than halfway across when she felt the hand on her leg, pulling her to him. She turned, treading water. "No fair," she protested, still breathing hard with effort. "We aren't done."

"I was winning anyway," he pointed out. "Decided I didn't want to wear you out this way."

"Maybe I had a burst of speed left in me. Did you think of that?"

"Nah." He was pulling her with him now, side-stroking toward shore. "Think you'd better accept it. You lose. And you know there's a price for that."

"Oh, yeah?" she got out through the rush of excitement as he reached to hold her, the water shallow enough for him to stand here. "I didn't agree to any rules like that."

"I just changed them," he told her, that gleam in his eyes again. She tried to stand herself, realized the water was still too deep for her, and held onto his broad shoulders instead as his mouth came down over hers in a long, heated kiss.

"What are they, then?" she asked, playing along, when he pulled his mouth from hers again and moved his lips over her cheek, his teeth closing on her earlobe. She had her legs wrapped around him now, her hands stroking over his shoulders and back, loving the feel of the shifting muscle under her palms. She bit his neck with an open mouth, felt a pulse jump there as she licked the salt from him.

"Hmm? What are what?" he asked, distracted, his hands cradling her bottom, rubbing her against him through the layers of wet fabric, each movement of his body bringing with it another flicker of sensation where he touched her.

"The rules. For when I lose." She licked again, used her own teeth.

"You take your togs off," he decided. "And then give me the prize. Which is whatever I want."

"Oh," she sighed. "Those are some pretty harsh rules. But I guess if I have to…"

"Oh, you have to," he assured her. "I'm dead serious about the rules. Take off your top."

"I'll go under and drown."

"I've got you. Take it off."

She kept her legs around him, reached behind her to unhook the back, then shrugged out of the wet garment, reached around his neck again, one hand clutching the wet bikini top, and looked up into his eyes. "Is this right?"

"Oh, yeh. That's right." He kissed her again, no laziness now, then shifted his mouth to her throat, pulling her up higher, the salty water helping to support her. He bent his head further, took a breast, white against the tanned skin around it, into his mouth.

"Nic," she groaned as his mouth moved over her, as she felt herself melting. "If somebody came by, they'd see me."

"Nobody here. And that's only step one. Take the bottoms off." He held her where she was, playing with her, his strong arms supporting her while she wriggled out of the scant piece of fabric.

"Tread water for a sec," he told her. He wrenched his own togs off with difficulty underwater, kicked them free, then grabbed for them and slung them over one shoulder before reaching for her again and pulling her into him, over him.

"This is the price of losing," he told her. "And this is what I get for winning. Always going to get it, too. I'm always going to get you."

Her mouth was on him again, at his throat, biting his shoulder as she hung on. They were breathing hard, lost in each other, when the wave broke over them, shocking them, pulling them apart. She tumbled for a moment, then was at the surface again, lungs working, trying to cough up the water she hadn't been able to avoid taking in at the sudden drenching.

Nic grabbed for her, began pulling her toward shore. "Are you OK?"

She coughed again, gasped for air. "Yeah," she got out at last. He set her on her feet and she stood gratefully, bent to cough some more.

"Geez. Sorry." He looked so chagrined, she had to laugh, coughed a final time, and felt her breath returning.

"That'll teach you to play games in the water," she got out.

"Seemed like a good idea at the time," he told her, grinning back in relief. "I forgot about that wee small thing called the tide."

"Oh, no! My bikini! I've lost it. Did you?"

He held up his togs to show her. "Pity. Reckon you'll just have to make a spectacular entrance, back at the resort. Good thing you *are* spectacular."

"Where *is* it? I'd better be able to find it. Shoot!"

He looked around, spotted a flash of hot pink in the distance. "Hang on. I'll get it." He bunched his togs in one hand and took off after the bits of pink. She saw him rise in the water again, wave the rescued bikini over his head, and swim back towards her again.

"Success," he said as he arrived. "Want to try again? Or would that be pushing our luck?"

She laughed. "Pushing our luck. Definitely. I'm probably getting an interesting sunburn anyway. I didn't put sunscreen everywhere. Missed a few spots."

"Then we should get you dressed again, and back," he decided. "Because those are some of my favorite bits. I need to keep them in good trim."

She held onto him once they were back in shallow water, steadied herself against him while she wrestled the sodden suit bottoms on, then untwisted the bra top to put it on.

"One sec." He put a big hand on either side of her ribcage, ran his thumbs over the pink nipples, watched them harden, took one into his mouth and gave it a gentle nip, then reluctantly let her go. "Just needed one last bit of that, before you put them away. And you still owe me, you know. Going to find a way to collect the full penalty, once we're back. Get you showered off, then show you what the price of losing really is."

She was lost in the memory, heated by it, remembering what the price of losing had been. Her shock when Nic had flipped her over on the big bed and blindfolded her. The heightening of sensation that had come with being unable to see, not knowing what was coming next. Everything he'd done to her, everything he'd had her do to him, his big, agile hands guiding her in her blindness. The way he'd turned her, moved her, talked to her, giving her more and more until she was limp, her body resonating with aftershocks, blissfully spent. And how tenderly he'd kissed her, how closely he'd held her afterwards while she fell asleep.

She looked up, startled, at the appearance of one of the rugby players. The game had broken up, she realized, blinking herself back to the present and wiping the foolish, absent smile from her face.

"Hi." He stood in front of her, shirt still off, a reasonable chest of his own on display. Blue eyes, a good smile, too. "Saw you over here, looking lonely. Want to join us?"

"No, thanks." She found herself responding to his friendly, ingenuous charm. "I'm not alone, actually." She gestured toward the play structure in the distance. "Just waiting for the kids to be ready for our swim."

"Minding them, are you?" he asked, still not clued in. He sank down on the bench beside her and used the shirt slung over his shoulder to towel his dark hair. Giving a fairly nice display of shoulders and back in the process, she had to admit.

"Nope."

"Mum!" It was Zack, racing toward her with the speed he'd inherited from his father, easily outpacing Graham. "Can we swim now?"

The young man looked up, startled, then back at Emma, eyes doing a quick, obvious reassessment. He got to his feet again, pulled the T-shirt on in haste. "Oh. Sorry. I didn't realize…"

"No worries." She smiled at him a bit sadly as Graham puffed up next to Zack. "Have a good day."

Too young for me anyway, she reminded herself, pulling out togs and towels and preparing for the trek to the changing rooms. However young she looked on the outside—and she knew she appeared quite a bit younger even than her twenty-seven years—she'd left that carefree girl behind a long, long time ago.

blues jersey

♡

Emma held Zack tightly by the hand as they made their way through the crowded Eden Park concourse and up the stairs to their entry door. He was wearing his prized Blues T-shirt, with a warm jumper over it in deference to the chill of the late April evening.

"I wish I had a Blues jersey," he'd sighed earlier as she'd pulled the thick sweater over his head. "Or a hoodie, at least. I could've worn it outside my jumper, so everyone could see. D'you think all the other kids will have jerseys?"

"Not everyone can afford that," she reminded him. "They're awfully expensive, remember? We're lucky to go tonight, though, aren't we?"

"Yeh!" he agreed, the jersey forgotten for the moment. He fidgeted as she grabbed her own jacket and reached for her ankle boots. "C'mon, Mum. We're going to miss it!"

"We aren't going to miss it," she promised. "Plenty of time." She pulled on one boot, reached for the other. One heel had a bad scuff, she saw with disgust. When had *that* happened? She hobbled into the kitchen and grabbed a Sharpie from the mug on the bench, colored the mark in with a few quick strokes. That was the good thing about black, she thought in satisfaction as she pulled the boot on and looked at it from above. Nothing visible from here. And nobody was going to be studying her feet that closely.

"Mum," Zack wailed. "Hurry."

They *were* well in time, she thought gratefully forty-five minutes later, searching for their row near midfield of the big stadium. Being on time wasn't always her best thing, but she hadn't wanted Zack to miss the sight and sound of Nic being announced, running onto the field. So she'd made a special effort, scuffed boot and all.

"Row 54," she said. "This is us." They edged into the row, murmuring their "Sorrys" as polite spectators stood or pulled legs aside for them. There would be other kids around, she saw. And lots of them *did* seem to be wearing jerseys, including the girls. Well, Nic had said there would be some players' families here tonight. Although not his fiancée. She wasn't able to make it. Emma felt a fresh surge of relief not to have to meet her right now, though she wondered at the same time why his girlfriend wouldn't be at a home game. Surely that came with the territory?

His love life is not your business, she reminded herself once again. *Just forget that part of it.* So hard to do, though, when she kept seeing him again, the coiled-spring way he still moved reminding her all too clearly of the past. How he'd looked. How he'd been. Wondered if he were doing all the things they'd done together with his fiancée.

Of course he is. But *she* hadn't. Had never done anything so exciting again. Her sex life since Zack, such as it was, had been pretty vanilla in contrast.

Stop thinking about your sex life. And his. It was anticipating watching him play that was doing it, she supposed. She shifted her attention back to the present, smiled at her neighbor as she found their seats at last. The woman, a pretty blonde with a beanie pulled over her long hair, smiled back at her in friendly welcome.

"You must be Emma," the blonde said. "And this must be Zack. Nic's good mate, I hear. I'm Hannah Callahan. Nic told me he had some special friends coming tonight. He asked me to look out for you."

Emma looked at her in surprise. She'd been grateful for the tickets that had kindled such a light in Zack's eyes when Nic had produced them over their hamburgers as a bonus prize for enduring the blood test on Wednesday. But she'd certainly never expected this kind of greeting. "Thanks. That's awfully nice of you. You're Drew's partner, right?"

"Wife." Hannah's warm, rueful smile took any sting out of the correction. "I just can't get used to that 'partner' thing. It makes me feel like we're in a business deal. But you know what I mean. Nic said you were American too."

"Mum used to be," Zack said. "But now she's a Kiwi, same as me."

"We're all Kiwis now, aren't we?" Hannah replied cheerfully. "I have a Kiwi boy at home myself. Too little to enjoy the game, though. Are you a Blues supporter?"

"Yeh," Zack told her earnestly. "They're my most favorite team, except the All Blacks."

"My sentiments exactly," Hannah assured him. From the wife of the Blues and All Blacks captain, Emma could well believe it.

"Who're you talking to?" A statuesque woman with classical Maori features peered around Hannah. "Hi." She held out a hand to Emma. "Reka Ranapia."

Emma introduced herself, then Zack.

"That's going to be boring for you, Zack, down the end like that," Reka told him. "Scoot over here and sit with the rest of the kids. Shift down, Emma."

"We all do what Reka says," Hannah laughed as Zack hurried to obey and she and Emma moved over in their turn.

"I'm not bossy. I just have good ideas," Reka grinned.

"That you do," Hannah agreed. "I love your sweater, Emma. And Zack's as well." She reached out to finger the heavy wool, the variegated shades of gray interspersed with white in a design of lightning bolts that had delighted Zack, as the boy squeezed past her. "Where'd you get this? And your own?"

"I made them," Emma told her, feeling a bit shy. She had decided to wear her own pale blue sweater tonight, with its dark blue trim, for obvious reasons. She might not have a jersey, but she could still wear the team colors. And her sweater was prettier than any jersey.

"Really," Hannah said, clearly impressed. She turned to look at Zack's sweater again. "I love that pattern. Exactly like a stormy sky. Where'd you find it?"

"I made it up," Emma said. "That's my hobby, knitting. Designing knits, mostly. Once I start working on the actual garment, I just want to hurry up and finish it so I can start the next thing."

"Oh, no," Reka groaned.

"Sorry," Emma said in embarrassed confusion. "Is this boring?"

"Reka knows she's just heard the last of me," Hannah smiled. "Because you're in my territory now."

"No worries," Reka sighed. "I'll just talk to Jenna and Kate. We'll look after Zack, Emma. Got heaps of kids over here."

Emma thanked her, then turned her attention back to Hannah. "What do you mean?" she asked. "Your territory?"

"I work for 2nd Hemisphere," Hannah told her. "The merino firm."

"I know who they are, of course," Emma said. "And I remember, now, that that's what you do. I'm jealous. I love merino, though I can't afford the yarn."

"Well..." Hannah scooted a bit closer and put out a hand to touch the lace pattern of Emma's sweater, bending closer to examine the crocheted edge. "I have a new venture with them, my own idea that I've been working on for a couple years now."

"The maternity wear thing?" Emma asked. "I saw the interview you did, last year. I loved the clothes. I wish I'd had them when I was pregnant." They'd have been beyond her budget, although, she thought practically, they'd last through several pregnancies. The breathable, lightweight, extra-soft wool was perfect for maternity wear, cool in summer, warm in winter.

"Don't tell, but I'm planning on doing another of those," Hannah said. "I want to get a couple of my friends to model this time. Reka's expecting again, and Jenna Douglas is, too, and the marketer in me can't help but think about the airtime we could get with that. But I haven't alerted them yet. I don't want to give them any time to think up excuses."

Emma smiled as Hannah continued. "But that isn't the latest. We're working now on a new line. Kids' things. For boys too, but mostly for girls."

Emma's eyes lit up with excitement. "Merino kids' wear. Oh, how fun. Skirts," she thought aloud. "Cardigans. Ooh. Stripes, and ruffles at the edges."

"Exactly. Do you work in design?"

"Not the kind you mean. CAD."

"But we do that," Hannah said. "That's how we produce our designs. In CAD."

"Really?"

"What kind of CAD do you do?"

"Engineering," Emma told her ruefully.

"Is that your field, then?"

"Not by preference," Emma admitted. "But it's what I've been doing, since I left University."

"Well, let's talk more another time," Hannah said. "If you'll be bringing Zack to more games. Because I'd love to get your thoughts. But we can't do it now, because here we go."

the mood spoilt

♡

Nic dropped his bag in the entryway the following Sunday, then thought again and took it upstairs to the bedroom. It would make Claudia happier to have it out of the way, and he didn't need to give her any extra agro just now.

Where *was* she, anyway? He finally ran her to ground in the exercise room, where she was riding the bike, headphones on. She pulled them off when she saw him, reached for the hand towel and wiped herself down. He went to her and gave her a kiss.

"Hi," she said with real warmth, returning the kiss with more enthusiasm than she'd shown him these past couple weeks. "Welcome home. Everything go OK? You looked good last night. Sorry about the loss, though."

"Thanks. A bit sore," he admitted. "The Crusaders were fizzing. Couldn't lift to match them. We're still top of the ladder, but it's got a wee bit too close for comfort."

"You can have a quiet day today, anyway. I've got nothing on, either."

He pulled her off the bike, kissed her again. "Hope you won't, have anything on that is. Because I've missed you."

♡

He hated to spoil the mood that afternoon, but on the other hand, this could be the perfect time to discuss the future, while they were feeling close, the bond tight again. "I got the blood test results back, Friday," he told her as they relaxed on the couch, her feet in his lap, the *Herald on Sunday* spread out between them.

And that was the mood spoilt, just as he'd feared. She pulled her feet away, sat upright and set the paper aside. "And?"

"No surprises. He's mine." He'd been changing after the Captain's Run at the stadium in Christchurch on Friday, had pulled out his mobile to see his doctor's text. His heart had skipped a beat, and it had seemed like an age till he was alone, could ring Frank back to get the word. It had felt momentous despite the certainty he'd have said he'd felt before. The biggest shock had been the relief.

A relief that Claudia clearly didn't share. She let out her breath on a long sigh.

"Not the news you were hoping for, eh," he said with a wry smile.

"It certainly does make life more complicated," she admitted. "What does Oliver say?"

"Haven't had a chance to ring him yet. But it's just a matter of filing the papers now, I reckon."

"That's it, then," Claudia said with a little nod. "Get it done, budget for that, and move on."

"Well, not quite," Nic pointed out. "There's still working out the visitation. That'll be a bit trickier."

"You're still planning on that, then."

"Course I am. Thought I'd made that clear."

"Don't you think it'll make everybody's life pretty messy? He's been getting on fine without you, all this time. Is it really fair to him to raise his expectations? I understand that you're obligated on the maintenance," she added hastily. "But putting him into a situation where he has to leave his mum and come here? How is that in his best interest?"

"It's in his best interest to have a dad who cares about him. I'm dead sure of that. And that means spending some time."

"And is his mum, what's-her-name, quite keen on that too?"

"Emma," Nic said sharply. "Her name is Emma. And I don't know. We haven't discussed it, like I said. Early days yet."

"Uh-huh," Claudia said skeptically. "All of this, and the stepmum thing too. I don't think any of this is going to be as simple as you think."

"I didn't say it'd be simple. But we'll work it out, all the same. In the meantime, I'll be spending time with him Mondays, playing a bit of rugby and having dinner. Starting tomorrow."

"She's agreed to that?"

"Emma? Yeh. For this week, she has. That's as far as we've got. Which is why I need to talk it over with her. Plus all this."

"She doesn't know yet?"

"Nah. Wanted to tell you first. I need your support on this, Claud," he admitted, taking her hand. "It's thrown me for a good old loop, I don't mind saying."

"I'm trying," she said. "But it's a big ask."

He scooted closer on the couch, took her in his arms. "I know it is. But we can do this, together. One step at a time."

♡

Emma finished cubing the avocado, slid it from the chopping board into the wooden salad bowl with the flat of the knife, then crumbled some feta on top. She wished she had something more exciting to offer than a precooked chicken from New World, the roasted vegetable salad she'd prepared the day before, and this green salad. But that was as much as she could manage on a Monday evening.

It wasn't about eating anyway. It wasn't a date. This dinner would merely be the transition between Nic's time with Zack, and the discussion the two of them needed to have.

Another lurch of anxiety at the thought, and she shook her head impatiently and shoved it down with an effort. She'd done an extra thorough job of cleaning yesterday, had even tidied up the lounge, attempted to bring some order to her desk, get rid of some of the papers that seemed to multiply of their own accord. And then had been annoyed at herself. So she wasn't neat. It wasn't Nic's place to judge her, and she was tired of apologizing for who she was. She'd resisted the urge to tidy her bedroom, anyway. Judgment or not, he wasn't going to be seeing that.

"Cheers for dinner," Nic told her once Zack was safely tucked into bed. Emma had decided on the lounge this time. It was more comfortable, after all. But she wasn't sitting on the couch with him. She took the small easy chair to one side, a safe distance away from where he sat, casual as usual in his track pants and T-shirt. She wished he'd wear long sleeves. And a turtleneck. And a bag over his head. Then she wouldn't be distracted by the sleepy eyes, serious now, without the glint of fun she'd seen in them so often.

Dinner. He was thanking her for dinner. "No worries. Zack loved having you here."

"Yeh." He got up and went to the entryway, fished an envelope from the pocket of his jacket, came back and handed it to her, reseating himself on the end of the couch beside her chair. "Here it is. The report."

She opened the envelope with hands that were suddenly cold. She'd known what it would say, of course, but she was still unprepared for what she saw there. The brief sentences, confirming that she and Nic were Zack's parents.

Father. There was the word that she once would have longed to see. Her fingers felt clumsy as she folded the paper again, shoved it back in the envelope and handed it to him without a word.

"Your copy," he told her. "I've got the other, to file. Rang Oliver—my attorney—today as well. He'll handle it from here."

She nodded, set the envelope down on the coffee table, took a comforting sip of tea just for something to do. "OK."

"I'd like to make this—this Monday thing—a regular deal," he went on. "You don't have to feed me again," he went on hastily. "I'll take him out, afterwards. And I've got tickets for you, for the two home games that're left, next couple weeks. If we end up playing any of the knockout rounds at home, I'll get you those as well."

"All right. On the Monday thing. For now." Zack certainly seemed to be enjoying himself, and that was what mattered. "And thanks for the tickets, and for asking Hannah to look out for us. That helped."

"No worries. Though she'll be wondering why, when you turn up next time. May be time to tell people I'm his dad, as well as Zack."

"Not yet," she said immediately.

"Why not?" he asked in frustration. "Isn't he going to wonder why I'm hanging about?"

"Of course he isn't. He's *six*. To a six-year-old, adults are a big mystery. They don't sit around analyzing our motivations. They accept what we do. He's thrilled to have you around. But I don't want to tell him you're his dad until I'm sure you're really ready to take that on."

"I'm sure. I'm doing it."

"I didn't say till *you* were sure. I said till *I* was. You don't have a great track record, do you?"

"I was twenty-two," he said impatiently. "And I didn't know what I was walking away from."

"We're not telling him yet," she said again. "Please, Nic. Promise me. This really matters to me."

"OK," he said reluctantly. "For now."

making progress

♡

"How're you going on those bridge revisions?"

Roger was standing over her, doing what Emma privately thought of as his looming thing. His fingers drummed on the work surface as if he barely had time for her before his next urgent appointment. As if she were holding him up.

"Fine," she said. "Everything's on track."

He nodded briskly. "See that you get them done. The deadline's Wednesday, remember, and we can't afford to miss it."

"If I'm not working fast enough, maybe Sean could help out," she suggested.

"He's on the Vogelsong project," Roger said impatiently.

"Well, then, I guess it's up to me, unless you want to take some of this."

"I have enough to do," he said. "You have no idea what my workload is. Having to check everything you and Sean do, as well as my own assignments. Not to mention the reporting."

"Well, I'll let you get back to it then, because I think Ryan has a question about the project too."

Roger turned, saw Ryan standing behind him. "Right, then. I expect to see those drawings first thing Wednesday, though, so I can look them over. I don't want any surprises."

It was amazing that she still had a tongue, as many times as she'd bitten it this past year, since Roger had been promoted. She should have had the job when Mike left. She was the best, and she'd thought, naively enough, that that would have counted. She knew why it hadn't. She was too young, too pretty. And had too many ovaries, she thought bitterly. And now, instead of a tolerable job that she didn't always enjoy, but that at least paid the bills, she dreaded every day.

Roger moved off at last, and Ryan came to take his place.

"Guess I don't have to ask you how my drawings are coming along," the young engineer said with a smile. "Looks like Roger already did it for me."

She made a little face. "They're getting done, no worries. Do you have a spec change for me, or something?"

"Nah. But I do have a couple tickets to the Yanni show at the Vector Arena for Saturday night, and I thought you might like to come along."

She'd rather poke herself in the eye with a sharp stick, actually. She hated Yanni. "Sorry," she said, offering Ryan a smile. "Thanks for the invitation, but I have a date Saturday night with my son."

"Pity," he said, recovering fast. "He's taking his mum out, is he?"

"He is. To the Blues game."

"Didn't know you were a rugby fan. Or a Blues supporter."

"Shows what you know about me, doesn't it? I'm full of surprises." She was enjoying flirting a bit now, watching his eyes light up in response. It *had* been a long time, and it was a whole lot nicer than being bullied by Roger. "I enjoy it, actually. And Zack loves it."

"You really are a dream date," Ryan said with a flash of teeth. "Beautiful, talented, *and* you like rugby. Maybe next week, then."

"Maybe," she said with a smile of her own. "We'll see."

♡

"Ouch," Emma said at once when Nic stepped into the entryway that evening, delivering Zack again after another session of rugby and hamburgers. She reached a hand toward the swollen red mass that was his left cheekbone, let it fall again without touching him. "That looks awful. Do you want to come in for a minute, while Zack's in the bath? Cup of tea? Tell me how it went, tonight?"

"Yeh. Cup of tea'd be good," he agreed.

"OK, then. Just a minute. Wow, you're a mess too, sweetie," she said to Zack, hanging up his jacket. "Let's get you cleaned up."

Nic was in the kitchen when she returned carrying Zack's backpack. She removed the crumpled school uniform and lunch bag, then set the plastic containers in the sink to be washed.

"Hope you don't mind," he said, handing her a mug. "I made myself at home."

"Thanks. Sit down. But here." She went to the freezer, pulled out a soft sports icepack. "Put this on. Cover it up, anyway, so I don't have to look at it. How did I miss that happening? I don't remember you being injured."

"This isn't injured. Just a bit of a knock. And it didn't happen during the game, is why you didn't notice."

"Then what? You didn't have training today, did you?"

He shook his head. "Last night. Outside that Belgian pub in Vulcan Lane, you know the one?"

"You got in a *fight?*"

"Not much of a fight," he said with a rueful grin. "I was standing there with Claudia and a couple friends, saying goodbye when this bloke ran up to me, gave me a good whack, and ran away again."

"What? Why?"

He shrugged. "Who knows why? Because I'm an All Black. A tall poppy, by definition. Because he had a bet on. Because he was pissed, and one of his mates dared him. Any of those."

"But couldn't you do something about it?" she asked in outrage. "Have him arrested, or something? He can just come up to you and *punch* you, do that to you?"

He smiled around the icepack. "Not likely to dob him in. That'd go down well, wouldn't it. Be a laughingstock then. What I would've done, if I weren't smarter than that by now, is chase him down, sort him out myself. But that wasn't on."

"Why not? Why shouldn't you be able to retaliate, if somebody hits you?"

"Because then there'd be an inquiry," he explained patiently. "And I'd be another brawling footballer. Drama, my name in the papers, a trip through the courts, most likely, and the All Black selectors looking at me askance, wondering what happened to my cool head, whether they should find another fullback for the Championship. Not to mention the World Cup." He shuddered. "Not taking that chance. Even if I weren't suspended. I can't afford it, in any sense. It's not worth it."

"But that's not fair."

"Like being a gunslinger in the Wild West. Fair game for anyone to challenge."

"That's not a challenge. That's just cowardice," she snapped. "I don't care how well known you are. I wish I'd been there. I would've gone after him. Nobody should be allowed to get away with that."

He got up, handed the icepack back to her. "Next time I go out, then, I'll have to get you to come along, be my bodyguard. My enforcer. I'll pop my head in, say goodbye to Zack on my way out. See you next week."

♡

No question, Emma decided on Saturday. She'd take a rugby game over a concert any day, at least a Yanni concert. She was sitting with Hannah again, watching the Blues take on the Highlanders, the southern team offering its usual stern challenge.

"They sure grow them tough down there," she said, wincing as Nic was pulled down in mid-stride by a particularly bruising tackle from one of the big Highlander locks. She breathed a sigh of relief as he bounced up again, seemingly none the worse for wear.

"How do they *do* that?" she asked. "Go down that hard and come back up?"

"I don't know," Hannah confessed. "Or even how they tackle that hard and keep getting up. I look at Drew the next day, and yeah, he's sore and bruised. But *I'd* be in a hospital bed."

Both women sat back in relief at the halftime whistle. "I wanted to ask you about something," Hannah said. "Do you think you'd be interested in coming in and discussing a CAD operator job with our technical manager? I'm not sure if we have an opening right this minute, but if you send me your CV, I'll pass it along."

"That would be amazing," Emma said, her heart beating hard. Could it be this easy? "I'd love to have the opportunity."

"It's not my department," Hannah cautioned. "So I can't promise anything. But I'm asking because it's not easy to find qualified people, so we do like to snap them up when we have a chance. I don't know that it would pay as well as what you're making now, but I think you might find it more interesting. And who knows, other opportunities might come up as well. The company's growing, and we do promote from within."

"I can't tell you how much I appreciate it," Emma told her fervently. "Because I'd love it. Where should I send my CV?"

"I'll give you my email address at work," Hannah said.

Emma pulled out her phone and entered it at Hannah's dictation. "Even if it didn't pay as much," she told Hannah, "it'd be great to be someplace where there was room to move up. When you're in engineering, and you're not an engineer, there's really no place to go, you know?"

"I can't promise," Hannah warned again. "But I will pass on your CV, and suggest that Madeleine might want to talk to you."

"That's plenty," Emma assured her. "If it doesn't work out, it doesn't." But she'd do everything she could to make sure she had the best possible chance, she vowed to herself. "And could I ask you a big favor?" she asked hesitatingly.

"What is it?"

"When I send you my CV. I'll work on it before I send it to you, and I'll have my sister look it over, too. She's an intermediate school teacher. But if you see anything that doesn't look quite right? Would you let me know, before you send it on? I'm not asking you to edit it, or anything. Just, if you notice, would you tell me and give me a chance to fix it? You'll know what they'll be looking for."

"Of course I will," Hannah answered, and Emma marveled again at her generosity. "But I'm sure what Madeleine will care about most is your CAD skills, not your writing skills. And your interest in knitwear, which I'll be happy to vouch for. Just watch out for the typos and spelling errors, and you should be fine."

♡

"I always like coming here," Nic said, accepting the inevitable cup of tea from her on Monday. Zack was already in bed, but Nic was lingering tonight. "It's so cozy."

"Well, thanks," she said with surprise. "I thought you disapproved of our modest accommodations."

"I don't mean I won't be glad to see you and Zack in something better. And that reminds me, Oliver says we should get the notice of the paternity determination soon. This week, maybe next. So you'll want to look out for that."

"OK," she said, taking another sip to calm herself. "I didn't realize it would be that fast."

"Fast as I can make it. And then we can get the maintenance sorted. I know money isn't that important to you," he went on hastily. "But I'll be glad."

"Why would you think money isn't important to me?"

"You have your priorities right, I mean. You realize money doesn't matter."

"The only people who think money doesn't matter," she said, "are people who have enough. Of course money matters. If you don't have it, it sure matters."

"But it doesn't make you happy," he argued. "Look at you and Zack. What you have here."

"It may not make you happy to have as much as you do. I wouldn't know. But I do know one thing. It can sure make you *un*happy, when you don't have enough."

"What's enough, though?"

She stared at him in disbelief. "I'll tell you what's enough. Enough is when you aren't lying awake at night, thinking about the electric bill. And then thinking about Zack's school uniform, and wondering how you're going to pay for both. Not to mention when the car is making that noise, and the Warrant of Fitness is due. And…" She broke off. "Never mind," she muttered. "You obviously don't get it."

"What about your parents?" he asked. "I thought they were both…teachers. Something like that. Haven't they helped?"

"Not like you mean. They paid for me to take the CAD courses when I found out I was pregnant. They helped with my rent, too, the first couple months. But they said I needed to learn to stand on my own two feet. That if they helped more than that, I would never become a responsible adult."

"When you were *pregnant?*" he asked incredulously.

"They have strong opinions," she said ruefully. "They were disappointed in me. And who knows, maybe they were right. I did mess up a lot, when I was younger. Failed a few exams, in high school. Couldn't decide what I wanted to study, at University. They thought I was flaky. They still do. But I'm glad, you know, in some ways, because if they *had* helped me more, if they were helping me now, I'd have to listen to them about those things, wouldn't I? They'd be criticizing what I did spend money on, telling me where to live, telling me I should like my job. And as it is, they can't."

"Don't they help at all?"

"They're retired now," she said. "Down in Hokitika. They're on a fixed income, and they're careful with what they do have. Yeah, it would have been nice if they'd helped more, before. It'd be nice if they helped more now, for that matter. Maybe I wouldn't be on the edge of disaster all the time. I like to think I would've behaved differently if my child had been in that kind of trouble, but like I said, they were disappointed. They thought I needed to grow up. And I don't mean they don't do anything. They've paid for rugby camp, these past couple years, which would've been quite a stretch. And they give Zack money for Christmas and his birthday. All that's helpful, and I try to be grateful, and not wish for more."

"Soon as we get this maintenance sorted," Nic promised, "that'll all be a thing of the past. I've got Oliver working on it now. So you should be thinking about a new place."

"Time enough for that. I'm just thinking about that electric bill," she said, a half-smile developing. "I've done my best on the money thing, but it's not my strong suit. Especially when Zack wants something, and I can't afford it. I hate that. But for me, too. I wish I could say that I don't care, that I'm more enlightened than that, but I do. I *try* not to be impulsive, but when I see some really special yarn, or some shoes that are a really good deal, even if I know I shouldn't buy them, it's so hard to resist. I'd love to be able to go into the MAC store in Britomart, and just buy what I want. I've never been," she said wistfully. "I look in the window, the way it's all packaged, all those eyeshadows, and think, better not tempt myself." She sighed. "I do love pretty things."

"Well, now you won't have to exert quite so much of that tricky self-control," he said with a smile of his own. "You've done without long enough, seems to me. And so has Zack. But it'll take a bit more time. And a couple weeks till I can see him again," he reminded her. "Two weeks in Safa."

"When do you leave?"

"Tomorrow. We'll lose that day getting there, then you want to get over the jet lag. Least we're not playing at Bloemfontein till the next week. That altitude, playing on the Highveld, that's a bugger. By then we'll have the body clocks acclimated, anyway."

"It's a short week as well, isn't it?"

"Yeh. Saturday one week, Friday the next. Last game of the season. And I want to ask you something," he went on, elbows on his knees, hands clasped, leaning forward to look at her, his heavily lashed brown eyes raised to her own. "I'd like to take Zack for the Queen's Birthday weekend, when I'm back. Sunday and Monday, anyway," he qualified. "We won't be back till late Saturday."

"Alone, you mean? To your house, with Claudia? He hasn't had that many sleepovers. I'm not sure…"

"Camping," he said. "Fishing. I go every year, with my brother and my dad."

"He doesn't know how to fish," she said doubtfully. "And overnight? Nic…"

"One night. With three adults," he pointed out. "And we'll teach him. How d'you think I learnt?" He smiled suddenly, the serious mood lightening. "He's a Kiwi boy, you know. Which means he needs to learn to fish. Your own dad hasn't taught him, I guess. You don't have a brother, right?"

"No. And you're right, my dad's not a big outdoorsman." She couldn't help smiling back. She'd never been able to resist Nic's smile, the way the corners of his mouth creased and his eyes lit up.

"Then we'll introduce him," Nic promised. "To being a real Kiwi bloke."

serious hair

♡

"How was it, going out last night?" Lucy asked, the following Saturday evening. She was sitting against the head of Emma's bed in her pajamas, a glass of Sauvignon Blanc in her hand.

Emma turned around on the embroidered stool of her floral-skirted dressing table where she was sitting in her underwear, finished wiping her eyeliner off with a cotton square. She reached for her nightgown on the bed, pulled it over her head, and crawled up to sit beside Lucy, picking up her own glass of wine from the bedside table. "Pretty good," she told her sister, wriggling under the covers and taking a sip. "Nice to go out for once, anyway. And considering I couldn't stay long, and I could barely have one beer, since I was driving home."

Ryan would have been glad to buy her another, she thought now. And to have continued the evening, too. It was gratifying, she admitted, to have somebody so obviously interested, though she'd decided to play it safe, go out with the group first instead. She'd worked with him for two years now, but she still didn't feel she really knew Ryan. Last night had been fun, though. He'd walked beside her to the pub where the younger members of the firm repaired after work, had poured her a beer from one of the pitchers on the table, laughed and flirted.

"I like the things you wear," he'd told her, leaning close to her ear to make himself heard above the din of conversation and music in the noisy bar. "You always look so soft. Not like an engineer." He took a honey-colored curl lightly between his fingers. "You don't even have serious hair."

"I wouldn't make a very good engineer, would I?" she asked. "It's more than the hair. Not serious about the subject, I'm afraid."

"I'm glad," he told her with a smile. "Wish we were someplace else, though. Someplace I could really talk to you. Too noisy in here."

She smiled back, took a piece of pizza from the pan on the table and bit into it. "Mmm," she said as the warm cheese hit her mouth. "Good. You want some?"

He was staring at her mouth, she realized. She licked into the corners to check for stray strands of cheese, grabbed for a serviette from the pile. "Do I have it on my face?" she asked him.

He shook his head, and she finished her pizza as they continued to chat—if you could call bawling into each others' ears chatting. She took a final swallow of beer, then leaned over to tell him, "I have to go. Can you slide over?"

He stood at the end of the bench, took hold of her elbow as she slid out and stood up. "I'll walk you to your car," he said.

"Thanks." She waved her goodbyes to the group, edged her way through the clusters of people crowding the bar area now, with Ryan close behind.

"Whew." She turned to smile at him when they were out in the cool air again, tugged her jacket on. "That was loud."

"We don't get you out with us often," he said, walking beside her up the sloping street towards the carpark. "You're not used to it."

"You're right. My Friday nights are usually a lot quieter than this."

"With your kid? Is it a boy or a girl?"

She knew she'd told him. Oh, well. "A son. Zack."

"How old is he?"

"Six."

"Six. I wouldn't have thought," he said, looking at her sideways. "You must get out, though, from time to time. How about a quiet dinner with me, Saturday next?"

"Sorry," she said. "Saturday doesn't work for me." Zack would be leaving for the camping trip Sunday morning. She didn't want to go out the night before. Unless she was mistaken, he was pretty nervous about the whole thing. Better to be home with him.

"Friday night, then?" he persisted.

"Hard," she admitted. "My sister picked Zack up from childcare today, but I can't ask her to do that two weeks in a row. How about lunch Friday instead? I could do that."

"I'll take a lunch," he decided. "If that's all I get."

♡

"So you're planning to go, huh?" Lucy asked as Emma finished telling her about the evening.

"Yeah. I'm not sure he's my dream guy, but he's cute. And not very...engineer-y. A bit more of an edge, maybe, which I like. As long as I go slow, why not? Because you know," Emma confessed, "I haven't even kissed a man for three—no, four months. I don't even want to *think* about how long it's been since I've slept with one. And I'm missing it."

"Because you still have an itch for Nic," Lucy pointed out.

"Wow. *That's* refined."

"Sorry," Lucy grinned. "But I'm right, aren't I?"

"I can't go there, though," Emma argued. "I have to keep seeing him, and that's so hard. Because I can't help but notice." She sighed and took another sip of wine. "If only he weren't so ridiculously *strong,*" she complained. "If he didn't have those arm muscles, or those big hands, maybe I could do it. Or those eyes. The way they turn down like that, you know?"

"Oh, boy," Lucy said sympathetically. "You really do still have it bad."

Emma groaned, dropped her head into a hand, and shook it in despair as her sister wrapped a comforting arm around her. "Plus he's about to get married to the elusive Claudia. And that's going to be even *worse.*"

"Still haven't met her?"

"No. And no chance now, not with Nic out of the country for two weeks. And I'm *relieved,* Luce. Because when I meet her, she'll be real. And then I'll *have* to make myself stop fantasizing about Nic."

"Better go out with this Ryan guy," Lucy counseled. "Sounds like you need some distraction. Or maybe to scratch that itch."

"I'm glad you're here tonight, anyway," Emma told her. "At least I have somebody to sleep with."

Lucy laughed. "In a manner of speaking." She set down her empty glass, reached out to turn off the bedside lamp, then snuggled down under the duvet. "I like being with you, too," she told her sister. "I hate it when Tom's out of town. I'm not used to living alone."

Emma snapped out her own light and curled on her side, her hands under her cheek, facing Lucy. "I miss you," she confessed in the darkness. "It's so much harder without you. Being the grownup. Because you know I'm not that good at this adult stuff."

Lucy reached out to rub her sister's shoulder. "Oh, honey. You are too. You're a great mum, and you're paying your bills, and you've fixed up this place so beautifully. I've always wished I were as talented and creative as you."

"Really?"

"Of course I have. All the things you make? You're really special. I'm sorry it's so hard. I'm sorry I couldn't stay with you. But…"

"No," Emma said, taking Lucy's hand. "You spent enough of your life with Zack and me. You needed to move in with Tom. It was the right thing. I'm just glad you're still able to come over sometimes and keep me company. Especially when I'm freaking out," she confessed, "the way I have been since Nic showed up." It was easier to say it, here in the dark.

"It's because you're still working it out," Lucy told her comfortingly. "You can't see what it'll look like, with Zack visiting him and all that."

"That's it," Emma said, letting her breath out in a sigh. "What am I going to do, when Zack's over there? Without my boy? I'm going to miss him so much."

"But it'll be good for him, being with his dad, won't it?" Lucy asked.

"I hope so. I *hope* so. Zack's so happy to spend time with him, it…it scares me. What if Nic hurts him, the way he did me? What if he changes his mind?"

"It doesn't sound like he's planning to do that," Lucy pointed out. "He's seemed pretty committed so far, hasn't he? And it might be kind of nice for you to have a little time to yourself. You haven't had much of that, that's for sure."

"But you're not *supposed* to have time to yourself, when you have a six-year-old," Emma tried to explain. "I'm supposed to be with my son. He's supposed to be with me. I'm supposed to take *care* of him."

"All you can do is see what happens," Lucy counseled. "And remember, it's not all tough stuff. He's going to be paying too, and that's going to make everything so much easier. I really think everything's going to turn out for the best, in the end."

"You think?" Emma asked in a small voice, her throat choked by tears.

"Oh, sweetie. I know it. Everything's going to be all right. You'll see."

♡

Lucy wasn't quite so positive the next morning. "Wha?" she mumbled when Emma slid out of bed. "What time is it?"

"Before six," Emma told her. "You don't have to get up. Zack and I are watching the game, that's all."

Lucy wandered out halfway through, thumped down on the couch with a sigh. "It's not even *seven*," she complained. "On Sunday *morning*. And you two are *loud*."

"It's the second half, Auntie Lucy!" Zack told her excitedly.

"Great," Lucy muttered dourly. She pulled half the afghan from Zack's lap to cover her legs. "OK," she yawned. "Is there any coffee?"

"Tea," Emma said distractedly. "But you have to go fix it. Because it's 14 to 10, and we're behind."

"We're?"

"The Blues," Zack explained. He held his breath, eased forward on the couch as the Cheetahs player sent a long kick downfield, and a Blues player ran forward and to the left to catch it, then took off into a gap, the two wingers falling in around him.

"It's Nic!" Zack told his aunt, bouncing up and down in his excitement. "He told me that bloke likes to kick to his right, because he's left-footed! And he did!"

Lucy looked at Emma, her expression quizzical. But her sister wasn't paying any attention to her. Her focus, like her son's, was all for the screen in front of her, where the players were all still running, the commentators animated now.

"Right," Lucy said with a sigh, hauling herself up off the couch. "Tea. Which I can see I'm making myself." Nobody was listening, and she got no response. Just a whoop from Emma, a shout of "Try!" from Zack, and a smack of palms in a high-five behind her.

bonding time

♡

"OK," Emma said, shoving one final pair of socks into the small duffel. "That's it, I think. A change of clothes, extra socks. Your toothbrush. Rain gear, gumboots. Because I'm afraid it's going to be wet up there. Toothbrush, toothpaste," she muttered. "I guess you won't be taking a shower."

"When's he coming, Mum?" Zack shifted from one foot to the other next to her. "How long?"

"Pretty soon," Emma assured him. "He'll text when he's on his way. Run and get your sleeping bag from your closet, OK?"

Zack dashed off, ran back trailing the flannel-lined thing behind him.

"I hope this is warm enough," Emma worried. "You've only used it for sleepovers, and this is outside. I may send a blanket too." She began to roll it, stopped when she felt the lump. "What's this?"

Zack looked a little hunted. "What?"

Emma reached inside, pulled out the spotted form, neck-first. "Are you sure you want to bring Raffo? You've been doing OK without him at Graham's, haven't you?"

"But this is *camping*. I may need him, for camping."

Emma looked into the worried eyes, reached out from her kneeling position to hold Zack close. "It's going to be OK," she assured her son. She kissed his fine blond hair, brushed it back from his eyes. "Nic asked you because he wants you to come. Because he wants to show you about camping, and fishing, and all that good blokey stuff."

"But I don't know *how*," Zack said anxiously. "And where's the toilet, in camping? What if I can't find it?"

"You ask Nic. Straight away, when you get there. Ask him to show you. And I'll leave Raffo in the sleeping bag, the way you had him. So he'll be there, just in case."

"He's a bit nervous," she said in a low voice to Nic when they were stowing Zack's gear in the back of the ute an hour later. "You'll look after him, won't you? He's never done this before, remember."

"I'll look after him," Nic promised.

"Where are your dad and brother?"

"Driving up from Tauranga. They'll meet us. And you'll want my home phone number, my address. Not that you'll need it, but the mobile service up there at the tip of the Coromandel can be a bit patchy. It'd be good for you to be able to reach Claudia, just in case."

Emma nodded, pulled out her mobile and punched the information in, then went to kiss Zack goodbye. He looked half-excited, half-terrified, strapped into the backseat, and she felt a lurch of fear for him.

"Have a great time, baby." She hugged him hard, then stood waving, blinking back tears, as Nic reversed out of the driveway. A quick wave from Nic, and they were gone. The last thing she saw was her son's anxious face peering out the side window, his hand waving frantically.

Nic wished the boy were in the front with him, but Emma had vetoed that on the grounds of safety. And had insisted on the booster seat for this trip, to Zack's disgust.

"I'm tall enough," the boy had argued. "You said."

"By half a centimeter," his mother had countered. "And that's not a good road, and it's raining. You can ride in the booster seat, or you can stay home." So that had been that. They had started out with a fair bit of conversation, centering around Friday night's win against the Cheetahs in Bloemfontein, but then Zack had fallen silent, and Nic had switched on some music for the hour-and-a-half drive to Thames, where they'd meet his father and Dan. Thank goodness Dan would be there.

He shook his head to clear the niggle of worry. "How you going back there, mate?" he asked, glancing into the rear-view mirror to the seat behind him.

"I need to pee," Zack said.

"Already? Didn't you go before you left? Only another hour to go."

"I *really* need to pee," Zack insisted. He was wriggling, Nic saw.

Right, then. "There's a service center in a few kilometers," he told Zack. "We're on the motorway, so I need to wait for that. Can you hold it?"

"I think so," Zack said dubiously.

"Do your best." Nic put his foot down a bit more, seeing the wriggling increase. Geez. Half an hour in. He pulled up in front of McDonalds. By the time he got around to Zack's side of the car, the boy was already out the door, dancing in place.

"OK. Run," Nic said. Zack raced through the entrance ahead of him, through the door Nic pointed out. Nic followed him in, breathed a sigh of relief as he saw that he'd made it to the urinal just in time.

"D'you want a fizz?" he asked Zack as they left the men's room. "As we're here."

"Really?" Zack asked.

"Why? Is that not on?"

"Nah, it's OK," Zack said quickly. "I can have one." A half hour later, pulling onto the verge and jumping out to race around the ute again, Nic had sussed out why it wasn't on. He'd bet Emma didn't give the kid anything at all to drink before a car ride.

♡

"You're late," his dad said with a scowl when Nic had pulled up at last beside George's own well-used ute in the big Pak 'n' Save carpark.

"Yeh. Couple unscheduled stops," Nic said, helping Zack out. "Zack, this is my dad, Mr. Wilkinson. And my brother Dan."

"Hi," Zack said shyly, offering his hand with the manners Nic had noticed from the beginning.

"Nic's mate, eh," Dan said with his engaging smile. "Ready for a bit of fishing?"

"Mr. Wilkinson?" George asked Nic. "Why the hell?"

"Because Emma wants him to get to know me first," Nic replied in a low voice. "Shh."

"Huh," George grunted.

"D'you want to take the Land Cruiser the rest of the way?" Nic asked him, changing the subject.

"Nah. I'll drive." Of course, Nic thought. He didn't respond, just went to the back of the ute and began shifting gear to his dad's smaller vehicle.

"Planning to stop in here for food?" he asked.

"We already did it," George told him. "While we were waiting for you."

Nic bit down the retort. "Right, then. I'll shift the boat." With his brother's help, and to the accompaniment of critical commentary from their father, he unfastened the dinghy from the top of his roof rack, transferred it to his dad's, then shifted Zack's booster seat to the other vehicle while George waited impatiently. It was the unpunctuality, Nic knew. Well, bugger it. Not like they had a schedule to keep. He wasn't about to apologize again.

"Let's use the toilet before we go," he told Zack instead. He'd learned his lesson. He ignored his father's annoyed sigh and took Zack into the cavernous building.

"Are we finally sorted, then?" George asked sarcastically when they returned.

"Yeh." Nic made sure Zack was strapped in properly, went around and hopped up into the other rear seat. "Ready to go."

The positive aspect of the two-hour drive that followed, Nic thought afterwards, was that they only had to stop once for Zack to pee, thanks to their newly instituted no-fizz policy. The negative side was that they had to stop three times for him to spew. He got carsick, it appeared. And the deeply rutted, incessantly curving metal road from Colville to Port Jackson was tailor-made for the purpose. By the time he was supporting Zack for the third time, hastily donned rain gear doing an inadequate job against the deluge that had begun minutes before, Nic was beginning to have serious doubts about the entire trip.

"Sorry," Zack said, tears swimming in the brown eyes and beginning to trickle down his cheeks under the hood of his anorak.

"That's OK," Nic said, pulling off his son's rain gear, then belting him in for the—fifth? sixth? time. He ignored his father's fingers, drumming on the steering wheel. "You can't help being sick. We're almost there anyway, aren't we, Dad?"

"No telling," his father ground out. "Depends how many more times we have to stop."

And that was the start of a fun-filled day. Turned out boats made Zack seasick as well. The frequent bouts of rain didn't help, either. Huddling under the concrete cooking shelter that evening, taking their turn with the electric cooker to grill the snapper that his dad and Dan had finally caught once they'd returned Nic and Zack to shore, eating with their fingers from paper plates, Nic had to wonder why he had thought this would be a good idea. It was a relief to dash through the rain again to the tent, after one final stop at the toilet for Zack.

"Time to get into those pajamas and get into that cozy bag, I reckon," Nic told him once they'd all wrestled off rain-soaked outer garments and stuck them at the front of the large four-man tent. Dusk was falling quickly thanks to the cloudy sky, and his dad turned on the lantern in silence and hung it overhead, where it cast weird shadows.

"I haven't brushed my teeth tonight, though," Zack objected. "Mum says."

"That's the beauty of camping," Dan told him cheerfully. "Nobody here cares if your teeth are clean or not. Or the rest of you, either. Your mum probably makes you take a bath too, doesn't she?"

"Yeh," Zack said doubtfully.

"See? We don't care that you're dirty. Because we're dirty too. Covered in fish guts." Dan made a comical face that had Zack giggling for the first time that day, and Nic offered his brother a grateful smile as he helped Zack out of his clothes and into his pajamas. Zack dove into his sleeping bag, then wriggled down to the bottom, head disappearing, before coming back up again.

"What's that you've got?" Dan asked, seeing a spotted something in Zack's hand.

"Nothing," Zack said in a scared voice.

"Got a teddy, have you?"

"It's not a teddy," Zack said indignantly. "It's Raffo." He pulled out the flocked giraffe to show them.

"Your mum should've taken that away by now," George grunted. "Soft, having a teddy, a big kid like you."

"Raffo's *not* a teddy," Zack insisted, his eyes filling with tears again, spilling over now. "And I only have him in bed, or at extra-special times. And Mum *said* I could bring him! She *said!*"

"Need to harden up," George said, glaring at Nic.

Nic felt his hands fisting, the familiar anger overtaking him. He shoved over to sit on his own sleeping bag, against the wall of the tent. "Bringing Raffo was OK," he told Zack. "It's a bit scary, I reckon, going camping the first time. Specially if it rains, and you're sick." He put a hand out, smoothed Zack's hair. "Everyone needs a bit of help sometimes."

"Really?" Zack asked doubtfully.

"Course they do," Nic smiled down at him. Ignored his father's snort of disgust and lay down next to Zack. "I'm knackered, though. Ready to give it a rest here."

"Because it's a long way," Zack said. "From Safa."

"Yeh," Nic gave Zack's back a bit of a rub. "You remembered, eh. It's a long way."

Zack really was exhausted from the long day, he saw. Within a few minutes, he was breathing peacefully.

♡

Zack made it through the night without further mishap, to Nic's relief, though they did have to make an early-morning dash for the toilets.

"Eggs for breakfast," George said when they returned, having started the gas cooker. He seemed to have recovered his good humor, Nic saw with relief. "And I've got the water on, make us a cup of tea. D'you drink tea?" he asked Zack. "Or d'you like cocoa better? Milo, maybe?"

"Yeh," Zack said shyly. "Cocoa, I mean. Please."

"Think I have a bit of that, in my camping box," George told him. "Have a look, will you, mate? Get your da—Get Nic to help you."

They were soon working on their camp breakfast of eggs and streaky bacon, accompanied by jam donuts from the Pak 'n' Save bakery that Zack seized on eagerly, but Nic refused.

"Watching your figure?" his dad asked with a raised brow.

"Training," Nic said. "I'll make another couple eggs instead. Semis in two weeks."

"A donut or two couldn't hurt, surely," George objected.

"Got a nutrition plan," Nic said evenly. "Worked out specially. And it doesn't include jam donuts."

"Huh. Probably for the best. Saw you missed a tackle the other night, handed the Cheetahs that try."

"And made five," Dan put in, taking another jam donut. "Plus a try of your own. Well done," he told his older brother. "Get to miss out on the quarterfinals, do you."

"Yeh," Nic said with gratitude. Trust Dan to accentuate the positive. "Let the niggles settle a bit. And play the semis match at home, which is always a bonus."

"Surprised you kicked that one back, in the fifty-third minute," George put in. "What were you thinking? Had some room to run, offload to Koti James. He was in the clear. If you'd scored then, that would've put the boot into them. As it was, you left it late, didn't you."

Nic thought about explaining, changed his mind. "Strategic decision," he said instead.

"Bloody unstrategic, you ask me."

"We'll see what the coaches have to say," Nic said. "If they didn't like my choice, they'll let me know, no worries."

Dan jumped in with a question or two, and the moment passed off. "Who's for fishing?" George asked when they'd washed up, stacked the pan and camp mugs to dry on a tea towel. "Tide's running strong this morning. Reckon we could get a couple snapper before we go home."

"Do I have to go in the boat?" Zack asked Nic quietly.

"Nah," Nic told him. "We'll see how we do from the rocks. I know a spot."

Zack held his rod obediently for a while, then began to shift back and forth, and finally sat down with a thump and began to wiggle the rod absently, watching the line play in the water. "Does it take a long time to catch a fish?" he asked presently.

"It can do," Nic responded. "Patience is part of it."

Zack sighed, and silence reigned for a while longer.

"D'you think they all went away?" he asked next.

"Who?"

"The fish. D'you think maybe they swam someplace else?"

"Nah. Just wait. We may get one yet."

The jerk, when it came, was on Zack's line, not Nic's. By that point, Zack was holding the rod with one hand, using the other to pick up pebbles, and the tug of the big fish pulled it straight out of his lax hold. Nic turned at his yell, only to see the rod slide and bounce across the rocks and into the sea.

"Shit!" Nic yelped. "Stay here," he instructed Zack. "Don't move." He bounded down the steep, boulder-strewn bank and dove into the sea, caught up with the rod, swam back with it and clambered out over the boulders again. Reached the spot where Zack stood, anxiously hopping from one foot to the other on the topmost rock, and finished reeling the big fish in. A couple kilos at least, he saw with satisfaction. He took the hook out of the gaping mouth and gave the head a smack on a rock to put a quick end to the animal after its ordeal.

"You killed it," Zack said with shock. "It's dead. Isn't it?"

"Yeh," Nic said, shivering now that the adrenaline was leaving him. "That's the idea. And you've got to hang onto your rod better than that."

Zack's eyes welled with tears. "I didn't know we'd have to *kill* it."

"Where did you think fish came from?" Nic asked in exasperation. "It's alive, you catch it. You kill it and you eat it. And if you didn't want it to suffer, you shouldn't have dropped your rod. If I hadn't gone after it, that poor fish would've had to drag it about till it died of exhaustion."

"Sorry." Zack's lip was trembling again, and Nic was suddenly overwhelmed with frustrated impatience.

"Never mind," he said curtly, shoving the fish into the chilly bin he'd brought for the purpose and snapping down the lid. He took the bin in one hand, the two rods in the other. "Come on. I need to get changed."

Zack lagged behind, and Nic cast a couple glances to make sure he was following. He dropped the rods and bin outside the tent, then went in and jerked off his wet things, replaced them with the change of clothes he'd luckily brought with him on account of the rain. Then took a few deep breaths, bundled the wet clothes away, and climbed out of the tent again.

Zack was sitting at the picnic table, his back to him, head bent, picking at the wood with one finger.

"Mate." Nic sat down across from him with a sigh. "It's OK."

Zack shook his head without raising it. He was crying, Nic realized. "I need your help," he told the boy. "Come help me clean this fish. It's caused us enough grief today. We may as well get a good lunch out of it."

Zack wasn't too squeamish about the cleaning, at least, Nic found with relief. His fascination with the fish's disgusting innards seemed to divert his mind from his misery, and he watched Nic's preparations with interest.

"And now we get to eat it," Nic told him when they arrived back at their campsite again. "Which is the point of the entire exercise."

"We had fish last night, though," Zack said doubtfully.

"Because we're fishing. That's what you eat, on a fishing trip. Fish."

"All the *time?*"

"Well, yeh. We didn't have it for brekkie, though, did we? Now, trout, that's a lovely brekkie. With some eggs, of course." The fish was frying in the pan now, turning a golden brown amidst the lavish slatherings of butter Nic had added.

"D'you have to go in a boat for trout?"

"Nah. Stand in a stream with your waders on, though. Gets a bit cold."

"Does it take a long time?"

"It can do. Not too keen on fishing so far, eh."

"I thought it would be fun," Zack admitted. "But it isn't so much, is it?"

Nic smiled. "Relaxing, that's what it is. Takes a bit of getting used to, maybe."

"I don't think I like relaxing," Zack said seriously. "Not as much as footy."

"Well, not as much as footy, no," Nic agreed. "Reckon footy's the best thing of all."

a bit of drama

♡

The trip home was just as miserable as he'd expected, Nic found. Worse, maybe, as all that fish that had gone down was now coming back up again, and his father's mood at the delay was even worse.

"Going to be late getting back," he grumbled. "I was counting on seven."

"And it'll be seven-thirty," Nic snapped back. "What's the bloody difference?" He could see his father's surprised, angry glance in the rear-view mirror. He didn't normally offer a retort. But his last nerve was frayed by now.

He pulled at last into Emma's driveway, relief and guilt warring for pride of place within him. Zack had been quiet on the drive back from Thames, worn out with carsickness maybe. At least Nic hoped that was it.

He pulled on his own anorak, ran around the car and opened Zack's door, feeling the rain soaking any part of him that might have stayed dry during all those spewing stops.

"Here." He helped Zack into his anorak, picked up the booster seat and grabbed the rest of his gear, slammed the car door and followed behind as the boy ran around the side of the house to his flat and dashed through the front door.

"Hi," Nic said, setting down his burdens.

Emma didn't seem to notice him in her haste to pull off Zack's anorak, help him out of his gumboots, before finally pulling her son into a fierce hug.

"You smell terrible," she told him, smoothing his hair back with a tender hand. "Were you sick?"

"Yeh," he said, burying his face in her side. "It was a really windy road, Mum."

She looked up at Nic at last. "How'd it go?"

"Could've been better," he admitted. "We had a few dramas. Didn't realize the road would make him so sick."

"It happens sometimes," she said. "It must have been worse because he was nervous. I should've given him something, but it can make him so sleepy and grouchy. Was it really bad?"

"Well, yeh. A few times. And it rained, which wasn't the best. Zack caught a fish, though, didn't you, mate?"

"Nah. I dropped it." He hung his head, fingered his mother's skirt, wouldn't meet Nic's eyes.

"A bit of drama, like I said. But the best part of a trip like this, sometimes, is coming home, getting warm and dry again," Nic said to Zack. "And now you're here with your mum again, and you can do that. I'll see you next week, OK?"

"OK," Zack said, still not looking up.

Emma glanced down at him, then up at Nic again with a puzzled frown.

He smiled awkwardly at her. He'd ring her later, he decided. Explain.

♡

"Thanks," Emma told her landlady forty-five minutes later. "I really, really appreciate it. An hour, I hope. Hour and fifteen minutes max."

"No worries, love," Lois said comfortably. "Makes no difference to me if I sit down here or up in the house. Gives me a chance to look at all your lovely bits and bobs."

The rain was really coming down now, Emma realized as she left the flat. She debated going back for her umbrella, but she didn't want to take the time. By the time she got to her car, she was regretting the decision. Too late now. She was already wet.

She turned up the heat on the drive to Nic's house, glancing down at every stoplight to check the map she'd printed out, then peering out again as her windscreen wipers tried and failed to keep up with the sheets of water streaming across them, until she pulled up the sloping drive and parked outside the garage. And was engulfed by rain again the moment she stepped out.

She dashed across to the front door, stood in the shelter of the vestibule, and rang the bell, then rang it again, impatient at the delay. After all this, he wasn't going to be home?

A third ring, and the door opened a bare twenty centimeters, a dark-haired woman glancing around it at her, then opening it reluctantly wider.

"Yes?" she asked, her gaze sweeping Emma and clearly coming away unimpressed.

"I need to talk to Nic." Emma could feel her hair plastered to her head, her sweater and jeans soaked.

"He's just out of the shower," the woman—Claudia, obviously—objected.

"I don't care if he's just off the boat from Siberia," Emma said furiously. "I need to talk to him about Zack."

"I suppose you're Emma," Claudia said with resignation. "You'd better come in."

Emma stepped into the entryway, all white walls, dark stone floor, and frosted light sconces, as Nic appeared in jeans and T-shirt, feet bare, rubbing his wet head with a fluffy white towel. "Who was it?"

He stopped, arrested, at the sight of her. "Emma. What are you doing here? Is Zack...Is something wrong?"

"Something's wrong, all right." She was shivering now, her teeth beginning to chatter. "And it's you. *You're* wrong." She was barely coherent in her rage. "Nobody asked you to get involved in his life! Nobody wanted you! Why'd you do it? Why hurt him?"

"Hang on. Wait." Nic gestured helplessly, looked at Claudia. "Come inside. Let's talk."

Claudia didn't echo the invitation, merely stared at Emma with the detached fascination she might have shown towards a wreck at the side of the motorway.

"No! I'm going to tell you right now. Do you know how excited he was? How much he was looking forward to this trip? He came back so quiet. So...so defeated. How could you *do* that to him?" She was crying now, shaking with cold and rage, the tears mingling with the rain soaking her. "Well, you're not taking him again. You aren't seeing him. This is it, do you hear? This is *it.*"

"Suits us," Claudia said at last. "Now, if you don't mind..."

"Claudia, no," Nic said. "This is between Emma and me. She can have her say."

Claudia looked at him for a long moment, then turned on her heel and left.

"Emma," Nic told her, coming forward to meet her where she still stood, barely inside the door. "Stop. Please. You're freezing, and you're too upset. Come on in, and we'll talk."

"No," she sobbed. "I don't want to talk to you. I changed my mind. Just...go *away.* Leave us *alone.*"

"Come on," he urged again. "You're here to tell me. But you're too cold, and too wet. Come inside and talk to me. I stuffed up, and I know it. Come in so we can find a way to make it better. For Zack's sake."

♡

That snapped her out of it, he saw. She nodded reluctantly, sniffed, wiped her hand across her face. He handed her the towel.

"Come into the kitchen, have a cuppa. Warm up." He took her beyond the dividing pillar and into the great room, across the expanse of wood floor to the breakfast bar. "Sit and dry off," he told her. He put the electric jug on, then had another thought. "Hang on a tick." He ran upstairs, came back with a charcoal gray fleece dressing gown, tossed it to her. "Put that on."

She pulled it around herself, clearly too cold to protest. She really had the shakes now. She huddled in his dressing gown, rubbed the towel over her hair and face, and he saw her attempting to blot the water from her sodden sweater and jeans while he made the tea.

He waited until she had both hands around the mug and was sipping the hot beverage, and he saw the shivers dying down. Though she wouldn't be really warm, he knew, until she got out of those wet things. He couldn't suggest that.

"I'm sorry," he said again. "I stuffed up, I know it. And let my dad say some things—" He broke off. "But I'll make it better."

"How?" she demanded. "How are you going to make it better?"

"Where is he now?"

"At home."

"Alone?"

"No. Of course not. What kind of mother do you think I am? My landlady's there with him."

"I'll come home with you now," he decided. "Talk to him."

"You can't. He'll be asleep."

He shrugged in frustration. "Tomorrow, then. Bugger. I have a sponsorship commitment after training. But I'll come after that, in the evening. Take him to dinner, talk to him."

"No. Not alone."

"What, then?"

"Come to dinner," she said, although he could see her reluctance. "So I can be there, hear what you say. Help him."

"Right. I'll be there. Six? Want me to bring a takeaway?"

"Yeah. Because I don't feel like cooking for you. But shouldn't you ask Claudia first? I don't think she'll be thrilled."

"I'll tell her. I don't keep secrets from Claudia."

♡

"So," Nic said to Zack the following night. The three of them were sitting around the little table, working on the Thai food Nic had brought. Not too spicy, per Emma's strictures. "Our camping trip wasn't one for the books, eh. Didn't work out quite as well as we'd planned."

Zack looked up at him warily, but didn't answer.

"Pity it rained," Nic went on. "That didn't help. And that you got sick. Not your fault," he went on hastily. "Can't help it when your tummy decides to go crook like that."

"And we had to stop too much, and come back in the boat," Zack volunteered at last. "That made your dad really angry."

"Aw. He gets angry anyway. Nothing new there."

"He didn't like me, though," Zack said, his voice small. "He said I had to harden up."

"Know how many times he's told me to harden up? Heaps. That's how many."

"But you're strong. You're a grown-up."

"I wasn't always. I was a kid, just like you."

"You prob'ly didn't ever cry, though," Zack said, making a little pile of rice with his fork, then aimlessly stabbing at bits of meat.

"Yeh, I did," Nic corrected him. "Not in front of my dad, it's true. But in our room, mine and Dan's? Heaps of times."

"Really?" Zack asked, eyes wide.

"Just ask Dan. He'll tell you all my guilty secrets. Anyway, camping's bound to be a bit rough the first time. Specially if it rains. And you've never fished before."

"Specially if you spew," Zack said.

"Yeh. Specially if you spew."

♡

"I was thinking we could try again," Nic told Emma later, after Zack was safely in bed. "Not fishing," he went on hastily. "Or camping. But what would you think about my taking Zack to the beach next Saturday? I asked Claudia to come along as well, so there'd be a female influence. Thought that might ease your mind."

Emma's brief experience of Claudia left her unconvinced. "I don't want you to take him without me," she said. "Not till I see for myself that things are better."

"Right," he sighed. "Come with us, then."

"You and Claudia, and Zack and me," she said dubiously. "Just one big happy family."

"Well, yeh." He smiled suddenly. "Or a double date. Think of it as neutral territory," he coaxed. "May be for the best, don't you think? For everyone to get to know each other?"

"Where would we go?" she asked, wavering.

"I was thinking Piha. Only an hour or so from here. If it doesn't rain, that is. A few hours, that's all. *With* a carsickness tablet," he added. "And no fishing. And nobody has to harden up."

She smiled back reluctantly. "OK. A few hours at the beach. No fishing. No camping."

"Zack and I've decided we like footy best anyway. We'll stick with that."

family time

♡

"Where's Claudia?" Emma asked in surprise when they got to the Toyota late Saturday morning. "I thought she was coming."

"Couldn't do it after all," Nic said, opening the door for Zack to clamber into the back seat and tossing Emma's beach bag in after him.

"Zack's going to wonder if she's real," Emma told him as she climbed into the passenger seat. "She doesn't seem too excited about getting to know us."

Nic shut her door after her, walked around and swung into the driver's side. "Yeh," he admitted as he put the ute in gear and pulled away from the curb. "She's having a bit of trouble with that."

They didn't talk about it more on the drive to Piha, mindful of Zack in the back seat. Instead, Nic good-humoredly answered Zack's questions about the training the team was doing for the semifinal. No stops despite the winding road, thanks to that tablet. Soon enough, they were driving slowly through the tiny town and ending up at the large Piha Beach carpark, sparsely populated today. No rain, just puffy white clouds and a brisk sea breeze.

"Let's go in the water!" Zack urged as they stepped over the berm and onto the wide beach.

"A bit cold," Nic said dubiously. "For you *and* your Mum. I'll go with you."

"I'll come too," Emma said. "For a bit, anyway. Till I freeze."

It *was* cold, she found. Frigid, in fact. Nic did stay with Zack, to her relief, braving the waves and allowing her to retreat to the shallow water near the shore. A few minutes, though, were enough for all of them. Emma ran for the beach bag she'd stashed at the edge of the high-tide mark, pulled out a big towel and rubbed Zack down, shivering herself, and wrestled his warmest jumper over his head.

"There. That'll warm you up," she told him.

"Do we have hot chocolate?" Zack asked.

"Luckily, yes." She reached into the bottom of the bag for the thermos.

Nic took it from her. "I'll pour it. Dry yourself off, get something on before you get hypothermia."

She took his advice. It might be best to cover up anyway. She'd wished this morning that she had a one-piece to wear. But she only had one choice, and it was a bikini, so that was that. Well, at least she wasn't shivering under a layer of cold, wet fabric. That was the upside. And it wasn't like Nic had never seen her body before.

She saw him staring at her, thermos in hand but hot chocolate forgotten, as she rubbed at the skimpy costume in an attempt to dry it. Whoops. She hadn't been to the beach with a man in too long. And maybe Nic having seen her body wasn't such a good thing after all. Just like it wasn't great that she'd seen his. She'd been right—he *had* added some muscle. And it looked terrific.

She wrenched her gaze away from the solid bulk of his shoulders, only to find herself captivated by the sight of the drops of water sliding slowly down his well-defined pectoral muscles toward the ridges of his abdomen, disappearing into his low-slung swim trunks. The extra weight in his chest and shoulders only set off his trim waist and narrow hips more, and there was just way too much of him on display, looking way too good, for her peace of mind. She forced herself to look away, dropped the towel and hastily pulled on her skirt, the heavy lace knit of cream-colored wool warming her, drew the ribbon drawstring tight and tied it in a bow, then wrapped herself in her pale pink cardigan before she found her comb and began working on her matted curls.

Nic finally looked back down at the thermos and cup in his hands. "Right. Hot chocolate." He poured it out, handed the metal cup to Zack, whose shaking hands promptly spilled half of it.

"Better to pour it halfway," Emma suggested.

"I see that," Nic said ruefully. "Hand me that towel." He rubbed hot chocolate off Zack's sweater, then used the towel on himself. And Emma figured out why he'd been staring at her. Because the sight of him drying off that broad chest, the play of muscle as he lifted his arms to work the towel over his back, had her watching again despite her best intentions. She was half-relieved, half-disappointed when he pulled his shirt and hoodie out of his day pack and tugged them over his still-damp torso.

"Drink up, mate," he told Zack, digging for the rugby ball he'd thrown in earlier. "We need to do a bit of running, get you warm again. We'll practice passing in the wind. Need that skill often enough."

Emma pulled a chunky black knit cap onto Zack's shaggy blond head. "This'll help too," she said.

"I like that," Nic commented. "Got the silver fern on there."

"It's not the real one," Zack told him. "It doesn't say All Blacks. Mum just put the fern on herself."

"Better," Nic said firmly. "Made just for you."

"Yeah, sweetie. Better watch it, or I'll embroider a flower instead of a fern on yours next time. Make it pretty, like mine,"

Emma told Zack with a smile, pulling on her own hat. Pink, with a delicate, multi-petaled knitted white flower on the side, pearly beads adorning its center. Completely frivolous and girly. And more importantly right now, nice and warm.

"Did you make that one too?" Nic asked.

"Yeah. Everything I have on, I made. Except the bikini. I bought that."

"You still like pink, I notice."

"I enjoy being a girl," she said, adjusting her hat so the flower sat just over one ear.

"Yeh. Noticed that too." He looked away, slung the pack over his shoulders, spun the rugby ball, tossing it back and forth in one hand in a complicated series of moves. "Ready, mate?"

"Yeh!" Zack said, handing his mother the thermos cup.

Emma followed behind as the two of them ran down the beach together, passing the ball back and forth. Nic sometimes had to lunge for Zack's passes when they went a bit wild, but her son wasn't too bad, she thought with pride. Nic had Zack run farther along, then kicked the ball to him, shouting in approval when Zack caught it, and encouraged Zack to kick it back, an attempt that went sadly awry. The ball sailed into the sea, and Nic had to wade out for it.

"Sorry," Zack called. Nic just waved at him, kicked it back. "Try again," he shouted. Zack's second attempt was a bit more accurate, and Nic made a ridiculously athletic leaping catch, pulling the ball in somehow with one big hand.

"Mum!" Zack came running to her some time later, Nic following behind, doing that flicking thing with the ball again, rolling it from wrist to elbow and back. Zack's cheeks were red with exertion and excitement, brown eyes alive with the joy of the day. "Did you see me kick?"

"I did," Emma told him with pride. "You did great."

"Well, not always," Zack said honestly. "Nic had to go back into the water a couple times to get it."

"Nah," Nic said, resting a hand on Zack's head, giving it a gentle shake. "Getting used to kicking it barefoot, that's all. Bit different."

"But Mum," Zack said, squirming. "I need to pee. Really bad. And I don't know where the toilets are."

"Oh." Emma looked back in the direction they had come.

Nic laughed. "That's the best part of being a bloke. The world's your toilet."

"Really? I can just go? What if somebody sees, though?" Zack looked around worriedly.

"Well, if it were a bit warmer, we'd just walk you out into the sea," Nic said. "Nobody about anyway, though. Come on. Over here, by this bit of rock."

They were back a couple minutes later. "Nic says it's OK, Mum," Zack told Emma earnestly.

"If he says so," Emma smiled at him, "I suppose it is." She pulled out a water bottle, ran it over his hands. "You still have to wash your hands, though. Rub. And then I'll give you a sammie."

They spread out another big towel, perched on it while Nic and Zack devoured the ham-and-cheese sandwiches Emma had prepared. She handed them each an apple, took one for herself, wrapped an arm around her knees to warm herself and looked out at the breaking waves, her ears full of their dull roar.

She took in a deep breath of salty air and knew that this was the best day she'd had in a long time. Seeing Zack so happy, after last weekend's misery. And being with Nic, with his obvious enjoyment of their company, their surroundings, the day. He had always had it, this quality of living in the moment, taking every bit of pleasure from it.

Just now, he was picking up a small stone, rubbing it between his fingers. "Look at this," he told Zack. "What does it look like to you?"

"A rugby ball!"

"Yeh. Exactly, doesn't it? It's even white, with a bit of blue. Just like the real thing." Nic passed the elliptical shape to Zack. "Smooth, too. That's spent a fair bit of time in the water, I reckon. Feel it."

"It's awesome," Zack said, closing his palm around it, then handed it back to Nic.

"You keep it," Nic said. "Souvenir of our day at the beach. Got a pocket there?" He helped Zack stow the stone in the small mesh pocket of his trunks.

"And our day at the beach is getting a bit cold," Emma remarked. "Time to start walking back, don't you think?"

Nic helped Emma gather the detritus of their picnic, shook the towel out into the wind, rolled it again, took the beach bag from her and stowed it inside, then set off with the two of them to retrace their steps. The wide expanse of sand, the wind, were exhilarating despite the chill, and he felt a bubble of happiness rise within him. He dropped the bags, took a few running steps, then turned a cartwheel and came up laughing.

Emma let go of Zack's hand and launched into four or five perfect cartwheels of her own, one after the other, a human pinwheel, and landed on her feet again, laughing in triumph, face flushed from the effort.

"Why didn't I know you could do that?" Nic asked as Zack came running up to join them.

"You never asked me," she answered cheekily.

"Show me how!" Zack demanded. "Please," he amended at a warning look from his mother.

"OK. Face me," Nic told him. "Legs apart, see? Now put your hands up over your head. Then just swing them around, and kick on over."

Zack gave a hop, swung both legs awkwardly without getting them close to vertical. "That's not it, though," he complained. "That isn't right."

"Here. Your mum can demonstrate, and I'll hold you," Nic said. "We'll show your body what it feels like."

Emma performed a slow cartwheel while Zack, with Nic's help, mirrored her movements. "Cool!" the boy said once he was upright again.

"Kick off a bit faster," Nic coached. "Get a bit of momentum going."

With their help, Zack was soon turning enthusiastic, if imperfect, cartwheels, and the three of them practiced until Nic suddenly kicked up instead into a handstand, then took seven or eight steps on his hands before landing neatly on his feet again.

"How about that?" he challenged Emma. "Got that in your repertoire, have you?"

"You're still the best at that one," she admitted. "I can get up there, just can't walk like you can." Her handstand was neat, toes pointed, her skirt dropping down around her shoulders to reveal the bikini—and the body—beneath, distracting Nic. Geez, she had pretty legs.

"Show me how!" Zack begged, prompting another bit of coaching.

"Here's one I bet I'm still better at," Emma told Nic. She moved slowly from a standing position into an arched backbend, turning her body into a perfect bow, then lifted her hands from the sand and came back the same way she'd descended.

"Well?" she challenged with a glint in her eye.

"Never tried that one," he admitted. "But I'll give it a go."

He wasn't sure he looked as good as she had, but he managed it. "Never knew you had these hidden talents," he said, looking up at her from his upside-down position.

"Gymnastics when I was a teenager," she explained. 'I don't think I could do much on the uneven bars these days, but I can still turn a cartwheel or two."

Nic bent his legs, lifted off without much effort and was upright again. "That'll get the spine sorted," he commented. "Reckon I grew a couple centimeters there."

"That or bugger it completely," she agreed ruefully, rubbing the small of her back. "I may have been a bit overenthusiastic, showing you my coming-up technique. It's been a while."

"I can't make myself go over," Zack complained. He was bent over backwards from the waist, waving his arms.

Emma laughed. "Here. Start lying on your back. Much easier." She dropped to the sand, to Nic's amazement. She didn't seem to mind how much of it she was collecting in her hair. He tried to imagine Claudia getting this messy, and failed utterly.

"Put your hands like this. Thumbs towards your head. No, other way," Emma was explaining. Nic stepped to Zack's head and repositioned his arms, grinning back at the little face looking up at him.

"Now push up. Use your legs," Emma instructed as she demonstrated.

"Like this?" Zack asked.

"That's brilliant," Nic told him. "You and your mum. What a picture." Upside down, heads turned to laugh at each other. It was a picture he needed, he decided. He ran for his pack, pulled out his phone and took a quick snap before the two of them thumped down to their backs again, sprawled on the sand to catch their breath.

A couple was approaching from the other direction, Nic saw, holding hands. He walked to meet them, held out the phone. "D'you mind taking a photo of the three of us?"

"No worries," the young man said cheerfully, reaching for it. "Tell me when."

"It's a special pose," Nic explained. "Give us a sec." He jogged back the few meters to Emma and Zack.

"Group shot," he told them. "Same as before. Can your back manage it?" he thought to ask Emma.

"One more can't hurt. Come on, Zack."

Under Nic's direction, they all dropped, their heads facing the photographer, then pushed up together.

"This is it," Nic called. "Quick, before Emma collapses."

"Ha! Before you do," she challenged, sticking her tongue out at him and making him laugh.

"OK. Look at me. Annnndd...got it," the young man announced triumphantly. Nic sank back down to the sand, then jumped to his feet and reached out a hand to pull a slower Emma up as Zack clambered to stand as well.

"That better have worked," Emma said as Nic took the phone from the young man with a word of thanks. "That's my limit, I think."

"Aren't you Nic Wilkinson?" the young woman with the photographer asked curiously.

"Yeh. That's me," he said, stowing the phone away again.

"How d'you think you'll go in the semis?" her boyfriend asked. "Who're you hoping to play?"

"Whoever turns up on the night," Nic assured him. "Prepared for both, but we'll get it sorted this next week, depending on what happens tonight."

"I've got a bit on you winning the Super 15," the young man said. "So here's hoping you get that right."

"We'll give it a go," Nic promised. "We're ready. Not too many injuries, that's the main thing."

"Good luck," the young man said. "To both of us."

"Cheers, mate," Nic said. He turned and saw Emma brushing the sand from Zack's back and hair. "We'll be getting on, then. Thanks for the photo."

"No worries." The young man and girl set off again with a single curious glance back at the three of them.

"No pressure, huh?" Emma asked wryly. She reached to brush off his own back, his shoulders, then seemed to change her mind, dropped her hand. "We'd better get on," she said. "Are you watching the game at home?"

"Yeh." He cleared his throat. "You've got a bit of sand in your hair yourself."

"Oh." She pulled off her hat, bent from the waist, scrubbed at her head vigorously, came back up with her curls in wild disorder, attempted to finger-comb them into place, then gave it up and put the hat back on again. Her cheeks were pink, her eyes sparkling. "Better?"

"Yeh," he smiled. "Better. But only a shower's really going to help any of us."

"A shower and then a bath, for me," she said. "After Zack has his. I showed off way too much there. I'm going to need a long soak tonight."

Her eyes met his, and he could see the moment when the memory hit her, too. When they were both thinking about the same thing. About the huge soaking tub that had held pride of place in one corner of the big *bure*. A pillow at each end, the multitude of candles surrounding the rim, all of which they'd lit that night, the only light other than the moon's soft illumination through the wide windows and doors. The scented oil in the water that had made both of their bodies slick.

They'd started at opposite ends, and he'd watched her sink lower, eyes closing in bliss as he'd massaged a slim, pedicured foot with its pale pink toenails, strong thumbs working on her heel, then moving over the arch with a lighter touch.

He ran his own foot up her inner thigh, rubbed it softly against her while he shifted his attention to her other foot.

"I should do you," she murmured. "But I'm too relaxed to move. And you're making me feel too good."

"Stay like that. I like you this way. Too sleepy to resist."

She opened her eyes halfway, gave him a secret little smile. "Hmm. What are you planning over there? Going to drown me? You already tried that, remember?"

"Nah." His hand was on her instep, thumb stroking the delicate spot at her inner ankle where the pulse beat. He could feel it picking up now as his own foot continued to move gently over her. "I'll try to make it more pleasant this time. Get you all the way there, too. But I do need you over here." He gave a little tug. "Time to shift yourself."

She came to him, because she always did. "Love how you do what I say," he told her. "Have I mentioned that?"

"Mmm. Just because you have good ideas," she murmured as he reached out to position her over him, raised his hands to her breasts, soft and slick with the bath oil. "I do like it in the water," she sighed.

"And I like it everywhere," he said, beginning to move her as she curled against him. "Every way."

It was true, he thought now, looking at her and knowing she was remembering too. It had all been so good. Slow and tender, or hard and fast. Like the time he hadn't been able to wait until they got back to the *bure,* after dinner, and had pulled her between two outbuildings, taken her against the wall. And had had to make it up to her later, which had been fun too.

Her eyes widened at the look in his own. She shifted her gaze, glanced down, then looked up again in confusion, the blush creeping up her cheeks.

"Sorry," he said ruefully. "Can't help it."

"It's not right," she said in distress. "You're engaged."

"Yeh. Thought we could do this, but better not, eh."

"Mum!" Zack was running towards them now, and they both turned to him in thankful relief. The boy was holding a piece of driftwood, twisted and shaped by the water into a sinuous curve. "Doesn't this look like a dragon?"

"Taking that home, mate?" Nic asked him.

"I'm going to put it on my shelf," Zack told him. "With my stone. It's a treasure. There are heaps of good things over here. Come see!"

"We need to get back anyway," Emma decided. "Time to go. Oh, my bag."

"I'll get it," Nic told her. He loped off and was soon headed back again. Emma took Zack's hand and set off, leaving Nic to follow behind, wrestling with his confused thoughts.

"See, Mum?" Zack said when they got to the spot where the angle of the shore had resulted in a collection of driftwood. "Isn't it cool? I thought you'd like it. Because they're interesting, aren't they?"

"They are!" she agreed with delight. She zeroed in on a short section of log that had been battered by time and tide, the cylindrical shape perfectly flat at both ends. "Wouldn't this be a great end table?" She ran her hands over it, taking obvious pleasure in the smooth surfaces, the dips and bulges. "I wish I could take it."

"Why not?" Nic asked.

She sighed. "I could get it back to your car if we were closer. We could roll it, huh, Zack? But it's too far."

Nic picked it up, tested its weight. "Not too bad. D'you really want it? I can bring it along, if you do."

"It's too heavy," she objected. "And too far back to the car."

He hefted it a couple times. "Nah. Not even twenty kilos, I reckon. And less than a kilometer to the carpark. No worries. D'you want it?"

"As long as you don't hurt yourself," she said dubiously.

"Do me a favor," he said, pained. "I may not be a forward, just a lowly fullback. But I can shift this."

"It's so awesome!" Zack was bouncing along next to her, hardly able to contain himself. "You get to have a new table, Mum! Because Nic's strong!"

Emma smiled down at him. "We'll walk fast, all the same. It's still a long way for him to carry that heavy thing, no matter what he says."

The carpark didn't turn up any too soon, Nic admitted to himself. He didn't want to think how much of his offer had come from wanting to impress both of them, because this thing was bloody heavy. He set it down next to the ute, careful to avoid any exhalation of breath that would have given away his relief at being shed of the burden, rummaged for his keys and opened the back, hefted the load into the Toyota and slammed the door on it.

"I can't believe you did that," Emma said. She had cast him continual worried glances on the walk back. "I really do want it, but you didn't have to." She toweled herself and Zack off as best she could to remove the worst of the sand, then handed the towel to Nic. "We're going to get things pretty sandy, too."

"That's why I have a ute," he reminded her. "That's the idea."

"Yeh, Mum," Zack put in. "When we went camping, it got really muddy, didn't it, Nic?"

"It did. That was a pretty wet trip, wasn't it, mate? Bit of a challenge."

"Yeh," Zack agreed, dropping his eyes.

"Oi," Nic said gently. "Look at me." He waited until Zack obeyed, then went on. "I told you, you did fine."

"I cried, though," Zack said in a small voice.

"Because you're six. And it was the first time, and you missed your Mum. Come on, now. Let's get you back home and into that bath. Because, mate. You're carrying enough sand on you to set up your own beach."

♡

He pulled up into the steep driveway in front of the house, brought the Toyota to a stop and set the brake.

"I'll just take this thing in for you, put it where you want it," he told Emma. "You OK?" he asked in a lower voice as she bent to gather their things.

"Yeah." She smiled briefly at him, then was out of the ute and ushering Zack to the front door.

He popped the latch on the back, pulled out the heavy piece of wood, then set it down to close the back again. She'd been so quiet on the way back. He could tell she was feeling awkward. No more of these outings without Claudia, he decided. It had felt too much like a family. Too confusing for all of them.

By the time he'd made it into the flat with the driftwood, she already had Zack in the bath. Nic shifted the load in his arms. "Where d'you want this?"

She ran to the end table between the chair and the couch. "Right here." She moved the lamp, then pulled the table aside to make a space.

He set the piece down where she indicated. "Got a particular way you want it?" He twisted and turned it until it was arranged to her satisfaction, then stood up again.

"Mind if I wash my hands?" he asked.

"Of course. Go ahead and use the bathroom sink. Zack won't mind. He's not that modest," she told him, her smile returning at last.

"Want me to take that other thing away?" he asked when he came back, indicating the end table. "Not good for much."

"No. I'll take it back to the Op Shop. That's where I got it in the first place. Recycling."

"I'll put it in your boot, then," he decided, picking it up.

"You don't have to do that."

"I know I don't. I will anyway. Walk me out, will you?"

She stood aside in silence as he stowed the table in the boot of her car, then slammed the lid and turned towards his own car.

"That was a good day," he told her as they walked down the driveway together. "More fun than I've had in ages."

"Too much fun," she said. She looked up at him, eyes troubled. "I don't want to…" Her voice trailed off.

"Yeh," he agreed with a sigh. He stopped at the ute, fingered the keys in his hand. "Too much history, I reckon."

"That's it," she said with relief. "Anyway. Zack will see you Monday. Have a good weekend. What's left of it."

the tipping point

♡

"I'm home!" he called out, shutting the oversized entry door behind him. "Claud?"

She came to meet him, pulled back at the sight of him. "What have you been *doing* to yourself? Rolling in the sand?"

"Yeh," he smiled. "Just about. It was brilliant, actually. You should've come. Did you have a good day?"

"Had lunch with Cassandra," she said. "We did some talking."

"Sounds good. I'll go take a shower, OK? And we can do some talking ourselves. Or whatever." He reached to kiss her, felt her withdrawal. "Something wrong?" he asked, pulling back with a frown.

"Go take your shower," she told him.

He came back downstairs afterwards, went to the fridge for a beer. The game wouldn't be on for a couple hours yet. He wondered if he should've made plans to watch with a teammate. Claudia hadn't been to a match since before he'd found Zack. And she hadn't seemed too keen on watching tonight's.

He went and sat on the couch next to her, took a pull at the bottle. Two was all he'd allow himself, with semis coming up. He'd enjoy every sip of this one.

"Wish you could've been there today," he told her again. "It'd be better, I think. Besides, you really do need to meet Emma and

Zack, because I want to get the visitation sorted, and she isn't going to agree to that if she's never met you. I was thinking, when we go to the bach after the final, maybe they could come up for a couple days."

"To *stay* with us?" Claudia asked in disbelief. "No."

"They could sleep in the Little House," he suggested. "I know it's all a bit irregular, but it's an irregular situation, isn't it? All you have to do is be civil to her, and get to know Zack a bit. That's easy. He's a great kid."

"No," Claudia said again. "If he really has to come, it'll have to be without her."

He sighed. "Remember what happened last time? She doesn't want him alone with me overnight. We'll have them up for a couple days, and that'll do it, I'm sure. Just relieve her mind a bit. I don't want to spend time with them without you anymore," he admitted, taking her hand. "It's not feeling like a good idea."

"It's not feeling like a good idea to me either," she said. She disengaged her hand, went and sat on the opposite couch, settling into what he thought of as her Lawyer Pose, perched upright, legs together, hands on her knees. "You need to decide what's most important to you, Nic. Your priorities have shifted, and it isn't working for me."

"What d'you mean?"

"I'm going to be your wife. I should be the most important person in the world to you. But you seem more interested in Zack, more committed to him, than you are to me. And that's not acceptable."

"He's my son. It's not a matter of choosing. It's fitting him into our life."

"But I don't want to fit him into my life," she said. "This isn't what I signed on for. I've given it a lot of thought, and this isn't going to work for me. Not the way you're doing it."

"What way, then?" he asked, his voice hardening. "What would work for you?"

"If you saw him on your own, the way you've been doing. I don't want to know him. I don't want to know her. Bad enough that you're planning to give away our money. But I don't want them infringing on our life together."

"That's too damn bad," he said, the anger rising. "Because he's there. He didn't ask to be, but he is. And I'm not going to shut him out."

"Then," she said, standing up, "we really have nothing else to discuss, do we?" One elegant hand went to her left ring finger. She pulled off the band, the brilliant stone flashing in the lamplight, held it out to him. "We're done here. That was my last gasp, just now."

He stared at her in shock, got slowly to his feet and took the ring from her. "You're willing to give up everything we have, over this?"

"Come on, Nic," she said impatiently. "It hasn't really been working for a while now. Don't tell me you haven't noticed."

He shrugged helplessly. "Just thought, you know, the stress of the wedding and all. Work. All that. Besides Zack."

"You've changed," she told him. "You used to be like me. Disciplined. Focused."

"Hang on, now. You can't say I'm not disciplined. That's all I am. All I've done, for years now. Meet my bloody obligations. Training. Meetings. Sponsorships. Public relations. What more d'you want me to do?"

"You aren't excited about the wedding," she said, beginning to tick her reasons off on long, slender fingers. "You seem like you want to be anywhere else, when I try to discuss it with you. You keep running off to spend time with Zack, wanting to do things that are 'fun.'" She made air quotes with her hands around the word. "But mostly, you aren't giving me the attention and consideration I deserve. I need to come first. I look at our future together, and I don't like what I see."

His jaw felt frozen. He could barely get the words out. "If that's how you feel. If you aren't even willing to try. Go to couples counseling, something like that, help us get through this."

"I need to come first," she said again. "And I'm not willing to deal with all this…this complication. That's the bottom line."

"Zack's not a bloody complication. He's a child. He's my *son*."

"Well, now you can do all the bonding you like," she snapped, then took a breath, shook her hair into place, gathered herself.

What kind of woman, Nic wondered, didn't even get upset when she was breaking her engagement? *He* was shaking inside, but she barely seemed flustered. How could that be? He might have become more emotional in the past few years, but surely she had got less so.

"I'll move out," she was saying now. "I'll take some of my clothes now, and come back later for the rest of my things. Thank God we hadn't combined our finances yet. But I want to take the art that's mine, the kitchen things."

"Whatever." What did this matter? "D'you have someplace to go?"

"To Cassandra's. We discussed it today."

"So you'd already decided."

"I decided to give you one more chance to choose me. And you didn't. So…" She shrugged again. "We're done, aren't we? It's been pretty good. It's gone now, that's all. I don't feel the same way about you I once did. And I suspect, if you look down deep, you'll say the same."

"I was still trying, though," he said. "Reckon that's the difference."

"No point in trying when it's over. Will you carry my suitcases down for me, please?"

"You already packed?"

"I was pretty sure. They're in my closet."

He turned without a word, climbed the stairs to the bedroom. Realized he was still holding the ring, shoved it into a pocket. Picked up the two big cases and brought them down for her. Second heavy load he'd carried that day, he thought fleetingly. What a difference a couple hours could make.

♡

"How'd it go?" Emma asked as she opened the door to Nic's knock on Monday evening. "You're early. Brrr. You feel so chilly." She rubbed Zack's back, pulled back to hold his hands in hers. "Wet and cold, like a little fish. Let's get you straight into the bath."

She looked up at Nic. "Want to come in for a minute?" she asked him. "Cup of tea? Because I'm sure you're cold too. "

"I could do with a cup of tea," he admitted.

"Can Nic stay for dinner?" Zack asked from inside his shirt as Emma pulled it over his head. "We didn't have it. Because we got wet."

"Can you?" Emma asked him. "Or do you need to get back?"

"I'd like to stay, if you have enough," he said. "I don't need to get back. And I could use the company tonight."

She looked at him sharply, started to say something, then went into the bathroom to help Zack get started.

♡

"Put your pajamas on when you're done," she said to Zack as she pulled the bathroom door shut to keep the heat in. "Get all cozy."

She came out to rejoin Nic in the lounge. "Come into the kitchen with me while I fix something," she said. He'd shed his jacket and shoes, she saw, was standing in track pants, hoodie, and socks. "I wish I had something warm for you to wear," she went on as he followed her. "But I suspect my dressing gown wouldn't work as well as yours did."

"Probably pink as well," he said with a little smile. "Or it has flowers on."

"How'd you guess?" She flipped the switch on the electric jug, pulled out the mugs, then went out into the lounge again and came back with the afghan.

"This isn't pink, anyway," she told him. "Wrap up a little. You're making me cold, looking at you."

"Not too bad." But he spread the warm yellow wrap across his lap, accepted the tea she was handing him.

"It's just going to be leftovers," she said apologetically. "I wasn't expecting you guys. Luckily, I have some chili and corn muffins in the freezer." She pulled them out, popped the plastic chili container into the microwave and set it to defrost, switched the oven on, then sat down across from him, poured milk into her tea, and stirred.

"Are you OK?" she asked hesitantly after a moment. "I hope you don't mind my asking. Because you look terrible, and you didn't play this weekend, so I know it's not that." He didn't exactly have dark shadows, but the usual gleam was missing from his eyes, and there was a weary look to his face and a slump to his shoulders she'd never seen.

He stirred his own tea slowly, looking down at the milky surface before meeting her gaze. "Broke up," he admitted. "Saturday, after our beach day."

"*What?*" She set her mug down. "You mean, you broke the engagement?"

"Nah." He grimaced. "She did."

"But...why? You'd been together so long," she said in distress. "It wasn't me, was it? She didn't get the wrong idea? Because I can ring her and reassure her that there's nothing between us, if that'll help."

"It wasn't you. That is, it was Zack, partly. But partly..." He shrugged heavily. "Reckon Zack was just the tipping point. That was when everything turned to custard. Least when I noticed it. I didn't realize anything was wrong, before that. I thought she was just a bit narked with me, over the wedding arrangements and that. That I wasn't rapt about the whole thing. But I guess it was. Wrong, I mean."

"Like what?" She got up to give the chili a stir, put it back in the microwave and started it up again. "What did she say?"

"That I wasn't putting her first. That I wasn't...disciplined enough for her anymore. That I didn't care about the wedding, like I said. But really, I think it was the putting her first thing. It wasn't what she'd bargained for, she said. Being a stepmum."

"It wasn't what I bargained for either," Emma pointed out. "Or you. That doesn't mean it's not a good thing. Anyway, if she loved you, wouldn't she want to support you?"

"She's always been what you'd call...high-maintenance, I suppose. Comes from being an only, maybe. All that focus from her mum and dad. I liked that, though, before. Her confidence. She's always known what she wanted, what she deserved. No insecurities. I admired that. Course, no need for me either, as it turned out. No need for support. And she didn't understand why I'd need it either."

"Doesn't sound that good, tell you the truth," Emma said. "To me, anyway. Not my idea of a partnership. Isn't that the point, that you help each other through the tough times, as well as enjoying the good ones?"

"I thought so," he said. "But I'm probably being unfair. It was a big ask, changing the rules like this."

"Huh." She didn't trust herself to speak. She got up again to stir the chili instead, wrestled an ancient, sticky drawer open to pull out a box of aluminum foil.

"So did you leave? Move out? Or did she?" she asked, tearing off a flimsy sheet and dumping the muffins onto it, beginning to crimp the edges.

"She did. My house," he explained.

"What did you do? Ring somebody?"

"Nah. Drank." He grinned at her ruefully. "Why I look so bad. You should've seen me yesterday. Least I had two days to get right afterwards. Not meant to do that, the week before a big game."

"And at least you didn't get on any planes, have any ill-advised flings," she offered with a little smile of her own.

"That's right," he remembered. "You *did* do that, didn't you? What did you do with the ring?" he asked suddenly. "After— what's his name? dumped you?"

"David. Best thing that ever happened to me. I'm not saying that's true for you," she went on hastily. "But wow, thank goodness we didn't get married. It wouldn't have lasted. At least I hope it wouldn't, because I think all the spirit would have been crushed out of me by now. Oh, and the ring? I gave it back, of course. Didn't think of it at the moment. I'd have liked to have thrown it at his head, not that it would've made much of a dent. Pretty small. But yeah, I left it with my dad to give back to him. He probably turned right around and gave it to Karen. He would've had to have it resized first, though. She had fat fingers."

"And a pig nose," he reminded her.

She laughed, saw his answering smile. "I told you that, huh? Yeah. Why? Did Claudia not give you back the ring?"

"Nah. She did. Of course. She's very...tidy. She'd never leave a loose end like that. But I have to tell you something terrible," he confessed. "I chucked it out, after about the fifth beer."

"What?"

"It was in my pocket," he explained. "And I went to sit down, felt it in there, and chucked it in the rubbish. I remember that much, anyway."

"You dug it out again, though, surely, once you sobered up."

"Nah. Collection day today. I put the bag in the bin, forgot it was in there. Realized a couple hours later."

She stared at him, aghast. "You're kidding. How much did it cost you? Oh, whoops," she realized. "You don't have to answer that."

"I don't mind," he said. "Not sure if I'm sorry, or glad. Twenty thousand."

"Twenty…thousand…*dollars?*" she asked incredulously. "And you accidentally chucked it *out?*"

"Yeh," he said, a smile growing now, turning into a laugh. "Reckon Claudia was right after all. I'm undisciplined, eh."

She began to laugh herself, pointed a finger at him. "You…are…an…*idiot,*" she got out.

"I know, right?" he managed to say before they were both overcome with helpless laughter.

"The divorce would've cost at least that much," he said at last, reaching for a paper serviette from the holder on the table and wiping his eyes. "Once I got over kicking myself, I decided maybe I got off cheap, at that."

"Mum!" Emma heard from the other room.

She got up hastily. "I forgot all about Zack," she told Nic. "Can you check those muffins, and give that chili a stir, please? Should be about ready."

♥

They didn't have another chance to talk until Zack was in bed. "I haven't seen anything about your breakup," Emma said. Nic was on the couch, and she'd reclaimed her afghan, was snuggled with it in her chair. "I'm sure it'll be in the *Herald*. Because I remember reading about the engagement there, when you announced it."

"Yeh. Rang the publicist today. That's one good thing. She'll take care of all that, 'alert the media.' Least everyone'll know then. I won't have to explain to everybody."

"What about your family?"

"Yeh." He sighed. "My family. They weren't rapt about it. They like Claudia. Specially my dad. I rang them today too."

"They wouldn't want you to marry somebody who didn't love you enough, though," she objected.

"Dunno. My dad probably thinks she's right," he said glumly, no laughter now.

"That's terrible. Though I know what you mean. I got some of that too, when David dumped me. The distinct impression that I'd screwed up. Again."

"That's it," he agreed. "'What did you do?' That's what he said. As if it couldn't possibly have been her."

"I can't imagine, though," she said slowly, running her fingers over the crocheted trim on the afghan. "Being a mum, I just can't imagine not having my first instinct be to support Zack. If I had to choose who was right and who was wrong, I'd be choosing him every time. Unfairly, I'm sure. But a mother bear doesn't stop to think about whether somebody has a right to approach her cub, does she? She just charges right in there to protect him. If bears know that, why don't human parents?"

"Dunno," he said again. "My dad isn't much of a bear, I guess."

"My mum either. My dad's a bit more supportive, thank goodness, though my mum talks more, so you get her opinion first. Her *strong* opinion. What did your own mum say?"

"She never says too much, when my dad's there," Nic admitted. "He can be a bit of a bully. She'll be kinder, I'm sure, when I see her alone."

He stood up, stretched. "And if I'm going to be any bloody use tomorrow at training, I need to go home now, get some sleep."

"Yeah. Me too." She set the afghan aside, got up to walk him to the door. "And if I didn't say it already, I'm sorry. I know how bad it feels, even if you're a bit relieved at the same time." She reached up to give him the hug she'd been longing to offer all evening. His own arms went around her in response, and he held her close for a moment, then let her go and stepped back.

"Thanks," he said, his eyes a bit damp. "And cheers for dinner. Next time, though, I'm bringing a couple beers with me. If I'm going to bare my soul like that, we could both use a bit of alcoholic help."

getting out

♡

"OK. How do I look?" Emma asked Zack on Friday night, coming out of her bedroom and giving a little pirouette. "Pretty," Zack said seriously. "I like your hair."

Emma gave the thin silver headband holding back her curls the barest nudge, making sure it was securely in place. "I like this too. What about the dress?" She cocked a hip, struck a pose. "Pretty good for half price, huh?"

Zack examined the coral-colored dress, her high-heeled sandals. "Yeh. You look pretty," he repeated.

Emma pulled the door leading to the hallway closed so she could look at herself in her only full-length mirror. The close-fitting bodice with its sweetheart neckline and wide straps *was* pretty, and the skirt wasn't *that* short. She shouldn't have bought it, back in the after-Christmas sales, but it had been too good a deal to resist. And now she had a chance to wear it at last.

She pulled on the delicate pale apricot shrug with its ribbon edging and eyed her image with satisfaction. "I think so too," she decided. "It's fun to get dressed up, isn't it?"

Zack looked at her dubiously.

"Don't answer that," she laughed. The doorbell rang, and she picked up her clutch. "That'll be Mrs. Harrison."

Her landlady stepped inside, looked her over with approval. "Don't you look lovely," she told her. "Your date's going to feel like a lucky fella."

"I hope so," Emma smiled. "Thank you so much for minding him. We shouldn't be too late. It's just dinner."

"No worries," Lois assured her. "We'll get on famously, won't we, Zack? Besides…" She held up the package in her hand and gave the boy a conspiratorial smile. "I brought chocolate biscuits. As I know they're your favorites. Once you've had your bath, we'll have a cozy time of it, make a bit of cocoa and eat our bikkies."

Zack was enthusiastic in his endorsement of the evening's program, and Emma laughed again. She still had her doubts about Ryan's potential as Mr. Right, but it had been months since she'd been on a proper date. Their lunch had gone pretty well, and it would be nice to be taken out, have somebody look at her with some heat. Somebody she could actually have, if she decided she wanted him.

Ryan, when he arrived a few minutes later, didn't disappoint. His blue eyes lit with appreciation at her appearance, a slow smile spreading over his face. The coral dress and high heels clearly worked for him, too. A few words to Lois, a parting hug and kiss for Zack, and they were off.

Ryan had spared no effort, Emma found, to make the evening romantic. She'd heard of Clooney's, but had never been taken there before. It was a far cry from her last dinner date, the hamburgers with Zack and Nic. She really should get out more.

He couldn't have chosen a more intimate dining experience, she saw as they entered the restaurant. Strings of black beads separated each table into its own little enclave, while the semicircular maroon banquettes and low lighting, cleverly offset by a small spotlight that allowed them to see their menus, encouraged murmured conversation.

Ryan was looking especially handsome tonight, his dark shirt tucked into dark gray slacks a contrast with the blond hair that shone in the glow of the little spot. He kept up a flow of conversation, mostly about his work, as they drank a spicy, savory Marlborough Pinot Noir that had her tastebuds humming in delight, and ate their small but exquisitely presented portions of meat and vegetables.

"So I decided they'd just have to extend the deadline. Sometimes you have to push back a bit. Don't you think?" he was asking now, his hand touching hers lightly to make his point, his foot shifting, coming to rest against her own.

"Hmm," she considered, taking another bite of her salmon. She left her hand where it was, but moved her foot. She wasn't quite ready for sexy games under the table. "Well, I'm not in a position to do much pushing back, so I can't really say."

"That's what I like about you," he said, taking her hand in his and smiling into her eyes. "That you don't do much pushing back."

She took a final bite, smiled noncommittally, took the opportunity to move her hand away under the pretext of setting her knife and fork neatly across her plate. "That was delicious," she told him. "Thank you. This was a treat."

"Nah," he said. "The treat was having you here with me. Because you're pretty delicious yourself." He smiled again.

Wow, she wondered, how many times had he used *that* line? OK, that went beyond smooth. That was just cheesy.

"Would you like a sweet?" he asked as the waiter came around again.

"No, thank you. But you go ahead, if you like," she said hurriedly. "I'm happy to sit for a bit."

"Want to get back, do you? So do I," he assured her. "We'll have the bill, please," he told the waiter.

"Thank you," she said again as he opened the car door for her. She had been unsurprised to find that he drove a dark, sporty late model with lush leather interior and all the gadgets. He closed the door after her before going around to his own side and sliding in, where he punched a few buttons to fill the car with soft, dreamy music, lush orchestrations and a male voice crooning about love.

It was all fairly effective, and the drive across the Harbour Bridge, through the dark streets in the warm car, soft music surrounding her, found its mark. By the time he had pulled the car to a stop in front of the house, she was feeling warm and had a few tingles. She *had* been missing being kissed, being touched. And it looked like she'd be getting some of that tonight.

She climbed out of the car, found Ryan close behind her. A bit *too* close, his hand touching the small of her back. Something about his touch sent a shiver down her spine—and not the right kind. Wow, it *had* been a while.

"Whew. Too much wine at dinner," she heard him say in her ear, his arm around her now. "Think you could fix me a cuppa?"

"Sure." She still had that vague sense of unease. But he was attractive, he was clearly interested, and a little fooling around was just what she needed. She was out of practice, that was all.

Not out of practice wanting Nic, her mind whispered. That was just memories, she reminded herself firmly. Long gone, and best forgotten. Time to set them aside for good, and this was her chance to start. She opened the door with her key, let Ryan in behind her, shrugged off her jacket and hung it up as she called a hello to Mrs. Harrison, ensconced on the couch with a paperback.

The older woman carefully slipped a bookmark into place, then rose to greet them.

"How'd it go, Lois? Any problems?" Emma asked her.

"No worries. A lamb, like always," Mrs. Harrison said fondly. "Had his bath, we had our cocoa and bikkies, then he cleaned his teeth and was off to bed like the good little fella he is."

"Please thank Fred for sparing you tonight, too," Emma said.

"Hmph. Don't think he missed me. Anyway, it's given me a chance to catch up on my reading, without the telly blaring away," Lois assured her. "I'll be off upstairs, then. Goodnight. Pleasure meeting you, Ryan."

"Likewise." He smiled briefly, held the door, then shut it behind her and came over to where Emma stood, still near the couch.

"I don't really want a cup of tea," he told her. "I know what I want." His mouth descended on hers as he pulled her onto the couch and came down over her. No softness, no romance now. She offered an instinctive protest that was smothered by his insistent mouth, the crushing weight of him. Her lips opened to tell him to slow down, and he took the opportunity to push his tongue into her mouth, even as he pulled her back towards the arm of the couch, so she was on her back. His hand went to a breast, and she uttered another ineffectual protest as she shoved against him once, then again, pushed him as hard as she could from her prone position. He paid no attention. Instead, he seemed to interpret her struggles as encouragement, deepened the kiss until she felt as if she would gag on it.

She felt the panic rising at the sensation of being trapped beneath him. This wasn't what she wanted. This was too much. Too fast. She had to get out.

He wasn't letting her go, though. Or letting up for even a moment as he continued to kiss her, his mouth bruising hers, his hands moving over her. Grabbing at her, pulling her against him. He drew back at last to reach a hand under the hem of her dress, onto her thigh, his knee pushing her legs apart, and she seized her opportunity, gave a convulsive heave and slid out from under him. She crashed into the coffee table on the way to the ground, bruising her shoulder badly against the edge, but barely felt the pain as she shoved off with her hands, made it to her feet and dashed around to put the end of the couch between herself and Ryan.

"No!" She was trembling, clutching the arm of the couch for support. "I don't want this. Stop!"

Ryan was standing himself now, staring at her, fists clenched. "Then why the hell did you invite me in?"

"Not to attack me!" Was he going to grab her again? She couldn't tell. She gave a fast glance around her. She could hit him with the lamp, if he tried. She reached for it, just in case. "You need to leave!" Her breath was coming hard now with effort and fear.

"What kind of a fucking tease are you?" he demanded angrily. "You dress like that, walk like that, invite me to come in? And then when I go to take what you're offering, you change your mind? What the bloody hell are you playing at?"

"Mum?" She whirled at the small voice from the doorway. Zack, his hair on end, the inevitable drooping sleeves and pajama legs puddling around him. His anxious gaze moving from one to the other of them. "What's wrong?"

"Baby." She moved swiftly across the room to him, pulled him to her. "Ryan's leaving."

"Too right I'm leaving." Ryan spat the words, then turned on his heel, grabbing his jacket from the hook by the door on the way. "Fucking waste of money."

Emma ran to the door, locked it after him and held onto the handle for a moment before she turned back to Zack, who had followed her anxiously. She smoothed his hair, unable to stop the trembling in her hands, before she pulled him close again. She wasn't sure if she were trying to comfort him or herself. She'd really thought, for a moment there, that Ryan had been willing to rape her. She still wasn't sure what he'd have done if Zack hadn't come in. How could she have been so stupid?

"He was really angry," Zack said against her waist. "I woke up, and I heard a big noise. His voice was really loud. I was scared."

"Oh, baby." She rubbed his shoulders. "It was OK. He's gone now, anyway. It's all over. Let's get you back to bed."

She got him off to sleep again with a glass of water, a song, and Raffo held snug against him, the hard, lumpy contours seeming to soothe him as always. But sleep, for her, was a long time coming.

Nothing had happened, she reminded herself again. She'd had a bad dating moment, that was all. But it would be a long time before she invited anyone else back to the flat, she knew. That had felt too close.

something in common

♡

Emma was thankful, the next day, that she and Zack had tickets for the semifinal. It wasn't just that she needed something else to think about. She'd felt jumpy and tense all day, had found herself double-checking that the front door was locked. She'd wished she could ring Lucy, but her sister had gone away for the weekend with Tom, and Emma hated to break in on that.

Nothing had happened, she scolded herself. Ryan wasn't coming back. It was all over. But she was still relieved when it was time to leave the flat and head into the City.

If she'd been looking for something to distract her, the first half of the game certainly provided it. She let her breath out with a *whoosh* and sat back with a grateful thump as the teams trotted off to the sheds at the start of the halftime break.

"It's awfully tight," Jenna said beside her.

Emma had barely spoken to Finn Douglas's heavily pregnant wife before. Tonight, though, she'd chosen to sit close to the kids, and that was where Jenna always seemed to be.

"I'm afraid this one's going to be close all the way," Jenna went on. "There's a lot of desire out there on both sides, it seems to me." She leaned to the left to have a word with her children, then was back with Emma again. "Sophie's pretty worried," she explained. "It's always such a physical battle with the South African teams."

"Well, if that's the case, the Stormers are living up to that tradition," Emma said. "I don't know as much about rugby as you do. Mostly what Zack tells me, and he's six, so…"

Jenna smiled, and Emma realized that what she had first taken for standoffishness was probably just shyness. "Sophie's been my tutor," the other woman confessed. "And Finn would laugh at the idea that I know a lot about rugby."

"He sure seems like he can keep up with anyone in a physical battle. He's been all over the field tonight, even I've noticed that. And boy, does he tackle hard. I'd hate to be on the receiving end of all that size and ferocity."

"He *is* impressive, isn't he?" Jenna beamed with pride. "He works so hard out there. But I'm sorry, I'm bragging. I can't help it. I love watching him play."

"You're entitled. How're you doing, though? How long to go?"

Jenna sighed. "A week. Or an eternity. Take your pick."

"Any action so far?"

"Not at all. And it's getting pretty hard to wait," Jenna admitted. "I made a pact with myself not to complain, because this is what I've wanted most in the world. But it's getting pretty hard to keep it."

Emma had to laugh at that one. "Zack was ten days late. Good thing I hadn't made any pacts, because the broken pieces would've been everywhere. Can I do anything, though? Take the kids for you tomorrow, maybe?"

"That's so kind," Jenna said, her eyes filling with what Emma recognized as hormonal tears. "Sophie's having some special time with her dad tomorrow, actually. They have a lunch date. Doing a little shopping, too. *Mysterious* shopping. I have a feeling I'm going to be getting a baby present of my very own. Would you and Zack consider coming over to visit Harry and me instead? I'd like the company. And the distraction."

"I'd love to," Emma said gratefully. More time out of the house, just what she needed. "They do seem to be getting on well."

"Six is a nice age. Harry's surprisingly uninterested in rugby," Jenna cautioned, "but he loves Legos, if that would interest Zack."

"Legos would go over big."

"Bring your walking shoes, and we'll take the boys up Mt. Eden first."

"Are you up for something that steep?" Emma asked in surprise.

Jenna laughed. "I said I was trying not to complain. I never promised anything about not trying to help speed up the process."

♡

"I still can't believe you're doing this," Emma puffed as she labored up the steep Mt. Eden hillside the next day behind Jenna, the two boys having run ahead. Zack was still so pumped up about the Blues' tough win in the semifinal, it was good for him to run out some of that energy.

"This is my back garden," Jenna explained, not sounding nearly as winded as she ought to be. She really had to increase her aerobic workouts, Emma decided. She was getting outperformed here by the nine-months-pregnant.

"And I used to run this almost every day," Jenna continued. "I stopped at about six months. Just too much of me bouncing around and hitting the ground again. Now I'm mostly swimming and walking, along with some gym stuff. I miss the running. This walk is good because I get the sweating thing too, get my heart rate up. I need that."

"All righty then," Emma said wryly, regaining her breath as they reached the summit at last. "I just wanted to float on my back at that stage, but whatever."

"I know!" Jenna agreed. "Especially because I feel *huge.* I tell Finn that's why I married him, because no matter how big I get with this baby, he's still going to outweigh me."

"I never thought of that," Emma laughed. "The hidden benefit of rugby players."

♡

"What are you making now?" Jenna asked when they were sitting in her wonderfully comfortable big kitchen, having a cup of herbal tea after a lunch of homemade chicken-vegetable soup, salad, and what Emma deeply suspected had been homemade rolls as well. The boys were happily immersed in Legos, Zack having been suitably awed by Harry's collection.

"A jacket," Emma said, holding up the black rectangle on her needles. "I'm just doing the back now, so it's hard to see. But here." She reached down and pulled the drawing out of her bag. "What do you think?"

"Oh, it's so cute!" Jenna exclaimed at the sight of the black zip jacket with its multicolored stripes on sleeves, hood, and sweatshirt-style pockets. "Did you design this?"

"Yeah," Emma said with her usual mix of embarrassment and pride. "The big news is, this is the first design I've done in CAD. Isn't that ironic? I only realized I could do that after Hannah set me up with an interview at her company. All these years of knitting and designing and being a CAD operator, and it's never occurred to me that I could use it that way."

"She mentioned that to me," Jenna said. "That she'd passed your name on, I mean. But I don't understand what it is. What *is* CAD?"

"Computer-Aided Design," Emma explained. "It's how all engineering designs are done now, of course. But it turns out it's how you do clothing design as well."

"So did the interview go well? If you're practicing?"

"Fingers crossed. So yeah, I've been studying up. It wouldn't pay as well, and I wouldn't have been able to consider it, before. But now..." Emma stopped. "My situation's got a bit better recently," she went on. "Which makes it possible to take a pay cut, especially if it means I'd enjoy what I did. And if I could help with designs...Boy," she sighed, "I'd *love* that."

"It sure sounds like more fun to me," Jenna said. "Cute little-girl clothes instead of, what? Buildings?"

"Oh, not just *buildings*. You've got your sewer tunnels, too," Emma said seriously, prompting a laugh. "Oh, yeah. Plus, the idea of working with people who like clothes. And..." She hesitated again, wondering how much was all right to share. "Being taken seriously," she said.

"Which doesn't happen now?" Jenna reached to refill Emma's cup.

"No. I'm too...female, I guess."

"Too pretty," Jenna translated. "And they can't see beyond the way you look."

"That's how it seems to me, anyway. I'm girly, I know it. I guess I could get some glasses I don't need. Cut my hair short. Wear more black."

"Heaven forbid. That's the last thing Auckland needs, another woman in black. And what is this, 1980? You shouldn't have to wear pinstriped suits with shoulder pads to be taken seriously."

Jenna lifted her teacup and clinked it against Emma's. "Anyway, here's to knitwear, and knitwear jobs. And to being a woman. And I wanted to tell you, along those lines, that you've done such a good job with Zack. He's a really nice boy."

"Thanks. I've done my best, but it hasn't always been easy."

"You're a single mum, I think," Jenna said hesitantly.

"Since the beginning."

"That *isn't* easy, I know it. I was raised by a single mum myself, since the beginning. Who *didn't* do all that well, so I know the difference."

"Yeah. We lived with my sister till Zack was almost four. That was better, but it's still not quite the same. Lucy's great— better than a lot of actual partners, I'll bet—but Zack isn't her kid, bottom line."

"It's hard to have all that responsibility on your shoulders," Jenna said. "Sometimes, when Finn's gone for a long stretch, and I'm feeling sorry for myself, I think, this is like being a single mum. And then I realize that it isn't even close. Because I have his support, and I know he's coming home to me again. I'm not in it by myself. And oh, dear. I'm sorry. That was insensitive. Blame the overemotional pregnancy thing. I keep blurting out things I shouldn't say at all."

"No," Emma protested. "There's nothing wrong with saying that. Because that's *exactly* it. How much the…the last resort you are. It's a relief to have somebody understand. And I'm happy for you. I really am."

She finished her row and shoved her knitting back into her bag. "But I'd better round Zack up, and get on with our errands. We're stopping by the Warehouse, since we're over here. High-end shopping. At least I know I won't be tempted by any fabulous clothes."

"Thanks for coming to visit," Jenna said. "I appreciate your hauling Zack all the way over here."

"Thank you for inviting me. I was surprised, actually," Emma confessed.

"It can be a little intimidating, sitting with the wives and girlfriends. Even though they're great," Jenna hastened to add.

"But it can still be awkward, not knowing if you fit in, if they'll accept you."

"Exactly!" Emma exclaimed. "That's exactly it! How did you know?"

Jenna smiled a bit sadly. "Oh, I learned that the same way I've learned everything else in my life. The hard way."

She gave Emma a warm hug at the door as she saw the two of them out. "I'm so glad you came to visit me," she told her. "And that I've had the chance to get to know Zack. Come back and see me again, when I have a baby to show you. Because I have a feeling that we have a lot in common."

when you're going through hell

♡

"Ready for a hot chocolate?" Nic asked Zack as they changed out of their rugby boots on Monday afternoon.

"Yeh. I'm starved!" Zack said. "Can I have a muffin too?"

"Your mum got a bit stroppy with me last time we did that," Nic reminded him. "Better not, not before dinner. I'm invited, remember. Don't want her to change her mind, turf me out."

Zack sighed. "OK. But a marshmallow?"

"Definitely a marshmallow," Nic agreed.

When they were sitting at a table in the tiny café next to the Domain, though, he saw that Zack wasn't quite as interested in his hot chocolate as usual. Instead, he kept looking up at Nic doubtfully.

"Got something on my face?" Nic asked, wiping his mouth with a paper serviette. "Or is it something on your mind?"

"D'you think you could lend me some money?" Zack asked him. "But I'm not sure how much," he added honestly. "How much does a cricket bat cost? It doesn't have to be a flash one. Maybe on Trade Me? Mum gets heaps of things on Trade Me."

"Course," Nic said automatically. "Didn't realize you didn't have one. Why d'you need it, though, this time of year? Thought you were focusing on the footy, for now. By the time you're using it, you may not fit it anymore."

"In case," Zack said obscurely.

"In case what?" Nic was bewildered now. "In case somebody asks you to play cricket this winter? Someone without a bat?"

"Nah. In case I have to protect Mum from a Bad Guy."

"You been watching those orcs again, eh," Nic guessed. "They aren't real, mate. Your mum's all right."

"I'm not a baby," Zack said impatiently. "I know there aren't really orcs. A real Bad Guy. In our flat."

"There's not likely to be a Bad Guy in your flat, surely," Nic said. "It's Northcote, not Darfur."

Zack looked at him blankly. "Huh?"

"I mean," Nic went on, "you live in a pretty good area. And I think your mum can keep you both safe. You don't need to worry about that."

"But I do," Zack insisted. "She said she wasn't, but she was scared. Because that guy was bad. He was yelling. He said the *f* word. And I think he hurt her. She has a really big bruise. I saw. And Mum's not very big, you know. Not for a grownup, she isn't."

"What?" Nic stared at him. "When was this? What happened?"

Zack's explanation only made him more confused. And worried. And more and more enraged.

"So will you lend me the money? And help me get it? Or can you buy me a bat, on Trade Me?" Zack finished. "I don't know how to do it. And they don't let kids anyway. Mum always does it for me. I'll pay you back, I promise," he went on hurriedly. "Only I spent all my money when I bought my Legos. I don't know how much bats cost. But if it wasn't too much?"

"I'll buy you a bat," Nic assured him. "But I don't want you to worry about this, because I'm going to get it sorted. No Bad Guy's going to hurt your mum again. That's *my* promise."

♡

"The other night. What happened?" he asked Emma when he was sure Zack was in the bath. He was leaning against the kitchen bench following a simple dinner of lamb chops and green beans, drying with a tea towel as Emma washed up at the dented stainless steel sink.

"What other night?"

He gestured impatiently with his towel. "Don't try to pretend. Zack told me. Something about a Bad Guy. Somebody who was in here, yelling. He was scared. He's worried about you."

She plunged her hands into the soapy water again, scrubbed hard at a plate, dropping her head so her hair fell over her face. "I hoped I'd convinced him I was all right. Because I was. Nothing happened."

"Who was it?" he persisted. "And what *did* happen? It was something, or he wouldn't have been so worried."

"It was...somebody I dated, Friday night. Somebody from the office. We came back here. I was thinking..." She turned to him at last, flushing with what seemed oddly like embarrassment. "I wasn't planning to do much. I wouldn't anyway, not with Zack here. He said I led him on. Maybe I did, saying yes to giving him a cup of tea, letting him in. It was stupid of me, I know. I *knew* something was off, and I did it anyway. I can't believe I got myself into that situation. And Zack too." She reached for a glass, swished the scrub brush around, but Nic could see that her hands were trembling. "But I'd been out with him before. I work with him. I *know* him. At least I thought I did."

"Inviting somebody in for a cuppa doesn't give him any rights." He was choking the life out of the tea towel, he realized, and forced himself to relax his grip. "You invited me, that first night here. I didn't jump you, and we have a history. What happened? Where's this bruise? Show me."

"He didn't do it," Emma protested. "Well, not exactly. It was me, hitting the coffee table. When I was trying to get away. I fell."

"Show me," he commanded again.

She sighed, pulled off her rubber gloves and laid them across the sink, then pulled down one shoulder of her sweater. An ugly patch about seven or eight centimeters across, he judged, on the outer edge of her shoulder blade, outside the thin ribbon of bra strap. Gone to black and blue now, three days later. Easy to see how the corner of the table had caught her there. And how hard she must have hit it.

"If you did it getting away from him, he did it," he said, pushing down the rage. She didn't need to see that. "Who was this?"

He got the story out of her in pieces.

"Nothing happened, though," she insisted at the end of her recital. "I don't know why I'm still so upset." She rinsed off the last pieces of silverware, handed them to him to dry.

"You thought he was going to rape you. A pretty good reason to be upset, seems to me." He hung the towel over its rack and turned to face her. "Because it scared the hell out of you, didn't it?"

She nodded, and he saw the sheen of tears in her eyes, the tremble of her mouth.

"Aw, hell." He finally allowed himself to put his arms around her, felt her soften against his chest, the tears starting. He held her until she pulled away again, wiping her eyes with the back of her hand.

"Sorry," she said. "It's just…I've felt so stupid for what happened, and for being so scared."

"You have nothing to feel stupid about, though," he insisted in frustration. "Zack's right, he was a Bad Guy. How the hell were you meant to know that? And of course you were scared. You had every reason to be. But you don't have to be scared anymore. That's one thing I can fix, at least. Give me your phone."

"What?"

"Your phone. Your mobile. Let me see it."

She fetched it from the corner of the bench where she'd set it earlier, handed it to him in wordless confusion.

"Why don't you even have a smartphone?" he asked.

"I don't need it. Or to pay for the data plan. I'm at work all day, and otherwise I mostly just text. This works fine."

He sat at the kitchen table as she took a seat opposite him. He scrolled down, found his contact number. "How the hell d'you do your speed dials?" he muttered. "Oh. Got it."

He looked up as Zack came back into the kitchen, in the All Black pajamas again. "Need to get you some of those in the right size," he told the boy as his mother reached out automatically for the rolling-up routine.

"I *like* these," Zack protested. "They're my favorites."

"I know. And they'd be even better if you fit them. Come here, mate." He reached around Zack as the boy came to stand next to him where he sat at the small round table, and felt him easing towards his knee. His heart melted at the trust in the gesture, and he cleared his throat, opened Emma's phone again. "D'you know how to do speed dial?"

"Course," Zack nodded. "Mum has Auntie Lucy on that. She's number two. I just hold it down to ring her."

"OK, then. And d'you know how to do 111?"

"Mum taught me," Zack said. "I've never done it for real, though. Only pretend. Only if there's a real emergency, she said. Like a fire. Or blood. *Bad* blood."

"That's probably number one on here, right?"

"Yeh," Zack agreed.

"Well, now there's number nine. This button at the bottom. That's me."

"I know which one's a nine. I know numbers. I'm *six.*"

"Right. But now you know, nine's an *N*, right? *N* for Nic."

"OK," Zack said. "So if I want to ring you, I can do nine."

"Yeh. And if your Mum's ever in trouble again," Nic told him seriously, pulling him closer, "if anything even worries you, you ring me. Push the nine. N for Nic. And I'll come straight away to help."

"Nic," Emma said. "You'll scare him."

Zack wasn't listening to her, though. He twisted around to look at Nic. "Really? You'd come? Even if it was in the night? Even if you were asleep?"

"Even if I were asleep," Nic assured him. "Straight away. I promise."

Zack exhaled, shoulders seeming to relax. "OK. But I still want the bat."

"What bat?" Emma asked.

"A cricket bat," Zack informed her. "Just in case."

"In case what? Oh." Emma looked from Zack to Nic. "Oh, no. You don't need to worry about that, sweetie. I told you."

"You'll get the bat," Nic promised him. "Just in case. But you don't need to worry about that bloke. He's not going to be bothering your Mum again."

When they'd got Zack off to bed and were alone together, though, Emma objected again. "I appreciated what you said to him. I would've thought it would make it worse, but you've clearly eased his mind. But it's not realistic, Nic."

"What isn't?"

"That Ryan's not going to bother me again. I work with him, remember? I could hardly face him today," she said with a shudder. "I'm doing his work, and it just makes me sick. He looked at me like I was..." She swallowed. "Dirt. Worse than dirt. And I'm afraid of what he's going to say."

"He should be afraid of what *you're* going to say," Nic pointed out.

"At work, though, it's almost all men. And I know it's wrong, but there are plenty of them who'd agree with him. That I was leading him on. And anyway, what could I say? That he kissed me too hard, and I didn't like it? He didn't actually *do* anything."

"He did enough," Nic said grimly. "And it doesn't sound like he was planning to stop."

"There's nothing I can do, though," she insisted. "Because there's nothing there, really. I have a bruise that he didn't even put on me. And a pretty strong dislike of him, which he obviously reciprocates. And that's all there is to it. Another thing to get through. When you're going through Hell, just keep going. Another one of those."

He stared at her. "That's it? That's your philosophy?"

"Sometimes," she admitted. "Days like today, it has to be. Just getting through till I get to something better."

♡

"Ryan something. Don't know his last name," Nic told the young receptionist. "An engineer. D'you know who I mean? And if he's still here?"

She was a bit flustered, he saw, on recognizing him. He gave her a reassuring grin. "I could use your help here. Ryan?"

"Ryan Aiken," she smiled back, the flush mounting on her cheeks. "He hasn't left yet, I don't think. Do you want me to ring him?"

"Please. And have him come meet me out here, will you?"

He felt a twinge of impatience as he saw her pick up the receiver at last and punch in the extension, her eyes moving to his as she spoke his name. He'd have been here sooner, if he could've been. Two days was more than enough for Emma to deal with this.

"Nic. It's a pleasure."

The bloke was wasted in engineering, Nic thought with contempt as Ryan came around the corner and extended his hand. Should've been a salesman.

Nic kept his own arms firmly folded across his chest. The intimidation pose. He saw Ryan drop his hand uncertainly at the lack of response to his friendly gesture.

"Ryan Aiken," Nic said, unsmiling. "Come outside a minute with me."

"What's this about? D'you want to chat to us about a house? Need some foundation work, do you? We could do that. Or anything else you need," Ryan said as they rode down in the lift. He was getting nervous at the continued silence, Nic saw. Good.

Nic led the way out through the historic building's double glass doors with their heavy brass hardware onto the wide Commerce Street pavement. He ignored the stream of passing foot traffic, forcing pedestrians to detour around him, and turned at last to face Ryan.

"Emma," he finally said.

"Emma?" Ryan looked at him blankly. "Emma who?"

"Have you attacked more than one woman named Emma recently?"

"Attacked? Me? Hang on."

Nic saw Ryan's eyes dart to the doorway. This kind of bully was always a coward in the end, he knew, when it came to someone his own size. His own lips twisted with contempt and he folded his arms again, to keep himself under restraint as much as to intimidate the other man. "Attacked," he said levelly. "Friday night. She's got a hell of a bruise on her."

"I didn't do that," Ryan objected. "I didn't touch her that way. Didn't do anything but what she was asking for."

Nic held himself back with an effort. "Because a woman goes out with you, she's saying she'll shag you?"

"If she invites me in, she is." Ryan was gaining confidence now. "And dresses like that. Bloody hell, mate. You know how it is."

"I'm not your mate," Nic ground out. "Ever hear of consent?"

Ryan flushed, one last bit of bravado. "Come on. Women like a man with confidence, someone who takes what he wants. They want it too, they just want us to do the running so they can feel overpowered. So they can say they weren't responsible."

Nic stared at him. "What kind of sick bastard thinks like that? That's rape."

"What're you?" Ryan sneered. "The White Ribbon ambassador?"

"I'm Emma's friend. One who's going to beat the hell out of you if you touch her again." Nic saw the other man's gaze shift uneasily under his own hard stare. "Find somebody else to do your bloody drawings. Don't talk to her. Don't talk about her. Got it?"

"No worries. I'm not interested. Wouldn't have been interested in the first place, if I'd known what she was like. Frigid bitch."

Ryan muttered it under his breath, but Nic heard it. He went still inside, and his voice was ice now. "You're one word away. One more word."

Ryan took a step back at last. He didn't get the message easily, from women or men, it seemed. "This is rubbish." His eyes moved from side to side like a trapped animal's, but he was still trying to salvage his pride. "I'm not staying here to listen to any more."

Nic reached out fast, grabbed the other man's arm just above the elbow. He'd resisted touching him, but now he allowed his hand to close hard, enough to let Ryan feel the force of it, the anger behind it. "You'll leave her alone from now on. Say it."

Ryan looked down at the hand gripping him, then up at Nic's face again, read the expression there. "Nobody else is as good as she is, though," he objected weakly.

Nic glared at him, increased the pressure. To anyone walking by, it'd look like one man reaching for another's arm in friendly enough fashion. But there'd be some pain now. He squeezed a bit harder, made it hurt a little more, determined to leave a bruise to match Emma's.

"OK," Ryan got out, fear and pain piercing the armor of his self-satisfaction as he realized his danger at last. "I'll get somebody else."

"And shut your gate about her at work," Nic prompted, keeping up the pressure.

"Yeh. OK," Ryan gasped, the last bit of resistance crumbling.

Nic let go of Ryan's arm, watched his hand go up to rub the spot, letting Nic see that it had hurt. Soft.

Nic nodded curtly. "That's it, then."

Ryan shot him one more frightened look and scurried toward the glass doors. Nic watched him go, then turned to walk back to the carpark. That was one thing Emma didn't have to cope with alone, anyway. Not this time.

some flower

♡

Emma had vacillated about taking Zack to the Super 15 final. The Chiefs and the Blues would be playing in Hamilton for the title, and she'd wondered about the advisability of driving two hours in traffic each way, and the late night it would mean for Zack. And, especially, about whether she could rely on her car, if she hit a long stretch of stop-and-go. She had it scheduled for service the next week, but it had been showing a dangerous tendency to overheat lately. An invitation to drive down with Jenna and the kids, though, provided the perfect solution.

"Are you sure you want to go right now?" she had asked Jenna dubiously.

"What, because I might have the baby? That's why I want you there. It'd be a pretty slim chance that it would happen right then. It feels like it's *never* going to happen, to tell you the truth. But just in case, I'd have you to drive my kids home then, wouldn't I? Plus, that's about the only way I can make sure Finn's there for the birth, to go along with him wherever he's playing. As long as I don't have to talk anyone into letting me on a plane, that is. I think that would be a hard sell."

"All right, then," Emma decided. "That sounds perfect." Her less-than-reliable little car was parked safely now at Jenna's house in Mt. Eden, and she and Zack had traveled in luxury in the Range Rover.

She was almost wishing now, though, that they'd stayed home after all. The tension was almost too much to bear, here in the packed Waikato Stadium, every one of its nearly twenty-six thousand seats filled for this ultimate event of the season. They were down to the final ten minutes now, and the usually sedate Kiwi spectators were anything but tonight. Surely there must be other Blues supporters in the stands, but what Emma heard was a home crowd in full cry for its team after a try and missed conversion that put the Chiefs up 22 to 20. A lead, but such a slim one.

She leaned forward, her hand gripping Zack's, as the Chiefs kicked off after their scoring try, and Nic took the kick at the 22. She saw one of his wingers falling in behind him, supporting him as he made his run up the left side of the field, the other staying back to cover the rear. Nic saw the tackler coming, passed to the wing but stayed with him, received the ball again in a lightning pass as the other player was going down in a tackle. A quick sidestep, and Nic was off.

Emma and Zack, together with the rest of the crowd, were on their feet now, the Blues supporters roaring their approval as Nic hit another gear and exploded down the field. Then the groan as a Chiefs player slid into him, hooking an ankle with his foot. The instant loss of momentum as Nic took an awkward hop on his left foot, then fell in a heap. He attempted to rise, but sank back to the turf again, and the referee ran in, blowing his whistle.

"Tripping," Jenna said grimly on Emma's other side. *"Yes,"* she hissed with satisfaction, watching Finn wade into the mix, straight into the player who had brought Nic down, before he was grabbed, held back by members of his own team. The trainer was on the field with his bag now, bending over a prostrate Nic.

"What happened?" Emma asked in confused worry. Zack was leaning against her, eyes wide. She pulled him automatically into her arms, watched Nic rise with the trainer's help and limp off the field. "He's OK," she told Zack, the relief overwhelming. "He's up. He's OK. He's hurt his leg, that's all."

They watched Nic's replacement run out, and the Blues line up so Hemi could take a kick at the goal. "What's happening?" she asked Jenna again.

"Tripping. That's a penalty kick." The stadium erupted as the kick went over, and the score went up, 23 to 22 in favor of the Blues. The giant screen showed a slow-motion replay of the offense, even as the teams took their places again for the Blues to kick off, only a couple minutes left on the clock now. Emma's attention was all for the action on the screen, the Chiefs player's body slowly sliding forward, his foot clearly coming out to hook itself around one of Nic's own flying feet, the sickening turn of the ankle at the unforeseen and sudden stop to his momentum.

"That'll be reviewed," Jenna guessed. "That was deliberate."

The Chiefs had the ball secured and were getting some momentum down the field, the crowd cheering its team on, until a huge, punishing tackle from Finn forced the ball from the player's hands and left the man lying on the ground for a moment before he clambered to his feet again.

"*Yes,*" Jenna breathed.

"Was that OK?" Emma asked doubtfully.

"Oh, yeah," Jenna said with satisfaction. "That was the guy who tripped Nic. Finn's not only made him turn the ball over, he's delivered the message too."

"And that's good?"

"He's delivered the message," Jenna repeated, her eyes not leaving the field. "That's his job. You didn't want to see that guy get away with that, did you?"

"No," Emma decided. "No, I sure didn't."

The Blues had the ball now, clearly determined not to let it out of their control again as the clock ran down. And, at last, the referee's whistle went, ending the match with a Blues win of the final, and Zack and Emma hugging each other in relieved gratitude.

♡

"How are we going to know if Nic's OK?" Zack asked as they made their way through the stadium, Jenna and Emma each keeping a tight hold on their tired children in the crowd.

"I texted him," Emma told him. She'd thought of it as soon as the game had ended, had pulled out her mobile even before they'd left their seats. She didn't know when he would see it. She hoped Nic would realize how worried Zack—and she—would be about him, and would answer when he could.

She heard the *ding* of the text when they were pulling into Jenna's garage, two hours later, pulled her phone from her purse with eager fingers.

"Baby," she said, a catch in her throat, reaching into the back seat to give Zack's knee a squeeze. "Time to wake up and get into our car. And I just heard from Nic. He says it's a sprain, that's all."

"Good news," Jenna said with relief.

"What does that mean?" Zack asked sleepily.

"It means his ankle's hurt, and he won't be able to play for awhile," she explained.

"Does it mean he can't play with the All Blacks?" Zack asked, anxious again.

"I don't know. I'm sure he'll be out for a bit. But we can ask him on Monday."

♡

"Thanks for cooking for me," Nic said on Monday evening. He had an ankle propped on a pillow atop the coffee table in Emma's flat, wrapped in one of the collection of cold packs he'd brought with him. "Because this is the boring bit."

"How long do you have to keep doing that?" she asked.

"Meant to be seventy-two hours, so until tomorrow evening. Ten minutes on, ten off. Only so much All Black game film a man can watch, eh."

"That doesn't sound boring," Zack chimed in. "That sounds *fun.*"

"Yeh." Nic smiled down at him. "It's a good treat. Not so much as a steady diet, though."

The buzzer went off on the oven, and Emma moved into the kitchen and came back a few minutes later with two plates that she set before Nic and Zack. "I hope this is OK," she said. "I wasn't sure steak and mushroom pie was on your diet plan, but it sure is tasty."

"A double slice of that, with the green beans and salad?" he said. "Works for me. I'm allowed a wee bit of indulgence anyway, just now."

"How long is it going to be?" she asked when she was settling herself with her own plate.

"A good five weeks till I'm on the field again," he said with a grimace. "Depending how the rehab goes, of course."

"You mean you don't get to play?" Zack asked. He and Emma were sitting on the floor, eating from the coffee table, and Nic smiled at the picture they made, before Emma hopped up to switch out his icepack. He could get used to this, he thought, shabby carpet and all. It was so snug and warm in here, and he loved looking at both of them. His son, and his...his son's mum.

He realized Zack was looking at him expectantly. "Pardon?" he asked. "What did you ask me?"

"You don't get to play with the All Blacks?" Zack repeated.

"Not for a bit," Nic said regretfully. "I'll miss the first two games, anyway. The road trip to Safa, then the Wallabies game back here. Hope I'll be fit for that second game against the Aussies in Melbourne, but we'll have to see how I go."

"What do you do to get better?" Zack asked.

"Whatever they tell me."

Nic accepted Finn's help to put away his dumbbells, then leaned down from the weight bench to grab his crutches from the floor. His workout range was limited just now, but he'd been going stark staring mad sitting around the house, and had greeted the invitation to meet Finn at the gym with relief. Thank goodness the big No. 8, always so disciplined about fitness, was seeking out extra workouts as well during his downtime before All Black training started up. Nic just wished he could be out there with the rest of the boys next week. He knew he'd be pushing his rehab to the fullest extent allowed by the training staff. When he did return to the squad, he meant to come back as strong as he could possibly be.

They made their way down the long hallway of the gigantic Les Mills gym toward the locker room, Finn matching his long pace to Nic's gait. Nic glanced into the big window of a group fitness room, then came to an abrupt halt, swinging around on the crutches to take a closer look.

Finn peered curiously inside, at a miked-up instructor calling out instructions to a crowded roomful of men and women balancing barbells on their shoulders as they dropped into a series of squats. "Looking for a bit more?" he asked Nic. "I knew you backs weren't up to any real work, but I didn't think you'd descended to Body Pump."

He gave Nic a light punch on the shoulder when he didn't respond. "Oi. Nico. What's up?"

"It's Emma," Nic said slowly. "There." He pointed at a trim figure in shorts and a tight, sleeveless top. "In the pink, see? In front."

"Ah. Emma," Finn said after a moment's perusal. "Can't see much from here, but if the front of her looks as good as the back, she must be as pretty as Jenna says. Your son's mum, eh."

That got Nic's attention in a hurry. "What? She told Jenna? I didn't think she'd told anyone."

"Nah, mate. She didn't say anything. But if you're going to have your kid and his mum coming to games and sitting with those girls, and he's going to look as much like you as Jenna says he does, they're going to pick up on that. I'd guess they all have a pretty fair idea."

"Zack doesn't know yet," Nic said with concern. "So I hope none of them says anything to him."

"No worries," Finn reassured him. "They wouldn't do that. Jenna told me, that's all, and I'm not much of a gossip. But I had no idea you had a kid, until she did say. That surprised me."

"Surprised me too," Nic admitted. "I found out by accident, a couple months ago. And that's what it was. An accident."

"I've heard that can happen," Finn said, a smile lightening his craggy face. "One of these days, I mean to find out what it's like to have one some other way."

"All of yours were?" Nic asked, startled. "You have one coming now, don't you?"

"Any moment." Finn pulled his mobile from his shorts pocket and checked it for what Nic realized was the umpteenth time that day. "Late already. We're just waiting for her, trying to be patient. But yeh, all accidents. *Happy* accidents, because I wouldn't trade any of them, I'll tell you that."

"Still getting used to it, myself," Nic said. "It's so much... responsibility. I want to do it right, and I don't always know how."

"It is," Finn agreed. "But there's nothing better. Footy's the best way in the world to earn a living, and it's a hell of a lot of fun, but it's not a life. My family, being a dad—that's my life. I cried like a baby when both my kids were born. And I'll cry this time, too."

"You?" Nic asked in shock.

Finn laughed. "Yeh. Me. Biggest baby in the room. I don't care how much of a hard man you are, when you see your kid come out, become a person, that's a miracle. And if you're lucky enough to love his mum, that's even better," he said, serious now. "Better for your kids, too."

"We aren't there," Nic said. "Not now, anyway."

Finn nodded. "Fair enough. You've been through some upheaval lately, I know that."

Nic turned away at last, and they started down the hallway again.

"But one thing I'll say," Finn said as he held the door for Nic to swing inside the locker room. "Do everything you can to stay in that boy's life. Because he needs you. And whether you know it or not, you need him too."

Nic took the final hop down the steps to Emma's front door the following Monday evening, one hand on the rail, the other awkwardly holding both crutches and the bag with the wine. Emma had invited him for dinner again, to his relief. The house had begun to seem much too big and lonely since his injury. The breakup with Claudia had meant the loss of most of their mutual friends as well, which only made sense, since they'd mostly been her friends in the first place. What hurt more was his exclusion from the squad, his real home. And there were only so many hours a man with one working leg could spend in the gym.

Zack opened the door at his knock, and Nic immediately felt better at the boy's warm greeting.

"Does your foot really hurt?" Zack asked once Nic was situated on the couch.

"Nah," Nic assured him. "Healing up pretty well now. I'll be off the crutches in another week, and into a brace. And back playing again in a few more weeks, touch wood." He knocked lightly on the coffee table.

Emma came out of the kitchen, cheeks a bit flushed from the heat of the stove, carrying two glasses of the Australian Shiraz he'd brought. Well, there were *some* compensations for injury. Wine, and being here with her.

"Dinner's almost ready," she promised. "Spaghetti. Another exciting culinary adventure, here at Chez Martens."

"Suits me," he said. "Nothing wrong with a bit of mince. And by the way," he remembered. "Meant to tell you. I heard that Jenna had that baby, on Saturday."

"At last," she said with relief, sinking into the armchair and picking up her glass. "And?"

"And what?" he asked in confusion. "She had it, and everyone's fine. Just thought you'd like to know."

"How big was she?" Emma pressed. "The baby?"

"How big?"

"How much did she weigh? How long was she?"

"*I* don't know. How would I know that?"

"Didn't you *ask?* Or didn't somebody say?"

"Not that I know of. Was I meant to ask?"

"Well, it would have been nice. Never mind. I'll find out. What's her name? I don't think they'd decided. Or I didn't hear before, at any rate. All I knew is that it was a girl."

"Can't remember. Some flower."

"Some *flower?*" she asked incredulously. "What the heck *do* you remember?"

"I told you. I heard she had the baby, and I thought you'd like to know, so I remembered to tell you. Don't I get *any* points for that?"

"Not many. Try harder. Rose? Poppy? Uh...Daisy? Violet? Lily?"

"Lily," he said with relief. "That was it. Lily."

"*Thank* you. I'll ring Jenna tomorrow," Emma planned. "And see if I can take Sophie and Harry off her hands, the next time Finn's out of town. I can deliver her baby present then as well. And see that baby, and find out how much she *weighed*."

♡

She brought the subject up again later, once Zack was in bed. Nic was pitching in on the drying as usual, crutches and all, while she did the washing-up. He seemed taller than ever, balanced on one foot beside her. His T-shirt was stretched tight over his chest, and her eyes kept drifting despite herself to his big, clever hands working the tea towel over the dishes, his solid forearms with their ridges of muscle, that bit of bicep revealed by his short sleeves. She could almost feel the heat radiating from his body. He'd always been warmer than she had, she remembered. Sometimes, in the tropical Fijian climate, he'd felt a bit too hot. But now, in a New Zealand winter...that heat would feel so good against her skin.

"The All Blacks will be in Australia this week, right?" she asked, trying to give her thoughts another direction.

"You've got the schedule memorized, I see. Yeh, they'll be gone from Wednesday morning, back Sunday."

"I'll see if I can take Jenna's kids Saturday, then. How are you feeling about not being with the team? Is it pretty bad?"

"Yeh. I'm gutted," he said bluntly. "Injuries are part of the game, and this one wasn't too bad. Being knocked out of the Cup, now, that would've been a real blow. But you always hate being left behind. On the other hand, it gives me a chance to spend some time with Zack. I was thinking about a few days at my bach, just outside of Leigh. School holidays now, right? And you said you were taking a holiday yourself next week."

"Right," she agreed cautiously.

"I was planning on going up next Sunday, soon as I'm shed of these bloody crutches, and coming back again on Thursday. I thought the two of you might like to come along, unless you've made other plans for your holiday."

"I haven't." She didn't want to tell him that she hadn't been able to afford to go away, even to visit her parents. Instead, she'd been planning a couple of museum visits, a trip to an indoor pool, playdates with Graham and Zack's other friends. A seaside bach might be the Kiwi holiday ideal, but it was as far out of her reach as another trip to Fiji. "The whole week, though?"

"Why not?" he asked reasonably. "Give Zack and me a chance to spend more than a couple hours together. And as long as you're there to make sure he knows where the toilet is, and that I don't damage him psychologically, where's the harm?"

"Don't joke about it," she warned.

"I'm not," he said, sobered. "Seriously, it'd be better if you were there, too."

"OK." She felt her breath coming a little faster, her heart beating a little harder, at the thought of spending nearly a week with him, and tried hard to focus. "It's a long time to take him by himself, though. If it rains, he could get pretty restless. And it's likely to do that, this time of year."

"I was thinking about a friend for him. Maybe invite Graham as well?"

"You want *two* six-year-old boys on your holiday?"

"I want Zack. And whatever makes that work."

"I'll check, then. But, Nic," she hesitated.

"Yeh? What is it?"

"Are there enough bedrooms?" she asked, unable to come out with the real question.

"Ah." He smiled ruefully. "Yeh. There's the original bach, what we call the Little House. I thought the boys could sleep there. It's just one room and a bath, but kids like it. A bit like camping out, in a good way. And another two bedrooms in the main house. One for you, and one for me."

"I just don't want you to be...expecting anything." Because she suspected he'd been having some of the same thoughts and feelings that had kept her awake and restless for weeks now. She wasn't sure what she wanted to do about them. Well, she knew what she *wanted* to do. She just wasn't sure what she *ought* to do.

He was looking annoyed now. "I'm not that bastard Ryan. I'm not *expecting* a bloody thing. A girl can even go out with me and say no afterwards without needing self-defense training. I'm asking you and Zack—*and* Graham—to come spend a few days with me, so I can get to know my son better. Are you asking if I'd like to sleep with you? If I want to start up again with you? Yeh, I do. I've wanted you from the first moment I met you, and nothing's changed. If we're talking about what I *want,* I want to kiss you, and touch you, and make love to you all night. I'd be doing it right now, ankle and all, if you said the word. But I'm not pushing it, am I? Because you *haven't* said the word."

She felt the color rising all the way from her chest to her face. And a flash of heat below as well, arrowing straight to the center of her, because she felt exactly the same way. "I don't know if I can, though," she said slowly, to herself as much as to him. "I can't do it for...for fun. Not like before. Because you broke my heart, Nic. You hurt me so much. If we got involved again...you could hurt me even more, now. And Zack too, this time. It feels too scary. Too risky. Not to mention that you're on the rebound. I don't want to be your consolation prize."

He shifted on the crutches to face her, completely serious now. "I know what I did, and I'm sorry for it. But I'm not that man anymore. If you give me your heart again, it'll be safe with me." He reached out to brush her cheek with the back of his hand.

She looked up at him, saw only sincerity in the dark brown eyes. "I'm not sure. It'd be a big step for me. Not casual."

He smiled a bit at that. "Not casual, no. And not about any rebound. It'd be about you and me. It's your choice to make. If you want to make it, I'm ready and willing. And if not...I'll be disappointed. But I'll still be here for Zack, whatever you decide."

gumboots and glowworms

♡

"Are we almost there?" Zack demanded.

"Pretty close!" Emma said cheerfully. "Good thing Leigh's not very far," she said quietly to Nic. "Just imagine if your bach was in Taupo."

He shuddered theatrically and grinned back at her. "Yeh. By the time we get there, it's going to have been a pretty long hour, eh."

"What are we going to do today?" Graham asked now.

"Well, let's see," Nic considered. "How about weeding the garden? I haven't been up there for a bit. It could probably do with some attention." He laughed at the groans from the back seat. "Nah. Just joking. And it's too cold for snorkeling, in July. But what would you boys think about going out around Goat Island on the glass-bottomed boat, seeing the fish at the marine reserve?"

"It's a boat made of *glass?*" Zack asked in puzzlement. "Doesn't it get broken? Wouldn't we get wet?"

"Or cut!" Graham chimed in. "My mum says to be careful, because glass can cut you. And then you can get bloody!"

"The *boat* isn't made of glass," Nic tried to explain. "It's the *bottom*...Oh, never mind. I'll show you when we get there, how's that?"

"When is it going to be?" Zack asked again.

"*Soon,*" Nic said in exasperation. "If your mum wasn't up here with her eye on the speedo, I'd be putting my foot down about now, no worries."

♡

"But this is really nice!" Emma exclaimed, when Nic had pulled up to the house with a heartfelt prayer of thanksgiving. "I was expecting something a lot more rustic, but it's beautiful!"

"Yeh, not too bad," Nic agreed, hopping out and beginning to haul suitcases and bags of groceries from the back of the ute. "Give us a hand, boys."

"Look at the view," Emma said with pleasure once Nic had the front door open. Wide ranch sliders on the back and side of the modern beach house opened onto a wraparound deck and offered a sweeping vista of the garden and the sea beyond.

"Yeh. Not big, and not too flash, but not bad either," Nic said.

"Would you *stop* with the Kiwi understatement?" she demanded with a laugh. "It's great!"

"Where do we sleep?" Zack asked, unimpressed with views.

"Ah," Nic smiled. "Let me show you. You boys get the best spot of all." He took them through a breezeway that led from the kitchen, and opened another door to a cottage set next to the larger, more modern building.

"*Cool,*" Zack and Graham breathed together at the sight of the single big room with its twin beds, large round woven rug, and wood stove in the corner.

"Look, Graham!" Zack said happily, pulling open the door and stepping onto the patio made of weathered brick. "We have our own place out here! We can play with our soldiers!"

"Got your bath, and even your own fridge and table," Nic showed them once the boys were back inside. "A cooker too, which you're *not* to use. A bit like a campervan, eh."

"This is the original building?" Emma asked him.

"Yeh. This was my great-uncle's bach," Nic explained. "When he died, I bought it, built the new house. But I kept this one too, partly out of memories, all the family holidays we spent in it. And partly because for some reason, the kids always want to sleep in here."

"You had *family* holidays in here?" she asked doubtfully.

He laughed. "Yeh. There was a big bed, and bunks for Dan and me. It was cozy, all right. But you can run straight down to the sea from here. I'll show you the track once we get all this gear unloaded."

"How did you manage the clean sheets and towels?" she asked, inspecting the bathroom.

"That would be Mrs. Jones. She lives down the road a bit, does the cleaning and that for me, keeps me from chipping my nail varnish when I'm up here. Because you know how much I hate that."

♡

The glass-bottomed boat had been a success. Nobody had got wet. *Or* cut. But they'd seen enough fish to keep both boys excited and well occupied, then had walked the shoreline and the rocky outcrops to find more, had let Zack and Graham explore before coming back for showers and a quick dinner of steak and salad.

Now the boys were in bed, and Nic was sitting on the couch with Emma, watching her curled up opposite him, the pale blue of her snug little T-shirt setting off the light flush of her cheeks from the heat of the wood fire and the wine they'd had with dinner.

"I shouldn't have had this second glass," she sighed. "I'm getting too sleepy. Can you drink the rest?"

"Reckon I could," he said with a smile. "As I'm on holiday."

She stood up and stretched languidly, her back arching, arms reaching overhead. He paused, arrested in the act of drinking, watching that little shirt ride up, exposing a couple centimeters of belly. Bloody hell. Did she have any idea what she was doing to him?

"I'm going to bed," she said, running both hands through her curls, her breasts lifting with the action and sending another surge of heat through him. "Being at the beach always does this to me. Makes me so sleepy. And I don't know what you have planned for us tomorrow."

He set his glass down, stood up as well. "Are you doing this on purpose?"

"What?" she asked in obvious confusion, her eyes widening.

"Being so...so sexy? I didn't think I was such rubbish at reading women, but I don't have a clue if you're trying to send me a message or not, so I'm just going to come straight out and ask."

"Oh. No. Unless...no. I wasn't meaning to."

He sighed. "I was afraid of that."

"Goodnight, then." She smiled at him. Too sweet. Too soft.

He reached for her, kissed her on the cheek, wanting so much more. His lips brushed her skin once again, then he lost the battle and gave her a soft kiss on the lips, held her close for just a moment more before he released her reluctantly and stepped back. "Goodnight."

Another smile, and she turned and walked to her bedroom. He watched her go, saw the outline of her bra strap under the snug little shirt, the smooth lines of her bum under the tight, faded jeans. Either she wasn't wearing anything under those, or it was a thong. Either way, it was making him ache. And he was going to bed alone.

♡

"What are we doing today?" Zack asked the next morning, when he and Graham were sitting at the scrubbed wood table with their bowls of Weet-Bix. "Are we going to the beach again? Or on the glass boat?"

"I was thinking about the cave, up at Waipu," Nic said. "See the glowworms, do a bit of exploring. What d'you reckon? Anybody scared of the dark?"

"A *cave?*" Zack said. "Sweet as, huh, Graham?"

"Yeh!" Graham agreed. "Cool!"

"Is it safe?" Emma asked doubtfully. "And is your ankle up to it?"

"Course. Long as we have torches. I've been there before," Nic assured her. "More than once. I know the twists and turns of it. *And* I'll wear my ankle brace, Mum. You coming to make sure of it, or would you rather stay here?"

"I'd like to come," Emma decided. "It sounds fun."

"You're not scared of the dark, then, yourself," Nic asked.

"Nah. Mum's just scared of spiders," Zack told him.

"Shh," she said with a laugh. "Don't tell Nic my guilty secrets."

"Spiders are good, though," Graham piped up. "They kill flies. And they won't hurt you. There aren't any bad spiders in En Zed. Not like in Aussie. You don't have to be scared, Emma."

"Thanks." She smiled at him. "I know you're right. But it isn't rational, I'm afraid. It's just that they're so...crawly." She shuddered. "It's all those *legs.*"

"She screams," Zack told Nic with delight. "When she sees them. And then she gets out the glass cleaner, and she squirts them, and she *really* screams. And then she picks them up with a tissue and flushes them down the loo."

"I don't *scream,*" Emma said, laughing but completely embarrassed now. "Unless they're those really big black ones. *Then* I scream, I admit. But usually I just...make scared noises. Because I *hate* them."

"Like this," Zack said, ever-helpful. "Ewww! Aahhhh! IHHH!"

"You s'posed to pick them up and put them outside," Graham told her as Emma succumbed to the giggles, seduced by Nic's burst of laughter. "You get a piece of paper and put it under them so they walk on it. Then you carry the paper outside and let them go, so they can catch flies!"

"Ugh," Emma shuddered, still laughing. "Ugh, ugh, ugh. They'd walk on my hand."

"Hardly ever," Graham assured her. "And then you just brush them off."

"Please stop talking about this," she moaned. "Let's talk about caves instead. I'm not scared of caves."

♡

"Right. Everybody ready?" Nic asked, coming into the lounge a half-hour later with his day pack. "Where are your gumboots?" he asked Emma.

"Oh, I just wear my trainers," she told him.

"It'll be wet in there," he objected. "Muddy, too."

"So I'll wash them, afterwards. It'll be fine."

"Thought you were a citizen," he said. "Didn't they check that you had gumboots, when they vetted you? Isn't that one of the rules? You have to know all the words to *Aotearoa,* own a pair of gummies, and be able to shell and eat a plate of prawns in under five minutes?"

"I can do the rest of it, but I don't have gumboots. Put the cuffs on me."

She held her wrists out, laughed up at him, and Nic was overcome by a flash of imagination that left him aroused and exasperated. This was ridiculous. He was a grown man, not a teenage boy.

"Yeh, well, guess you'll have to get muddy then," he said, doing his best to stay cool. "Ready, boys?"

"Yeh!" Zack said enthusiastically.

"Let's go, then."

But as they were walking down the steps to the car, with the boys running ahead, he called them back.

"Why are you walking like that?" he asked Zack. "Something wrong? A blister? Let's get that sorted, before we go."

"Nah," Zack said, embarrassed. He glanced at his mother, then hastily away. "My gummies feel funny, that's all."

"Hang on." Nic reached down to feel his foot in the boot, then glanced sharply up at Emma. "His toes are curling under," he told her. "These are too small for him."

"What?" She knelt down, felt Zack's toes. Nic was right, she realized. "Oh, sweetie. Why didn't you tell me you needed new boots?"

Zack glanced uncomfortably at Graham, dropped his eyes. "I didn't want to say," he muttered. "Because."

"Because why?" she asked.

"Because you said," he told her reluctantly. "That we're not s'posed to spend money. Because of the car. You *said*, Mum!"

"Oh, baby." She went to hug him, but he squirmed away.

"*Mum,*" he said, scarlet with embarrassment. "Don't. Can we go now?" he pleaded to Nic. "I can walk."

"Yeh," Nic said, unsmiling. "We'll go by way of Warkworth. With a stop for gumboots."

The trip was a success despite its inauspicious start, to Emma's relief. Nic had insisted on buying her a pair of gumboots as well, when they'd reached the shop. She'd picked out an inexpensive black version of the knee-high rubber boots, but he'd seen her longing glance and had asked the salesman to bring out the floral ones with pink edging.

"I love them," she said when she'd slipped them on, stood admiring herself in the mirror. "I don't need them, though. Black is OK."

"Why ever would I buy you black boots now that I've seen you in those?" he asked. "If anyone was ever meant to wear gumboots with flowers on—which I'd have doubted, before—it's you."

He turned to the young salesman. "We'll take them, and the others, the kids' ones, as well."

Zack had insisted on black boots rather than anything more colorful. "You have black," he'd told Nic. "I want ones like yours." Then had looked down, shy again.

♡

Theirs was the only car in the Waipu Caves carpark, and the boys were delighted to find horses pastured in the paddock that also served, in typical New Zealand fashion, as the start of the walking track and cave entrance. After a pause for petting and carrot-feeding—taking care of most of the vegetable content in the lunch Emma had packed so carefully—they made their way to the sign marking the cave entrance.

"Why didn't I know this was here?" Emma asked, switching on her torch to enter the cavern.

"Because you needed somebody to show you," Nic said smugly. "And here he is."

"Are you sure you know the way, though?" she asked with concern as they penetrated more deeply, leaving the light at the entrance behind. She was glad for the gumboots with their ridged soles. They were skirting a running stream now, its banks muddy and slippery.

"Dead sure," he said. "Look at this, fellas," he told the boys, playing his torch over a large formation hanging down from the ceiling. "D'you know what this is?"

"It's a stalactite. Or a stalagmite," Emma said when the boys confessed ignorance. "I can never remember."

"Stalactite. 'The mites go up, the tights come down,'" he quoted. "That's how to remember."

"Ew," she said. "Nasty imagery. But effective."

"Shut off the torches, now," he directed them. "And you'll see something."

"Glowworms!" Graham said, looking at the pinpricks of light overhead. "Like at Waitomo!"

"Been there, have you?" Nic asked.

"I haven't," Zack said.

"We'll have to take you, then, another time," Nic told him. "But there're heaps of glowworms right here for us to find ourselves. First, though, we have to make it through this tricky bit. Torches on. And if you come along in back, Emma, we'll just keep them between us. I can help them over, if they need a bit of a hand."

It *was* tricky, Emma found, wading through the water, climbing up and down through rocky passages and edging around corners. Some of the boulder-scrambling was too much for the boys, and Nic did have to reach down and give them a hoist over. She was glad he seemed to know where they were going, because her sense of direction was soon thoroughly confused by the twists and turns in the dark.

"Are you sure you've got this right?" she asked him nervously as he directed them to a right at a junction of passages, developing an uncomfortable mental image of the four of them, lost and cold in the deserted cavern. "Should we have brought string or something?"

His voice echoed back to her. "Nah. Don't need string. I know where we are. Another turn or two, and you'll really see something."

Five minutes on, and she realized what he meant. They dropped down out of a passage to find themselves in a huge underground space with a level floor. They shone their torches around at the carved, twisted rock surfaces, the spectacular stalac-*'tites,'* Emma reminded herself, hanging down from the ceiling.

"And here's the real show," Nic told them. "Let me give you a bit of a boost, and you'll see what I mean."

He lifted the boys up onto a large, flat rock formation, like a king-sized bed in the middle of the room, then offered Emma a hand up.

"Now lie on your backs," he instructed. "Torches off. And enjoy."

It was a full glowworm panorama, Emma found with delight, for all the world like a night sky, the distances deceptive here in the dark.

They lay in silence, resting after the effort of climbing through the tunnels, and as she lay next to Zack on the hard stone, listening to the stream, its sound magnified a hundred-fold by the echoing rock passages, looking up at the multitude of little glowworm stars, Emma realized that she was, at this moment, absolutely, perfectly happy.

a couple of chaperones

♡

The journey out was slower, a bit more difficult. The boys were getting tired now, requiring more help to clamber over the boulders in the dark. They remained enthusiastic, though, to Emma's relief, encouraged by Nic's good humor. And when they were once again blinking in the daylight outside the cave entrance, the horses grazing peacefully in the paddock beyond, she had to laugh.

"I've never seen anything so muddy," she told them. "How did you manage to get mud all the way up to your *necks?*"

"That's why there's a shower over here," Nic told her, leading the way to the toilets which did, Emma saw, feature an outdoor shower on one side. "And why I had you bring them dry clothes."

"I don't have to take a shower, do I?" Zack asked dubiously. "It's going to be *cold.*"

"Not a real shower," Nic assured him. "But you do have to get some of that mud off. Drop your gear, and we'll get to it. Sooner you're clean, sooner we can eat."

Emma ran for the bag of clean clothes and the big towel, tossed them to Nic in deference to Graham's modesty, then went into the ladies' toilet herself to change and clean up. It was such a relief to have somebody else taking charge, not to have to look after Zack before she could think about herself. She could hear

Nic joking with the boys, their squeals as he scrubbed their muddy arms, necks, and faces in the freezing water.

She waited until she could tell by the conversation outside that they were finished, then popped her head out. "Everybody decent? Safe for girls?" she asked.

"Good as gold," Nic told her. He was scrubbing his own arms and hands under the tap now, rinsing the worst of the mud off his gumboots, and she went to join him.

"It's *freezing,* Mum!" Zack said happily.

"Brr," she shivered. "It is." She reached for the towel, dried herself off, handed it to Nic. "Thanks," she told him.

"For what?"

"For taking care of them."

"No worries. Hoping you did a proper job on that picnic, though, because you've got three hungry men here."

♡

The boys were quiet on the twisting road home, the winter dusk falling early, the interior of the ute warm and cozy. Thank goodness Nic had thought to warn her, and Emma had been able to give Zack a carsickness tablet. Both boys were nearly asleep by the time Nic pulled into the bach's driveway, but rallied themselves enough to climb into the big shower together and scrub down the rest of the way under Nic's direction. Emma could hear him in there, washing hair and issuing instructions. She caught the high-pitched sound of their excited responses as she threw muddy gear into the washing machine in the laundry alcove nearby.

"Have them put on their pajamas when they're done," she called in to Nic. "I'll fix them a quick tea in a bit. Early bedtime tonight after all that."

He did as she asked, then settled the boys in front of the big TV to play a racecar videogame, to Emma's disgust. "It's not good for them," she complained. "Those games are addictive."

"I don't think it'll warp their characters too much," he said. "It's not every day. Just a bit of fun on holiday."

"Why do you even have that thing?" she asked. "Do you play it? That's hard for me to imagine."

"Not much, though I've been known to take a turn driving a racecar. If Graham weren't here, you'd probably see me having a go with Zack. And sometimes a mate will borrow the bach, or one of my rellies, with kids. Just one of those things that's nice to have. *Holiday* things," he added firmly. "Indulgences. You can go home again, read the Great Works to him, discuss art history. Playing a videogame for an hour isn't going to lower his IQ, I promise. Just a bit of blokey fun."

He went on more seriously. "Anyway, I want to talk to you. Come outside with me, will you?" He grabbed his hoodie from the rack, tossed her jumper to her, and opened the ranch sliders off the lounge, led her out onto the wooden deck that wrapped around half the house, around to the back where steps led to the garden, and the darkness beyond that was the sea.

"Sit down," he told her. "Because we need to have a chat about money."

"Why do I feel like I'm in the headmaster's office?" she asked, looking at him in the faint illumination cast by a single outdoor bulb. "I think I'd prefer to stand, if you're going to yell at me about Zack's gumboots. I didn't know he'd outgrown them, or I'd have bought him new ones. We had a bit of car trouble last month, and things were tight, that's all. And why do you get to criticize how I'm taking care of him, anyway? Or how I'm budgeting? I appreciate your buying him new ones, but that still doesn't give you the right."

"Wait, what? I'm not criticizing you. I'm just saying, money shouldn't be tight now. Because I know you got that first maintenance payment, beginning of the month. No need for him to worry about telling you his boots are too small. And time to think about looking for a new place, too."

"With one payment? That let me pay off the card, after that car trouble. And gave me some peace of mind," she admitted. "And I *told* you. I'd have bought him new boots, if I'd known. That was *last* month, that I was worried. But it's way too early to think about shifting house."

"I don't like you living in that dodgy place, though. You *or* Zack. With spiders," he reminded her.

"I don't think spiders confine their activities to cheap flats. And Zack's settled at school. If we moved, he'd end up someplace new, and that's way too much change. Besides, there's nothing wrong with my flat. All right, it's not flash. And it isn't tidy, but that's not the flat's fault. I have Mrs. Harrison there, and that's massive. Not just that she's willing to watch Zack from time to time, but that I know she's there in an emergency, and so does Zack."

"But you should be someplace better," he said in frustration. "I'm...I'm embarrassed to have you both there. To have people know you're there. To have you living like that, while I'm... while I'm where I am."

"Well, I'm sorry you feel that way. But you must see, that's not my problem. I have to do what's right for *us*. And anyway, you've paid me once. *Once*. I'd be stupid to assume my life's all roses now, and get in over my head. The deposit alone, and the payment to the realtor—that's a month's rent. Which I don't have. And then the moving expenses, and the higher rent..." She made a helpless gesture. "I told you, money's not my best thing. But at least I've learned, now, to think first. To recognize when something's beyond my means."

"And I told *you*," he said impatiently. "Oliver's working on that lump sum. And I can help, in the meantime."

"I'm not spending that! Come *on*, Nic. That'd be beyond irresponsible. That'd be crazy. That's Zack's insurance! I mean to put it aside for him. For his education. And for an emergency, in case something happens to me. I have life insurance if the worst happens, but what if I got sick, or in an accident? I lie awake nights, worrying about that."

"He'd have me, wouldn't he? There's no reason for you to lie awake at all. And I'm not planning on putting all my money in gold mines, you know. It'll be there, when it's time for Uni. And so will I."

"I hope so," she said. "I hope you will. But I know maintenance ends at eighteen. And I have to be *sure*. He's my responsibility. I'm all he has."

"Nah, you're not." He could feel his blood pressure rising, the frustration mounting. Why wouldn't she *see?* Why'd she have to be so bloody obstinate? "You're *not* all he has. He has me. Legally now as well. And I'm not going anywhere. Why can't you wrap your little mind around that?"

"Don't call me stupid," she warned him, her posture becoming rigid. "Don't you dare! I am not stupid!"

"What the hell? I never said you were stupid!" How was this conversation getting away from him so badly?

"You said my mind was little. My mind isn't little. My mind is just as good as yours!"

"I didn't mean…" He stopped. He couldn't see any way out of this. Suddenly, instead of being in the right as he knew he was, he was on the back foot, struggling for territory. "Aw, shit. You're stubborn as hell, you know that?"

"I'm stupid *and* stubborn?" Her eyes were flashing nine kinds of danger signals now.

"You're stubborn. Not stupid. I didn't *say* that. And I want to kiss you, damn it!"

"What?"

"That's what I'm asking myself. You're frustrating the hell out of me just now. So why do I want to put my hands on you so badly?" He took a step closer, rested a palm on the wall behind her. "Right. Trying to focus here. I want you out of there. I want you both someplace better. And I'm ready and willing to help you do it. I wish I could make you do it now, but I can't see how."

"You can't," she told him, her eyes intent on him, her lips parting as he leaned over her. She was leaning into him a bit too, he could tell, her breath still coming fast. "You can't make me."

"Reckon I'd better just kiss you, then."

He pulled her into him, and she felt as good there as she always had. Soft, and warm, and curvy, fitting him like she'd been created just for him to hold. He settled his mouth over hers, did his best not to grab her, to keep it gentle. Felt her sigh, her mouth parting for him, and suddenly it wasn't gentle at all. Her arms came around him, her hands went to the back of his neck, slid down his back as if she wanted to feel all of him, the same way he wanted to feel all of her. And then her hands were under his T-shirt, moving greedily over him, and he was backing her all the way up against the wall. Kissing her neck, reaching his own hand inside the neckline of that stretchy shirt to hold her. Feeling the softness of her, the perfect shape of her breast filling his hand, the warmth of her skin. Hearing the moan she couldn't suppress as his teeth grazed the side of her neck, his thumb moved over a nipple that hardened at his touch. He reached the other hand around, cupped her bottom in the soft denim, lifted her off her feet, and pressed himself into her. Felt every centimeter of her body melting against his own, and wanted to keep going, closer and closer, more and more, until he was inside her. Now.

"Nic." Her breathless voice came dimly through the roaring in his head. *"Nic."*

She was pushing at him, he realized. He came back to himself with an effort, set her down. She moved away from him, breathing hard, and he leaned his forehead against the wall, tried to compose himself.

She ran her hands over her hair, smoothing it back into place. "Wow," she said shakily. "I didn't know *that* was going to happen."

He stood up straight to look at her, his heart rate slowing a bit at last. "I thought I could keep my hands off you. It's just that you still look so good. Everything about you. Like exactly what I want. And ever since I saw you again, it's like my body... remembers. And it wants to do it all again." He smiled at her ruefully. "My brain doesn't seem to have a lot to say about it."

"Yeah," she sighed. "That's pretty much it, isn't it? But not...not now. Not with the boys right there. I think we'd better go back inside, get our own showers, and find a couple of chaperones to keep us under control. For now, anyway."

angel wings

♡

She was glad they had the boys, an excuse to take some time and regain her equilibrium before she made any decisions she might regret. It felt right to be working in the kitchen with Nic to fix a simple dinner of bangers and mash, to give him the sausages to fry while she mashed potatoes and put together a salad. To eat at the big table while Nic displayed his surprising knowledge of cave formation and geology, drew pictures to show the boys how stalactites and stalagmites were formed.

"How do you know all this?" she asked him.

"Did a couple geology papers at Uni. And I grew up in En Zed. I've spent a fair few hours in caves."

"Wait a minute. Back up," she commanded. "I thought you didn't finish Uni."

"When did I tell you that?"

"On the plane, remember? To Fiji?"

"You *remember* that?"

"Why? I wasn't *that*—" She broke off, glanced at the boys, started over. "I wasn't so...far gone that I don't remember."

"Did my first year and a half," he explained, "while I played. And then it got too hard to do both, so I quit. I do plan to go back once I'm done playing."

"And study what?"

"Haven't decided. Engineering, maybe. What's funny? You don't think I can? I'm pretty good at maths."

"No," she got out, giggling helplessly into her serviette. "I can't tell you now. Later."

♡

"Right," he said when they had the boys in bed and were sitting on the couch in the lounge, a bottle of wine on the table in front of them and glasses in hand. "Why is the idea of my being an engineer so bloody funny?"

"It's not you," she said, the giggles rising again. "It's me. *You* weren't drunk. Maybe you remember what David—my reluctant groom—did for a living."

"An Assistant Professor of Sanitary Engineering," Nic quoted.

"Yeah," she smiled. "And where do I work now?"

"An engineering firm." He began to laugh himself. "You seem doomed to repeat your mistakes."

"I'm starting to think, though," she told him, "that there are engineers and engineers."

He pulled her to him, kissed her forehead. "Think I'll be able to avoid getting dull, do you?"

"Yeah," she sighed, letting him hold her. "I think you just broke the mold."

They stayed like that a minute longer before she sat up again. "You said you'd like to see some pictures of Zack, so I brought his baby book. Want to look at it now?"

"Shifting gears again, are we?" He smiled. "Yeh, I'd like to see it."

She got up and went into her bedroom, came out again with the scrapbook.

"You spent some hours on this," Nic commented as she opened it to Zack's newborn photo. "It looks professional."

"I wanted it to be nice," she said. "I wanted him to have it when he was grown, and to know that he was...wanted. Loved."

"Yeh." He cleared his throat. "Yeh, I see that. He wasn't a looker, though, was he?" he asked doubtfully, looking at the swaddled figure, puffy eyes scrunched shut, skin peeling, a tuft of black hair sticking straight up. "And why is his hair black?"

"He was beautiful," Emma said hotly. "He was a newborn. He was big, and late in coming, and he got a little squished, that's all. And their hair falls out, and comes back in the color it's going to be. Didn't you know that?"

"Nah. Haven't been around many babies."

He peered at another picture, taken a week or so later. "Looks a bit better in this one," he offered. "Are you sure this is the right baby, though? Because his eyes are blue."

"All Pakeha babies' eyes start out blue, too. Same thing. Takes a while."

"Is there a photo of you, earlier?" he asked.

"You don't want to see that. I was as big as a house."

He looked down at her, the smile reaching all the way to his eyes. "I want to see. House and all."

She sighed in resignation, turned back a page. "Don't say I didn't warn you."

"Whoa." He looked at the taut round belly swelling heavily over the top of her bikini bottom. "You weren't joking. Who took this?"

She smiled softly in remembrance. "Lucy. Of course. Taking me to the beach so I could float in the salt water, defy gravity for a bit. I got pretty grouchy there, that last week when he wouldn't arrive. It was hot, too, which just made everything worse. I said we'd be scarring everyone else there for life, showing them that, but she insisted. And it was fun. I was so scared, and so tired by then. But that day was fun."

"I'm sorry," he said, sobered. "That you had to do it alone."

"I wasn't alone. I had my sister. Then, and afterwards."

"She lived with you by then?"

"Yeah. I don't know what I would have done, without her. While Zack was tiny. When I went back to work. No sleep, not knowing what I was doing, just trying to cope." She touched another picture of herself, belly still huge but covered this time, next to her sister, their arms around each other.

She looked up at Nic, her eyes filling with tears as she remembered. "Why'd you do it?" she asked. "Why didn't you ring like you said you would? The truth. Why?"

"I was too young," he said slowly. "Stupid. I thought, because this had come along, because *you* had come along, and it was so good, that my life would be full of things like that. Of girls. Of things that good, times like we had. I didn't realize it was special."

"I did," she said. "I knew."

"You were smarter than me," he admitted. He reached a hand up, ran the back of it along her cheek. "Still are, I reckon."

She turned from him, folded the book shut, reached out to set it on the table, and felt his arms come around her from behind.

"You were so pretty," he said, nuzzling the side of her neck, pulling her back against him. "When you were in my lap, on that plane. Remember that?"

"Yeah," she breathed. "I remember."

"Those angel eyes," he said, his lips moving over the honey-colored curls. He reached a hand to pull them aside, kiss the skin beneath. She shivered under his touch, the feel of his lips against the sensitive skin. "You looked so innocent. I wanted to keep holding you, just give you a cuddle, and at the same time..." His voice trailed off.

It was easier to ask, without having to look him in the eye. "What? I've always wondered. If you were just looking for some company, and I fell into your lap. Literally, I know. So easy."

He reached a hand up under the stretchy top, over the thin band of her bra, the satiny skin of her sides, her back. At her sigh, he worked the top up to expose more of her. Both hands were on her now, running up her ribs to her breasts. He pulled her against him, into his lap, and bent his mouth to the back of her neck again as his hands moved over her.

"Nah. It was this," he said against her skin, his thumbs stroking over her shoulder blades. "All this softness. Made me want to cuddle you, but also...it made me want to do dirty things to you. Pull you down there with me, rub those angel wings in the mud. Watch your eyes close, see that pretty mouth on me."

His hands were on her breasts now, the light, lacy cups of her bra no barrier. His teeth scraped against the side of her neck, his hands continued to roam, and she offered no resistance when he finally turned her around again to face him.

"You're so sweet," he told her, pulling the top all the way off now, exposing the lacy peach bra, disordering her curls. "And it kills me. It did then, and it still does. I only have to see you, and I want you again, even more than I did the first time."

She sighed, her eyes drifting shut as she felt him reaching around to unfasten the bra, pulling it off. His mouth closed over hers, one hand pulling her more tightly against him, the other moving over her breast, thumb caressing the nipple, each touch sending a jolt of pleasure directly to her core. The flames were licking her, and she was starting to burn.

"This is a probably a bad idea," she moaned. "But it feels so good."

"Let's just feel good, then," he coaxed. He shifted her over him before bending his head to take that same nipple in his mouth, his hand moving to the other breast, beginning to play. She gasped at the dual sensations, reached out for his shoulders and held on.

He lifted his mouth to hers again, nudged her legs apart with his hand, cupped her there as he continued to kiss her, to touch her. She felt her body pulling toward him, opening for him. Needing him.

"I need to take your clothes off," he told her at last. "I've been waiting to see this again for months now, and I just can't wait any more. But I'm going to ask. You OK doing this?"

"Yes," she sighed. "I need it too. So, yes. Please. Now."

He stood, lifting her in his arms, and carried her to his bedroom, kicked the door shut behind them, found the way to the bed in the darkness, laid her down on the white cotton duvet, and reached a hand out for the bedside light. "I don't want to do this in the dark. It's been too long. I need to see."

"Nic." She reached for him, pulled him down to her. Kissed his mouth, reached under his T-shirt to feel him, run her hands over his chest. "Lock the door. In case."

He pulled away from her reluctantly, went to do as she asked, turned again to see her there, on the bed. His pulse was hammering, but he wanted to go slowly. Let it build, make it as good for her as it had been before. One thing he was sure of, he still remembered how to please her.

Her hands went to the stretchy leggings, and he was back at the bed again, coming down over her. "Hold still. My job to undress you."

He reached for the waistband, saw her lift her hips from the bed to help him, and pulled the material down over her legs, exposing the skin to him. He needed to taste all that. Everything. He began to move down her body, felt her clutching at his shoulders, holding him, running her hands over him.

"Lie still," he told her again. "Because I need to kiss you everywhere tonight. And you need to lie still for me."

He was at her breasts again, lingering there. Moving lower, running his hand over the band of peach lace at her hip, down her thigh. Then up her inner thigh, the skin like silk. Slowly, now. Drawing it out. Making her wait until, at last, he settled his hand over her, rubbed. Felt her jerk at the touch, the dampness of the fabric under his hand.

He kissed her through the material, softly at first. Then, slowly, began to pull the insubstantial things off her. Watched her shift, saw her struggling to open to him as he drew them down her legs, finally freed her from them. Then ran both hands up her again, until the thumbs met at the center. Put a hand on each thigh to push her legs apart, slid a finger inside her, then another, felt the heat there, the desire she couldn't hide anymore, heard her begin to whimper as he touched her. And, finally, bent his head to her as his hand continued to move. She wasn't waxed now, he saw. Didn't matter. Either way was good. Really good.

She was gasping, panting against him, held fast by his fingers inside her, his hand pressing her down, his mouth against her. He brought her up, and up further, felt her excitement build, the way she was writhing under him.

He'd been right. He remembered everything. How she liked it. What made her squirm. What made her moan. And what made her, finally, convulse around him, her torso rising from the bed as she called out in incoherent abandon.

The spasms slowed, and she was pulling him up to her, grabbing at his T-shirt, pulling it over his head.

"Inside," she got out. "Please, Nic. Please." Her hands were unsnapping his jeans, pulling the zipper down, impatiently trying to help him get rid of the rest of his clothes. Then she was holding him again as he struggled to get the condom on. Running her hands over him, as if she couldn't wait.

He wanted to do everything, feel all of her. He was moving her, turning her, giving her instructions, just as he always had. And getting the thrill he'd remembered so often, seeing her respond, doing exactly as he told her. Doing everything he wanted.

Finally, though, it had to be simple. He needed her under him, needed to look into the blue eyes, to see her mouth open, hear her breathing hard, calling out to him, her legs and arms wrapping around him.

"Nic." Her voice was urgent now, her hips pulling at him. "I need...I need...*Please.*"

He shoved his hand down between them, raised himself off her, rubbed her as he moved, heard her breath catch, felt the change as she began to climb again. He brought her to another shuddering, gasping orgasm and, as he felt her clenching around him, finally found his own release, swearing aloud with it, over and over again.

♡

He grabbed an edge of the duvet, pulled it over them both as he lay with her, still breathing hard, then gathered her close and kissed her, long and lingeringly, and that felt just as good as the rest of it had, because this was Nic, and he was hers again, and she was his.

She sighed against him. "You said I killed you," she murmured, finally opening her eyes to look at him, her smile soft. "But you kill me too, you know."

He reached a hand out to brush the curls from her cheek, kissed her there, then lay back again and tightened his hold on her. "No leftovers, then? After what happened?"

"After *what* happened?" she asked in confusion.

"Ryan," he said reluctantly. "Wondering if I should've been less...less aggressive. Didn't think about it, though. As soon as we started, I just wanted all of you, all for me. The way I always have."

"No," she said immediately. "Don't change. You've never scared me. And it's what I want, too. It's how I like it, and I've missed it so much." She ran a hand over his chest, levered herself up so she could move over him, leaned down to kiss him. "I want it exactly the way you do it. But I need to go get into my own bed, in case the boys wake up."

"I'd rather you stayed with me," he said, pulling her leg over him so she was straddling him, then reaching for her breasts, running a thumb over each pink nipple until they hardened at his touch. "We've got some catching up to do."

"I know we do," she sighed, shivering as he continued to caress her. She couldn't help rubbing herself against him, just for a minute, because it felt so good. "But I can't." She pulled her leg across him reluctantly, leaned over the bed and groped for her underwear and leggings on the floor. He ran a hand over her bottom, down her legs, and held her there a moment, pressing her down, before he pulled her up to join him again.

"Tomorrow, then," he said. "Seeing that is giving me ideas, now that I've got the green light. Tomorrow night. Same time, same place."

"I'll be here," she smiled, kissing him one last time before she got up and went to the door. "You've got a date."

a very nice walk

♡

"I don't think this is going to be a beach day," Emma said on Wednesday morning, looking out at the lowering clouds through the wall of windows that made up the back of the bach. "I'm afraid it's going to be raining on us pretty soon."

"Pity," Nic agreed. He looked at the boys, tucking contentedly into their eggs and bacon. "Reckon you lot'll end up playing the racecar game a bit today. Think you can feature that?"

He smiled when they eagerly assented to his plan. "I did bring along something for a rainy day as well, just in case you get bored with the racecars." He disappeared into his bedroom, came back with a couple of bags and handed one to each boy. "See if this'll keep you busy."

"Awesome!" Graham yelped. "A Lego robot!"

"I got a dinosaur!" Zack said excitedly. "T-Rex!"

"What do you say?" Emma asked, prompting a flurry of thank-yous. "And finish your breakfast before you open the boxes, please," she told them. "You can look at the pictures on them now, and then we'll clear off the table so you can start working on putting them together. That way you won't lose any pieces."

"You're such a mum," Nic told her.

"Yep. That's me. And thanks," she said as he finished the last of his own breakfast and rose to put the plate in the dishwasher. "That was a great idea. And very thoughtful."

"I may just get the hang of this boy thing yet, d'you reckon?"

"You just may."

"If you don't mind a bit of wind, yourself," he said, "I did ask Mrs. Jones if she'd be willing to mind the boys this morning. Seeing as we've got them well occupied, I thought you and I could take a walk on Pakiri Beach. I know the weather's not the best, but you've got gumboots now, haven't you? There's something about all that space that always appeals to me, no matter what. May give us a chance to have a chat, too. Or we could go into town for a coffee, if you'd rather."

"A walk, please," she said at once. "If we get wet, we can always dry off afterwards, can't we?"

♡

An hour later, they stepped off the boardwalk and onto the sand. Not another soul was visible in this weather, just the curved expanse stretching on for kilometers, as far as they could see in either direction. The surf was running strong, the water an angry green, foaming white where the waves broke. A mass of dark gray threatened overhead, the sun out one minute, obscured by fast-moving clouds at the next.

"This may be a good time to talk about telling Zack that I'm his dad," Nic suggested after they had walked in silence for a few minutes.

"Already?" Emma hesitated.

"What d'you mean, 'already?' It's been two and a half months, I'm paying the maintenance, and it's time we sat down with my schedule, worked out a way to get him over to stay with me every week. You can come too, you know. I'm hoping you'll want to. So there's nothing to be afraid of, is there? It's past time for him to know anyway, don't you think?"

She had to admit that he was right. No matter how uncritically and delightedly Zack accepted his weekly outings with Nic, it was a big leap from that to staying overnight at his house. And she could no longer tell herself that she was unsure of Nic's intentions. She hadn't entirely lost her concern about the long term, but he'd been nothing but determined and committed so far.

"All right," she said. "Not now, while Graham's here. But soon."

"I want to get his room set up, at my place," Nic went on. "Once we're back. That'd be a good time to tell him, and that he'll be staying with me some of the time."

"Next week. OK. But I want to be there, because it'll be a lot for him to hear."

"We'll do it together," he promised. "After all, we made him together, didn't we? And in case I haven't said this, we did a hell of a job."

"We did, didn't we? He's pretty great."

"Yeh. Pretty good raw material, if we say so ourselves, and you've done well too. I'd never have imagined the girl I knew then as a mum. You've surprised me, I'll admit."

"We've both grown up since then, I guess, one way or another." She struggled to zip her anorak as the wind picked up, shivering a little.

"Too cold?" he asked, taking her hand and threading his fingers through hers. "Want to go back?"

"No," she said, loving the feeling of her hand in his. Something so simple, but it felt so good. Warm, and strong, and comforting. "Our beach experiences this time around have been a bit different, haven't they?"

"You're right. Heaps more clothes on." He smiled down at her, his cheeks wind-reddened under the All Blacks beanie. "Not quite as easy, is it? In any sense."

"No. But still good," she assured him. "Do you still remember?" she went on hesitatingly. "What it was like?"

"I don't think I've forgotten a single minute. How about you?"

"Me neither, but I haven't had much to compare it with. And I suspect you have, haven't you?"

"D'you really want to know?" he asked, serious now.

"No," she decided. "Probably not."

"Good. Because I don't want to tell you. It's enough to say that, yeh, I remember. Because it was the best."

The clouds that had been threatening since they'd started walking suddenly decided to make good on their promise, the first drops of rain spattering them, hitting the ground hard and creating pockmarks in the sand.

"Beach walk's over," Nic decided, pulling her around again. "Back to the car."

They began making their way back across the broad expanse of sand, hurrying now. The drops increased, and then the cloud was directly overhead, and the rain was pelting, and they were running, gasping with the cold and wet, laughing, Nic matching his pace to her slower one. They found the track to the carpark, made their way up over the sloping approach, heads bent against the driving rain. Nic had his keys out, was pressing the remote. He pulled her door open, helped her out of her anorak before he ran around to the driver's side and jumped into the ute himself.

"Bloody hell," he swore, yanking off his own anorak before turning the key in the ignition and shifting the heat to full. "I'm freezing. Whose idea was it to take a romantic walk on the beach?"

"Yours," she said, a bubble of laughter escaping her. Then they were both laughing as she reached over to pull off his beanie, soaking wet now. He grabbed her hand, pulled her against him, and kissed her, his mouth still curved in a smile. And suddenly, they weren't laughing anymore. His hands were under her sweater, and she was pulling up his hoodie and the T-shirt beneath in her turn as they continued to kiss, lips and tongues exploring.

He sat back at last. "Back seat," he got out. "Come on. Quick as you can." He opened his door, dove into the back and pulled her between the seats to join him.

"What if somebody comes, though?" she moaned as he yanked her sweater over her head, reached for the clasp of her bra. "They'll see."

"Nobody here to see. And the windows are steamed up anyway," he pointed out practically, turning his attention to her sodden jeans. "Geez, these are tight," he complained. "Hard as hell to pull down. And get those boots off, or we'll be stuck, good and proper."

She reached down to pull off her gumboots and socks as he did the same, then wriggled out of the jeans with his help. "You saying I should change my wardrobe?" she asked, helping him get rid of his shirt and hoodie in her turn. "You don't like my tight jeans, or how I look in them?"

"You know I do." He was unfastening his ankle brace, divesting himself of his track pants with her eager assistance. Their sodden clothes lay in a heap on the floor, the car was steamy and warm, and they were kissing again, their hands moving over each other.

"Lie down here." He was pulling her towards him, pushing her down on the seat.

"There's not enough room," she protested.

"Shift round." He pulled one of her legs into the gap between the front seats, shoved the other one up over the top of the rear seat. "Like this. Stay there."

She saw him grabbing for his pants again, searching the pockets, pulling out the condom, and suddenly realized how she must look, how exposed she was. She wriggled to pull her legs down, to sit up again.

"No," he told her sharply, pushing her down again, shoving her leg back up. Then amended his tone. "Please. Stay there. Like that."

"But I look..." she said in embarrassment.

"You look," he said, finally reaching to kiss her, to touch her, "like every man's dream. Open. Ready. Waiting for me."

She moaned as he moved over her. "I shouldn't let you do this," she got out. "Oh, no." The leather was cold under her bare skin, her legs were splayed uncomfortably, and her arms were fluttering, trying to find something to hold onto, reaching behind her for the door handle, hanging on.

And none of it mattered. Every bit of her was focused on where he was touching her, how hard he was driving her.

"Come on," he was telling her. "Give me some of that. Give me what I want. You know it's mine." He was touching her, kissing her in exactly the right places, in exactly the right ways, and she was going up fast, forgetting where she was, her awkward, exposed position. Up, and up higher, hearing him urging her, until she reached the top and went over with a broken cry. Before she was done, he was finally, blessedly, inside her, and her arms were around his back, finding the purchase they needed.

It was hot, and hard, and fast. And when it was over, and she was in his lap, his hand stroking her hair, she let her breath out in a long, audible sigh. "Wow. That wasn't at all what I was expecting, this morning. Funny how you just happened to have a condom with you, wasn't it?"

"Mmm. Lucky," he agreed.

"That has to be the most...adolescent thing I've ever done," she mused. "If I ever *had* had sex in the back of a car, I can't imagine it would have been that good. Because you always make sure I get there first. Even in the back of a Toyota, in the rain."

"That's because I'm a gentleman," he told her with his lazy grin. "Ladies first, that's my motto."

"Is *that* what you are? Who knew?"

"Oi," he protested, dipping his head to nuzzle the side of her neck, making her shiver. "Are you complaining?"

"No," she sighed, her arms tightening around him. "No complaints here. Not from me."

♡

Getting dressed again was a cold, clammy business, accompanied by a fair amount of swearing on his part and giggling on hers.

"Now I know why I got the Land Cruiser instead of the RAV4," he told her, wrestling his way back into his sodden pants and pulling on his boots. "That was a tight enough fit as it was. I would've strained something."

"You should just be smaller," she told him saucily, working on her own socks and boots. "I fit fine."

"D'you want me to be smaller, then?" he grinned at her.

"Well, no," she said, considering. "On second thought, I think you should stay big. If we're talking about what I like."

♡

Back at the bach again, they endured a clucking lecture from Mrs. Jones. "What an idea," she scolded Nic. "Taking this poor girl out in the rain, getting her so cold and wet. Go on, pop yourselves into the bath and into some dry things before you catch your death. Meantime, I'll make a pot of tea."

"Did you have a nice walk, Mum?" Zack asked when they were warm and dry again. Mrs. Jones had come through with cocoa and cinnamon toast as well before she'd left, and Emma smiled at the brown mustaches, accented by sprinklings of cinnamon sugar, that both boys were sporting.

"We had a very nice walk," she assured her son. "The nicest walk ever."

♡

"I don't want to leave," Emma sighed as she packed up the contents of the fridge the next morning. "This was really good. The best holiday I've had in years. Maybe seven years," she decided with a laughing glance at Nic.

"It *was* pretty good, at that," he agreed with a warm smile. "This ready?" he asked, indicating the chilly bin she'd just filled. He hefted it at her nod, then set it down again as a thought struck him. "How about extending it a bit? D'you think you could get that neighbor of yours to mind Zack tomorrow night, so I could take you to dinner? I don't think I've ever seen you dressed up to go out, you know. I always like how you look," he went on hurriedly. "But I'd like to see some high heels again. Think there's a chance of that?"

"Let me ring Lucy first," Emma decided. "She may be able to take Zack, since she's on holiday too. I hate to ask Lois again so soon."

"OK."

As he continued to look at her expectantly, she faltered. "What? You want me to ring her right now?"

"Now's good. Because I want my date."

She went into her bedroom for her mobile, came out again a few minutes later. "She says she can take him overnight, actually," she said, trying to sound casual.

What Lucy had said, in fact, was a lot more than that. "You've just been on holiday," she had complained. "Why do you need another night out?"

"Because," Emma said, her color rising as if her sister could see her, "Nic wants to go out to dinner."

"Oh. *Oh*. What happened?" Lucy demanded. "Did you..."

"Yeah," Emma said, laughing. "I did. We did."

"Oh, boy," Lucy breathed. "Can't say I'm entirely surprised, but wow. Wow. OK, here's the deal," she decided. "I'll take him all night. Because you've been up there with *two* six-year-old boys, gettin' busy in a *bach?* Not exactly a honeymoon."

"Would you really?" Emma asked gratefully. "That would be amazing."

"*In* return," Lucy continued inexorably, "for you coming over tomorrow and giving me the whole scoop."

"Trust me," Emma said, "you don't want the whole scoop." She just wished she had *more* to keep from Lucy. She'd had more great sex in the last few days than she'd had in the last few years. But despite her reassurances, she could tell that Nic was still holding back a bit. An overnight, though...an overnight could be just what they needed.

"OK. The expurgated version," Lucy decided. "Seriously, Em. Come over and talk to me. I need to make sure you're OK. That's my babysitting fee."

♡

"Overnight?" Nic said now. His eyes had that gleam in them again. "So what you're saying is, this is going to be a really *good* date."

"I don't know," she said, tossing her hair a bit and turning back to the fridge, then peeping back at him over her shoulder, sticking out her bum just a little. It was so much fun to push his buttons. "I guess that depends on you."

He laughed. He could see exactly what she was doing, she could tell. Oh, yeah. The overnight was going to work.

"I do like a saucy woman," he said. "I'll see what I can do."

something special

♡

No Emma answering Nic's knock at the door the following night. Instead, there stood Zack, already dressed for bed in—what else—his favorite pajamas.

"Hi, Nic!" Zack said happily. "Mum's not ready. She's getting pretty. And that always takes a *long* time."

"Bet it does," Nic said seriously, following Zack into the lounge. "But you're ready, eh."

"Because boys go faster," Zack explained, plopping himself down on the coach. "I get to spend the night at Auntie Lucy's, did you know?"

"I heard. What'll you do over there?"

"I get to sleep in the guest room. The bed's really big, like Mum's. It has heaps of pillows, too. And then, in the morning, Auntie Lucy says we can make Mickey Mouse pancakes! With chocolate bits in, she says."

Emma interrupted this catalog of delights. She was still in her dressing gown, Nic saw. And he'd been right, it *was* pink. With flowers on.

"Sorry," she said, looking a bit flustered, but so pretty. Her makeup was done, he could tell, and her hair, too, falling in soft ringlets around her face. It wouldn't be too long, then.

"It's OK," he told her with a smile. "Looks like it'll be worth the wait. I can always ring the restaurant, change our booking."

"Five minutes," she promised. "I just have to get dressed."

She appeared not too much later than that. "I was right," Nic told her, standing to greet her with a decorous kiss on the cheek, mindful of Zack. "Definitely worth the wait." Because her skirt was a silvery gray, a bit clingy, a bit short. With it, she was wearing a soft, fine sweater in a deep blue. That was clingy, too, with a wide V neckline leading to a row of tiny square buttons down the front, buttons he knew he'd be unfastening in a few hours. She put a hand on his shoulder, crossed one leg over the opposite knee, and reached down to buckle the strap on her high-heeled sandal.

"OK," she announced, switching hands to buckle the second shoe. "I'm ready. And wow, you look gorgeous. Guess this really *is* going to be a date."

He looked down at the white-on-white stripe of his dress shirt, the black jacket, dark gray pants and black shoes. "Pretty simple for me. Shined my shoes, gave myself a bit of a shave. That was about it."

"Well, it worked. I'm going to have the best-looking date in the whole place, aren't I, Zack? Get your pack and your jacket and let's go, OK?" She pulled her own short wool coat from the hook and Nic took it from her, held it for her to slide into.

"OK," Zack said. "I put Raffo in, though. D'you think Tom will say I'm a baby? That I have to harden up?" He glanced at Nic, then looked away.

"Nah," Nic answered. "Like you said, it's just at bedtime. Everybody needs something to cuddle with at bedtime." He ruffled Zack's hair. "Now let's get on, or I really *will* have to ring the restaurant."

He got both of them settled in the car. "Devonport, right?"

"Right," Emma said. "Just off King Edward Parade, on Church Street. We're putting you to a lot of trouble. Having to drive over to collect us, then back again and down to Devonport before we even go out. I could have met you there, I just realized."

"Didn't you know that collecting the girl is one of the best parts of the date? Tip for you," he told Zack, catching his eye in the rear-view mirror. "This is Boyfriend School, so pay attention."

"Are you Mum's boyfriend?" Zack asked with interest. "I thought you were *my* friend."

"Reckon I'm both now."

"Good," Zack decided. "Because you're not a Bad Guy."

"Too right," Nic said firmly. "No more Bad Guys for your mum. She's done with that."

He pulled up outside Lucy and Tom's flat, the bottom half of a house, one of a group set back from the road, and reached to grab Zack's backpack. The boy ran ahead to ring the bell, and Nic took the opportunity to tell Emma, "You look gorgeous, by the way. In case I didn't tell you."

"Thanks. I was afraid you'd be angry that I was running late."

"Nah. No rush. We have all night." He smiled down at her as, ahead of them, the door opened, the light falling on Zack's blond head. "And now's when I get vetted by the family," he added. "Bit scary."

"Yeah, right," she smiled back, taking his hand and stepping into the warm flat to give her sister a kiss hello.

In truth, Nic *did* feel like he was being checked out. Because no question, Lucy was looking him over critically, and Tom, coming up behind her, was doing the same. The other man's handshake was firm, his gaze direct. A good bloke, Nic thought at once.

"Thank you so much for taking Zack tonight," Emma was telling them. "He's been looking forward to it."

"We're going to watch something special, on telly," Tom promised Zack.

"A film?" Zack asked. "A cartoon?"

"Nah, mate. Got the final of the last World Cup on DVD, so you can watch Nic here doing his stuff. Scored the only try in that one, didn't you?" he asked Nic.

"I did," Nic agreed. "But it was the forwards who shone that night, I reckon. Drew was Man of the Match. The only choice, really. Because we wouldn't have won it without the Skipper. It was too close. Lots of the boys were getting a bit nervy. Not him, though. The hotter it gets, the cooler he stays. Settled everyone right back down, helped us hang on to the end."

"You're known to have a bit of a cool head yourself, though," Tom said.

"If I have, I've learnt from the best," Nic assured him.

"Well, this is all very fascinating," Lucy broke in. "And I'm sure you boys could stand here and talk rugby all night. But I think you have someplace you're meant to be, don't you?"

Nic laughed. "We do. And your sister's too pretty to keep waiting about. Got to go show her off to the world. Or to Auckland, anyway." He shook hands again with Tom and Lucy, gave Zack a quick squeeze around the shoulders, and waited while Emma pulled her son in for a goodnight hug and kiss.

Outside again, he took Emma's hand. "My palm's not sweating," he told her. "Reckon I *am* cool, at that, at least on the outside. Think I passed?"

"You know you did. Good thing you have that instant bonding mechanism."

"I wasn't talking about Tom. I meant your sister."

"Oh. Lucy." Emma laughed. "Yeah, she's a tougher customer. I suspect the probation period will be a little longer with Lucy."

♡

He drove away from the house, turned a corner, and pulled the car to the side of the road, put it in Park.

"Why are we stopping?" she asked. "Did you forget something?"

He turned to her, clicked open his seatbelt, then hers. Put one hand on the side of her face, thumb stroking over her cheek, then tugged her to him with the other arm and kissed her, feeling her soft little mouth opening under his.

"Couldn't wait," he said, drawing back a little, still caressing her cheek. "We've got all night, finally, and a house to ourselves. Time and space for everything we want to do. But first, I'm taking you to dinner. D'you realize we've never been on a real date? I've never had you dress up for me like this. Never collected you at your house and taken you out. Never walked through a flash restaurant behind you. How many times have we made love? But I've hardly even bought you a dinner. Nothing since that hamburger with Zack."

"I want to go on a date with you." She traced the parentheses at the sides of his mouth, her touch delicate against his skin. "I want to go a restaurant with you, too, hold hands under the table, then have you drive me home. But, Nic."

"What?" he asked, his forehead against hers. "What do you want? Anything." He kissed her cheek, drew back to look at her.

"Can we make it...special? Can we do something special, tonight?"

"Special how?" He hoped she was talking about what he thought she was talking about.

"Like...something unusual," she said breathlessly. "Different. Special. The kind of thing we did before. I haven't done anything like that in so long. Not with anyone but you."

He felt the heat go straight to his groin, but forced himself to pause, to think it through. "That wouldn't scare you, though? After what happened to you?"

"But it's not the same at all," she insisted. "It's what I told you. This is *you*. And I can't stand the idea that what he did could...change me. That it could keep me from doing what I want, or keep you from doing what *you* want. Whatever you want. If you have things you've wanted..." She hesitated. "Things you've wanted to do with me, I want you to do them. If you do, I mean," she trailed off uncertainly.

"What did you have in mind?" he asked, his voice sounding a little strained even to himself. "Anything you'd like to try? Maybe you'd like to tie me up, be the one in control for a change. Not my first choice, but I reckon I could live with it. I could sacrifice myself for the good of the cause, eh."

"If you want me to," she said doubtfully. "But it's not my first choice either. You know I'd rather be more..."

He brushed a hand over her cheek, felt the way she leaned into it. "Yeh. I know how you'd rather be. Lucky for me, because that's how I like you. That'll do me. No suggestions for me, then?"

She shook her head. "I want you to say. I want you to be... what you said. In control. If that's all right with you. If you want to."

She was blushing, he could tell, even in the dark. And she already had him well on his way. "Oh, I want to. That's going to work for me. Have to go to dinner first, though, so I can think about this. Plan something good enough for you."

"Yes, please," she said with a relieved sigh, snuggling up to him, running her hands down his arms. Making him feel like a man, in that way that only she could.

"Step One," he decided. "Reach down and pull off those undies for me."

"What? Now? Before dinner?" she asked, faltering.

"Yeh. Before dinner. You're not going to be needing those anymore, so you can just give them to me right now."

"This skirt is short, though," she objected.

"Then you'd better be careful how you sit, hadn't you? So nobody sees but me. Come on, now. Take them off."

He watched in the darkness of the car as she finally reached under her skirt, pulled the wispy material down her legs, over the high heels. He saw her hesitate, held out his hand. "Give them to me. Mine now."

He reached across her, shoved them into the glove box, pulled the key from the ignition to lock them away. "That's it, then," he told her. "That's us started. Because you don't get to put those on again till tomorrow."

aubergine

♡

She could never remember, afterwards, what they had talked about on their date, or what she had eaten, except that he'd watched her take every mouthful. And had held her hand under the table, just as she'd asked. And that she'd looked back at him, had seen that his eyes had that gleam in them again, and had had to restrain herself from asking him to take her home, right now.

He finished the last bite of potato, set his fork down. She laid her hand over his large brown one, traced slow designs on it as he used his other hand to wipe his mouth with the cloth serviette, then laid it next to his plate.

"Still hungry?" he asked. "You didn't finish."

"No," she said. "I'm not hungry, I mean."

"D'you want dessert? Coffee?"

"You're just teasing me now. You know I don't."

"Maybe I do, though," he said. "Maybe I'll ask to look at the menu again."

"*Nic.* Please."

"Love how you say that," he said, the smile in his eyes reaching his mouth at last. "Reckon you're going to be saying that a few more times before this night's over." He leaned closer on the banquette and whispered in her ear, "How're you going down there?"

She couldn't help it. She wriggled a little, and he noticed, she could tell.

He raised a hand for the bill, laid down his credit card. "Maybe I won't get that sweet after all," he told her as the waiter took the folder away again. "Because there's something else I'm going to want tonight, and I need to save a bit of room for it."

She felt his eyes on the silk of her skirt, the length of her legs during the walk through the restaurant. He held the door for her, took her hand for the trek to the car.

"OK walking in those shoes?" he asked. "Because I could still bring the car around. Don't know how you can do that."

"I'm good at walking in heels. Lots of practice. I like them."

"Lucky for me, because I like them too. First time I met you, you were wearing them, remember? I put one of them back on for you. Down there looking at your gorgeous legs, wanting to run my hands right up them." He threaded his fingers through hers, pulled her a bit closer. "I've wanted you from the first moment I met you. And every moment since."

"Are you doing this on purpose?" she asked breathlessly.

"What?"

"Saying these things. Making me..."

He swung her around, pulled her to him, and bent to give her a kiss, right there on the busy pavement. It got away from them, heated until he was holding her close against him, her hands were around his neck, and she was kissing him back, lost in it, oblivious to the passing pedestrian traffic.

"What?" he asked at last, smiling down into her eyes. "What am I doing to you?"

"You know," she breathed. "And you *are*. You *are* doing it on purpose. Making me feel like this."

They reached the car, and he saw her into it before going around and getting into his own seat. He reached for her again, ran a hand up her inner thigh, all the way to the top. Then his hand stilled.

"Emma," he said hoarsely. "Did you get yourself waxed again? Did you do that for me?"

The heat rose up her throat, into her face, as his hand moved over her. Embarrassment, excitement, nervousness, it was all mixed together. She was so ready, she was afraid that if he kept touching her like that, she was going to orgasm right here. "You seemed to like it last time," she said uncertainly. "I thought you did."

"Oh, I do." One hand was around her waist, reaching under her, lifting her for him, while the other moved under her skirt. "I could just touch you a bit here. Because I think you're about to come, aren't you?"

"Nic," she gasped. "I can't. Not here. What if somebody sees?"

"Then they'll have a thrill, won't they?" His hand was still moving. "Come on, now. Lie back and give them a show."

She knew nobody could really see, here at the back of the dark carpark. But his words had ignited her. His fingers were inside her, stroking over her. And he was still talking, and she was lost.

"I'm going to take you home," he told her. "I'm going to fuck you so hard tonight, you're going to be walking funny for days. I'm going to do things to you that you've only heard about. And you're going to love it. You're going to be crying, and screaming, and begging me for more. You aren't going to know your own name by the time I've finished with you."

She couldn't stop herself. Her breath came in gasps and her body stiffened as she spasmed around his hand, her back slamming against the leather seat. He held her there, kept going until she finished, then took her in his arms for another deep kiss.

"That was a pretty good start," he said against her hair. "Now let's go home so I can do the rest."

♡

It was a pity they'd gone all the way into the City, he thought. Because he was so hard, he was aching with it. After twenty minutes that seemed more like an hour, he was pulling up the steep driveway, punching the button for the garage. He pulled the car in, turned it off, and closed the garage door again before he turned to her once more.

"I need to tell you something," he said seriously. "Before we start."

"Before we *start?* What did we just do?"

He smiled. "Warmed you up, that's all. I have heaps more planned, before I let you go. And that's what I want to talk to you about. I don't want to do anything you're not comfortable with, or anything that feels wrong to you. I'm going to be pushing it tonight, so if you really don't want something, you need to tell me."

"You aren't planning to hurt me, are you?" she asked uncertainly. "That isn't what I meant. Not...not pain."

He reached out to kiss her, ran a hand over her cheek, closed it gently around the back of her neck. "You know I wouldn't hurt you. I'll never hurt you, and I don't want to scare you. So if it's really too much, if I push you further than you want to go, if you want me to stop. Say...say 'aubergine.' That's your word. Not one you're likely to be using tonight, otherwise. I know you're going to be saying things like 'wait.' And 'oh, no.' Because it's going to be so much for you to take. And I'm not going to know if you really mean it. But if you say 'aubergine,' I'll stop straight away, no matter what I'm doing, or how much I want to keep doing it. I promise."

"I'm nervous," she admitted. She was, he could see. Those big eyes looked up at him pleadingly. He kissed her again, gently this time.

"You should be nervous," he told her. "You shouldn't be scared, but you should definitely be nervous. Because you wanted something special, and now you're going to get it."

He led her into the house by the hand, flipping lights on, and took her upstairs to his bedroom, then changed his mind and took her into another room instead, one that had the bed he needed. He tossed cushions onto the floor, pulled the duvet back.

"Go wash up, if you like," he told her. "Do whatever you need to do to get comfortable. Then come back and lie down here."

"Where are you going?" she asked anxiously.

"Need to get a few things. Then I'll come back. And when I do, I want you here, lying down. Don't take anything off," he thought to add. "I'm going to do that."

"OK," she said. Still nervous, he saw. Good.

♡

She was lying on the bed when he eased back into the room again a few minutes later, his arms full. She'd taken her shoes off before arranging herself, but had followed his instructions and left the rest of her clothes in place.

The excitement was a physical thing now, overwhelming her body, the thrum and pulse in every secret part of her keeping pace with her rapid heartbeat. But the nervousness had increased along with it, and she found that she was hugging herself, arms folded across her chest, legs crossed.

She shivered with anticipation as he set his burdens on the nightstand, then sat down on the bed next to her and leaned down for a kiss. "Good work getting on the bed for me," he said. "Now we'll just do the next thing."

"What's the next thing?" she asked, her pulse hammering.

He lay down beside her, moved over her as he continued to kiss her, took one of her hands in his. She jerked in surprise as he looped the necktie around it, then fastened it to the post on the headboard with a quick knot.

"I never liked these anyway," he said conversationally, taking hold of the other hand and fastening it in its turn." So tug all you want. I won't care."

"*Nic,*" she pleaded. She struggled against the restraints, but he'd tied her too securely. Her wrists were held tight, her arms stretched overhead, and she was throbbing with arousal now.

"Remember your word?" he asked. "Aubergine. D'you want to say it?"

"Oh. Oh, no." Her breath was coming in shallow gasps. "No. I don't want to say it."

His smile started slowly, then grew as he looked down at her. "Good. That's good. You're doing so well. And now I'm going to get you naked, so I can play with you."

He drew it out, though, spent torturous minutes unbuttoning her sweater, one tiny square button at a time. Running his hands over her skin at every stop, before he finally, so slowly, unfastened the front clasp of the lacy bra. He used his hands and mouth on her as she felt the little skirt riding up her thighs, and she pulled desperately against the fabric binding her to the bed, writhed at his touch.

"Touch me," she got out. *"Please."*

"Where?" he asked, his hands playing at her breasts as his teeth grazed her neck, fastened on her earlobe. "Where d'you want me to touch you?"

She moved her legs as far apart as the skirt would allow. "You know. Please. I need it."

"Not yet. You're not in charge now, remember? I am. And I say it's not time yet."

At last, when she was whimpering under him, he untied one knot, helped her pull her arm through her sleeve and bra strap, then quickly refastened her. He did the same on the other side until she was tied again, naked to the waist.

"Oh, yeh," he said with satisfaction. "That's brilliant. That's gorgeous. That's how I want you." He reached around the back of her skirt for the zip, pulled it down, then eased the silky material down over her hips, over her legs, until she was, finally, naked beneath him.

He stood back, still fully dressed. She looked up at him, felt her arms being stretched taut, saw the hunger on his face, and was nearly undone.

"I thought about tying your legs down, too," he told her, reaching down to run a slow hand over her body, making her shiver, her body straining into his caress. Down her arm, over her breast, her belly, her thigh. And still, maddeningly, not where she needed him most. "Like my very best fantasy. Having you all the way tied up for me, helpless. That'd be too much, I know. So I'm just going to have you spread your legs, make you hold still for me."

"No. It's not too much. You can do that. You can tie me down," she got out through another surge of excitement. Her torso rose from the bed, and she shuddered, her legs moving apart as if of their own volition.

"You won't be able to move, once I do that," he warned.

She couldn't answer, could only whimper and shift, her back arching, trying to get closer to him. She needed him so badly now, she was burning with it. Aching for it.

He didn't ask again, just grabbed at something beyond her vision. Then he was fastening the tie around her ankle with a quick jerk, pulling it toward the post at the foot of the bed. Stretching her out, tying her down, then moving around to do the same thing on the other side before standing over her again, looking down at her where she lay, open to him.

He'd lost every bit of his own composure, she saw. He was breathing hard, almost as hard as she was herself. She twisted against her bonds, heard him swear under his breath. Then, finally, he was unbuttoning his shirt, pulling off the rest of his clothes, moving to the head of the bed, reaching for a condom amongst the supplies he'd brought, unwrapping it.

"We're going to play more later," he promised as he came down over her, eased inside her. "I'm going to do everything to you tonight. But right now, I'm going to fuck you."

"Nic," she moaned. "*Nic.*"

He started slowly, pausing before each stroke as she strained towards him, teasing her until she was making urgent, incoherent sounds, trying and failing to pull him into her, to hurry him. At last, when she was panting with frustrated arousal, he gradually began to increase the tempo.

Faster and harder, over and over. Being held like this, unable to move, was forcing every bit of her awareness onto the slide of him inside her, the friction of his body rubbing over her where she was most sensitive. Each stroke was pushing her higher, until it was past bearing. He was resting his weight on his hands, driving hard now, and she was beginning to keen. It was too much, too strong. She couldn't take any more.

"*Nic,*" she begged. "Please. Untie me. I can't...I can't..."

"Not going to untie you," he told her, his voice ragged with effort. "I want you to know I've got you, that you can't move. That you're mine, to do anything I want with. Because you are, aren't you?"

"Yes. Yes," she said on a sobbing breath.

"Say it, then," he ordered roughly.

"I'm yours," she got out, barely aware of what she was saying. "I'm yours."

"Too right. You belong to me. You're mine, and I'll do anything I want to you."

His words pushed her over the edge. She began to spasm around him, her wail sounding loud in her own ears, tears coming to her eyes as her pleasure grew, nearly painful in its intensity. He was grabbing a bound wrist in each hand now, holding her down even more tightly as wave after wave of delicious convulsions overpowered her. And then he was shouting, slamming into her, his excitement fueling her own, and she was crying out with him, utterly and completely lost.

She was still jerking and shaking when he rolled off her, moved to untie her wrists and ankles, pulled her arms down. He grabbed tissues to clean both of them up, handed her a few for her face. She wiped her eyes, took a deep, shuddering breath.

"You OK?" he asked, running a hand down her body.

She felt herself trembling, her body quivering under his touch. She nodded, then pulled him to her. He wrapped his arms around her in response, held her close.

"That scared me," she said against his chest. "Feeling that much."

He kissed her gently. "Scared me too, a bit," he admitted. "Never been that out of control. Are you hurt? Inside? Did I bruise you?"

"No. No. I'm just…limp."

"I brought some other things," he told her, pulling the sheet and duvet over them both. "But I'm too shattered just now, and you are, too. So I think we'll sleep for a while. Then we'll have some wine, and we'll try the next bit."

♡

By the time he woke the next morning, his internal alarm going off as always at seven, Nic felt as if he'd been through a cyclone and back again. He'd managed to get through a few more of the fantasies he'd had about her, and they'd all lived up to their advance billing. He'd explored every centimeter of her with his hands and mouth, and a few other things, too. Had turned her over, tied her up again that way, and kept her there for a good long while. Had lost count of the number of times she'd come, and had gone through two more condoms himself.

But it was her response that had devastated him. She'd called his name again and again, cried out in pained ecstasy, and begged him for more, just as he'd told her she would. Her openness, her vulnerability, her utter surrender to her own pleasure had pushed him to a place he'd never been. She'd given him everything, and he'd given her what she'd asked for. Something special. A night they would both remember for a long, long time. And she'd never once said "aubergine."

♡

Emma winced as she sat up in bed, muscles and tissues protesting against the treatment they'd received. There wasn't a clock in here, but the sun was coming through the open plantation shutters. She listened, but couldn't hear Nic, so she got up with a groan and went into the ensuite bathroom.

A hot shower eased some of the aches, but she wished she had her toothbrush. Too much of the chilled white wine, in the night. And the ice in the bucket he'd brought, dripped onto her. Then his warm mouth, heating her again. She flushed at the memories. She'd asked for something special, and he had delivered beyond anything she could have imagined. Under his inventive guidance, she'd been able to abandon herself completely to the joy of rediscovering her body, and all the pleasure it could feel.

"Morning." Nic came into the bedroom to find her wrapped in a towel, picking up her discarded clothes. "Cup of tea?"

She turned to look at him, suddenly shy. She could feel the blush creeping up her neck as she remembered all the things they'd done, then realized what he'd said. "Cup of *tea?*" she asked in disbelief.

"Yeh," he said in surprise. "Why not?"

She started to laugh. "It just seems a little…incongruous. After what we just did."

He grinned in response. "I'm good, but even I need to take a break sometimes, have a cuppa. Labor laws, you know. Mandatory smoko."

"Then, yes, I'd love a cup of tea. But my toothbrush is in my purse, in your car. At least I think I left it there. Could you look? That would make me feel a lot more human."

"I'll look," he promised.

He came back in a few minutes with two mugs of tea, set them down on the bedside table, then pulled her little travel toothbrush and a tube of toothpaste from the pocket of his jeans. "And voila."

"Great," she said with gratitude, taking them from him and disappearing into the bathroom.

When she came out, he was sitting propped against the pillows, the picture of casual innocence, sipping his tea. He patted the spot next to him.

"I should get dressed," she said.

He reached for the dressing gown he'd brought, tossed it to her. "Put that on, get cozy here with me for a minute. Oh, and here." He lifted himself to reach into his jeans pocket, pulled out the scrap of silvery lace. "You may want these again now. Though if you decide to leave them off, I won't complain. Because I'm going to take you out for brekkie before we collect Zack. You could probably do with a large coffee, this morning. I know I could."

"Don't you feel a little…embarrassed?" she asked, snuggling next to him wrapped in his oversized dressing gown, picking up her mug.

"Nah," he said decisively. "I feel happy. And worked out. How about you?"

She laughed. "Worked out. Yeah, I guess that would describe it. Worked out. Worked over. Shagged up, down, and sideways, the way someone once promised me he could do."

"I did, didn't I? Took a while to make good on that, but I reckon I've done it now."

"You have, so I guess you're entitled to look that smug. I don't think I'm going to be forgetting this night in a hurry."

"No...cobwebs?" he asked, serious now. "You good?"

"You blew them away. As long as I stick with you, looks like I'm golden."

"As long as you stick with me, reckon we both are."

He leaned over to kiss her cheek, sat up again with a grin. "And by the way. Anytime you want something special, just give me the word. Because I enjoyed that, and I'd be happy to do it again."

the boy in the tower

♡

"Now that we've had one adventure," Nic said on the drive back to Devonport, "it's time for the other one, don't you think?"

"Which one?" Emma asked. She was feeling relaxed, a bit sleepy again despite the bowl-sized latte she'd consumed with breakfast. Must be all those good sex endorphins, she supposed. Or just too much sex and too little sleep.

"Telling Zack I'm his dad."

That got her attention. "Oh. Wow."

"It's time, don't you think?" Nic asked again. "Step back a sec and look at it. I'd like him to come stay with me on the weekends I'm here, and that's not many, you know. Just the next few weeks, and then I'm off to Aussie and on to Argentina, if the ankle's fit again. Back for a few more weeks, bar some days in Wellington and Dunedin, and it's off again to England for the World Cup. Assuming I'm fit, and in form, and selected, touch wood. That'll be a lot of time away, and not much here, all the way till the end of October. So I'd say we should do it now, wouldn't you? Give him some time with me to get used to the idea?"

"Yeah," she forced herself to say through a throat that had tightened. "It should be now."

He shot her a quick glance, reached a hand out to grip her own briefly. "I'm not going to take him away from you, you know," he said gently. "I'm not trying to make his life harder. Or yours. I'll be doing my best to make it better, for both of you. But I want him to know he's my son. I want him to *know* he can ring me. That he can count on me if he needs me."

She really couldn't think of an argument against that. "All right. When do you want to do it?"

"Today, I thought. The game will be on at five-thirty tonight," he added practically. "Maybe we could all watch together, afterwards. May break the ice, so to speak. Settle a few of the collywobbles."

"It's on that early?" she asked, distracted.

"Sydney time," he said patiently. "Where d'you want to do it?"

She felt rushed, but knew it wasn't his fault. He was right, he'd waited long enough, and it was time. "Our flat," she said with decision. "Where he's comfortable, and safe. And I think your idea about the game is a good one. Maybe before that?"

"Not now?"

"No. I need to shift gears, not to mention getting out of these clothes. Let me go home first, finish getting things squared away after our holiday."

"OK. What about food? Want me to bring a takeaway? We could heat it up again, after, eat it during the game."

She had to laugh a little in spite of her tension. "Food. Sure. You're in charge of food. But, Nic," she said, sobering. "This is a big deal. Don't underestimate it."

"I know it's a big deal," he said seriously. "It's a big deal for me, too. I'm shaking inside. Never been more nervous."

"Really?"

A rueful smile appeared at the corner of his mouth. "Oh, yeh."

♡

He brought Chinese. The same restaurant, the same menu as the first time.

"Potstickers," he told Zack, holding up the bag. "Our favorite, eh. But first, your mum and I want to talk to you about something. I'll just pop this in the fridge, and we'll have a chat."

"Did I do something bad?" Zack asked anxiously as they took their seats in the lounge. Emma had chosen to sit on the couch where she could be with Zack, leaving Nic perched on the edge of the armchair next to them. "I spilt the juice at Auntie Lucy's," Zack said uncertainly. "But she *said* it was OK. She *said.*"

"You didn't do anything bad," Emma said hastily. "This isn't a bad thing. It's a good thing." She found herself wanting to run away, to avoid this, to escape into her bedroom, pull the quilt over her head.

You're the mum, she told herself, trying to quell the feeling of panic. *Be the mum.* She gathered her courage and plunged in. "Remember when I told you your dad had to go away?"

"Yeh," Zack said slowly, his eyes searching hers.

She took his hand in hers. No way to say this except straight out. "Your dad was Nic, sweetie. He was your dad. He *is* your dad."

Zack's eyes flew to Nic's. "Nic is?" he asked doubtfully. "Like a stepdad, you mean? Like Stephen has, in my class?"

"Nah, mate," Nic said, his voice a bit gruff. "I'm your real dad. Your...your birth dad." He stopped, looked at Emma in mute appeal.

She took over again. "You know everyone has a mum and a dad who make them. Well, before you were born, Nic and I knew each other, and we made you. And then Nic had to go away, like I said."

"I did," Nic put in. "I went away. I went to play for Bath, remember? And I didn't know we'd...made you. I didn't know I had a son until I saw you and your mum at Rob's camp. It was a surprise. That's why you didn't know about me before, because I didn't know either. But I did make you, and I'm your real dad."

"Are you going to live here now?" Zack asked. "Because mums and dads live with their kids."

"Not all of them do," Emma reminded him. "Stephen's dad lives in a different house, right?"

"Right," Zack remembered.

"And he stays with him, some weekends, doesn't he?"

"Yeh. He has a big house. Stephen's mum has a flat, like us. But he has heaps of toys at his dad's. He told me."

"That's how this is going to be too," Emma said, choosing to pass over the comment about the toys. "You're going to live with me most of the time, but you'll stay with Nic sometimes too. You'll have another bed at his house."

Zack looked at Nic. "Not *my* bed?" he asked in alarm. "Do I have to?"

"We'll make you a special room," Nic promised him. "Your own room. Your mum can bring you to my house tomorrow so you can see it."

"Is it going to be always? I don't get to be with you anymore?" Zack implored his mother.

"No, it's not going to be always," she assured him. "It's going to be sometimes. Some nights. Just like you see Nic now, and play rugby with him. You'll just sleep there, that's all."

"Like camping?"

"Nah, mate," Nic said with a little smile. "Not like camping, I promise. A real bed. You'll see, tomorrow. We'll get it sorted."

"Can I bring Raffo?"

"Course you can. And anything else you need, to be comfortable."

"Mum." Zack tugged at Emma's sleeve until she bent her head to him. "What do I call him?" he asked in a clearly audible whisper. "If he's my dad?"

243

Emma shot a look at Nic, who was clearly taken aback at the question.

"That's for you to choose," he finally answered. "You can call me Dad, if you like. Because that's what I am. But if you'd rather not," he went on quickly, seeing the look of alarm on Zack's face, "you can go on calling me Nic."

"OK," Zack said with relief. "Can we have potstickers now?"

Emma laughed a little shakily, saw Nic smiling with what looked like the same relief. "Yeah. I'd say it's time for potstickers. And a rugby game, too."

♡

"Do heaps of people live here?" Zack asked the next afternoon, head tipped back to take in all three stories of the villa rising above them.

"Nope. Just Nic." Should she be saying "your dad," she wondered? It felt too strange, though.

"It's like a castle," Zack said, still dubious. "It has a tower."

"A turret," Emma agreed. "That's what you call those. Just like on the canisters I painted."

"He must get lonesome," Zack decided. "When I'm big and have a house, I'm going to have you live in it with me."

"Mmm. We'll see about that," she said with a smile.

Zack clung to her hand as he saw Nic coming down the brick-lined concrete footpath to join them. "Do I have to live here now, Mum?" he asked nervously.

"No," Emma promised. "Just a visit, that's all, like we talked about. Like a sleepover."

She lifted her face for Nic's kiss, feeling more settled as always by the sheer solidity of him. "Hi," she said.

"Hi." Nic dropped a hand to Zack's head, gave his hair a rumple. "How ya goin', mate?"

"Fine," Zack said shyly, dropping his gaze.

"Zack thinks your house is pretty big," Emma told him. "He's wondering if you ever get lonesome."

"I do," Nic said seriously once Zack was looking at him again. "Heaps of times. That's why I want you and your mum to come stay with me."

"Mum can come too?" Zack asked.

"Course she can. If she wants to, that is."

Zack breathed a windy sigh of relief. *"Can* you come, Mum?" he begged.

"I think I could manage that," she said with a smile at Nic. "That'd be fun."

"Then let's have a wander round," Nic said. "Take the tour."

Zack wasn't much interested in the lounge, kitchen, dining room, and study that took up most of the ground floor, however impressive they still were to Emma. He showed a bit more enthusiasm, though, for the patio outside.

"You have a spa pool!" he said with delight. "Is it really hot?"

"Yeh," Nic said. "And you're not to go in that unless your Mum or I are with you, understand?"

"Maybe a lock for the cover," Emma said to Nic quietly. "Just to be on the safe side."

"D'you ever practice in the garden?" Zack asked, looking longingly at the level patch of grass beyond the patio.

"Never had anyone willing to do it with me," Nic said. "Maybe you'd like to help me out with that, when you're here."

"No kicking," Emma put in hastily. "Or that'll be the end of your windows."

"Oi. I'm more accurate than that," Nic protested.

She laughed. "I wasn't talking about you, and you know it."

Zack's interest waned again on the first floor, until they reached the exercise room. "Cool," he said, looking at the sets of weights stored on specially built racks, the ranks of dumbbells and heavy round plates meant to fit onto the long barbell rods, all stacked neatly against the mirrored wall that stretched the entire length of the room.

"You have just about everything, don't you?" Emma asked, taking in the weight bench and bench press rack, the state-of-the-art exercise bike and treadmill, the exercise balls and stretching mats arranged in the corner. "I wouldn't need a gym membership if I had all this."

"You wouldn't be able to take those classes, though," Nic pointed out.

"How do you know about my classes?"

"Saw you there one day," he admitted. "Working out. D'you go often?"

"Most days, at lunch. I get a membership as part of my job. One of the few perks."

Zack had climbed up onto the bike, was trying in vain to reach the pedals. "Where am I going to sleep?" he asked Nic. "When I'm here?"

"Got a spot in mind for you." Nic led them up yet another flight of stairs, opened a door at the end of another gleaming hardwood passage. "This is what I was thinking," he said. "Come in and tell me how it strikes you. A bit like a treehouse, see?"

"Yeh," Zack agreed, going over to gaze out the big window into the treetops beyond. "It's cool."

He was still uncertain, Emma could tell. And she was, too. It all felt pretty new. Pretty strange. "Nice ceiling," she said encouragingly. It did, indeed, slope on both sides, here at the top of the house. "It makes it cozy, but it's still a good height."

"Where do these stairs go?" Zack asked, standing on the first step of the twisting iron stairway that stood in an alcove at one end of the room.

"Ah," Nic smiled. "Why don't you go on up there, see for yourself?"

"*Awesome!*" they heard a moment later. "Mum! Come see!"

246

Emma emerged at the top, closely followed by Nic. "It's the turret!" she exclaimed. "How great!"

Zack was kneeling on one of the window seats that lined two walls of the little tower, peering out. "You can see the sea, Mum!" he told her excitedly.

"Thought you might like that," Nic said with satisfaction. "It's a pretty good place to read a book, or just look out at the kite surfers, watch the storms come in, check the tides. A good place to be a boy. And a person could even build a Lego set up here," he suggested with a twinkle, pointing out the built-in desk on the third wall. "If he had a new one, of course."

"It's so *cool*," Zack said again. "Can I sleep up here, too?"

Nic laughed. "You may be more comfortable in a bed, but it's your room. Come on down and see the rest of it."

Zack left the little tower reluctantly.

"Be sure to hold the handrail on the way down," Emma cautioned him. "And to watch yourself on these twisty steps."

"*Mum*," Zack said with exasperation. "I'm not a *baby*. I can do *stairs*."

Downstairs again, he eyed the room a bit dubiously. "This bed is really big. And fancy." He looked at the pale green satin duvet cover, poked it gingerly.

"I thought we could get you something more your size," Nic suggested. "That'd make a bit more room in here, too. So you could have a desk, shelves, all that."

"A desk? Like a real one?" Zack asked.

"Yeh," Nic assured him. "A real one. Don't look so excited. You're meant to do your homework at it."

"D'you think Graham could come sometime?" Zack asked him shyly. "To see my room?"

"Don't see why not. Give you a bit of company."

"Bunk beds," Emma said. "If you think so," she added hastily with a look at Nic. "But it'd be better, if you mean it about Zack being able to have a friend over. We could put them against this wall," she planned.

"Wow," Zack breathed. "Bunk beds would be *awesome.*"

"Bunk beds it is, then," Nic decided. "And a desk, and shelves. And clear out the rest of this clobber."

Emma had to laugh at that. Any one of the pieces of "clobber" in this room would, she knew, have cost more than all the furniture in her little flat.

"How d'you want it to look?" Nic asked Zack. "When it's done?"

"What d'you mean?" Zack asked blankly.

"I mean, decorated," Nic explained. "The paint, and that. Want the walls white like they are, or colors, like at your mum's?"

"*Can* I have colors?"

"Course. It's your room. You can have what you like."

"Black, then," Zack said firmly. "I want an All Black room."

Emma and Nic shared a look. "Teach you to issue open-ended invitations like that," she grinned. "Boy, do you have a lot to learn."

She explained to Zack, "The whole room being black would be too dark. It'd be like a cave in here. But I know," she went on as his face fell. "How about if we did a wallpaper border up at the top? I'm pretty sure I could find that. Keep the walls white, but with a border. Black, with the silver fern and 'All Blacks' on, all the way around?"

"Yeh," Zack decided. "That'd be choice. And can the rest of the room be All Blacks too? Can I bring my posters from home, maybe?"

"Nah," Nic told him. "We'll get you new posters. So you'll have them both places. And," he told Emma, "if there's anything, sheets, duvet, and that, that he wants. All Black stuff. I think you can get that kind of gear. Since we've got a theme going here."

"Can I, Mum?" Zack asked eagerly.

"Sure," she smiled down at him, "if Nic says."

"Right," Nic decided. "I don't know what to buy, though. What would suit him. Maybe you wouldn't mind buying the furniture, and all the rest of it. And a carpet, too," he realized, using a toe to flip up the edge of an Oriental carpet in a delicate pastel paisley pattern. "Because this isn't going to work, eh. Just tell me how much it was, and I'll put it back into your account."

"Uh…" She stopped. "Sweetie, I need to talk to Nic for a while," she decided. "Let's go get you set up with the TV, just for a few minutes, OK?"

♡

"I need to tell you," she said when she and Nic were in the room again, alone this time. "I can't, actually. Buy the furniture and everything, I mean." She was embarrassed, but it was better to be honest. "I told you, money's not my best thing. And a few years ago, I had a pretty big problem. I spent too much on my credit card, then I had some car trouble, and…" she trailed off. "Anyway, I got it all paid off, finally. Took forever. But I lowered my credit limit, so I couldn't do that again. I only have a few thousand dollars on there, for emergencies. Which happen a lot," she admitted. "There isn't enough to buy all this," she finished, feeling ashamed as always when she talked about money, but relieved, too. He might as well know the worst.

He didn't say anything, just pulled his wallet from his back pocket, selected a credit card and handed it to her. "Right. Use this, then."

She looked at him in puzzled surprise. "You're giving me your card to use? After what I just told you?"

He shrugged. "What did you tell me? That you had a problem, and you took care of it, and saw to it that it wouldn't happen again. Why would that make me not trust you? What am I missing here?"

"I just…" She stopped in confusion, put the card into her own wallet, snapped her purse closed again. "I'll only buy stuff for Zack," she promised. "And I'll try to remember to save all the receipts for you."

"No worries. I'll see the statement," he reminded her. "Besides, that card doesn't have much of a limit on it itself. If you tried running away to the Gold Coast for a flash holiday, you wouldn't get too far. So I'm not taking much of a risk, after all."

"But you should tell me," she said as a new concern occurred to her, "how much I can spend on it. What *your* limit is."

"Were you planning on antiques, then? Are there designer bunk beds I don't know about?"

"No, of course not. Well, maybe there are. I wouldn't know. But there are different options. Normally, I'd try the Op Shops first, then go to the outlet stores, if I couldn't find anything. There's always a cheaper way."

"No Op Shops. I'm not saying there's anything wrong with that, but you don't need to do all that, not this time. Just go to the regular shop." He gave a frustrated gesture. "Whatever that is. I have no idea. Claudia did all the rest of this, with the decorator. But go where you think will be good, buy what he needs, and we'll be golden."

"OK," she said. Well, that was easy. Nice to have money.

"Oh, and come look at this with me, will you?" He took her down the stairs and along the hall to the main guest bedroom, the one, Emma realized with embarrassment, that they'd used two nights earlier.

"The nights Zack's here, like I said, I'm thinking I may be able to talk you into coming too," Nic told her with a smile. "And that you may want to sleep in here. Wake up in here, anyway."

"I will," she said with relief. "I want to be with you, but I don't want Zack to know we're sleeping together. It's too…complicated, just now. He has enough to deal with. I was wondering how to do that."

"Well, this is it, don't you think? Anyway, this is yours. It has a bath—but you already know that. Has the right bed, too, in case we ever need to use that again."

She looked at the carved posts, and could feel herself turning red. "Yeah," she said, her voice sounding constrained in her ears. "A bath would be nice."

He smiled. "And the bed? How about that?"

"Nic," she pleaded. "Quit it. I'm so embarrassed, I can't stand it."

He took her face in his hands and gave her a long kiss. "Sorry," he said, though he didn't look sorry in the least. "You're right, I'm teasing. We'll use my bed. It's bigger. Just keep this one for special occasions. That suit you?"

"That does," she agreed, turning her head to rub her cheek against his hand. "Special occasions. That works for me."

"What I really brought you in here to say," he told her, releasing her reluctantly, "is that when you're buying that stuff for Zack, if you need anything for this room, sheets, towels, duvet cover, like that, you should go ahead."

"But you have those things already," she said. "It's all done."

"Yeh." He rubbed the bridge of his nose ruefully with a thumb. "Just thought, you know. Colors, and that. They may not suit you."

She looked at the light-charcoal walls with their chalk-white trim, the silver-gray duvet cover and white linens, envisioned the gray towels in the bath. "Well, I wouldn't say they'd be my first choice," she conceded, "but it's very elegant. And the color scheme matches the walls. Too much work to change everything. No point."

"I want you to be comfortable, that's all," he said. "So you'll be here as much as possible."

"It's fine," she said. "I'll focus on Zack's room. That's going to be plenty, no worries."

theme bedroom

♡

"Did my bed come?" Zack asked on Wednesday afternoon, as he'd asked every day since they'd bought it, never mind Emma's explanations of delivery schedules.

She opened the car door and slung his pack into the back seat, made sure he was fastened. "Well, you know what?" she told him happily as she climbed into the driver's seat and prepared to leave the childcare center carpark. "It did! Nic texted me that all the furniture was delivered today, and the guys got everything set up. *And* he invited us to come over and get your room ready tonight, if you want. So it'll be all set for you when we go to stay this weekend. But maybe you're too tired," she added seriously. "Maybe you'd rather wait till Friday."

"*Mummmm,*" Zack wailed, then saw the smile peeping out of the corner of her mouth and laughed in relief. "Can we really go? Straight away?"

"Almost," she promised. "We need to stop by the house first and get the other stuff we bought. And get me changed into some jeans, if I'm going to be hanging your wallpaper border and crawling around on top of a bunk bed. Plus you need to eat something before we go. A quick tea. Beans and toast, how's that?"

"OK. But can you drive really, really fast?" Zack pleaded. "Because I can't *wait.*"

♡

He was out of the car and running for the door, when they eventually did get to Nic's, before Emma even had the boot open. She came up behind him, loaded down with a bulging bag of bedding, just as Nic opened the door to find Zack dancing impatiently on the doorstep.

"Hi, there," he said. "Come to do a bit of redecorating, eh. D'you need to pee?" he asked in alarm, seeing Zack's wiggly performance.

"Nah," Zack said indignantly. "I'm just *excited.*"

Emma laughed. "You catch on fast, don't you?" She gave Nic a quick kiss. "There's a bunch more stuff in the car."

"Got it. Leave that thing there. I'll fetch it all, bring it up. Meantime, go have a look."

♡

Nic came through the door of the bedroom, dropped his armload of purchases. "Shit!" he yelped, making it across the room just in time to catch Emma as she overbalanced and tipped off the seat of Zack's desk chair, the wheels rolling out from under her.

"What the hell were you *thinking?*" he asked in exasperation, setting her down. "Standing on something with wheels? It *rolls,* you know? That's the bloody idea. Why didn't you wait for me, ask me to get a stepstool?"

"I just wanted to start hanging the border," she said, looking flustered. "I had the chair shoved up against the wall. I thought it'd be OK."

"You're too bloody impulsive. Are you *trying* to get yourself hurt? You need to think, damn it!"

"Don't shout at me. It was stupid, OK? I admit it. And I was scared, when I started to fall. I don't need you to shout at me."

"Aw, geez." He reached for her, gave her a cuddle. She was trembling a bit, he realized. It really *had* scared her. "Sorry. But you scared me, too."

"Anyway," she said, rallying now, "you haven't always minded my impulsivity, have you?"

"Nah," he said with a smile. "You're right. I haven't."

"You said a *lot* of bad words, Nic," Zack told him from his perch on the upper bunk. "Mum says I'm not allowed."

"You're not," Nic said. "Slipped out, that's all. And I'll go get a stepstool, do the rest of this," he told Emma. "You go put sheets on, or something. Something *safe.*"

"I can do it," she objected. "I've done everything at our flat, you know. All the painting, hanging everything. I own an electric drill. I even kill my own spiders. And if you'll get me the stepstool, I'll do this, too."

Nic sighed. "Right. You're competent and strong. *And* clever. Even though I stand by the stubborn bit. So let me ask this another way. Would you please *allow* me to hang the wallpaper border, participate in this decorating exercise?"

"Are you patronizing me?" she asked suspiciously.

"Nah. I'm not. Really not. I still think the rolling-chair thing wasn't your best moment. But I'll acknowledge that you could do it. I'm asking you to let *me* do it."

"Would *somebody* please do it?" Zack pleaded. "I really, really want my All Blacks room. *Please?*"

Emma had to laugh. "We'll do it together," she told Nic. "Just yell when you need me to hand you something."

By the time he had the rest of the border hung, with very little help needed from her, she had to admit, Emma had both beds neatly made with their matching All Blacks duvets.

"I still wish we'd got the sheets," Zack sighed, sitting on the bottom bunk and bouncing experimentally. "Then I'd have everything."

"Boy, give you one thing, and you're a regular conspicuous consumer, aren't you?" Emma chided him. "They're ridiculous. These white ones have a higher cotton count, *and* they're a quarter of the price. It's all those licensing fees. We spent enough of Nic's money as it was."

"Oi," Nic protested. "Those licensing fees pay my wages, you know. Looked at another way, you're just putting a bit more back in the pot for later, when my agent's negotiating my next contract. So you could view all this as an investment, eh," he said with a wink at Zack.

"Yeh, Mum!" Zack said triumphantly. "It's a vestment!"

Emma laughed. "You don't even know what an investment is. And for the record, that means when you put your money, or you work hard, toward something that's going to be earning you money back later on. Like working hard in school helps you get a good job when you're big."

"I don't need to work hard in school," Zack protested. "Because I'm going to be a rugby player when I grow up, like Nic."

"Hang on," Nic said. "Even if you *are* a rugby player, you have to be able to do sums, and read and write, don't you. Otherwise, how are you going to count all that lovely lolly you're getting? Or read your contract? And besides," he went on more seriously, "rugby only lasts so long, no matter how far you get, and then you have to go do something else. So I'm afraid it's going to be homework at that desk, like I said. And not just looking at those photo books about footy."

"*Thank* you," Emma told him. "He has a one-track mind, that's the problem. Boys."

"Not all boys," Nic protested. "My mind runs on at least two tracks." He grinned at her, and she laughed and stuck out her tongue at him, and he suddenly felt that there was nowhere in the world he'd rather be right now than here, with the two of them.

"Well, since you're so smart, and so handy, and have a step-stool," she said, "maybe you'd like to hang these posters, too.

And the bulletin board, over the desk. Though they're pretty big," she said doubtfully, beginning to lug a large framed image of the All Blacks in mid-haka toward the wall where she wanted it. "And heavy. Do you have the stuff?"

"Do me a favor. What kind of a Kiwi d'you take me for? Course I do. And stop that. Wait for me to shift them. *Please.*"

He returned in a few minutes with a toolbox and a plastic case for a serious electric drill. "Right, then. Show me where you'd like them."

The two of them, working together, had all three items hung within a few minutes. Emma collected the last of the rubbish, stacked it outside the door, and they all stood back to admire the room.

"This is a theme bedroom, is what this is," Nic pronounced. "Nobody's going to be walking in here and asking, "So, Zack. What are your interests?""

"It's so cool!" Zack said happily. "When can Graham come? Friday? I want him to see it!"

"It should just be us at first," Emma told him. "We'll have Graham over next time. If it's OK with Nic," she said, looking at him.

"Course," he agreed. "My mate Graham needs a bit of help on his offloading anyway. Got a wild arm. You know, though, there's one more thing this room needs. Hang on a tick, and I'll get it."

Zack gazed longingly at the distinctive black Champions bag Nic brought back with him. "That's the real bag!" he told Nic. "From the shop. What's in it?"

"The real deal," Nic promised. "Something you may need this weekend. Because when you shift house, you know, people give you a housewarming present. Reckon this is your bedwarming present." He handed the bag to Zack. "Open it and see."

Zack dropped to the floor, opened the big bag.

"*Wow,*" he breathed, pulling out the set of All Black pajamas. "Can I put them on now?" he begged his mother.

"I don't see why not," she smiled. "Wear them home, if you like. Because it's time for bath, and bed."

Zack pulled off his clothes impatiently, tugged on the new pajamas. "I fit them!" he told Nic excitedly. "Mum doesn't have to roll! And they have tags on!"

"Yeh, mate." Nic cleared his throat. "And they look awesome."

"Thank you," Emma told him quietly as Zack ran to examine himself in the bathroom mirror.

"Got an ABs jersey for him too," Nic said. "For him to wear Saturday night, when we all go to the match."

She hugged him. "He's going to love that so much. How did you know what size he was, though?"

"I had a squiz at some of his gear when we were at the bach," he confessed. "Been wanting to get him those pajamas for a fair few weeks now. This seemed like the right time."

housewarming party

♡

"Sorry," Emma said on Friday evening when Nic was once again opening the door to the two of them. "I know we're really late. I hope you're not too starved."

"What happened?" he asked.

"Hard day at work. I'll tell you later, OK?"

He nodded, hefted her roller bag. "Whoosh. What d'you have in here, bricks? It's only two days."

"If it's too heavy," she said with a flash of spirit, "I'll carry it myself. You want me to look nice, don't you? That doesn't happen by accident, you know. Curling iron, shoes…it all adds up."

He laughed. "I think I can still shift it. Come up with me. We can see how Zack's getting on, then you can help me put dinner together. Only the very best for you. All ready-prepared by somebody else."

♡

"Whew," Nic said once Zack was safely in bed, and he and Emma were in the lounge again. "Alone at last."

It had taken awhile. Zack had been unable to decide on the upper or lower bunk, until Nic had hit on the proposal to spend tonight on the bottom, and Saturday on the top. "Then you can decide scientifically," he told Zack seriously.

"Getting both sets of sheets dirty," Emma protested.

Nic scoffed at that. "What, Graham's going to come to spend the night, and say, 'Oh, Zack! These sheets have been *used*, I can tell! How will I ever, ever sleep in such *filth?*'" He made his voice high, slapped both hands to his face in mock horror, and had Zack helpless with giggles.

"We're boys," Nic finished with a grin at Emma. "We don't care too much if our bed's had a prior occupant or not."

Now the two of them were finally sitting on one of the big leather couches, the gas fireplace making a cozy display, and sharing the second half of a bottle of wine that, Nic had insisted, was necessary for their "housewarming party." Emma was already a little tipsy, feeling relaxed for the first time all day as she snuggled with him. She thought lazily about working on the sweater she had started for Reka's baby, but couldn't be bothered. Besides, she'd probably lose the pattern.

"So what happened today?" Nic asked her. "In your hard day at work?"

She sighed. "I almost hate to tell you. I wish I handled this stuff better. Why do I let myself get so *upset?* Why can't I just say what a guy would say?"

"What would a guy say?" Nic asked in confusion. "About what?"

"You know. Eff you."

"Can't even say the word, eh," he said, rubbing the back of her neck. "You're such a girly girl. I think you'd better tell me, though. Explain why you'd be swearing at somebody. If you were a bloke, that is."

"Roger called me over," Emma said reluctantly. "He was with Aaron, one of the project managers. There'd been a problem with some of the drawings. An important spec change that hadn't made it onto the final version, they said. But it wasn't my *fault*. I didn't think it was at the time, but I couldn't think of how to prove it. And I got all flustered. Because Roger didn't give me a chance, he just laid into me. Going on about how I'd made the company look bad, made Aaron look bad. He was saying things like, 'This is a very serious error. I have no choice but to write you up for this.' And then I went back and checked," she said, tears filling her eyes, "what I'd been given. And that—that change—wasn't on there. I went back over there, tried to explain. And Aaron insisted he'd told me, and Roger was standing there *berating* me, for everyone to hear."

She lost the battle with the tears, couldn't stop them from spilling down her cheeks. "I just felt so...so small. I couldn't think of the right thing to say. And Roger was loving it, I could tell. I was so *angry*. I wanted to scream at him. I wanted so much to walk out. To quit right there."

Nic pulled her into his lap, wrapped his arms around her as she finally let the tears go that she'd been holding back all day. It was such a relief to be held, to be comforted, that, perversely, it made her cry all the harder. He didn't try to talk to her, just reached for the tissue box, then held her against his chest until she was cried out, and was blowing her nose and wiping her eyes.

"Feel better?" he asked.

She nodded shakily, took a deep, shuddering breath and blew her nose again, grabbed another wad of tissues and tried in vain to blot some of the moisture from his T-shirt where she'd soaked it.

"Why *don't* you tell that Roger to go fuck himself?" Nic asked. "See, I can say the word. Bet you could too, if you practiced enough."

"Want me to practice on you?" she asked with a watery smile, pulling back to look at him.

He laughed. "Nah. But maybe you *should* quit, have you thought of that?"

She sighed, rested her cheek against his chest again as he continued to stroke her hair. "Every single day. But I can't. I need my job, and Roger knows it. He knows I won't quit, unfortunately."

"I thought you were talking to the people at Hannah's place. Have you heard back from them?"

She shook her head. "I had the interview, and they're interested in hiring me, but they need to get their new line going first. The kids' line," she reminded him. "Probably November, they said. I don't want to look for a new job, if this is a real possibility. Because it's exactly what I want. I just have to hold on till then, that's all."

"I'm surprised you've held on this long, if it's been this bad."

"It's only been the past year that it's been this bad, just since Roger. At first, I thought he'd get over it. That he was just proving he was my boss, showing me he was in charge. I thought if I didn't challenge him, he'd settle down."

"Not if he's a bully," Nic said with certainty. "That just makes them push more, if they think they can get away with it. You have to push back, with that type."

"Yeah," she sighed. "I figured that out, a little too late." She reached for her wineglass, took a sip and handed it to him. "Finish this, will you? I'm already a little drunk. That's probably why I cried."

He took it from her and obliged. "Wish I could go in there and talk to him," he said with frustration. "I'd like to sort him out."

She snuggled up against him. "Like you did with Ryan?" she asked, listening to his heart beating under her cheek. She felt his start of surprise and smiled with satisfaction. "You thought I wouldn't find out about that, huh? Not too hard to figure out. Suddenly he was avoiding me like the plague. And then I heard, third-hand, that somebody'd seen you talking to him outside the office, that next day."

"Yeh," he admitted. "I had a word."

"Well, thanks. If you hadn't done that, I might *really* have had to quit, and then who knows where Zack and I would be."

"You'd be OK," he promised, running a hand down her back and setting the wineglass back down on the coffee table. "I wouldn't actually let you starve, you know."

"Mmm." She nestled a little closer. "Anyway, thanks."

"If you really want to thank me, you'll come upstairs with me. Because it's bedtime, you know. And we've got a bit of bedwarming to do ourselves tonight. Got a pressie for you, too, along those lines."

"All Black pajamas for me too?" she asked, climbing off his lap and walking to the stairs with him, her hand in his. "Why, Nic. How thoughtful."

He laughed. "I'm sure you'd be adorable in them. But nah. I went in a little different direction."

"Better not be red and black, or crotchless either," she warned him.

"Why don't you just be quiet, and let me show you what it is?" he scolded, pulling her through the door into his big bedroom. He went to the closet, pulled a pale blue box from the shelf, tied with a white ribbon. "Here." He handed it to her. "Happy bedwarming."

She sat on the gold satin duvet cover, pulled off the bow, opened the box and pulled back layers of tissue to find a short gown in the palest pearl pink silk. The bodice was made entirely of lace, and the same pale pink lace edged the hem and the edges of the side slits. She set the box aside and stood, holding the beautiful thing up to herself, looked into the mirrored closet doors at the halter neck, the deep V of the neckline.

"It's gorgeous," she breathed. "Is this real silk? It feels like it."

"Meant to be," he smiled. "How'd I do? Sorry it isn't red and black, or crotchless. Didn't know that was what you were expecting."

She wrapped her arms around him, still holding the gown. "It's brilliant," she told him fervently. "It's so pretty, and the silk feels so luxurious. I just need to try it on, make sure it fits."

"It should do. Because I had a wee look at some of your things, too, for the size," he confessed. "I didn't have a clue, other than that you're pretty small. And they'd have thought I was pervy, standing in the shop, holding out my hands to show how big you are." He demonstrated tracing her curves in the air. "But don't let me stop you trying on your bedwarming present, because I'd like to see it. Though you know I'm planning to take it straight off you again."

"I'm going to take a shower first," she said. "Wash my face. Too much crying. And I want to get pretty, and put lotion on, before I wear this." She reached for him, kissed him again. "I'll be back in a little while. Then I'll show you."

♡

He was waiting, sitting up in bed, bare chest brown against the white linens, when she reappeared in her dressing gown.

"You ready for this?" she asked, her hand on the tie.

"Ready and waiting," he assured her. He hitched himself up a bit further, watched her take off the flowered dressing gown and lay it on a chair.

"It fits perfectly, see?" she asked, smoothing her hand over the silk. "And it feels wonderful."

"You need to let me feel it too," he said, his eyes warm with appreciation. "But first, turn around, let me see the back."

"Well?" she asked, looking over her shoulder at him. He'd got out of bed, was standing behind her, pulling her against him, running his hand down the silk.

"Felt good in the shop," he said huskily. "But I reckon I needed to see it on the model to get the full effect. Because you're so damn beautiful."

He leaned down to kiss the side of her neck. "Too easy," he murmured against her skin, beginning to pull the gown up over her thighs with one hand, the other sliding inside the lace to cup a breast as he watched their reflection in the mirror.

"What is?" she asked breathlessly, her eyes drifting shut.

"You. All I have to do is say something like that, and you're mine."

"No." She opened her eyes to smile tenderly at his reflection, gave a long sigh as the gown fell to the floor in a drift of silk. Both his hands came up now to cover her breasts, to move over her, play with her as he watched in the mirror. When she was boneless and sighing against him, he finally sent one big hand on a leisurely journey down her body, drifting over her sides, her belly, before settling in at last to caress her.

"No," she repeated, arching back against him, barely able to support herself as his hands continued to move. Her legs parted under his touch, and the view in the mirror, the sight of his big hands holding her, moving over her pale skin, was doing as much for her as she could feel it doing for him. "All you have to do is look at me, and I'm yours."

He groaned, pulled her with him to the bed, lay on his back and lifted her over him. "I keep thinking I've got you. Then you say something like that, look at me the way you do. And I realize that you've got me."

He pulled her down to kiss her, finally settled her over him and began to move her, so slowly, for long minutes. Then turned her so he was on top, held her, caressed her, kissed her again and again as the heat built. Brought her up, step by slow step, watched her lose herself in him. And this time, it was her name he groaned out, in the end.

in the stands

♡

Emma woke to the sight of the charcoal-gray walls, the sound of the door opening.

"Morning," Nic said, sitting next to her and carefully setting down a steaming mug on the bedside table. "Brought you a coffee."

"Thanks." She hauled herself up and pulled an extra pillow behind her. "A coffee?" she realized. "Not a cup of tea?"

"I bought one of those K-Cup things yesterday," he confessed. "Because you're too exciting. If my nights are going to be this eventful, I decided I was going to need some serious caffeine."

"Ha. You thought *I* was going to need it, that's the real truth."

"Well, yeh. That too. You look just as pretty in that nightdress in the daylight, by the way. And I wish you'd stayed with me, last night. Because I'm not sure when Zack wakes up. Too late now." He gave a disgruntled sigh.

"What time is it?" she asked, taking another grateful sip of hot, milky coffee as she stretched out a knee to rub it against his side. He didn't disappoint, reaching for it and stroking her skin. And he'd even put honey in her coffee, she could tell, even though he shuddered every time she added it.

"A bit after seven," he said, letting go of her knee and standing up again with another sigh of regret. "I was about to use the gym, before breakfast. I really came in to ask if you wanted to join me."

"Sure. Let me get dressed, and I'll be right there."

♡

Half an hour later, she was beginning to realize that she was in for a serious workout. Nic was a demanding coach, keeping a critical eye on her form.

"You don't have to help me, you know," she said as he set down his bar to put a hand behind her lower back, another on her upper chest. He gently nudged her more upright before he picked up his own bar again and resumed counting off squats and dead lifts to the accompaniment of pumping music from the room's built-in speaker system.

"This is meant to be your workout," she went on breathlessly. "It's for you. I'm just...ugh...tagging along. And enjoying watching your...muscles flex."

"You're missing your class today," he pointed out, shifting his grip a bit on the heavy barbell he held across his back. "Twelve more. And this *is* for me, because I like looking at your bum while you do this. It's my entertainment."

"You do?" she asked as she bent over to perform the set of dead lifts he ordered next.

"Looks good that way too," he said, somehow keeping track of the count and the conversation while he watched her. "Just like that time I saw you in your class. Much better now that I know I get to touch it. And that's it," he finished, lifting his bar over his head and setting it down as the song ended. He grabbed a couple towels from the bar nearby, tossing one to her. "Shoulders next."

"Mum?" Zack came into the room in his new pajamas, hair sticking up in all directions in wild abandon.

"Morning, baby," Emma said, pulling him in for a hug and kiss. "You slept late."

Zack was looking at Nic's barbell with awed fascination. "Wow. That's *huge.*"

Nic laughed, gave his son's head a rub and reached to turn the music down. "Don't tell the forwards that. They'd fall about laughing. That's why the backs like to train together, avoid those embarrassing comparisons. You have a good night in your new bed? How'd that lower bunk suit you?"

"Good," Zack said, leaning close as Nic wrapped a sweaty arm around his shoulders.

"We're still working out for a while longer," Emma said. "Why don't you go brush your teeth and get your clothes on? Then you can go play in your tower, if you like, or come down here with your Tintin book while I finish. Breakfast soon, I promise."

"And, mate," Nic added. "You may want to check your shelves in that room, because I think there may be something on there now. I hate bare shelves." He gave the boy a wink that had Zack scurrying for the door again.

"New Lego set," Nic said at Emma's questioning look. "Something for here, for him to do this weekend." He picked up the barbell again, took off a plate from either side in preparation for the next group of exercises while she did the same. "It's a bit different," he said thoughtfully.

"What is?"

"Having a kid. Having to think about what he's going to do, so you can finish your workout."

She laughed. "*If* you get to finish. It's nice that he's six now and can do more for himself. But you're right. Your life isn't nearly as simple. Or as spontaneous."

"I'm discovering that," he admitted. "Elbows out. Lift to chest height," he demonstrated. "Twelve of these."

"Are you regretting taking it on?" she asked as she followed along.

"Nah. I said it was different. Not that it wasn't better."

♡

"That's a pretty picture," Nic said, coming back into the house with Zack after an afternoon rugby session. He leaned down to kiss the top of Emma's head as she sat cross-legged on the couch, her lap full of pale green skirt.

"What, me knitting? I don't look like your sweet granny?"

He laughed. "Not exactly. What're you working on now?"

She held up the large circular needle to show him. "A skirt for my sister."

"I like those…holes in it," he said.

"The lace pattern," she smiled. "Yeah, it's pretty, isn't it? I'm going to weave some silk ribbon through, in this horizontal band between the two main patterns. That's why I've made bigger openings there."

"How d'you do that? Make the holes?" he asked, coming to sit beside her.

"You really want to know?" she asked in surprise.

"Yeh. Why not?"

She demonstrated the pattern for him. "Looks tricky," he said.

"Yeah, lace can be. It's a challenge to pay attention, not to make a mistake. I can't knit lace during rugby games anymore. I end up with the pattern all over the place. And if I'm watching you, I can't knit at all."

"Another dream realized. I'm more fascinating than knitting. And we have an hour," he announced, glancing at his watch. "Before we need to head out to the pub, if we're not going to be rushed getting to the game."

"OK. I'll finish this row, then I'll get Zack and me ready," she promised.

Zack pulled at Nic's arm until his father bent over. "That's what she always says," the boy confided in a low voice. "But she takes a long time. We'll be *late*."

"Hey. I heard that," Emma protested. "I'm not saying I won't be rushing around at the end, but I *have* to finish my row."

"No worries," Nic smiled, watching her needles fly. "We'll be on time." Because they actually had an extra fifteen minutes. He had Emma's little issue with time sussed out by now.

♡

"Nice jersey, Zack," Reka said with a warm smile as the three of them edged into their seats in the stands well in advance of the start, thanks to Nic's strategic planning. "I see you've decided which team you're supporting tonight. Not turning up in a Boks jersey."

"This is the real All Blacks jersey," Zack told her seriously. "The new one, this year's. And I have All Black pajamas, and an All Black bedroom, at Nic's. I have *everything*."

"At Nic's, eh," Reka said, her gaze moving amongst the three of them, curiosity evident. Emma edged around her with a word and a hug, gave Hannah and Kate a quick kiss hello, enquired after Jenna and the baby.

"Yeh," Nic said, pulling Zack to him with an arm around his shoulders. "At my house. I see you've got to know my son, Reka. So you will've already learnt that he has good taste when it comes to sport."

All the women looked up at that, Nic saw with satisfaction. Well, if you had something to announce, telling Reka was the surest way.

She recovered quickly. "Go on down past Kate," she told Zack. "Show the other kids that flash new jersey. They have an extra flag for you, too. Brought it along especially."

♡

"I hope you don't mind that I won't be paying too much attention to you during the game," Nic told Emma as they settled down to await the teams' entry onto the field. "I need to keep a sharp eye out tonight, see how the Boks've decided to play us, as I'll be out there against them myself in a few weeks."

"No worries. I'm sure Reka will keep me company."

"I'm sure she will," he said with a smile. "I know that put you on the spot, but Zack needs to know, too. That I'm his dad, and I'm happy to tell anyone about it."

Emma had cravenly hoped that Reka would be too interested in the fast-moving game for further discussion. Pity tonight's referee was one of those who seemed to enjoy picking up every infraction. The game was a stuttering stop-start affair, interrupted by countless scrum resets and lineouts. Plenty of time for Reka to get a few questions in.

"Nic seems chuffed about Zack," was her first sally. "I wouldn't really have expected less of him, but I'm guessing it's been a bit complicated, with Claudia and all."

"Yeah," Emma agreed. "It was. Nic's been nothing but involved since he found out. He's done everything right, really, but it hasn't been easy."

"That's what broke off the engagement, eh. We all wondered, because she made a dead set at him from the start. It was hard to imagine her giving him the push. Which of them was it, in the end? *Was* it her? Or him?"

Emma wondered if she should say. But she knew what Reka was really asking, and she wanted to scotch that rumor from the start. "It was her," she said. "But not because of me," she went on hastily. "Nic and I hadn't...we didn't...I think they were having problems anyway," she finished lamely. "And then, Zack."

They fell silent for a few minutes, watching the game, until the referee blew the whistle for another scrum.

"So he told her he had a kid," Reka guessed. "And that was one hill too far."

"Yeah," Emma said with relief. "I think so."

"No loss," Reka said. Emma couldn't help a surprised burst of laughter, which had Reka joining in. "Just couldn't warm up to her," Reka confessed. "Nic's a sweetheart. He deserves someone better. Somebody warmer." Her glance was speculative again.

"She was beautiful, though," Emma said. "I only met her once, but I saw lots of pictures. She's stunning, and really intelligent, from what I hear. She's going places, I think."

"Huh," Reka sniffed. "I asked Hemi once, and he said, *too* perfect. He said, you want a girl you can rumple a bit." She grinned at Emma. "Sorry. That's my hubby talking."

Emma laughed, but she was glad when the teams went into the changing sheds at the break with the All Blacks up by a measly three points and she could turn to Nic again. He sat back with a frustrated sigh, a frown making an unusual appearance on his normally cheerful face.

"Bad?" she asked tentatively.

"Not getting any quick ball," he complained. "Their forward pack has us on the back foot, and we're not able to play any kind of expansive game. And all those penalties the ref is blowing, they're not helping a bit. All chop and change, not able to get into any kind of rhythm."

"Would it be better if you were there?" she asked.

He grinned suddenly. "I'd like to think so, wouldn't I? Because I always figure into it more when we play the Boks. I sometimes wonder why they don't move away a bit from that kick and chase strategy, but on the other hand, they have the best record of any team against the ABs, so you could say it works for them. Keep it amongst the forwards, keep us from playing our best game. Anyway, win or lose, you know you've played a match the next day."

"You mean you figure into it because they kick it away so much," she guessed, zeroing in on the part of his speech that had caught her attention. "And then you kick it back, or run it, or pass it to one of the wings, or whatever. Depending."

"Yeh." He smiled at her again. "Depending. Are you asking, depending on what?"

"Not right now," she decided. "I'll wait till you have time to really explain it, because I'm afraid you're going to have to be drawing me pictures."

"I'll just go get you a beer, then," he said. "If I'm going to be watching from the stands, may as well take full advantage and have a bev while I can." He leaned around her, touched Reka on the arm. "Can I get you something?" he asked her. "Or any of the others?"

Reka relayed the offer down the line, turned back to Nic. "A beer for Kate, she says. Nothing for Hannah. And definitely nothing for me. I'd just end up spending the second half queuing for the toilets. Thanks, though."

He looked a bit startled, and Emma laughed. "You're presuming too much pregnant-lady knowledge, Reka. It's your bladder," she explained kindly to Nic. "When you get that pregnant, the final trimester. The last three months," she translated. "The baby's pressing on everything, and you don't have much room in there."

She laughed again at the look on his face. "Go get the beers," she told him. "Escape before we start talking about hemorrhoids."

That had Reka laughing as well, and Nic scooting off in a hurry.

"He's facing a fair learning curve, I can see," Reka said, as Hannah and Kate leaned forward to join the conversation.

"What did we miss?" Kate asked, eyes sparkling. "Because I'll bet Reka's got it all out of you, Emma. Come on, catch me up."

"You're as bad as Reka, Kate," Hannah told her. "I swear, you're becoming Maori yourself. Show a little Pakeha restraint."

"I'm Italian," Kate complained. "That's already halfway to Maori. And the other half, Koti's been working on. You want restraint, go sit with Emma and be blonde and proper together. Leave Reka and me in the Fun Kids section. So Nic's ditched Cool, Capable Claudia, eh, Emma? Did he come to his senses, or did she decide she fit the role of Wicked Stepmother a little too well?"

"Kate!" Hannah gasped. "That's bad, even for you. That's going too far."

"Whoops." Kate looked chagrined. "Sorry, Emma. I do get carried away when I'm having fun."

"No worries." Emma had been laughing in spite of herself. "I already told Reka. I may as well tell you, too. It was Claudia's idea, as far as I know. And I don't know her, so I can't comment on her personality."

"But you and Nic are an item, eh," Reka asked.

Emma flushed. "Uh…"

"Poor Emma," Hannah protested. "Shift over, Reka. I *am* going to sit with her. We need some blonde power over here. Stop pestering her, you two."

"Can you check with Zack how he's doing, Kate?" Emma asked. "If he needs to use the toilet, or anything?"

Kate leaned over for a consultation, then turned back to Emma. "He says he already went. That Ariana took him, before the break."

"Oh, no," Emma said with shock. "I'm sorry. I should have asked sooner. I didn't realize they'd be wandering about on their own."

"Ariana loves it," Reka assured her. "Being the oldest, she thinks she's everybody's auntie. I'm going to have to watch out, or she's going to be taking over this one entirely." She wrapped a protective hand around the mound of her belly.

"She's a good little manager," Hannah told Emma. "Even at nine. Wonder where she gets that from."

"Oi," Reka protested. "We're *capable*. That's what we are."

All the women looked up as Nic edged down the row of seats again, handed Emma the tray with the beers. He leaned over to give her a quick kiss before sitting down himself. "In for a penny, in for a pound," he announced, looking at Reka with a laughing smile. "Because I know you were wondering."

♡

Emma twisted in the seat of the Lexus to check on Zack. "Asleep," she told Nic. "That was a lot of excitement, last night and today. He'll need a quiet day tomorrow, because school starts again on Monday, too. Maybe we should go on home in the morning."

"Why?" he asked. "Why can't we all have a quiet day? What would you be doing differently if you were at home?"

She considered. "Maybe having Graham over for a few hours."

"Well, why can't we do that? Ring his mum and ask, why don't you? I know Zack'd love to show him his tower. And I meant to ask you to go to the flat anyway tomorrow, pack a few more things. You could collect Graham then. I thought you and Zack could stay with me until I'm off to Aussie on Thursday."

"I have to go to work, though. And Zack has to go to school."

"And your point?"

She really couldn't think of one.

"It's not much more driving," he said. "And I'd be able to take Zack to school on Monday, collect him as well, give him a bit of a shorter day. You wouldn't even have to do as much. Rose'll be coming by every afternoon."

"*Every* afternoon?"

"Monday through Wednesday, yeh. She comes and does my washing, a bit of a shop, fixes me something for dinner, as well as cleaning."

"Wow. You have somebody to fix your dinner every night?"

"Weeknights, when I'm home. Because I have to eat right, and there are only a few things I know how to make," he confessed. "Can't have steak and salad every night, or scrambled eggs. Besides, I don't like cleaning, but I like it clean. What's a fella to do?"

He went on more seriously. "I'll be back at training on Tuesday, and off to Melbourne on Thursday, start that long stretch away. We don't have that much time. I'd like to spend as much of it as I can with you and Zack."

"It won't be that exciting," she warned him. "He's tired at the end of the day, and so am I. And if any of those days are too tiring, we may have some tears, a meltdown. Can you handle that?"

"I've already seen you cry," he pointed out. "I think you know I can handle it."

"I meant Zack."

He smiled. "I know you did. Whoever has a meltdown. Even if it's me. I can handle it."

the real thing

♡

It felt strange to be at home again once Nic had left for Australia. Back to the regular routine that had been their normal life, but that felt so flat now to her, and to Zack too, Emma suspected. Watching the game helped. Talking to Nic the next day, as the team were preparing to get on the plane for the flight to Argentina, helped more.

"Here's where he is," Emma explained to Zack after they'd rung off, pulling up a world map on the computer. "Here's us, in New Zealand, see? And here's Melbourne."

"In Aussie," Zack said seriously. "I know where that is."

"Right. Because you've been there."

"And then where does he go?" Zack asked.

"Here. A long, long, way. He'll have to fly past New Zealand again, see? And then all the way across the Pacific Ocean to Buenos Aires, in Argentina. Almost halfway around the world."

"Does it take a long time? Like Safa?"

"Even longer. Fifteen hours. That's a whole long day, from the time you get up in the morning, to the time you go to bed. That's how long."

"Do they do training, when they're going on the airplane?" Zack wondered.

She laughed. "I think that'd make the plane tip over. Not really," she hastened to add when he looked alarmed. "But there isn't room. No, they're tired anyway, after their game. They're resting from that, and putting ice on the sore places, probably, like Nic did on his ankle, remember? And sleeping, and eating, and watching some films."

"And *then* they do training. When they get there," Zack guessed.

"Yeah," Emma smiled. "They'll be doing heaps of training. I think you can count on that."

♡

The difference in time zones meant that Zack couldn't talk to his father during the long week while they waited for the game against Argentina, and they had to rely on the emails Nic sent. At last, though, it was Saturday noon in Auckland, Friday night in Argentina, and he called. Emma let Zack go first, then gratefully took the phone herself, the first time that week that she'd felt free to talk for more than a few minutes, the first time she hadn't been at work when Nic rang.

"How'd the Captain's Run go today? Are you guys ready, with the jet lag and everything?" she asked. "Are you all the way over it?"

"Yeh, it's been enough time now, and we feel pretty good. With the day you gain coming over here, it turns out that it's a long week. Coming back, losing the day, that'll be tougher."

"How do you win, though?" she wondered. "When you *have* been traveling, and you're playing in the other team's home stadium, and everything? Why does it work?"

"Because we're a bit better, maybe?" he asked with a smile in his voice. "No, seriously. A lot of it's conditioning, being fit enough. And good coaching, everyone being on the same page, doing his part on the pitch. And something you'd think would be a disadvantage, like travel, can work for you too, in a funny way."

"How? How could that be?"

"What really loses you footy games," he explained, "assuming you're fit enough, that you've trained enough together, that you have the players and the coaching, is looking past the week. It's not thinking it'll be hard, it's assuming it'll be easy. Do that, lose that mental edge, and you've lost the game before you've even started. The difference at the international level isn't that much. It's maybe five percent that separates teams. When you're talking about a few of the teams, the Boks, the Welsh, the French, the English, it's less than that. And any team can sting you, if you've let your guard down."

"So if you know it's hard…"

"Right. If you know it's going to be hard, if you've been traveling for three weeks, you can lift to overcome that. Never assume, that's the trick. And that can be hard to do, when everybody else—the journos, the public—thinks it'll be easy. Out here on the sharp end, we know it's never easy."

"It never looks easy to me," she said. "But then, I've seen you afterwards a few times now. So you aren't just a…a pinball out there. Not to me."

He laughed. "Glad I'm not a pinball. And it's good to know that you'll see me after this one, too. Just a few more days."

"I miss you," she sighed. "I can't wait to watch you tomorrow, but I miss you *now*."

"That's good. Because I miss you too."

"You do? You aren't too busy? Or just used to it?"

"You're joking, right? That's the hardest part of all, specially this trip. Leaving you and Zack, just when I want to be with you most. But that's what's better this time, too. It'll be so different flying back, knowing I have the two of you to come home to."

"When *are* you back?" she asked, warmth filling her at his words.

"Tuesday noon, about then. And it's off to Wellington again on Friday, ready to play the Wallabies next Sunday. It'll be a short week, like I said, which means they'll be rotating the squad a fair bit during both games. I told Zack I wouldn't be starting tomorrow, so he won't be disappointed. But can you bring him over after work Tuesday? Can the two of you stay, those few nights there before I'm off again?"

"Of course we can, if you want us to."

"Oh yeh," he said with a little laugh. "I want you to."

♡

Back and forth, then. The surging happiness when he came home, spending those paltry three nights together, then seeing him off to Wellington, welcoming him home a few days later. A brief Sunday afternoon before the work week began, and then he was off again, to Dunedin this time, to play the Springboks once more. Then, finally, the Championship won, and having time stretching before them at last.

"Seems funny, doesn't it," Nic said. They were sitting in the spa, decorously clad in their swim togs in deference to Zack, who'd spent a bare five minutes with them before declaring it "too hot and boring" and heading back into his tower to begin to put together the new Lego set Nic had brought him from Dunedin.

"What does?" Emma asked, lifting her legs to lay them on top of his under the bubbling water.

"Being so glad to have two weeks with you. Like our non-honeymoon, but in reverse, eh. You'll be going to work, and I'll be training, but just knowing you two will be here with me until I have to leave again for England..." He trailed off, picked up a foot in his hands and began to massage it. "That's pretty special."

"Mmm," she agreed with a blissful sigh. "I'm happy about it too. But you should let me do the foot massaging. You're the one who needs it."

"What I *need*," he corrected her, "is to put my hands on you. And since this is as far as I can go till tonight, I'm going to do this, for now."

♡

"Do you have Reka and Hemi's address?" she asked him later that afternoon. "I finished their baby present, and I want to send it off tomorrow."

"Course." He pulled out his phone, read off the address as she copied it down on the big mailing box. "Let's see how it turned out, then."

"Sure, if you really want to. It's the same as what I made for Jenna," she said, opening the gift box and carefully removing layers of tissue. "Pretty simple." She pulled out the little hat and sweater with their pink ribbon trim, the tiny matching booties.

"Aww," he said. "Those are really cute."

"The cream color's a bit problematic, of course, but at least spit-up's white. We'll just cross our fingers about the baby poo."

"They can't get poo on shoes, surely. Or sweaters."

She laughed. "Trust me, they can get it on *everything*. Even the hat may not escape. You've never seen a diaper disaster, I guess. But it's washable. Plus, with cream, I can just switch out the pink ribbons for blue and change the buttons from these flower ones, if they need it. Though Reka swears this is it. She says she's tired of having babies and Hemi not being there for them."

"Yeh, and four's a lot," Nic said. "But I wouldn't take any bets on that, all the same, because he's likely to be around after this. I know he's planning on retiring. Everyone wants to be part of the squad that wins the World Cup for New Zealand twice in a row, touch wood. He's held on for that these past four years, along with a fair few of the older fellas. But at some point once you're past thirty, your body's telling you that enough's enough. So, yeh, Hemi's had a good run, but I think it's coming to an end, and he'll be home. And besides, they're Maori. Even if they do decide to stop at four, there's bound to be a cousin to pass these on to." He ran a finger over the seed stitch pattern on the edge of the tiny sweater. "You're really good at this, aren't you?"

"Oh, baby things are easy. Everything's so small, it goes fast. And you can use better yarn, too, because it doesn't take much. This is cashmere, merino, and silk. Doesn't it feel nice?" she asked, fingering the sweater herself.

"Yeh, it does. I'm sure Reka'll love it."

"Thanks." She placed the little items carefully back in their box, wrapped the tissue paper around them and put the lid on again. "And thanks for indulging me and asking. I know it's a little estrogen-rich for you, admiring knitwear, talking about babies."

"I like it, though. I like your girly things."

"You do?" she asked doubtfully.

"Course I do. My life's pretty blokey, you know. I'm not interested in having a woman I can arm-wrestle, who's trying to prove she's tougher than me. I tried that," he admitted. "It didn't work out so well for me. I've decided I quite like indulging my soft side a bit. Especially when it wins me sensitivity points," he added with a grin.

"That makes it sound like you want me to be weak," she said slowly.

"That's not it," he hurried to explain. "I'm just saying you're different from me, and I like that. Because, you know, competition's for out there." He gestured toward the windows. "When I'm holding you, or kicking the footy with Zack, it's not about being tough, then. It's about the other side of me."

He shrugged with frustration. "I'm not saying this right. What I'm trying to say is, I like being with you. I like the way you look, the way you smell, the things you talk about. You remind me about that other side. And you make me feel good."

She reached up for him, pulled him down for a soft kiss. "I'm glad. Because you make me feel good, too."

♡

"D'you remember?" he asked while he was still holding her close, late that night. "When I told you I loved you, in Fiji?"

"Yes," she said, lifting her head from his chest to look up at him. "I remember."

"I thought I knew what that meant, then," he said. "How much I loved being with you, making love with you. How you made me laugh, made everything so much fun. Turns out I didn't have a clue."

"What do you mean?"

"If I'd felt then the way I feel now, I'd never have been able to leave you the way I did. Because it's so much more than that, isn't it?" He stopped, went on again slowly. "It's wanting to hang the wallpaper border for you, hold you when you cry. Having something funny happen at training, and thinking, I need to tell you about that. Wanting to come back to you when I'm gone."

"Bloody hell," he finished in exasperation. "I can never say what I mean. And this would be a good time to tell me you love me too." He scowled down at her. "I'm twisting in the wind here."

She reached out to trace those curved lines at the side of his mouth. Lines that had been faint, back then, were etched into his skin now by time, and work, and the countless hours of training in the sun and wind, and smiling. Smiling, most of all.

"Of course I love you," she said, her eyes shining with tears. "I did then, and I've never stopped. And you said it just fine. You said it perfectly. But it was more selfish back then for me, too. You're right about that. Some of what I thought was love was me looking for someone to...prop me up. To keep me from having to grow up by myself in the scary world. Maybe to keep from having to grow up at all. And now I know I can be in the scary world by myself, if I have to. But it's so much better with you. And if I haven't told you," she finished, "well, that's because the boy's supposed to say it first, everybody knows that. But I love you, and I'll tell you so. And I need to hear it from you too, if you can manage it."

"I can manage it," he promised. "To love you, and to tell you I do, too. Count on me for that."

a hell of a nerve

♡

"Sorry I wasn't ready," Emma apologized, stuffing a final pair of shoes into her suitcase and fastening the zip. "I had a little trouble getting dressed."

"Needed help, did you?" Nic asked. "Pity I wasn't here, then."

She laughed. "You're not the least bit helpful when I'm putting clothes *on*, and you know it. But seriously. Is this OK, for meeting your parents?"

He inspected the flouncy little flowered skirt, fine-knit cardigan, and tights that she was wearing with her low boots. "It works for *me*," he said. "Makes me want to unfasten some buttons." He reached for the sweater.

She slapped his hand away. "That's *not* the reaction I'm hoping for," she complained, a smile trying to escape her would-be stern expression. "Does it look...suitable?"

"Yeh," he said. "It looks suitable. You look pretty. I can't help it that everything you wear makes me want to undress you."

"All right," she said, blowing out a nervous breath and smoothing a hand down her side. "Zack, baby!" She ran lightly up the stairs, calling to him. "Time to go!"

"Are you ready, Mum?" Zack asked, coming down the staircase holding the banister with one hand, his Lego T-Rex in the other. "All the way ready?"

Nic laughed. "I think she's ready at last. C'mon, mate. Help me get this stuff to the car. You take this bag of…whatever this is, and I'll do my best to stagger out with your mum's suitcase. Good thing I've done some training."

"It's wine," Emma cautioned, unable to keep from laughing herself. "In the bag. So be careful, sweetie. And some chocolates as well. It's all I could think of to bring for your mum, Nic."

"She'll love them," Nic assured her, hefting her suitcase with a groan that had Zack giggling.

♡

"Is your dad really my grandpa?" Zack asked from the back seat when they were on the motorway. "My *real* grandpa?"

"Yeh," Nic assured him. "And my mum's your granny, too."

"I already have a grandpa and grandma, though," Zack pointed out. "So how can they be, too?"

"Everyone has two sets, baby," Emma explained. "Your mum's parents, and your dad's parents, remember?"

"Oh," Zack said. "Because Nic's my dad?"

"Yeh," Nic said with a smile for his son in the rear-view mirror. "That's it."

♡

"We were expecting you an hour ago," were the first words out of his dad's mouth when they arrived in Tauranga two hours later, both Nic's parents hurrying out of the house at the sound of the Toyota pulling into the driveway.

"My fault, I'm afraid," Emma said.

Nic gave his mum a quick kiss, then went to pull out their bags.

"Hi," Emma said, holding out her hand with a sunny smile. "I'm Emma, and this guy here is Zack."

Nic's mother took her hand in both her own and gave it a warm squeeze. "I'm so glad you're here. I'm Ellen, and Nic's dad is George. But you knew that, didn't you?" She laughed. "Sorry. I'm so excited, I barely know what I'm saying." She bent over, her hands on her knees, and smiled at Zack. "D'you know who I am?" she asked him. "I'm your granny! And do you know, you have such a look of your dad when he was a little boy. I've got a photo of him that's so like you, you wouldn't believe it!"

"I brought his baby book," Emma told her. "Nic thought you might like to see it."

"Wasn't that thoughtful of you," Ellen said, her pleasure evident. "I'll love having a look at that. I'll pull out those old photos of Nic, and we can compare them."

"Not the one of me naked in the bath, Mum," Nic said with exaggerated pain.

"Oh, we *especially* want to see that," Emma said. "Don't we, Zack?"

He giggled and nodded, and Ellen laughed again. "Come on into the house, then," she urged. "We'll have a lovely cup of tea and get to know one another properly."

His mother was a much safer landing spot for Zack than his dad, Nic thought with relief as he carried their suitcases inside.

"We've put you in your old room, of course, Nic," his mother said. "And we've popped Emma and Zack into Dan's bedroom, as it has the two beds."

Nic caught Emma's eye behind his mother's back and made a disappointed face that had her stifling a laugh in response. "Better plan on sleepwalking tonight," he murmured in her ear.

"When you're settled, come out and give me a hand with the garden, why don't you," George suggested.

"I don't mind," Nic said with relief. Working with his dad was the most congenial way to spend time with him, he'd long found.

"You two do that," Ellen said. "Emma and Zack are going to come have a chat with me while I make a pudding for tonight. And maybe you'll want to lick the bowl for me, eh," she told Zack with a conspiratorial smile.

"Yeh!" Zack agreed enthusiastically. "That's my favorite! What kind of pudding will it be?"

"Sticky date. Because that's your *dad's* favorite. Come into the kitchen with me and help me get started, then."

"When's Dan coming?" Nic asked his dad, heaving Emma's suitcase onto one bed and dropping Zack's little satchel onto the other.

"Dinnertime," George replied in some disgust. "I asked him to come by earlier and give me a hand, but he's off somewhere with a mate."

"Good job I'm here, then," Nic said. "And you're not allowed to run off with my brother," he told Emma. "Because he's the handsome one."

"I think I already know which one I like better," she said, smiling back at him.

"Good. I'm holding you to that. You OK if I leave you with my mum for a bit?" he asked, taking hold of one of her curls and rubbing it between his fingers.

"Your mum doesn't seem too scary. You go ahead and help your dad. I'll be fine," she said, so he gave her a quick kiss and reluctantly left her to it.

"What did you have in mind?" he asked his father when they were in the big, neatly arranged garage.

"Time to cultivate the vegie garden," George said. "I borrowed Geoff Harris's tiller for the weekend. Hope you've brought your work boots."

"Yeh, I did. Let me get them out of the ute. I'll be glad of the loan of a pair of gloves, though."

One thing you could say about his dad, Nic decided a few minutes later, having hauled the rototiller into the garden and looking over the vegetable bed, he did keep a tidy garden. The expanse of grass extended into the neighbors' plots on either side, which had given him plenty of room to practice kicking as a kid, but the row of hedges at the back was as neat and regular as ever. Closer to the house, trees, ferns, and flax plants existed in harmony with the rhododendrons and azaleas his mother loved.

He bent his attention to his task, setting the choke and starting up the heavy tiller, enjoying the exertion of working his way down the length of the plot and back again. Meanwhile, his dad took the wheelbarrow and hauled bags of soil amendments from the shed, began to rip them open and distribute the contents over the areas Nic had tilled in preparation for the second go.

They worked in harmony for an hour or so, conversation brief and limited by the roar of the machine. Finally, though, Nic pulled it to the side of the big plot and shut it down. His dad handed him a hand cultivator, and they set to work breaking down the larger dirt clods left by the machine.

"Looks like you're getting on well with Zack these days," his dad said after they had worked in silence for a while.

"Yeh. They've both been staying with me, whenever I'm home. And they're nice to come home to, I'll tell you that."

"Seems like you got involved with Emma pretty fast, after the break with Claudia," his dad pointed out.

"A month or so," Nic agreed, willing himself to stay calm. "But then, I fell in love with Emma a long time ago. Falling in love again wasn't too hard at all."

"I can see she's a good time," George said. "But it takes more than that, you know."

Nic had never come closer to hitting his father. He turned away, walked a few steps toward the back of the garden, still clutching the cultivator, and stood staring unseeingly at that neatly trimmed hedge. He took some deep breaths, deliberately loosened his grip on the tool, and finally turned to face George again.

"If you ever say something like that again," he told his father, his voice quiet, "that's the last you'll see of me."

"What?" George asked in genuine surprise. "Just trying to give you the benefit of my experience."

"I've had more experience than you could even dream of," Nic told him bluntly. "I sure as hell don't need the benefit of yours."

"You've gone potty on this girl, that's what it is," George argued. "I would've thought that by now, you'd know how to avoid the ones who're looking for a sportsman with a bit of lolly. Now, Claudia—"

"I think I know which of the two of them was more interested in my money, and what being with me could do for her. Who wanted to be taken to flash restaurants. Who insisted I buy that house that's too big for me, then spent all that money doing it up. Who walked out on me the minute she was asked to front up, as soon as things stopped being comfortable. So don't talk to me about gold-diggers," Nic said, talking straight over his father's attempt to interrupt. "Because my experience in that area is the same as in the other. A hell of a lot more than yours."

♡

They'd finished the rest of the job in silence, Nic glad of the opportunity to take his frustration and anger out on the dirt clods. But even the largest garden plot eventually got tilled. His father made a few gruff remarks as they put the tools away, and Nic went inside to shower and change, then sought refuge in the kitchen with the rest of his family.

Fortunately, Dan put in an appearance before too long and, as always, his easy, laughing presence helped dissipate the tension between his father and older brother. Nic found himself relaxing over dinner, encouraged to share stories about training in rugby-mad Argentina and playing before the raucously enthusiastic crowd in La Plata.

"I looked up when we came out of the tunnel," he said with a grin, "saw all these blokes holding oranges. I thought, good on them for eating such healthy snacks. Didn't realize they meant to chuck them at us."

"They *threw* them at you?" Emma asked with shock.

"Didn't hit us. Splattered around a bit, that's all. But they're good buggers. They support their own team, and they're passionate about it. They could give a few lessons to those polite En Zed crowds. But all the same, they stood up and gave us an ovation for our performance when we came off the field. They've been chuffed to play in the Rugby Championship, to get the chance to lift their own game. And they may not be at the top level yet," he said seriously, "but you discount them at your peril. They'll give a good account of themselves at the World Cup. Because they play, like they say?" He thumped his chest with a fist. *"Con corazón."*

♡

"Emma and I'll do the washing-up, Mum," he said when his mother stood at the end of the meal to clear plates. "Least I will," he said with a glance at Emma. "Maybe I shouldn't be volunteering you, eh."

"Of course you should," she smiled back at him.

"We've got quite good at it," Nic told his mother. "Become a team, haven't we, as she doesn't have a dishwasher."

"Oh, that takes me back," Ellen said sympathetically. "I can still remember when I first got one. And the old days without it, when it seemed like I spent half my life with my hands in the suds."

"Well, it isn't that bad," Emma said. "It's just Zack and me. And Nic, sometimes, but he helps, so that doesn't count."

"Hope you don't mind," Nic said when they were alone in the cozy kitchen, filling up that same dishwasher and scraping out serving plates.

"Of course not," Emma said. "It gives me a chance to talk to you. Your mum's really nice, but I can't help being a little nervous about what she thinks of me, after Claudia."

"You'd never get her to compare," he said, "but if you could read her mind, I'd bet any money that you'd win."

"Really?" she asked doubtfully.

"Really." He smiled down at her. "Besides, you come with a ready-made grandchild, don't you. Contest's over right there."

She laughed. "You could be right about that. You'll notice Zack's perfectly happy to be left with her."

"He's no fool," Nic agreed. "Bet he's getting an extra chocolate out of her right now."

They finished, were wiping down surfaces. "And one more thing," he said. He brought his dishcloth around to her side of the room, stealthily wiping closer and closer until he finally gave up the pretense, set it down, and put his arms around her from behind, pulled her into him. He bent his head to the side of her neck and kissed her there. "Have I mentioned that you're pretty?"

"Mmm," she said, leaning back into him. "I don't think you have. Maybe you could tell me now."

"Yeh," he sighed, turning her around and pulling her close for a proper kiss. "You're pretty, and you look so cute twitching round in that little skirt. If we weren't quite so well chaperoned, I'd be flipping that skirt up right now and showing you a thing or two."

He was working on telling her a few more things when the kitchen door opened with a bang to admit Dan.

"Whoops," his brother said with a laugh. "I didn't realize there was so much action in here. I've clearly been in the wrong room."

"What d'you want?" Nic asked, turning his head but not releasing Emma. "I'm busy here."

"Yeh, bro. I see that. Came for a beer, and one for Dad as well."

Nic stepped away from Emma reluctantly, opened the refrigerator and pulled out two beers. "Here. Go."

"Geez, Nic. Have a heart. Let me at least *talk* to her. Some of us poor lonely blokes don't even *have* a girlfriend, never mind a hope of landing one this pretty. What could possibly have interested someone like you in this ugly bugger?" he demanded of a laughing Emma. "When there are so many better choices out there, like, say, me?"

"Get your own girl," Nic told him with a mock-scowl. "This one's mine."

"Afraid so," Emma said, her eyes dancing. "Nic was right—you *are* the handsome one. Too bad he's got me under his wicked spell."

"Tell me you have a sister," Dan begged.

"I have a sister. And she has a partner too, so I'm afraid my family's out. It *is* a pity that you don't have any looks or charm of your own to rely on. I guess you're destined to remain lonely forever."

Dan heaved a heartfelt sigh. "Well, if he doesn't treat you right, you know where I live."

"Sorry. I make it a point these days not to fall in love with more than one brother at a time. I find it makes my life so much less complicated."

"Out," Nic said sternly, opening the door and giving his brother a shove. "Let me finish kissing my girlfriend in peace."

♡

Pity he couldn't do that for the entire evening, Nic thought. Luckily, Dan stayed another hour and kept the conversation lively. At last, though, he got up to leave.

"I'll walk out with you," Nic told him. He waited while Dan said goodbye to Emma with a brotherly kiss on the cheek and a laughing glance in his direction. Emma took the opportunity to whisk Zack off for a bath, and the two brothers walked out to Dan's car.

"Thanks for coming by," Nic said with real gratitude. "I already had a moment today when I was ready to load everybody up and head back to Auckland. You saved me for another day. Wish I could laugh it off like you do, but…" He shrugged. "Can't, that's all."

"Yeh, nah," Dan said, leaning against the car and tossing his keys in his hand. "It's easier for me, that's why. All the expectation's on you, isn't it. He's so proud of you, that's what makes him push so hard."

"Is *that* it," Nic said wryly. "And here I thought it was the opposite. Seems like nothing I do is ever good enough. If I score a try, he wonders why I didn't score two. Good job Drew's got the captaincy locked up, and they'd never select a back anyway, or he'd be wondering how I'd failed at that."

"I don't know why he thinks he has to keep on like that," Dan agreed. "Not much further for you to go, is there."

"Yeh," Nic said. "Anyway, good to see you."

"I'll be barracking for you, next couple months, you know that," Dan told him. "Good luck over there. You're a bloody hard act to follow, but you're not bad as a brother, all the same."

"Cheers," Nic said with a grin.

"And all joking aside," Dan added. "Zack and Emma? You're a lucky man."

"All joking aside," Nic said, "I know it."

♡

"When's the announcement of the squad for the Cup?" George asked the next morning as they sat over a cup of tea.

"Tomorrow," Nic answered.

"Has Pete talked to you?" George pressed.

"Yeh. Anyway, I'm in form. I wasn't expecting to be left behind. Doesn't mean I'll be starting every game, though."

George grunted. "I would've felt better about it if you hadn't started from the bench those first two matches after you came back."

"Resting my ankle," Nic explained. "Giving me a chance to ease back in. I wasn't the only one rested, and I won't be the last. It's a matter of rotation, giving the new caps, and the boys without much experience, a chance to get a feel for the pace of test footy, in case they're needed. The World Cup, on top of the Championship—that's a big ask. You'll see the Skipper rested, is my guess, during one or two of the pool games, the ones against the minnows. And that almost never happens."

Time to change the subject. "Want to go into the back garden, kick the ball a bit with me?" he asked Zack. He was feeling tense and edgy, the way he always did after a day with his dad. It was even worse this time, because he could tell Zack was feeling the same way. He was subdued this morning, and had been slow to eat his Weet-Bix at breakfast, a sure sign of distress. Running around would help both of them.

"Yeh," Zack said with relief.

"Run and get a warm jersey on, then," Nic instructed, getting up and putting his teacup into the dishwasher. "Want to join us, Emma?"

"No thanks," she smiled. "I think my kicking's beyond hope. Anyway, your mum thinks she can teach me to make an apricot slice. I'm not much of a baker, but I'd like to learn."

"I'll come," George said, wiping his mouth and standing up from the table. Ellen whisked his cup away, and Nic wondered for the thousandth time if it would kill his dad to help out a bit around the house, and then realized with dismay what his dad had said. So much for his plan to get himself and Zack out from under that critical eye for a bit.

"Run on down to the end of the garden," Nic instructed Zack once they were outside. "We'll give you a bit of work under the high ball."

"Your technique's looking a bit dodgy off the right foot," George commented after watching a number of Nic's easy kicks back to his son. "I was noticing it looked different, these last games."

"I've changed it a bit," Nic said. "Lets me get the ball away faster."

"Sure it's a good idea to change up now?" George asked.

"If I weren't, I wouldn't be doing it," Nic answered shortly. Despite his best efforts to control it, his temper was beginning to fray.

He called Zack back. "Passing practice," he told him. "Want to help out here, Dad?"

"I don't mind," George said.

The three of them set off, tossing the ball behind them, then letting the ball carrier run ahead to pass back in his turn. All went well for a while, until Zack's pass to George went awry. The older man reached for it, but couldn't pull it in. He stopped running with a curse, went back for the ball. "Got to look where you're passing it," he snapped to Zack.

"Sorry," the boy said, looking chastened at the tone.

"Never mind," Nic said. "Start again." This time, Zack was the one who missed George's pass, which had been a bit high for his six-year-old frame.

"Focus!" George barked. "Watch the ball! Watch my arm!"

Zack's lip was trembling, and Nic quickly started him running in the opposite direction, caught his wobbly pass with ease, then sent it back to him again. If his dad was going to be that much of an arsehole, he could just stay out of it.

Zack, though, was thoroughly rattled by now, and his return pass to Nic was far off the mark. Nic got a hand on it, but couldn't pull it in, had to jog over to pick it up out of one of the flax plants at the edge of the wide expanse of grass.

"Thought you'd been working with him," George accused. "You had a more accurate arm than that by the time you were five."

"You've got him doubting himself, is why," Nic shot back.

"He needs to harden up, then," George insisted, "if a suggestion or two can do that to him. Because he's bloody useless this morning."

"Dad. He's right here," Nic warned.

"So?"

"So quit telling him what he's done wrong, or to harden up!" Nic snapped, completely exasperated now. "You're not helping!" He put an arm around Zack, who was openly crying by this time.

"Big kids like you don't cry," George told his grandson. "And why shouldn't I coach him, just like I did you? I try to give you both the feedback you need, and all I get is agro for it. When did you get so soft that you couldn't take a bit of criticism?"

"Right. That's it. That's enough," Nic decided. "Mate," he told Zack, handing him the ball, "go on back inside and see your granny. Maybe she'll give you a bit of that apricot slice, when it's done." He reached a thumb down, wiped the tears from Zack's eyes. "Oi," he said softly. "It's OK. Just give me a sec, and then I'll be coming in too."

Zack nodded and trudged off with the ball after one final scared look at his grandfather. Nic turned back to his dad. Time to put him right. Well past time.

"When I'm out there on the paddock, under the high ball," he began, "that's a pretty lonely place. I have to back myself. The last thing I need out there is doubt. I have heaps of people to give me advice. I don't need an earbashing from you after every match. Or to have your voice in my head every time I miss a tackle, telling me I'm not good enough."

"Watch how you're talking to me," George began to bluster.

"Nah, Dad." Nic interrupted his father again. He'd never done that before this weekend, and now he wondered why not, because it felt damn good. "Watch how you're talking to *me*. And how you talk to my son, if you want to keep seeing either one of us."

He saw the shock, and went on all the same. "I spent half my life with you telling me to harden up," he told his dad. "Right, now I have. And if I think Zack needs any help learning how to be a man, I'm here to give it to him. He doesn't need your criticism. He doesn't need your disapproval. What he needs is your love."

"What kind of a pussy are you trying to make him?" George asked incredulously. "How's he going to turn out with that kind of soft attitude?"

"Like a decent man, I hope. A good New Zealander. A loving son to his mum. A good mate. And yeh, he'll harden up. Heaps of time in his life for him to learn that, and for me to teach him. It's not your job, and I'm not going to let you do it. Because the way you do it hurts, and I'm not going to let you hurt my son."

"You're telling me I *hurt* you? That's your gratitude for everything I've done? If it hadn't been for me pushing you, you'd never even have made the Super 15, let alone the All Blacks. Have you forgotten all the times I worked with you? How many hours I spent practicing with you?"

"Nah, Dad," Nic sighed. "I haven't. And I'm grateful for it. Just like I know that you did the things you did, said the things you said, because you thought I needed to hear them. That you were trying to make a man of me."

"Too right I was," George grunted, barely mollified.

"But I *am* a man now," Nic said. "Time for you to see it. I'm a pretty damn good footballer, too, and I know a hell of a lot more about rugby than you do. And I'm a father as well. I can take care of myself, and I can take care of my family. I don't need you to tell me how to live my life, how to do my job, how to choose a woman to love, how to raise my son."

He saw the danger signs, the vein bulging in his father's temple, his face reddening, and plowed on regardless. "I want you in my life, Dad. I want you in Zack's life. But it's going to be on my terms, or it's not going to happen. And here's what they are. You'll treat Emma with respect. Not asking you to love her, though I can't imagine why you wouldn't. She's a bloody fantastic person, and she's done a damn good job of raising her son without any help from me, the help she should have had. I'm going to do everything I can to make it up to her, because she deserves it. And as for Zack? You can either be a decent grandpa to him, or you can not see him at all. Your choice. No telling him to harden up. No suggestion that he isn't good enough, strong enough, tough enough for you. If he needs any criticism, or any discipline, that'll come from his mum, or me."

"You've got a hell of a nerve," his father said, his face purple with rage now.

"Yeh, I have," Nic told him levelly. "Finally. I'll say goodbye to Mum, and we'll be off. We won't be staying for lunch. Let me know what you decide."

He left his father standing there, staring after him. Turned and walked back to the house without another word.

a bolt from the blue

♡

"You all right?" Nic asked.

"Yeah." Emma turned her head briefly to smile at him. She'd taken the morning off work to drive him to the airport for the long journey to London, and the World Cup. Nic had driven Zack to school earlier so they could say their own private goodbye. Now it was just the two of them, this final half hour in the car.

"I know it's a hell of a long time," he said now. "Eight weeks. But I'll ring you every morning I can, talk to you before you go to bed. Not as good as being there with you, but it's the best I have to offer."

"I'll take that," she told him seriously. "And we'll get to watch you, remember. That'll help. It's not like you're being deployed. We'll talk to you, and we'll watch you, and we'll be here supporting you. The rest of the team too, of course," she added. "But mostly you."

"Soon as I'm back," he said, "we'll go on that holiday, take some time together. With Zack too."

"Are you telling me," she asked him gently, "or convincing yourself? I'll be here, Nic. We both will."

♡

For all her brave words, it *was* hard without him. The phone calls helped, and the emails and photos they exchanged. And watching

him throughout the four rounds of pool play, the All Blacks winning all their games as predicted in this eighth World Cup, the
expectations stratospheric for the reigning World Champions. But
by the time the team had won their quarterfinal match to secure
their spot in the semis, Emma's longing had become a physical ache.

"You looked so good," she told him on the phone late Sunday
night. "You did so well."

"And how d'you know that?" he asked, the smile in his voice
coming through clearly.

"Zack said," she admitted. "And the commentators too,
about how you did. But how you *looked?* That was all me."

He laughed. "Didn't realize it was all down to how I filled
out the jersey. Here I thought I was meant to be playing well."

"If I were a selector, it'd be all about the jersey. And I miss
you. At the weekends especially, with Zack, we both do. And at
night, like now?" She sighed. "I *really* miss you."

"Miss you, too. I look at the photos on my phone before I go to
sleep. That one of us doing the backbend? That's my favorite. But
I'm wishing I had something better to remember you by, at night."

"Want me to send you something?"

"Yeh. I would. Maybe a photo you wouldn't want to put in
an email? Something like that."

"What, take it in front of the mirror?"

"Yeh, that'd work. That'd be choice."

"I'm not going to send you some porn shot. No...major body
parts. That'd just be icky."

"Not asking for a porn shot. But if there were a bit of skin there...
I wouldn't mind that, would I. I wouldn't mind seeing that at all."

♡

Nic saw the red light blinking on the hotel phone as he and Koti
James came into the room after dinner on Thursday. Koti picked
up the handset, punched buttons to listen to the message.

"Parcel at Reception," he informed Nic. "And sadly, it isn't for me."

A moment earlier, Nic had been looking forward to having a bit of a lie-down, watching a film on his laptop. But now, he grabbed his keycard and headed to the lift. He collected the flat, thin parcel from the reception desk with a word of thanks and began to open it in the lobby, then checked himself. If it was what he was hoping, he was going to need privacy for this.

Five minutes later, he was on the phone, a huge, stupid grin on his face.

Three rings, then Emma's cautious voice on the other end. "Nic?"

"Hi," he said. "You at work?"

"Yeah. Let me go out into the passage." Thirty seconds of silence, and her voice again. "OK. I can talk now."

"Got your parcel." He laughed. "That was bloody brilliant. That'll do me."

"You liked my photo, then?"

"Loved your photo. Very artistic. Loved the candlelight. Gave me some good ideas, for when I'm home again. But what gave me even better ideas?" He rubbed the silvery lace of the filmy underwear between his fingers. "That other item you put in."

"I was hoping it might bring back some memories," she said, her voice sounding a bit breathless now. "I'm living on those memories, myself. And I need a little refresher."

"I'll give you a refresher," he assured her. "Give you more than that, in another week or two. That's a promise."

♡

Three days later, their playful conversation was the last thing on Emma's mind as she sat beside Zack on the couch and anxiously scanned the screen in front of her for Nic's number 15. Fewer than fifteen minutes remained in the semifinal match that would determine the team to face the Springboks in the final. Churches were reported to be nearly deserted in favor of this game, being played on Saturday night in England and shown live here in New Zealand on Sunday morning. Rugby was New Zealand's real national religion, the old joke went, and Emma knew from the frenzy of the last World Cup just how true that was.

Today, the French side was testing that staunch Kiwi faith in their national team. After playing the entire tournament like a disorganized mob who seemed to have got their wins on pure luck, the French had chosen this occasion to put together their strongest performance. The forwards in particular were surging, wrapping up the New Zealand side, not allowing the backs to break the line or play their expansive game. Nic's play had been solid, but the French lockdown had meant a lack of spectacular moments from him, too.

The All Blacks, in fact, didn't seem to be firing on all pistons. It was what Nic had said, Emma suspected as her tension mounted. For all the effort she knew the team had put into mental preparation, they had allowed themselves to relax a bit too much, to look past this game to the final. There had been too many missed tackles, and two rare misses on penalty kicks from Hemi had left six points on the field. The score was tied at 12 all, and the French had the ball.

The All Blacks *couldn't* lose now, Emma thought in despair. Being knocked out by the French again, after the heartbreaking defeats of World Cups past—that would be too cruel.

The ring of her mobile startled her. She glanced at it. Lucy. Why on earth would she be ringing now? She had to know that they'd be watching the game. She picked up the phone, keeping her eyes on the screen. "Luce. We're *watching.* Is it an emergency?"

"It's urgent. Have you seen the Sunday *Herald?*"

"What? How can that be urgent? I'll ring you back when this is over," Emma said hurriedly as bodies piled into the ruck and the announcers' voices rose. "I've got to go."

She tried without success to make sense of what was going on. "What happened?" she asked Zack.

"The French knocked on," Zack said. "We get a scrum." He was clutching Raffo tightly around the neck with both hands, squeezing in his tension.

The scrum was clean, and the All Blacks forwards were holding the French back, giving the backs quick ball. Emma checked the time. Ten minutes. She could see the pattern being set up on the open side, four players running together. At last, a flicking pass to Koti James, the big centre. Koti plowing through one defender as if he weren't there, sidestepping two more. And finally putting on a burst of speed that left the chasing French behind, diving across the try line at the corner, arms outstretched, a grin on his face, as the stadium exploded. And Zack and Emma, together with most of New Zealand, leaping from the couch, jumping and shouting.

Hemi's kick was straight between the posts this time despite the difficult angle, and suddenly New Zealand was seven points up, with six minutes left to run on the clock. The French gave it a game effort, but there was no way, Emma saw, that the All Blacks were giving up this game now. They tackled like men possessed, Drew Callahan forced another turnover, and then it was the All Blacks' ball, and they were plowing forward, meter by meter, until at last, mercifully, time was up. One last kick into touch by Hemi and the game was over, the All Blacks advancing into the final, and the French going nowhere but home.

Emma and Zack were hugging again, Zack laughing, Emma crying. She could hear, even from the back of the house, the shouting and cheering filling the morning air as neighbors came outside to celebrate. The relief was as great as the tension had been.

"If the final's like that," she sighed at last, sitting back on the couch with a thump and wiping her streaming eyes, "I'm not sure my heart can take it. Maybe I'd better not watch."

"*Mum,*" Zack said with alarm, "you *have* to watch! It's Nic!"

She laughed shakily. "I'm just talking, baby. I'm going to be watching. But I'm afraid it's going to be just this tight. I was hoping, yesterday, that Wales would win. South Africa...that's going to be an awfully tough match, on top of this one."

"They can do it," Zack assured her. "They can do *anything.*"

A knock at the door had Emma hurrying to answer. Lucy stood there, the Sunday paper in her hand.

"I came as soon as the game was over," her sister said, no smile on her face. "I need to show you this."

Emma laughed. "Aren't you even happy? They *won,* Luce! They're going to the final!"

"I need to show you this," Lucy repeated, going into the kitchen and spreading the paper on the table. "Here. I'm going to go talk to Zack, get him distracted with something else."

Emma sat down, looked where Lucy had pointed. A photo of an attractive middle-aged woman she didn't recognize, holding a large framed photo. Of Nic and Claudia, she realized. And then the headline. *Nic Wilkinson's double life.*

She began to read, her heart sinking further with every word.

> Even close friends were stunned when one of New Zealand's most prominent and glamorous couples, rugby heartthrob Dominic Wilkinson and his gorgeous bride-to-be, lawyer Claudia Parker, announced recently that their longstanding engagement was off. For the first time, the *Herald on Sunday* can reveal the reason behind the shock split: Wilkinson's double life with his longstanding mistress and their six-year-old son.
>
> Elizabeth Parker, Claudia's mother, has shared her story with the *Herald* in an effort to quell rumors that Wilkinson initiated the

breakup. "Nothing could be further from the truth," Mrs. Parker insists. "Nic begged Claudia to stay. But when she knew what he really was, and the secrets he'd been keeping all this time, she really had no choice but to go."

Turns out that All Black stalwart Nico, as he's known to his teammates, isn't just popular with rugby supporters. The handsome fullback is a hit with the ladies as well—and according to Mrs. Parker, he hasn't been shy about spreading his attentions around, especially when on the road with the Blues and All Blacks.

The final straw came when his fiancée discovered that Wilkinson had a six-year-old son he'd never acknowledged nor supported—and that he had continued to maintain a relationship with the boy's mother, 27-year-old Emma Martens. While Wilkinson reportedly spent hundreds of thousands doing up a posh house on the North Shore, his son and the boy's mother have been living in substandard conditions in a shabby basement flat nearby.

"Why any woman would be willing to stay involved with somebody under those circumstances, somebody who wasn't even willing to support the child they had together, I have no idea," Mrs. Parker says. "Fortunately, Claudia has more self-respect than that. As soon as she learned of the boy's existence, and Nic's involvement with his mother, my daughter called a halt."

"I can't help but feel sorry for that boy," Mrs. Parker notes. "He didn't ask for the parents he got. Who knows, maybe Nic will step up to his responsibilities, now that everyone knows what he really is. I can only hope that public shame will force him to do what his own conscience couldn't."

The article went on to say that the newspaper wasn't naming the child in question, due to concerns for his privacy.

"Some help," Emma said when Lucy returned to the kitchen, after giving her time to read the damning article twice more. She could barely speak for fury. "My name's in there. How hard is that going to be, for people to figure out who the kid is? And how could she *say* that? I can't believe Claudia told her that. Surely it can't be what *she* believes. Nic said he told her even before we got the blood tests. That's why they broke up, because of his wanting to pay for Zack, and get involved with him! So how could she *say* that?"

"Are you sure it's not true about the other women, though?" Lucy asked. "He sure took up with you fast, in the beginning. And this latest time too, for that matter."

"What evidence does she offer for that?" Emma flashed back. "For his seeing other women? Absolutely *none.* I took up quickly with *him*, too, both times. Does that mean I'm some kind of slut?"

"No." Lucy backed off. "No, of course not."

"Well, neither is Nic. I don't believe a word of it. It's all innuendo, taking a little bit of truth and twisting it so it sounds just as bad as possible. I'd like to kill that woman. How could she do this to him? How's he supposed to defend himself against this?"

"Uh…she's done something to you, too," Lucy pointed out. "You're named in here, Em."

"So?" Emma asked fiercely. "Are my family and friends going to believe this? Did you? Did you read it and think, my, I never knew my sister was such a spineless tramp?"

"And what about Zack?" Lucy asked quietly.

"Yeah," Emma said, sobered now. "That's the worst, isn't it? But his friends aren't big *Herald* readers," she said, rallying. "And he *isn't* named. And anyway, it isn't *true.* Nic *is* paying the maintenance, and he *has* acknowledged Zack. We're not going to let this beat us, or let it beat Nic either."

the heart of a lion

♡

Despite what she'd told Lucy, Emma found herself sick with anxiety after her sister left. This wasn't going to do Nic's previously sterling reputation the least bit of good, or help his endorsement contracts, either. She knew how quickly the New Zealand public could turn on a sportsman, an All Black in particular. Members of the national rugby team weren't just supposed to be the best at the game, they were meant to behave like champions off the field as well. There was no tolerance for anything less.

Why did he have to be so far away, and the time so different? He'd just played a brutally difficult match, she reminded herself. He'd be sleeping. She'd have to wait until late evening, morning his time, to talk to him, that was all. She didn't have anything to ask him anyway. But she'd like to have heard his voice all the same.

She decided to clean the flat. She needed to move, and that was as good a way as any. When vacuuming and dusting, scrubbing the tub weren't enough, she attacked the worn lino on the kitchen floor with a scrub brush and a vengeance, working on her hands and knees until it shone. Her flat was too small for any really satisfactory release of energy, but at least it was clean now.

After resisting for hours, she finally gave in to temptation and looked at the story online, read the public comments that followed the article. And was immediately sorry she had. Her spirits plummeted further as she saw that fully eighty-six New Zealanders had already taken the trouble to weigh in on the topic, even in the face of a major World Cup victory. Any hope she'd had that Nic's performance in today's semifinal would have lessened the ire towards him was quickly dispelled.

"Disgusting sense of entitlement." "Those boys are paid well to be role models. If he can't even behave with common decency, the All Blacks don't need him." "What's wrong with our national values when this kind of thing is acceptable?" And those were some of the more measured remarks. Screen after screen of them, almost all negative. The least vitriolic merely unconcerned. "He's a sportsman, not a Boy Scout. Who cares what he does off the field?" Nobody seemed to have any problem at all believing the rumors.

Next came the concerned call from her parents. They too were quick to believe the story, she found. To believe anything bad about Nic, despite her earlier explanations, her assurances now that the allegations were false.

"He's made four maintenance payments so far," she reminded them. "And that big back payment too, which was all him. He had no obligation to do that. And here's what I want to know. Should I ring the paper and tell them?"

"You'll just draw more attention to it," her mother counseled. "Why pour fuel on the fire? You can't be popular right now, being cast as the other woman, breaking up that relationship, and they aren't going to believe you. The whole thing is going to be bad enough for Zack. Let it die down. Let it go, and it'll become yesterday's news."

"But it's not fair," she protested. "Nic hasn't done anything wrong. How can I sit here and let people attack him like that?"

"Life isn't fair," her mother said. "You know that. You're talking like a child."

"What does that saying even mean?" Emma demanded. "That it's not fair, and I should just accept that? Well, I'm not going to. Not this time. Life may not be fair, but I am. I have to go. I've got something I need to do."

♡

"Nico." He felt the touch on his shoulder, reached out an arm to pull Emma close, encountered only a pillow. He emerged slowly from the fog of the dream he'd been having about her, opened his eyes to see Koti standing over him.

He closed his eyes again with a groan. "You're pretty, mate, but you're not who I want to see this morning. Go away."

"You need to see this," his roommate insisted. "Wake up."

"What is it?" Nic asked reluctantly, seeing Koti holding his open laptop. "You shouldn't read your own press, you know. And I'm sure as hell not interested. If you want somebody to tell you that your try was the most magnificent piece of football they've ever seen, ring your wife."

"I'm not joking, Nico," Koti insisted. "Sit up and read this."

Nic realized his seriousness at last. He sat up, a cold dread suddenly filling him. "Is it Zack?" he demanded. "Emma?"

"In a manner of speaking. Not hurt," Koti went on hastily as Nic paled. "Just…just read it, cuz."

"Bloody hell," Nic said when he saw the headline. He continued to curse softly as he finished the article, then looked up at Koti furiously, finally at a loss for words.

"She's touched a nerve with that," his roomie said with sympathy. "Heaps of comments, too."

Nic gave his terse opinion of what everyone could do with their comments.

"Not true, I take it," Koti said.

Nic rubbed a thumb over the bridge of his nose and sighed. "Nah. Not true. But how am I meant to prove it?"

"Somebody's had a whack at it for you," Koti said. He swiveled the laptop around, clicked a few times. "She must be a hell of a girl. That took some nerve."

"Oh, no," Nic groaned. "Emma." A photo of her looking pretty and defiant. And plenty of quotes. She really *had* thrown herself in there.

"Nic and I had a short relationship when we were both very young," he read. "Unfortunately, I wasn't able to let him know at the time that that relationship had resulted in a child. He didn't find out, in fact, until this year, when he was already engaged to Claudia. But as soon as he discovered it—and I mean the day after he discovered it—he was involved. He's acknowledged paternity of our son, he's paid the full maintenance every month since, and he's set up a schedule of visitation which he's kept to. I have no idea why Mrs. Parker would say the things she has. But I want to state for the record that Nic has done everything he should have done, everything he could have done, for his son."

He scrolled down, read the rest. "In response to the allegations of an ongoing relationship between herself and Wilkinson, Ms. Martens responded, 'We were not romantically involved while Nic was engaged to Claudia.' She refused further comment on the subject."

"That's something Kate would do," Koti said when Nic looked up again. "Not many women would come out swinging like that, though, without thinking about what kind of abuse they were letting themselves in for."

"She looks like a fluffy little kitten," Nic said. "But she's got the heart of a lion."

"That's mana," Koti agreed. "Good on her."

"I need to ring her," Nic realized. "This happened, when?" He checked the first article again. "Yesterday. Bloody hell. I need to talk to her."

"Coming down for breakfast?" Koti asked.

"Tell them I'll be down in a minute. I need to do this first."

After ten her time, he realized. "Hi," he said when she answered. "Am I waking you up?"

Her laugh was shaky. "Not exactly. I'm so glad to hear your voice. It's been...a hard day."

"Aw, Emma," he pleaded. "Don't cry. Come on, sweetheart. Don't cry."

"Can't help it," he heard through the sobs. "Give me a minute, OK?"

"Has it really been bad?" he asked when she'd got herself under control again. "Your family?"

"No," she said, her voice a bit sniffly still. "It's all right. Lucy, my parents...Did you see what your dad said?"

"Oh, no," he groaned. "What did he say? Do I want to hear this?"

"It's not like that. It's good. Are you online? Look for it. I'll wait."

A minute of silence, then, "Did you find it?" she asked.

"Yeh. Hang on. I'm reading." Short and sweet, he saw. "'Nic's never been anything but a credit to us,' the elder Wilkinson asserted. 'I trust him to do what's right, because that's how he was raised. I know this is all bollocks, because I know my son. *And* my grandson. I don't know what Claudia's mum's on about, and that's all I have to say.'"

"Well, that's set them right," he said with a smile.

"Yeah," Emma said. "He's on your side, no doubt about that."

"I'd better ring them too, this morning," he said. "Nah, too late now. Tonight, then. What a bloody cock-up. But talking of people who're on my side, what you did? I appreciate it, but you shouldn't have. You don't have to fight my battles."

"Of course I do. What did you expect? I'm not going to let people say those kinds of things about you. Why would Claudia's mum even say that, though? It's all over. I don't get it."

"I don't know," he said, almost as perplexed as she was. "I can't believe that's what Claudia told her. I guess it's how she twisted what she heard. She was so wrapped up in it all—the wedding, the publicity, the whole 'glamour couple' thing. She had a scrapbook, you know? Like you did with Zack, that baby book. But instead, it was full of all Claudia's press clippings, the adverts we did together. She'd got herself so invested. That was her career, being glamorous Claudia's mum. And now, all the World Cup publicity, thinking about what might have been..."

"She needed somebody to blame," Emma finished.

"Reckon she did. At least until Claudia marries a politician, or becomes one herself. Only a matter of time. And I need to say something else," he went on, serious now. "There's nothing in the rest of what she said, either. About my being—whatever the hell it was. 'Popular with the ladies.' I don't spread anything around. I hope you know that."

"I do," she said, and he heard the catch in her voice. "But it helps to have you tell me."

He grimaced. "That's it, isn't it. How do you prove you *didn't* do something? Because if it *were* true, I'd say the same thing, wouldn't I? But it's not. I promise it's not."

"I know it's not," she assured him again. "You don't need to worry about me. I didn't believe it. I never doubted you."

He sat a moment in silence, feeling shaken and humbled by her faith in him, especially given his disastrously poor performance the last time around. He'd been wracking his brain for a way to reassure her, and hadn't been able to come up with a single thing. It was such a relief to know he didn't have to. He wished he knew how to tell her that, but he couldn't think of what to say. The phone just didn't work well enough, he thought in frustration. He needed to see her, and hold her. To be able to show her how he felt.

"How's Zack?" he asked at last, abandoning the attempt to express himself. "Least she didn't name him. Be thankful for small blessings, I guess."

"He doesn't know. I didn't see any point in telling him. It's over, I hope. And oh!" she exclaimed. "I can't believe I haven't said! Congratulations on your win."

He laughed a bit in grateful relief. "Yeh. The win. It *was* nice, at the time."

fallout

♡

School holidays had been shifted about to accommodate the semifinals and final of the World Cup, to Emma's amusement. Only in New Zealand. Zack would be off this week and next, which meant that when Nic came home the following week, they could spend some time with him.

Maybe she could arrange a day or two off herself, she thought as she was hurrying Zack through the Monday morning routine before dropping him at the childcare center. She'd heard from 2nd Hemisphere again, and late November was looking like a real possibility. If Roger was annoyed, well, maybe it didn't matter quite so much, not if she could finally, mercifully look forward to the day she could quit this job.

She'd thought it would be easier to keep working there, now that she was looking at the possibility of leaving. To her surprise, the opposite was true. One foot, it seemed, was already out the door, with the rest of her longing to follow. Especially today. Anything Elizabeth's article hadn't accomplished, she knew, her own picture and defense of Nic would have finished off. She'd be Topic A today, even amongst an office full of engineers.

Well, that was just too bad, she told herself bracingly. Because she needed her paycheck, and so did Zack. She walked into the office at her usual time, headed straight for her desk without saying hello to anyone, and immediately switched on her computer and pulled up the Emirates Building revisions. Let someone take issue with *that.*

Her self-imposed Zone of Isolation did its business, and she worked through the morning undisturbed, until her mobile rang just before noon. Lucy.

"Can you talk?" her sister asked.

"If it's important. I'm trying to get these drawings done."

"You didn't see, then."

"What didn't I see?" Emma was getting alarmed now. "What are you talking about?"

"Oh, man. I hate to tell you, Em. But…go look, online. It's the *Herald* again. And then ring me back."

Nic Wilkinson's double life…Or is it a hat trick?

Emma skimmed down the story, past a photo of a buxom young woman with a glass in her hand. Down to the pertinent paragraph.

> "…I don't usually do this kind of thing," Ms. Soames, a vivacious brunette, said. "But when I first met Nic at post-match party a couple years ago, he needed somebody to talk to. That's all it was, at first. His girlfriend didn't really understand the pressure he was under, he told me. We ended up talking all night. He was so unhappy, and so grateful to have somebody who understood him and was willing to listen. He just wanted to be comforted. He appreciated that so much. And ever since, we've had something really special. He comes to see me whenever the team's in Wellington. I don't think he has anyone in his life who loves him for who he is, not the way I do."

The phone rang again as she read the final lines. Lucy. Of course.

"So did you see it?" her sister asked impatiently.

"Yeah. Hang on." She walked out of the office with her mobile, out into the passage. "Yeah, I saw it."

"I hope you aren't going to start excusing him again," Lucy warned. "Even you can't find a way out of this."

"I don't know what I think," Emma admitted. "Nic just swore to me—just *yesterday*—that he doesn't cheat. And what Claudia's mum said, the other stuff, I *know* that wasn't true. If it'd been up to Nic, Claudia would've come along every time we were together. So if that was a lie, why wouldn't this be?"

"This girl's just lying, then?" Lucy said. "Come *on*, Em. You don't really believe that."

"I don't know what I believe," Emma said, more firmly this time. "And I'm not going to decide until I talk to Nic."

"And when will that be?" Lucy demanded.

"Well, not *now*. It's...almost midnight there. And I have to go back to work. I'll ring him tonight, when I can talk, and he can too. I have to go."

"Em..."

"I have to *go*, Luce."

The thought of walking back into the office, past the desks full of men who would, she knew, have read both stories, made her quail. No hope for it, though. She'd have to face them some-time. Back to the drawings, she told herself. She could do this.

It was even harder than she'd imagined, because there was Ryan standing near her desk, talking to Sean. Her colleague looked at her with some sympathy, but Ryan openly smirked as she walked by. Whatever Nic had said to him, it had kept him quiet these past months, but there was no question he was enjoying her discomfiture now. She ignored him and opened her document again, feeling sick inside.

A trip to the gym at lunchtime helped, as always. At least nobody in her class knew her name, or who she was. She was just another body to them. She'd go back to work, finish the Emirates drawings, go home and ring Nic.

Another call on her mobile, though, soon after she'd got back to her desk, put an end to those plans. Zack's childcare center. Oh, no. Not today.

"Hi, Emma." It was Zoe, the center's director, sounding a bit harassed. "I'm afraid I'll have to ask you to come get Zack."

"Is he ill? What does he have? How bad?"

"He isn't ill," Zoe hastened to say. "It's not that at all. But he's been fighting, and you know that's not on."

"Fighting? Zack?" Emma couldn't have been more surprised. "How? Why?"

"What was in the paper yesterday," Zoe said reluctantly. "And this morning as well, I hear. A couple of the boys said some things. I gather that Zack felt he had to defend his... his father. It would have been better if you'd told me about this, so I could have looked out for it. As it was, I didn't know anything till one of the aides explained it to me. I don't read the *Herald.*"

"Sorry," was all Emma could think of to say. She opened her desk drawer, pulled out her purse, hastily saved her document and began the process of shutting down her computer. "Is he hurt? Is anyone else hurt?"

"Nobody's badly injured," Zoe said. "A few scratches and bruises, that's all. But it's a center policy that we don't allow fighting. He'll have to go home and cool off. I'm talking to the other parents as well. It wasn't unprovoked, and I don't antici-pate serious consequences. But you'll need to impress upon Zack that no matter the provocation, fighting isn't allowed. And he'll need to make some apologies. But we can discuss it more when you bring him in tomorrow. Just now, you have a very unhappy little boy, and I think it's best if you take him home and get him calmed down before we go any further."

Emma was already on her feet, on her way to Roger's desk. He was in the midst of a discussion with one of the project managers, and Emma waited, shifting from one foot to the other, until they'd finished.

Roger didn't cut it short, kept her waiting a good five minutes, turned to her at last. "Yes?"

"I need to leave," she said abruptly. "For the day, that is. I need to collect Zack from childcare. I'll be back in the morning, maybe a bit late."

"You have a deadline," he said sharply.

"Sorry. He can't stay there, and I need to go."

"I could write you up for this," he threatened.

"Why? Because my kid has an emergency?" All the frustrations and injustices of the past two days boiled over into rage. "All right. I'll tell you *I* have an emergency. I have an emergency, and I need to leave. I'll finish the Emirates revisions first thing in the morning. It'll take me two more hours max. It's an *internal* deadline, and you know it."

"You need to watch your tone," he said, bristling.

"And you need to watch yours," she snapped. "Because I have the legal right to use my sickness benefit for myself *or* my child. Anything else is discrimination, and it's illegal. And my son needs me, and I'm leaving."

She left him gaping after her, and didn't look back.

♡

She drove as fast as she dared, cursing the distance, the traffic across the Harbour Bridge, finally pulled into the carpark and hurried into the center's office.

"Hi," she told Zoe distractedly. "I got here as quickly as I could. Where's Zack?"

Zoe looked at her in surprise. "I thought you'd already got him."

"What?" Emma felt the unease rising like a cold tide. "What do you mean?"

"No worries," Zoe hurried to say. "He must have got confused and gone back to the room. I came back in and he wasn't here, so I assumed you'd collected him. Let's go have a look."

Emma tried to calm her racing heart as she walked down the hallway with Zoe. They stuck their heads into the big activity room. Empty.

"The big kids must be playing in the back," Zoe decided.

Another walk out to the enclosed play yard, full of boys and girls running, swinging from overhead bars on the play structure, going down the slides. But no Zack.

"Let me just ask," Zoe said, looking a fraction less calm. Emma kept searching the crowd of moving children, turning to look around her, assuring herself that she'd see her son at any moment.

Zoe came back with the lead teacher, concern clear on both their faces. "Joan says he didn't come back after she took him to the office," Zoe said. "That she told him to wait there for you. Nobody else could have collected him, I take it."

"No," Emma said. Her voice sounded as if it were coming from someplace far away, and the fear was like a tangible being, sitting on her chest, clawing at her.

Zoe nodded, still maintaining her calm demeanor. "Come on back to the office. We'll have the teachers take a look round the center. He can't have gone far. He'll just be hiding, maybe. Afraid he's in trouble, and not wanting to face you. That can happen, you know. We'll find him, I'm sure of it."

Back to the little office again. Zoe ringing the other teachers as Emma fidgeted in her visitor's chair, frantically trying to think of something—anything—she could do to find her son.

She wanted to get up and run through the center searching for him, but she forced herself to stay where she was.

He's here, she assured herself over and over. *He's hiding, and he's here.*

Ten minutes? Fifteen? of Zoe taking calls, before the director turned to Emma with a sigh. "That's everyplace searched, and no sign of him. I'm afraid we have to assume he's left the center. The most likely thing is that he would have walked home. I'll go with you, and we'll drive the route."

"He wouldn't do that, though," Emma protested. "He doesn't have a key, and he wouldn't *do* it."

"Children do funny things when they're upset," Zoe said. "Running home can seem perfectly logical to a six-year-old, even though you or I wouldn't consider it. Let's just have a check for him, before we do anything else."

"Like ring the police, you mean. We need to do that right now. We're wasting time here."

"Let's check first," Zoe coaxed. "He could be sitting outside your front door this minute."

"No," Emma said. Her hands were gripping the arms of the chair, and she'd lost the battle with the fear that consumed her. "No. Ring the police now. They can see if he's at the flat. They can check more quickly than you and I can."

They waited, not talking, after Zoe made the call. Emma stared at the phone on the desk, willing it to ring with the news that the police had found Zack, safe and sound, at home. But it remained resolutely silent.

There were two police officers in the doorway, then, a man and a woman, faces serious under the familiar caps with their checkered bands.

Emma jumped up. "Did they find him?"

"Sorry." For a horrible moment, she thought the man was telling her something else. "We haven't found him yet. Not at your flat, not on the route. We're calling in a search team now."

"Oh, God." Emma put a hand out to the back of the chair, and the female officer came forward.

"Why don't you sit down," she suggested, then turned to Zoe. "Maybe a cup of tea, because we need to ask some questions."

"Who's looking?" Emma asked desperately. "What search team? Who?"

"We've rung the right people," the man assured her. "They're looking now, near the center. Going door to door and asking if anyone's seen him. But in order for us to direct them, we need some answers from you."

Emma answered their questions automatically, pushing down the terror that lurked just below the surface. No, there was nobody else who could have come to collect Zack. Noplace else she could think of that he would have gone. Nobody who knew he was meant to be leaving early.

"Why *was* he leaving early?" the female officer asked.

"He'd been fighting," Emma said.

"Was he unhappy?" the officer asked Zoe. "Upset? Would he have thought he was going to be in trouble?"

"Yes," Zoe confirmed. "Very upset. I don't know about in trouble."

"No," Emma protested. "I mean, yes, he'd have been upset, I'm sure. But he wouldn't have thought…he wouldn't have been worried about what I'd do. I don't think so."

"What about his dad?" the male officer asked. "He wouldn't have collected him? Did you ring him?" he asked Zoe.

"Oh." Zoe looked confused. "No."

"His dad's in England," Emma said. "With the All Blacks. His dad's Nic Wilkinson."

Both officers sat up straighter at that. "But the boy's name isn't Wilkinson," the man said.

"No. Zack has my name."

"Would anyone else know who his dad was?"

"Yes," Emma said, a new wave of cold fear engulfing her. "Anyone who read the *Herald* yesterday could know."

"And come here to kidnap him?" Zoe protested. "We do have precautions. People can't just walk in off the street and abduct a child."

Emma froze at the words. *Kidnap. Abduct.* She turned her anger and fear on Zoe. "Like you had precautions against Zack walking out? How do we know nobody took him? Has anybody asked? *Is* anybody asking?"

"Do you have security cameras?" the male officer asked.

"No," Zoe said. "We've never needed them."

"I need to ring my sister," Emma said. "And Zack's dad. I need to ring Nic."

Ringing Lucy was harder than she could have imagined. Saying the words. *Missing. Gone.* Emma found herself choking on the story.

"Please come," she finally begged. "Please come be with me."

She rang off, looked at the mobile again, then took a breath and picked it up to ring Nic.

Four rings. Five. It was…what was it? Two o'clock? Three? She couldn't think. Then his voice, fuzzy with sleep. "'Lo? Emma? What?"

The tears, then. "Zack," she got out. "He's gone, and they can't…Oh, God, Nic. They can't find him."

"What?"

She explained in halting sentences, her breath coming in shallow gasps. Saying it didn't get any easier. It just made it more real.

"Who's looking? Where?" he demanded. "What are they doing to find him?"

"I don't *know,*" she wailed. "They say they're looking. And they asked about…" She swallowed, forced herself to go on. "About security camera footage. In case somebody…in case somebody took him." She was shaking so hard, she nearly dropped the phone. "Oh, God, Nic. What if somebody took him?"

"Emma," he said sharply. "No. Nobody's going to have taken him. He was in the center, right? Somebody would've had to come in. That won't have happened. For ransom? Not in En Zed. He's walked someplace, is what it is. But why?"

She explained about the fight.

"Shit," he said, his voice shaky with emotion. "Bloody hell. He's run away. Because he thought…Bloody *hell*. But they'll find him. They're going to find him. Let me talk to the police. Is somebody there with you?"

Emma handed the mobile to the female officer, heard her answering Nic's questions about the search team.

"I'll be escorting your…Ms. Martens to her home shortly," the woman said. "If the boy's wandering about, he could arrive home at any time. She'll be more comfortable there as well."

Another pause. "Yeh, I'll be staying with her," she confirmed. A few more sentences, and she handed the phone back to Emma.

"Nic," she said, hugging herself with the arm that wasn't holding the phone, rocking back and forth in distress. "Oh, God. Zack."

"I'm coming back," he said. "I'll find out when I can get a flight. But it takes so bloody *long.*"

"No," she said at once. "Please. I need you to be there. I need to talk to you. I can't have you be gone, not be able to ring you, for more than a *day.* And they'll find him before that, won't they? They have to find him."

"Ring me when you're back at the house, then," he commanded. "Tell me what's happening. I'll check flights, but I won't leave now. Because of course they will. They'll find him."

♡

The next hours were an endless fight against panic. Sitting in the lounge, holding her sister's hand, her body stiff and frozen with fear and dread. Trying to force her thoughts away from images of Zack, of what could be happening to him. Images she couldn't bear to entertain, but couldn't keep from her mind either. Waiting for the phone to ring, and fearing the call at the same time. Lucy ringing their parents, explaining. Leaving Emma periodically to step outside and ring them again, only to tell them that there was still no news of Zack. Waiting, with Nic ringing for updates that she couldn't give him. And, to her surprise, his parents' arrival.

"Oh, darling." Ellen folded Emma in a hug as both women's tears flowed. "Nothing yet?"

"No," Emma got out around the lump in her throat. "No."

"What do you know?" George asked, face set and grim. "What have you heard?"

"Nothing," Emma told him shakily. "They've been out looking. But nothing."

"Who's out looking?" George demanded of the female officer, still sitting patiently in the side chair. "What are they doing?"

"We have a team out," she assured him. "And volunteers as well. They've fanned out from the center, searching."

"Right. I'll be helping with that," he decided. "I'm no bloody use here. Ellen'll stay with you, Emma. Make you a cup of tea or something. But I'm going out to look for Zack."

Emma nodded stiffly. Ellen on one side of her, Lucy on the other. Praying. And waiting.

When the call finally came over the police radio, all four women in the room jumped. Emma's heart was beating so hard, it seemed as if it might actually leap from her chest. She couldn't breathe as she listened to the woman answering. She saw the relieved grin flash on her face, the thumbs-up, and dissolved in racking sobs. She was folded into Ellen's arms, Lucy hugging her from behind, as they all cried together.

"Onopoto Domain," the policewoman said, pushing the button to end the call. "Lost. But they've got him. I'll take you. All of you."

"Nic," Emma got out through her tears. "I need to tell Nic."

"In the car," Lucy said. "Ring him on the way."

♥

He answered on the first ring, as he had every time.

"They found him," she said, her entire body shaking with the release of tension. "They *found* him."

"And?"

"He's OK. He's safe. Thank God. He's safe."

His ragged, indrawn breath, then a choking sound. And another voice on the line.

"Emma? It's Koti. What's happened?"

"He's OK. Zack's OK. They found him at the Domain. We're here now. I see him. Oh, thank God. I'll ring Nic back. Tell him."

Then she was out of the car, running through the darkness to her son. She vaguely registered George, standing in the little group of police around the small figure, before she was pulling Zack into her arms, sinking to the ground with him. Crying, and taking his sobs, his tears, into herself.

"Oh, baby," she finally got out. "I was so *worried.* What were you *doing?* What happened?"

"It was my...s-s-stone," Zack stammered through his tears. "I w-w-wanted to...chuck it back in the sea. But I couldn't *find* it," he wailed. "And I thought you'd be angry, so I tried to...I tried to go home. I just wanted to go *home,*" he sobbed. "But I kept getting loster, and then I got scared because it was dark, and there might be animals, so I hid behind a tree so they couldn't get me. And I was so *scared,* Mum!" He buried his head in her side as he wept.

"Oh, baby." She smoothed his hair again and again with a trembling hand. "What stone, though? Why?"

"The one Nic gave me," Zack said, his lip quivering. He put his hand into his shorts pocket, pulled out the white oval. "From the beach. I had it in my pack. And I wanted to chuck it away."

"But why?"

"Because he doesn't *want* me." The tears, starting again.

"Oh, sweetie. Yes, he does. He *does*. He's been so worried."

"No, he doesn't! Liam and Connor *said!* I said it wasn't true, but they said it was in the paper. They said he did wrong things. I said he didn't, but they said it was news, and news is *true*. And they said…" He broke off, crying hard now. "They said he…he didn't want to be my dad. I told them he gave me an All Black bedroom, and I have a jersey, and *everything!* But they said he didn't want me. They said he *said.*"

"They were wrong," Emma told him fiercely. "Nic's your dad, and he does want you. He loves you, and he wants you. That's *true*."

"But it's *news*," Zack sobbed.

George had been standing nearby with Ellen, but now he squatted on his haunches next to Zack. "Mate," he said. "You know I'm your Grandpa, don't you?"

"Yeh," Zack said doubtfully, his woebegone face turned up to his grandfather's.

"That means I'm your dad's dad. And it means I know your dad. And I can tell you. Your dad wants you, and he loves you." His voice was gruffer now, but he plowed on. "Just as much as I love him, that's how much your dad loves you. And that's heaps."

"Really?" Zack asked uncertainly as he sniffed.

"Really," George assured him. He put out a work-hardened hand to tousle his grandson's hair. "Just that much. I'm his dad, and I know."

"And right now," Emma said, standing up, holding her son to her, feeling weak with relief and emotion, "we need to ring your dad. So he knows you're OK, and he can talk to you himself."

cane toad

♡

Ellen and Lucy fixed dinner while Emma ran Zack a bath and sat with him while he took it. She couldn't bear to leave him, not tonight. He recovered quickly under the influence of warm water and hot soup, and was soon showing his grandparents his Legos and All Blacks poster. Emma's own recovery, though, wasn't nearly as quick. By the time she'd got Zack off to sleep with a story and a song, she didn't think she'd ever been more exhausted in her life. Lucy offered to stay, but Emma knew she needed the quiet, time alone to recover.

She'd thought she had no more tears left, but they'd started again in earnest once she had shut the door behind the others. Tears of remembered terror, of relief and gratitude. For what she'd feared, and for not having to endure it. And in the midst of it, the ring of her mobile. She groped for it. Nic. She took a deep, shaky breath, pushed the button to answer.

"Hi," she said, the tears welling up in seemingly inexhaustible supply. "Aren't you...aren't you at training, or out with the team, or something?"

"You're joking, right?" His voice didn't sound much firmer than her own. "I'm buggered. All I want to do is to be there with the two of you. How's Zack?"

"Asleep at last."

"And how're you?"

She laughed a little, and was amazed to find she still could. It seemed like so long since she had laughed. "Better than I was. That was...it was the worst. For you, too, I know."

"And we haven't even—" He stopped, started over. "There was something else in the *Herald* today. I just heard about it, since...since Zack. Since I found out he was OK. It hardly seemed to matter, when I heard it. But then I started worrying that you'd seen it, and that you would've believed it. Because it isn't true. None of it."

"It isn't?" She wanted so much to believe. Thoughts of Zack had driven everything else from her mind for hours. But once he was safe at home again, the remembrance of the story had seeped back in, a niggling unease at the edges of her consciousness. "I did see it. And I didn't know what to think."

"I wouldn't do that. I *didn't* do that." His voice sounded pinched and tight, far from his usual deep, controlled tone. "I didn't cheat on Claudia, ever. Even with you, however tempted I was. And you know nobody else could've tempted me as much as you. I sure as hell haven't cheated on you."

"Why would she say it, then?"

"*I* don't know," he said in frustration. "Publicity? Her moment in the spotlight? I barely recognize her. Couldn't have told you her name. One of those girls who hangs about when we're celebrating after a match. I won't say she hasn't taken anyone back to her place, any of the younger boys. But I don't do that anymore. I was a fool and lost you once. I wouldn't risk that again."

She was silent, digesting what he'd said, not sure what else to say. What to ask.

"If you need somebody to vouch for me," he went on hurriedly. "My roomie during any of those trips, any of the other boys. Everyone knows who goes after what's on offer, and who doesn't. And I don't. I realize there's no way I can prove it. I'm gone too much. All I can ask you to do is believe that I love you, and I don't want anybody else. I need you to believe that."

"Lucy said that Cooper's is talking about canceling their contract with you," she said slowly. "And that some of the others were considering it too."

"Yeh," he admitted. "Because 'mums buy bread,'" he mimicked savagely. "And I'm not looking good to mums just now. That's what my agent told me. But that doesn't matter. That's the least of it. What matters is you, whether you can still trust me. Don't give up on me, Emma. Please. I need you to believe in me."

"I do," she said, the tears coming again now. "It's going to take a lot more than that for me to give up on you. I believe in you, and I love you."

"Oh, God." She heard the ragged sound of his indrawn breath. "Give me a sec here."

He came back a minute later. Exhaled down the line, a long breath. "All this. I just…I can't do this. I'm buggered. This was too bad, today. It's too hard, being here alone. I need to see both of you, to have you here. Would you come be with me?"

"What? Now?" she faltered. "To London?"

"I need you here. It's not the reputation thing, or the endorsements," he hurried on. "Everyone else I care about, everyone who knows me, my teammates, my family, they'll know what to believe. It's not about that. It's about you and me, and Zack too. I know it's a big ask. It's so far. And I know it'd be a leap of faith. But…can you?"

It was a leap, she realized, that she'd already taken. "If you need me," she promised, "I'll come. I'll bring Zack, and we'll both come."

"You will?" He sounded startled.

"Of course I will. That's what loving someone means, doesn't it? Being there for you, when you need me?"

"I don't deserve you," he said, his voice shaky again. "I know I don't. But I'm going to do my best to try."

"I just don't know...what." She tried to think, but her mind was mush. "How to do it."

"I'll do it," he promised at once. "There's a flight at twelve-thirty tomorrow afternoon. I know that, because it's the one we took. If you can get to the airport tomorrow by ten-thirty, I'll email you the tickets, for you and Zack. Don't be late," he warned her. "Don't leave it to the last minute, not this time. I'll get someone to find a room for you, too, and send you the booking. All you need to do is email me your passport info. Numbers, full names, expiration. You do have them, don't you?" he asked in sudden alarm. "Passports?"

"Yeah. We both do. Tomorrow morning? I'll have to go into work," she realized. "I can't do it on the phone. It's going to take some time to sort all the projects out. And I don't know what Roger will say. I don't know what'll happen."

"Whatever happens, it doesn't matter. Because I'm here for you. You know that."

"I do," she said. "I know. And I'm here for you, too."

♡

Lucy was already asleep when Emma rang.

"What?" her sister asked fuzzily. "What happened? Zack? Something else?"

She was alarmed at Emma's recital. "I know it's been a bad day. It must be hard to even think straight. But...you *believe* him? Enough to drop everything and *go* there? How can you?"

"Because I do," Emma said helplessly. "Because I love him, and he loves me, and I believe that he's telling me the truth. And we need to be together right now."

"He has *no* track record," Lucy reminded her. "OK, I believe that he cares about Zack. That was obvious, today. But he told you once before that he loved you, remember? What did that count for?"

"That was then, and this is now. What has he done, these past months, that's been less than honorable? What?"

"Nothing. That you *know* of," Lucy pointed out.

"And what do I know now?" Emma challenged her. "I know what Claudia's mum said, which wasn't true. He's rung me almost every night he's been gone. *Including* when he was in Wellington. Maybe there are men out there who can hook up with some girl, and then ring their partners a half hour later to say 'I love you,' but Nic isn't one of them. Bottom line," she told her sister. "I can believe the man I love, who's given me absolutely no reason to doubt him these past months, and who *needs* me right now. Or some woman I've never met, making allegations that don't even *sound* like Nic. 'We talked all night?'" she quoted furiously. "'He just wanted to be comforted?' *Nic?* Not bloody likely. If I need proof she doesn't really know him, there it is right there."

"You need to think harder about this," Lucy cautioned. "You need to stop and think it through before you make this kind of decision. You can't just jump in impulsively here, Em, the way you do. I think Nic needs to prove himself."

"And I know he already has. This *isn't* impulsivity. This is trusting my own judgment for once, and trusting Nic too. But the reason I rang you," Emma went on when Lucy would have argued, "is to ask if you'd take Zack for a couple hours tomorrow morning, while I go in to work and get that squared away."

"Get it squared away?" Lucy asked dubiously. "How's that going to go over?"

"Like a lead balloon, I expect," Emma admitted. "But I can't worry about that."

♡

She was at Lucy's door before seven the next morning, holding Zack by the hand.

"You're early," Lucy said with surprise. "I couldn't see how you'd do this, with packing and everything."

"I did everything last night. Everything's in the car, ready to go."

Lucy looked at her more closely. "All night? Did you get any sleep at all?"

"Not much," Emma admitted. "I tried, but I just couldn't. And I was all fired up last night, but now I can't help worrying. You know Roger's going to make it as difficult as possible. He's going to be furious."

"Tough," Lucy said roundly. "Sometimes life happens, and I'd say this is definitely one of those times."

"So you aren't angry with me, still?"

"It's your decision, not mine," Lucy said reluctantly. "I don't want to see you hurt again, that's all. But you know best."

"That's right," Emma said, straightening her shoulders. "I do. I really do." She bent to give Zack a hug and kiss goodbye. "I'll be back on the eight-forty-five ferry," she told him. "And then we'll be off."

"To the airport, right?" Zack asked anxiously. "We're going to be with Nic?"

"We sure are. Just as soon as I go in and get my work figured out, and talk to Roger about needing this week."

♡

It didn't turn out to be as simple as that, however.

"I know it's unexpected," she told Roger as they stood by his desk. She tried to make her tone businesslike instead of pleading. She hated explaining, telling him about her private life, but she couldn't see any way around it. "You will've seen the news. Nic's going through a hard time, and he needs us. And I need to go be with him."

"Go anywhere you like," Roger said, his pale scalp reddening. "But if you leave here today—*again*—don't plan on coming back afterwards. How'm I meant to get all this lot done without you? Are we supposed to tell our clients that your boyfriend *needed* you so he could kick the ball straight? What, you're vitally important to the squad? They can't win without you? It's been clear to me from the start that you can't decide if you're a mum or a CAD operator. Now you've found something else that your feminine sensibilities are telling you to put above your work. What's next, you need to stay home because you have PMT?"

"You're not allowed to say that, and you know it," Emma said angrily. "And I'm not making any such choice. You're the one putting it that way. All right, I don't get the perfect attendance award like you. Because I have a son, and a damn *life*. But I get more done than anyone else, you know I do. And I haven't missed any more time than Sean. Probably less, in fact. I've never used more than my benefit, other than that one year when Zack and I both had flu. We couldn't help that, and we can't help this either. *I've* sure never missed work because I was hungover, unlike plenty of people in this office. You can't say I don't put my work first. And you can't do this."

"I can't give you the sack for walking out on me without notice?" Roger asked incredulously. "Too right I can."

"No." She could feel her hands trembling, her breath coming fast, but she looked Roger straight in the pale blue, protuberant eye. He looked like a cane toad, she decided. An ugly, nasty, warty cane toad. She was shaky with exhaustion and emotion. Furious. And, suddenly, just plain fed up. She'd had enough of Roger, of this place, of this job that sucked her soul dry every single day. "You can't. Because I quit. You've wanted to get rid of me from Day One. Because I'm better than you, and you know it.

You're jealous, and you're a bully, and you're pathetic, and you're a…a lousy manager. So you know what? You can take this job and shove it straight up your ass! Because I *quit!*"

Roger gaped at her, his lips actually quivering with rage. Emma saw Sean stifling a fit of the giggles behind him. Others had turned to gawk as well, now. She stalked to her desk, grabbed the framed photo of Zack. What else did she need from here? Not a damn thing. Let the next unlucky occupant have the bottle of Panadol. Lord knew they'd need it.

"Don't think you'll ever work here again, after this," Roger recovered himself enough to shout across the room. "You come crawling back here asking for your job back, you're going to find it's long gone."

"No worries," Emma snapped with all the contempt she'd stored up during this last long year. "I'm going on to bigger and better things. You're going to be hearing about me someday. I'm going to be somebody. And all you're ever going to be is an asshole."

She grabbed her purse and got out of the building as fast as she could, and made it all the way onto the ferry before she burst into tears.

the man i ought to be

♡

"Nico. You'll want to see this," Nic heard the moment he stepped back into the hotel room. He'd taken advantage of the time apart from the team to take a walk through Green Park, past Buckingham Palace, trying to calm himself, regain his composure.

"What now?" he asked, the fatigue he'd barely shaken enveloping him again at the sight of Koti holding up his laptop. What *else* could happen today? he thought bitterly. Was he going to hear about some girl in Argentina now?

"Nah, mate. This is good news," Koti promised. "C'mon, and I'll show you." He waited impatiently for Nic to pull his shoes off, then went with him into his bedroom, handed him the laptop as he sat down on the bed. "Check out the video," he commanded.

"Claudia. What the *hell*," Nic began, then stopped short at what she was saying. He let the clip play out for its entire short duration, then went back to the beginning, played it again to make sure he'd understood correctly.

She sat there in front of the cameras, poised and beautiful as always, not a hair out of place. And *defended* him.

"Nic was my partner for more than three years," she said. "And no matter what you may have heard elsewhere, he never gave me any reason to doubt his commitment to me, or his fidelity. Yes, he discovered he had a child. And when he did, he took responsibility for his son, financially and otherwise. Our relationship didn't work out, for reasons entirely unrelated to that."

Well, *that* bit wasn't true. Never mind.

"He had no physical relationship with his child's mother while he was involved with me," Claudia was saying now. "He even asked me to come along during any time he spent with the two of them."

Which she hadn't, but never mind that, either. A few more sentences, and her statement was over, the screen going dark again.

"I'd say your troubles are over, mate," Koti said with a satisfied smile. "Well on their way, at least."

"Yeh," Nic said slowly. "Zack and Emma are on their way here, that's the main thing. Arriving late tonight, or early tomorrow, I should say."

"All that way?" Koti asked, startled. "That's dedication."

"Nah. That's Emma. She puts her heart on the line, and the rest of her goes right along with it. If she loves you, she's in, boots and all. No half measures for Emma."

♡

As soon as dinner was over that evening, he was back in the room again. Eight in the morning, Auckland time. Time to ring Claudia.

"Nic." The voice sounded the same as ever. Perfectly under control, beautifully modulated. Not surprised. Not exactly brimming with enthusiasm to talk to him, either.

"Hi, Claud." He stopped, not sure how to go on. "Just wanted to say, thanks," he said lamely. "For what you said. I know it couldn't have been easy."

"You're welcome. But I did it for myself, actually. I couldn't stomach the idea of people being sorry for me. Poor Claudia, being dumped for somebody else. I was never angrier with Mum than after she did that. I've had a few words with her about it. Making me look like your fool."

"You're not that. You were never that. You're nobody's fool. And whatever you say, it was still a decent thing to do, and a tough one, too. And I appreciate it more than I can say."

"And now we're done," she said. "My mum did wrong, and I've done my best to make it right. I wish you well, but there's no reason for us to talk again. Don't ring me, and I won't ring you."

It was one thing to make decisions in the heat of the moment, Emma found. And another thing entirely to think about them in the darkness of an airliner, her entire being dragging with exhaustion. Twenty-five hours in the air, two more spent slumped in a tiny waiting room at LAX between flight legs, Zack sleeping with his head in her lap.

Nic had arranged for them to fly Business Select, to her immense relief, but even fold-flat beds and all the amenities couldn't fix her internal clock, or still the dark thoughts that her racing mind insisted on producing. At least Zack had slept reasonably well, and the seatback movies had kept him entertained as well as a six-year-old could be on a flight that long. But by the time they had endured the endless wait that was British Customs, Emma felt ready to drop where she stood.

"What time is it?" she asked the London cabbie who had loaded their bags into the boot before hopping back into the driver's seat. She smoothed Zack's hair, made sure his seatbelt was fastened.

"Just gone one," he said cheerfully. "Long journey?"

"From New Zealand," she said wryly. "Yeah, pretty long."

He whistled. "Here for the Cup final, are you? No, what am I saying?" he decided. "You two can't be Kiwi rugby fans. No resemblance whatsoever."

"That's what we are, though," she sighed.

"Cor," he said, looking at her in the rearview mirror. "I'd never've thought it."

She was half-asleep herself by the time he pulled up outside the big hotel and pulled her bags out, where they were immediately whisked away by a bellman. *Tip,* Emma fuzzily remembered. She'd been in New Zealand so long, she'd almost forgotten. She wrestled with the unfamiliar notes she'd changed back in the Auckland airport, what seemed like days ago, paid the cabbie and remembered to tip the bellman as well.

At last, they were in their room. She briefly considered a shower for Zack, then gave up and helped him into the big bed in one room of the suite she'd been astonished to find had been reserved for the two of them. She got his clothes off, opened his suitcase with hands that felt like they belonged to somebody else, and pulled on his pajamas. Then dragged herself into the shower, fell into her own wide, white bed, and dropped instantly down into bottomless slumber.

A night's sleep helped. And so did a note from Jenna, pushed under the door sometime before Emma woke up at nine the next morning, inviting the two of them out for an afternoon of sightseeing.

"I'm so glad you've come," the other woman said as she pulled Emma into another warm hug. A substantial English breakfast had done its work in restoring both Emma and Zack to reasonable spirits, a joyous reunion with Harry providing the bonus. The two boys were in the other bedroom of Jenna's suite now, already engrossed in Legos.

"Finn's been keeping me updated on what's been going on, and how hard it's been for Nic," Jenna continued, gesturing Emma to a seat on the couch and sinking down next to her, taking her hand. "It's all so *awful*. Having Zack go missing…" She shuddered. "You poor thing. I can't even imagine how horrible that must have been. And this other, this latest, that's just doubly unfair. Especially because there's nothing to it, Finn says. And he'd know," she insisted. "He says Nic's straight as a die. And as Finn's the same way himself, you can believe him when he says that."

"Thanks," Emma said. She'd teared up yet again at Jenna's warm greeting, her defense of Nic, and now she wiped her eyes with a little laugh. "I appreciate that. But I trust Nic. I just wish there were somebody who *could* say that about him. To the press, I mean. Because he can't defend himself. There's really nothing he can say. 'I didn't do it, honestly?' He can barely say that to *me*, let alone New Zealand."

"But somebody else *did* say that," Jenna said with surprise. "Haven't you heard?"

She went on to explain Claudia's surprise defense, and the effect it had had. "I'm not sure about his endorsements," she finished. "Unfortunately, retractions never have the same sensational effect as revelations, do they? But at least he's got some vindication out of it. And I know you must be dying to see him, after all this. But since it won't be until tonight, we may as well go see the Tower of London, don't you think?"

Emma found herself enjoying the tour despite herself. She'd never been to the U.K.—had never been farther away, since moving to New Zealand, than the Fiji trip and a couple quick visits to Australia—and London was one big distraction.

"Plus, we don't have to worry about not looking right, and getting squished at the pedestrian crossings," Jenna had pointed out cheerfully.

Emma had been glad for the outing, for Zack as much as herself, and for Jenna and the children's company during dinner that evening. But it was with a sense of immense relief that she shut the hotel room door at seven that evening and got Zack into the bath and then in his pajamas. Nic had promised to join them as soon as he'd had his own dinner with the team. He'd only have a couple hours even then, he'd warned her. She didn't care. She just wanted to see him, and hold him.

When the knock finally came, she was sitting on the bed with Zack, reading to him as he held Raffo tight. She jumped at the sound, then dashed to the door and was with him at last. She hadn't realized how much she'd missed the security of his arms until they were around her again and he was holding her tight, kissing her as if he couldn't bear to let her go.

♡

Nic reached out for Zack, standing behind his mother and clutching Raffo. "Come here, mate. Come have a cuddle as well." He pulled Zack into his arms, felt himself tearing up at the feeling of the small body pressed against his own, and stood back, finally, to look at the boy.

"You're all ready for bed, I see," he told him. "What did you think of your first flight to the Northern Hemisphere?"

"Long," Zack said.

"Yeh," Nic had to laugh a bit at that. "Still want to be an All Black? I should warn you, you'd end up doing a fair few of those journeys in the course of a year."

Zack nodded. Still shy with him despite everything, Nic saw.

"Come have a chat with me," he told his son. He looked at Emma, saw the agreement on her face. "Show me where your bed is."

He took a seat on the edge of the bed, waited while Zack climbed up to sit beside him. "Another big bed with heaps of pillows, eh," he said, then paused, not sure how to begin.

"You've heard some things about me, I know, while I've been gone," he told Zack at last. "And I know it's got you a bit confused. That's why I'm so glad you're here with me now, so I can talk it over with you face to face, put things right."

Zack looked up at him doubtfully, held Raffo a bit closer. Nic saw his hands running over the giraffe's little horns, pulling at the ears, and his heart twisted with pain for his boy.

"For example," he went on, "I know you heard somebody say that I didn't want you. That I didn't want you for my son."

Zack had his head bent now. Nic had to lean close to hear the words, spoken so softly. "You prob'ly wanted a different boy. Somebody who didn't cry. Somebody brave, like you."

"Nah, mate," Nic said around the constriction in his throat. "I wanted somebody exactly like you. Somebody who loves footy as much as I do. Somebody who loves his mum enough to ask me for a cricket bat so he can protect her from a Bad Guy. That's the kind of brave boy I want. And that's the kind I've got. Because you're *my* boy. You're my son, and you always will be. And dads always love their sons. That's forever."

Zack turned to him, looked up at him. Tears were streaming down the little face, the eyes, so like Nic's own, staring beseechingly into his. And then Nic was crying too, and pulling Zack to him, holding him close, the way he'd always wanted to.

Emma looked cautiously in at the door. Nic looked up, laughed through the tears that were spilling down his own cheeks now. "Come on in," he told her. "Come join this party. We're just in here having a regular old father-son weepfest."

She came to sit on the other side of Zack, reached out to stroke his head. The boy's sobs eased at last, and Emma got up and went into the bathroom, came out with a handful of tissues. She handed a batch to Nic with a smile, then cleaned Zack up, gave him a hug and kiss.

"OK," she told him gently. "Bedtime. You and Raffo get snuggled down here. Because your dad and I need to have a talk ourselves."

Zack got under the covers obediently, his eyes still red and swollen. He accepted his mother's goodnight kiss, then turned to Nic again.

"Can you kiss me too?" he asked. "Dad?"

♡

"Aw, geez," Nic said, taking a shuddering breath on the bed in Emma's room five minutes later. He'd really let go after that. He'd known it felt good to hold her while she cried. He'd never have guessed that the roles could be reversed. Or that he'd be all right with that.

Emma held him to her, rubbed her hand over his back. "The thing about kids is," she said, "they take your heart. And it's never entirely your own again. A piece of it is always with them, forever."

"Yeh." He blew his nose again. "Yeh. Between you and Zack," he smiled crookedly, "reckon my heart's pretty well parceled out by now. Because I need you both so much. I need you to help me become the man I want to be. The man I ought to be."

"Oh, Nic," she said softly. "Don't you know? You already are."

epilogue

♡

Emma's memories of that World Cup final were, forever afterwards, a mixture of impressions colored by emotion. The monstrous stadium at Twickenham, filled to its capacity of eighty-two thousand with supporters from all nations, but especially, of course, those from South Africa and New Zealand. Singing along to the familiar strains of Aotearoa during the anthems, seeing the commitment on the faces of the men in black jerseys, the silver fern blazing over their hearts as they represented their country tonight. Watching them perform the spectacular Kapa o Pango haka reserved for the most important occasions, their ferocity seeming, as always, completely genuine. The tense battle of the first half, the lead shifting back and forth, hinging on the penalty kicks. And Nic, putting on a complete show under the high ball, pushing the attack, making his lightning decisions before the ball even reached him, seeming as always to be able to see three plays ahead. Spectacular as the last line of All Black defense. Making it all look so easy.

The lessons of the previous week hadn't gone unlearnt, it was clear. Nobody was taking victory for granted tonight. But that didn't mean it was going to come easily for either squad. When the teams trotted into the sheds at the halftime break, the score was a bare 9 to 6 in favor of the All Blacks, and several players on each team had already retired to the blood bin. Whoever won, as Nic had said about that earlier game against the Springboks, the All Blacks would know they'd played a match tomorrow.

The second half was shaping up as more of the same, a tough defensive struggle, the flashes of offensive brilliance limited by the grim determination of both forward packs. And then there were a bare nine minutes to play, and the score was 9 to 11, with the Springboks leading. And, worse, in possession of the ball near the All Black 22, attempting a short kick and recovery that would all but put the game away, if they scored. After all this, Emma thought with her heart in her mouth, all the sweat and pain, all the hours and kilometers in the air, were they going to lose now?

The kick, though, misdelivered in the heat of the moment, going out of touch near the All Black 5, and a lineout awarded to the New Zealand side. The hooker throwing the ball in, the jumpers on both sides being lifted by their teammates to swat at it. The expectancy in the stadium like a physical thing.

A hand on the ball, and it was on its way back to Nic, standing far behind the tryline, with three Springboks coming for him. If one of them got to the ball and went to ground with it, the game would be won, the deficit nearly impossible to make up.

Nic, catching the ball in those sure hands and somehow sending it instantly off his right boot again. Low and hard, to the right of the surging Springboks. Not just kicked out of danger, kicked with pinpoint accuracy to an All Black wing who took it and ran.

Down the pitch, hand to hand, closer and closer to their opponents' tryline. A punishing Springbok tackle 40 meters out. Too punishing, as it turned out. A high tackle, and the All Black fans in the stadium emitting a cheer in unison at the awarding of the penalty kick. So far out, and the angle made it worse, but Hemi had made more difficult kicks, even this night.

The crowd on its feet now. Kiwi hands clasped to mouths, hoping, praying for the kick to go through, fans in green roaring their support for their team. Hemi setting up, his expression intense, calculating angles. And then running to the ball, kicking it away. The cheer that began as the ball seemed certain to sail through, turning to a groan when it bounced off the post and back out onto the field. Drew Callahan, the captain somehow, always, just that fraction more alert than anyone else, catching it on the bounce, less than ten meters out. Charging straight through the defenders, caught by surprise, and across the line. Touching down to score the try, to win the match.

A half second to grasp what had happened, and the stadium erupted. Emma was crying, pulling Zack to her, as, around her, the rest of the players' friends and families did the same. Jenna, holding her sleeping baby, was weeping as well. The two women turned to each other, laughed at each others' tears, then watched as Hemi slotted the conversion through.

The score was 16 to 11, the game was over, and the World Cup was somehow, impossibly, miraculously in All Black hands once again.

They stayed for the awarding of the trophy, of course, and the sight of the team standing on the risers, medals around their necks. The speeches and the confetti, the celebration in the stands. Jenna's baby woke in the middle of it all and began to cry, and the two women looked at each other and smiled.

"Finn would say that's a reminder of what's really important," Jenna said, pulling out a receiving blanket and preparing to feed Lily. "And that we need to get these kids back to the hotel pretty soon."

Emma laughed, still lightheaded with relief and happiness. "You're right. It's after ten, and Lily's not going to be the only one crying, any time now."

Waiting, back at the hotel, for Nic. Putting Zack to bed, then unable to sit still. Turning the TV on, then off again. It was after three by the time she heard the knock, and by then, she had at last fallen asleep. She didn't bother with a dressing gown, just ran to the door and pulled him inside.

She laughed as his arms came around her, as he lifted her off her feet and kissed her, his mouth still tasting of champagne, as he walked her backward toward the bed. He was laughing too, laughing and pulling his shoes off at the same time. And she was pulling off his warmup jacket, his T-shirt, as heedless for once of the bruises and scrapes beneath as he was himself. Falling backward with him on top of her, feeling him pushing up the pink nightdress, for once not managing to take it off her.

One more affirmation. One final celebration. One last World Cup victory.

♡

"Where are we going?" Emma asked as the taxi pulled up outside Paddington Station the next morning. "I thought you said lunch."

"We *are* having lunch. And then we're taking a rail journey."

"What? Why? Zack…"

"Is safe with Jenna and Finn," Nic said firmly. "And they know we'll be gone for a bit."

♡

"This is us," he said as the announcement for Bath came over the loudspeaker and the train pulled slowly into the station. He got up from the seat in the first-class compartment and took her hand.

"Bath? That's the mystery destination?" she asked, her confusion now complete. "Why?"

"It's a surprise," he said. "A good one."

"I've heard of going to Disneyland when you win," she said, stepping down onto the platform. "But Bath is a new one. Are

348

we revisiting your old haunts? Is that it? You want to show me where you played, when you lived in England?" A bit insensitive, but she couldn't really be upset with him. Not any more.

"Yeh," he said. "Less than a kilometer to walk, and it's quite pretty. Ten minutes or so. Want to do that, or get a taxi?"

"Walk," she said immediately, looking at the graceful buildings that prevailed here in the center of the ancient city. "I can do ten minutes, even in heels." And besides, she wanted to walk with him. To hold his hand, hear him talk about the evening before, or be quiet. Either way. Just to be with him.

"So we really *are* revisiting your past," she said at the end of their short journey. "That has to be the stadium."

"Yeh," Nic said. "The Rec."

"I guess it's good to see it, but it's not my favorite thing to remember, you know, that time when you were here."

"And that's exactly why we're doing it," he said. "It's because this is where I came, after I left you. Where I was while you were pregnant with Zack, and while he was a baby too. That's why it seemed like a good idea to bring you here now, today, the way I wish I'd done back then. Full circle, or something like that."

She still didn't understand, but it was obviously important to him. "So what was it like for you?" she asked, walking with him along the long pathway towards a side gate.

"Exciting," he admitted. "Terrifying, sometimes. Lonely. Another Kiwi overseas."

"Not that lonely, I'll bet," she said with a sidelong glance at him. "I remember what you said. You didn't want to be safe. You wanted to have every adventure."

He laughed. "You could be right, at that. Not very delicate of you, referring to my wild younger days. We're meant to just draw a blank over that bit. I *did* settle down, like I told you, once I was back home again. I was just young, and thoughtless, and stupid. As we both know."

They had reached the gate now, and it was being pulled open by a lean older man in coveralls, who greeted Nic with a friendly handshake, and offered the same to Emma on Nic's introduction.

"Cheers, mate," Nic told him. "Frank here was kind enough to agree to let us in today," he told Emma. "He hasn't quite forgotten me, it seems, though it's been a wee while. Course, he won some money on the boys and me, back in the day."

"And this time as well," Frank said. "I had a bit on, on the All Blacks that is. Don't tell them down the pub, but I did at that. You had me worried a couple times, but you won me a bit of beer money in the end, didn't you? Course, the odds weren't good," he acknowledged. "But you can't have everything."

"I knew there was a reason we were working so hard for it," Nic told him with a grin. "Should've guessed, it was your beer money. Glad to see you still have some judgment, even without me here to put you right."

Frank grunted. "You were always a pretty good bloke. For a bloody Kiwi."

"And so were you. For a bloody Pom," Nic returned.

"Quite the love-fest you two have going on," Emma said with a smile.

"Nah, Nic's all right," Frank said. "Always ready with a word. No side to him, that's the main thing. Didn't strut about like he owned the place just because he could kick a ruddy ball."

"Aw, mate," Nic said with another grin. "That's just being a Kiwi, is what that is. You want someone to beat his chest, you gotta look to an Aussie."

Frank grunted out a laugh. "They're not bad blokes either, I have to say. So you doing all right, down there in the Antipodes? They treating you OK?"

"Yeh. Treating me better, now that they've sent me over my best girl. Got a son, too, though he's back in London today."

"Well. Congrats on that. That's a good thing, that is, being a dad. You won't want to stand round here, though, flapping your gums with me. Go do what you've come to do. But mind you come back and find me, when you're done. I'll be in the little office. Wouldn't want you to get locked in."

"Thanks, mate," Nic said. "I owe you one."

"Nah. It's all for love, and all that." Frank winked at Nic, then turned and left them, a shambling figure in his workmen's coveralls.

Nic kept hold of Emma's hand, took her down the long concrete passage, on out through the gate and onto the wide grassy field. She stumbled, her heels sinking into the turf.

"Hang on," she said. "I don't understand why we're going out here, but if we are, I need to take these off." She steadied herself against him in the way he loved as she reached down for first one shoe, then the other. "Oh. Brrr," she complained, her bare toes shrinking against the cold grass.

Nic laughed and swung her up into his arms. "Didn't even think about that. You can see why I need your influence in my life." He carried her down the field, all the way to the 22, marked with its white line. To a spot at dead center, where he gently set her down.

"See here," he told her, gesturing with an arm across the expanse of field ahead of them. "This is where I live, down the back. Where I can see everything that's happening. I have the best view from here of how the game's going. The long view. So I know what I need to do, what my wingers need to do as well."

"OK," she said dubiously. "That's interesting. But..."

"Shush. I'm not finished. I practiced this." He took a breath, started again. "That's my job, to see the game, to decide fast based on what I'm seeing. And then to back myself. Once I decide, I have to be committed. All the way. No hesitation, no turning back."

"And what I'm seeing now," he said, reaching for the shoes she was still holding, dropping them to the turf, then taking both her hands in his and turning her to face him, "taking the long view? Is that I love you, and I want you with me forever."

He let go of one hand, reached inside his jacket pocket and pulled out the small velvet box. Flipped it open with his thumb, then turned it so she could see it. "If you don't like it," he said hurriedly at her silence, "we can take it back. I thought it was pretty. Feminine, like you. But you can choose something else, if you'd rather."

She looked up at him, eyes shining. "Oh, Nic. It's not that. I love it. Of course I love it. It's beautiful. But you need to be sure. For Zack, and for me."

"I'm sure. It's what I told you. I'm in, a hundred percent. It's the only way. We've both done this before, I know. And that's why I know this is right, because it feels so different. It's not that it's the right time, and I don't have a clue what the pluses and minuses are. But I'm in. All the way. All my life. I'm just sorry it's taken so long, that you've had to be alone this long. But you'll never have to be alone again, I promise you that."

"*I'm* not, not really. Sorry, that is," she explained hastily at his look of surprise. "I had some growing up to do, like I told you. I never felt like a full-fledged adult, not for years. And now I do, and that's important. But it's been so *hard* sometimes, to do it by myself. To be the only thing Zack has. To be the only thing *I* have."

"You're not the only thing anymore," he promised. "Because from now on, you have me. Always. And I have you. Because I need you to marry me, you know. Once rugby's through with me and my knees are buggered, I'm going to need a famous knitwear designer to support me in my old age. So really, this is my clever plot."

She smiled mistily up at him. "Well, I can't promise to be famous. Or that I'll even be a knitwear designer, though I hope so. I'm sure going to give it my best shot. But one thing I *can* promise. I'll never chuck your ring in the rubbish, or let you do it either. Because it isn't coming off my finger, ever. Not from now on."

"It's coming off once. Because there's a matching band. And I can't wait to take this off, so I can put that on you."

He took her hand in his, slid the platinum band onto her finger. It looked as gorgeous there as he'd thought it would, he decided in satisfaction, the two side stones in their butterfly setting framing the brilliant two carats of flash in the center.

"And it's time to say yes now, you know," he added gently. "Because you haven't done that yet."

"Oh!" she gasped, then laughed shakily. "Yes. Yes. You know I'm saying yes." She pulled him to her, kissed him. When she drew back again, he saw tears in her eyes.

"No long engagement, OK?" she pleaded. She still hadn't really looked at the ring, he realized. Hadn't looked at anything but him. "No big wedding, no *Woman's World* deal. I don't think you want that anyway. And I know I don't."

"Nah. I hear December's a pretty good month for weddings. What d'you think? We may need to start working on a brother or sister for Zack, too. Because he's going to make a fantastic big brother."

"I'd like that," she agreed, curling against him, one arm around his neck, the other holding tight around his waist. "December, and some baby-making practice too. I'd like to have a little girl someday."

A little girl who looked like her, he thought. Curls, big blue eyes, and all. Wouldn't he be the lucky man then. He leaned down to kiss her again, rubbed his thumb across her cheek. "Know what else I've heard?"

"No, what?" she asked, holding him so close. Next to her heart, where he'd always be, from now on.

"I've heard that you can have a pretty good honeymoon in Fiji. And that it's the best place in the world to make an awesome baby."

The End

Sign up for my new New Release mailing list at www.rosalindjames.com/mail-list to be notified of special pricing on new books, sales, and more.

Turn the page for a Kiwi glossary and a preview of the next book in the series.

a kiwi glossary

A few notes about Maori pronunciation:
- The accent is normally on the first syllable.
- All vowels are pronounced separately.
- All vowels except u have a short vowel sound.
- "wh" is pronounced "f."
- "ng" is pronounced as in "singer," not as in "anger."

ABs: All Blacks

across the Ditch: in Australia (across the Tasman Sea). Or, if you're in Australia, in New Zealand!

advert: commercial

agro: aggravation

air con: air conditioning

All Blacks: National rugby team. Members are selected for every series from amongst the five NZ Super 15 teams. The All Blacks play similarly selected teams from other nations.

ambo: paramedic

Aotearoa: New Zealand (the other official name, meaning "The Land of the Long White Cloud" in Maori)

arvo, this arvo: afternoon

Aussie, Oz: Australia. (An Australian is also an Aussie. Pronounced "Ozzie.")

bach: holiday home (pronounced like "bachelor")

backs: rugby players who aren't in the scrum and do more running, kicking, and ball-carrying—though all players do all jobs and play both offense and defense. Backs tend to be faster and leaner than forwards.

bangers and mash: sausages and potatoes

barrack for: cheer for

bench: counter (kitchen bench)

berko: berserk

Big Smoke: the big city (usually Auckland)

bikkies: cookies

billy-o, like billy-o: like crazy. "I paddled like billy-o and just barely made it through that rapid."

bin, rubbish bin: trash can

bit of a dag: a comedian, a funny guy

bits and bobs: stuff ("be sure you get all your bits and bobs")

blood bin: players leaving field for injury

Blues: Auckland's Super 15 team

bollocks: rubbish, nonsense

boofhead: fool, jerk

booking: reservation

boots and all: full tilt, no holding back

bot, the bot: flu, a bug

Boxing Day: December 26—a holiday

brekkie: breakfast

brilliant: fantastic

bub: baby, small child

buggered: messed up, exhausted

bull's roar: close. "They never came within a bull's roar of winning."

bunk off: duck out, skip (bunk off school)

bust a gut: do your utmost, make a supreme effort

Cake Tin: Wellington's rugby stadium (not the official name, but it looks exactly like a springform pan)

caravan: travel trailer

cardie: a cardigan sweater

chat up: flirt with

chilly bin: ice chest

chips: French fries. (potato chips are "crisps")

chocolate bits: chocolate chips

chocolate fish: pink or white marshmallow coated with milk chocolate, in the shape of a fish. A common treat/reward for kids (and for adults. You often get a chocolate fish on the saucer when you order a mochaccino—a mocha).

choice: fantastic

chokka: full

chooks: chickens

Chrissy: Christmas

chuck out: throw away

chuffed: pleased

collywobbles: nervous tummy, upset stomach

come a greaser: take a bad fall

costume, cossie: swimsuit (female only)

cot: crib (for a baby)

crook: ill

cuddle: hug (give a cuddle)

cuppa: a cup of tea (the universal remedy)

CV: resumé

cyclone: hurricane (Southern Hemisphere)

dairy: corner shop (not just for milk!)

dead: very; e.g., "dead sexy."

dill: fool

do your block: lose your temper

dob in: turn in; report to authorities. Frowned upon.

doco: documentary

doddle: easy. "That'll be a doddle."

dodgy: suspect, low-quality

dogbox: The doghouse—in trouble

dole: unemployment.

dole bludger: somebody who doesn't try to get work and lives off unemployment (which doesn't have a time limit in NZ)

Domain: a good-sized park; often the "official" park of the town.

dressing gown: bathrobe

drongo: fool (Australian, but used sometimes in NZ as well)

drop your gear: take off your clothes

duvet: comforter

earbashing: talking-to, one-sided chat

electric jug: electric teakettle to heat water. Every Kiwi kitchen has one.

En Zed: Pronunciation of NZ. ("Z" is pronounced "Zed.")

ensuite: master bath (a bath in the bedroom).

eye fillet: premium steak (filet mignon)

fair go: a fair chance. Kiwi ideology: everyone deserves a fair go.

fair wound me up: Got me very upset

fantail: small, friendly native bird

farewelled, he'll be farewelled: funeral; he'll have his funeral.

feed, have a feed: meal

first five, first five-eighth: rugby back—does most of the big kicking jobs and is the main director of the backs. Also called the No. 10.

fixtures: playing schedule

fizz, fizzie: soft drink

fizzing: fired up

flaked out: tired

flash: fancy

flat to the boards: at top speed

flat white: most popular NZ coffee. An espresso with milk but no foam.

flattie: roommate

flicks: movies

flying fox: zipline

footpath: sidewalk

footy, football: rugby

forwards: rugby players who make up the scrum and do the most physical battling for position. Tend to be bigger and more heavily muscled than backs.

fossick about: hunt around for something

front up: face the music, show your mettle

garden: yard

get on the piss: get drunk

get stuck in: commit to something

give way: yield

giving him stick, give him some stick about it: teasing, needling

glowworms: larvae of a fly found only in NZ. They shine a light to attract insects. Found in caves or other dark, moist places.

go crook, be crook: go wrong, be ill

go on the turps: get drunk

gobsmacked: astounded

good hiding: beating ("They gave us a good hiding in Dunedin.")

grotty: grungy, badly done up

ground floor: what we call the first floor. The "first floor" is one floor up.

gumboots, gummies: knee-high rubber boots. It rains a lot in New Zealand.

gutted: thoroughly upset

Haast's Eagle: (extinct). Huge native NZ eagle. Ate moa.

haere mai: Maori greeting

haka: ceremonial Maori challenge—done before every All Blacks game

hang on a tick: wait a minute

hard man: the tough guy, the enforcer

hard yakka: hard work (from Australian)

harden up: toughen up. Standard NZ (male) response to (male) complaints: "Harden the f*** up!"

have a bit on: I have placed a bet on [whatever]. Sports gambling and prostitution are both legal in New Zealand.

have a go: try

Have a nosy for…: look around for

head: principal (headmaster)

head down: or head down, bum up. Put your head down. Work hard.

heaps: lots. "Give it heaps."

hei toki: pendant (Maori)

holiday: vacation

honesty box: a small stand put up just off the road with bags of fruit and vegetables and a cash box. Very common in New Zealand.

hooker: rugby position (forward)

hooning around: driving fast, wannabe tough-guy behavior (typically young men)

hoovering: vacuuming (after the brand of vacuum cleaner)

ice block: popsicle

I'll see you right: I'll help you out

in form: performing well (athletically)

it's not on: It's not all right

iwi: tribe (Maori)

jabs: immunizations, shots

jandals: flip-flops. (This word is only used in New Zealand. Jandals and gumboots are the iconic Kiwi footwear.)

jersey: a rugby shirt, or a pullover sweater

joker: a guy. "A good Kiwi joker": a regular guy; a good guy.

journo: journalist

jumper: a heavy pullover sweater

ka pai: going smoothly (Maori).

kapa haka: school singing group (Maori songs/performances. Any student can join, not just Maori.)

karanga: Maori song of welcome (done by a woman)

keeping his/your head down: working hard

kia ora: welcome (Maori, but used commonly)

kilojoules: like calories—measure of food energy

kindy: kindergarten (this is 3- and 4-year-olds)

kit, get your kit off: clothes, take off your clothes

Kiwi: New Zealander OR the bird. If the person, it's capitalized. Not the fruit.

kiwifruit: the fruit. (Never called simply a "kiwi.")

knackered: exhausted

knockout rounds: playoff rounds (quarterfinals, semifinals, final)

koru: ubiquitous spiral Maori symbol of new beginnings, hope

kumara: Maori sweet potato.

ladder: standings (rugby)

littlies: young kids

lock: rugby position (forward)

lollies: candy

lolly: candy or money

lounge: living room

mad as a meat axe: crazy

maintenance: child support

major: "a major." A big deal, a big event

mana: prestige, earned respect, spiritual power

Maori: native people of NZ—though even they arrived relatively recently from elsewhere in Polynesia

marae: Maori meeting house

Marmite: Savory Kiwi yeast-based spread for toast. An acquired taste. (Kiwis swear it tastes different from Vegemite, the Aussie version.)

mate: friend. And yes, fathers call their sons "mate."

metal road: gravel road

Milo: cocoa substitute; hot drink mix

mind: take care of, babysit

moa: (extinct) Any of several species of huge flightless NZ birds. All eaten by the Maori before Europeans arrived.

moko: Maori tattoo

mokopuna: grandchildren

motorway: freeway

mozzie: mosquito; OR a Maori Australian (Maori + Aussie = Mozzie)

muesli: like granola, but unbaked

munted: broken

naff: stupid, unsuitable. "Did you get any naff Chrissy pressies this year?"

nappy: diaper

narked, narky: annoyed

netball: Down-Under version of basketball for women. Played like basketball, but the hoop is a bit narrower, the players wear skirts, and they don't dribble and can't contact each other. It can look fairly tame to an American eye. There are professional netball teams, and it's televised and taken quite seriously.

new caps: new All Blacks—those named to the side for the first time

New World: One of the two major NZ supermarket chains

nibbles: snacks

nick, in good nick: doing well

niggle, niggly: small injury, ache or soreness

no worries: no problem. The Kiwi mantra.

No. 8: rugby position. A forward

not very flash: not feeling well

Nurofen: brand of ibuprofen

nutted out: worked out

OE: Overseas Experience—young people taking a year or two overseas, before or after University.

offload: pass (rugby)

oldies: older people. (or for the elderly, "wrinklies!")

on the front foot: Having the advantage. Vs. on the back foot— at a disadvantage. From rugby.

Op Shop: charity shop, secondhand shop

out on the razzle: out drinking too much, getting crazy

paddock: field (often used for rugby—"out on the paddock")

Pakeha: European-ancestry people (as opposed to Polynesians)

Panadol: over-the-counter painkiller

partner: romantic partner, married or not

patu: Maori club

paua, paua shell: NZ abalone

pavlova (pav): Classic Kiwi Christmas (summer) dessert. Meringue, fresh fruit (often kiwifruit and strawberries) and whipped cream.

pavement: sidewalk (generally on wider city streets)

pear-shaped, going pear-shaped: messed up, when it all goes to Hell

penny dropped: light dawned (figured it out)

people mover: minivan

perve: stare sexually

phone's engaged: phone's busy

piece of piss: easy

pike out: give up, wimp out

piss awful: very bad

piss up: drinking (noun) a piss-up

pissed: drunk

pissed as a fart: very drunk. And yes, this is an actual expression.

play up: act up

playing out of his skin: playing very well

plunger: French Press coffeemaker

PMT: PMS

pohutukawa: native tree; called the "New Zealand Christmas Tree" for its beautiful red blossoms at Christmastime (high summer)

poi: balls of flax on strings that are swung around the head, often to the accompaniment of singing and/or dancing by women. They make rhythmic patterns in the air, and it's very beautiful.

Pom, Pommie: English person

pop: pop over, pop back, pop into the oven, pop out, pop in

possie: position (rugby)

postie: mail carrier

pot plants: potted plants (not what you thought, huh?)

poumanu: greenstone (jade)

prang: accident (with the car)

pressie: present

puckaroo: broken (from Maori)

pudding: dessert

pull your head in: calm down, quit being rowdy

Pumas: Argentina's national rugby team

pushchair: baby stroller

put your hand up: volunteer

put your head down: work hard

rapt: thrilled

rattle your dags: hurry up. From the sound that dried excrement on a sheep's backside makes, when the sheep is running!

red card: penalty for highly dangerous play. The player is sent off for the rest of the game, and the team plays with 14 men.

rellies: relatives

riding the pine: sitting on the bench (as a substitute in a match)

rimu: a New Zealand tree. The wood used to be used for building and flooring, but like all native NZ trees, it was over-logged. Older houses, though, often have rimu floors, and they're beautiful.

Rippa: junior rugby

root: have sex (you DON'T root for a team!)

ropeable: very angry

ropey: off, damaged ("a bit ropey")

rort: ripoff

rough as guts: uncouth

rubbish bin: garbage can

rugby boots: rugby shoes with spikes (sprigs)

Rugby Championship: Contest played each year in the Southern Hemisphere by the national teams of NZ, Australia, South Africa, and Argentina

Rugby World Cup, RWC: World championship, played every four years amongst the top 20 teams in the world

rugged up: dressed warmly

ruru: native owl

Safa: South Africa. Abbreviation only used in NZ.

sammie: sandwich

scoff, scoffing: eating, like "snarfing"

second-five, second five-eighth: rugby back (No. 9). With the first-five, directs the game. Also feeds the scrum and generally collects the ball from the ball carrier at the breakdown and distributes it.

selectors: team of 3 (the head coach is one) who choose players for the All Blacks squad, for every series

serviette: napkin

shag: have sex with. A little rude, but not too bad.

shattered: exhausted

sheds: locker room (rugby)

she'll be right: See "no worries." Everything will work out. The other Kiwi mantra.

shift house: move (house)

shonky: shady (person). "a bit shonky"

shout, your shout, my shout, shout somebody a coffee: buy a round, treat somebody

sickie, throw a sickie: call in sick

sin bin: players sitting out 10-minute penalty in rugby (or, in the case of a red card, the rest of the game)

sink the boot in: kick you when you're down

skint: broke (poor)

skipper: (team) captain. Also called "the Skip."

slag off: speak disparagingly of; disrespect

smack: spank. Smacking kids is illegal in NZ.

smoko: coffee break

snog: kiss; make out with

sorted: taken care of

spa, spa pool: hot tub

sparrow fart: the crack of dawn

speedo: Not the swimsuit! Speedometer. (the swimsuit is called a budgie smuggler—a budgie is a parakeet, LOL.)

spew: vomit

spit the dummy: have a tantrum. (A dummy is a pacifier)

sportsman: athlete

sporty: liking sports

spot on: absolutely correct. "That's spot on. You're spot on."

Springboks, Boks: South African national rugby team

squiz: look. "I was just having a squiz round." "Giz a squiz": Give me a look at that.

stickybeak: nosy person, busybody

stonkered: drunk—a bit stonkered—or exhausted

stoush: bar fight, fight

straight away: right away

strength of it: the truth, the facts. "What's the strength of that?" = "What's the true story on that?"

stroppy: prickly, taking offense easily

stuffed up: messed up

Super 15: Top rugby competition: five teams each from NZ, Australia, South Africa. The New Zealand Super 15 teams are, from north to south: Blues (Auckland), Chiefs (Waikato/

Hamilton), Hurricanes (Wellington), Crusaders (Canterbury/Christchurch), Highlanders (Otago/Dunedin).

supporter: fan (Do NOT say "root for." "To root" is to have (rude) sex!)

suss out: figure out

sweet: dessert

sweet as: great. (also: choice as, angry as, lame as…Meaning "very" whatever. "Mum was angry as that we ate up all the pudding before tea with Nana.")

takahe: ground-dwelling native bird. Like a giant parrot.

takeaway: takeout (food)

tall poppy: arrogant person who puts himself forward or sets himself above others. It is every Kiwi's duty to cut down tall poppies, a job they undertake enthusiastically.

Tangata Whenua: Maori (people of the land)

tapu: sacred (Maori)

Te Papa: the National Museum, in Wellington

tea: dinner (casual meal at home)

tea towel: dishtowel

test match: international rugby match (e.g., an All Blacks game)

throw a wobbly: have a tantrum

tick off: cross off (tick off a list)

ticker: heart. "The boys showed a lot of ticker out there today."

togs: swimsuit (male or female)

torch: flashlight

touch wood: knock on wood (for luck)

track: trail

trainers: athletic shoes

tramping: hiking

transtasman: Australia/New Zealand (the Bledisloe Cup is a transtasman rivalry)

trolley: shopping cart

tucker: food

tui: Native bird

turn to custard: go south, deteriorate

turps, go on the turps: get drunk

Uni: University—or school uniform

up the duff: pregnant. A bit vulgar (like "knocked up")

ute: pickup or SUV

vet: check out

waiata: Maori song

wairua: spirit, soul (Maori). Very important concept.

waka: canoe (Maori)

Wallabies: Australian national rugby team

Warrant of Fitness: certificate of a car's fitness to drive

wedding tackle: the family jewels; a man's genitals

Weet-Bix: ubiquitous breakfast cereal

whaddarya?: I am dubious about your masculinity (meaning "Whaddarya...pussy?")

whakapapa: genealogy (Maori). A critical concept.

whanau: family (Maori). Big whanau: extended family. Small whanau: nuclear family.

wheelie bin: rubbish bin (garbage can) with wheels.

whinge: whine. Contemptuous! Kiwis dislike whingeing. Harden up!

White Ribbon: campaign against domestic violence

wind up: upset (perhaps purposefully). "Their comments were bound to wind him up."

wing: rugby position (back)

Yank: American. Not pejorative.

yellow card: A penalty for dangerous play that sends a player off for 10 minutes to the sin bin. The team plays with 14 men during that time—or even 13, if two are sinbinned.

yonks: ages. "It's been going on for yonks."

Find out what's new at the **ROSALIND JAMES WEBSITE**.
http://www.rosalindjames.com

"Like" my <u>Facebook</u> page at facebook.com/rosalindjames
or follow me on <u>Twitter</u> at twitter.com/RosalindJames5
to learn about giveaways, events, and more.
Want to tell me what you liked, or what I got wrong? I'd love
to hear! You can email me at **Rosalind@rosalindjames.com**

by rosalind james

Cover design by Robin Ludwig Design Inc.,
http://www.gobookcoverdesign.com/

Read on for an excerpt from
Just My Luck
(Escape to New Zealand, Book Five)

fear and loathing in the climbing gym

♡

Nate Torrance knew he was going to fall that day. He just didn't realize how far he'd go.

He reminded himself desperately that he was wearing a safety harness. That the harness was clipped into a rope, that the man on the other end was his most trusted friend, and that he, unlike Nate, actually knew what he was doing. But none of those messages seemed to be reaching Nate's sweating hands.

Now he understood the reason for the bags of chalk many of the other climbers in the gym wore clipped to the back of their harnesses. Too bad he didn't have one. He made the mistake of looking down, and actually felt his arms tremble. He was a good fifteen meters up, with another five or so to go to reach the top. And he didn't think he was going to make it.

"Another foothold for your right foot, just up and to the right."

He heard the voice coming from beside him, looked across in surprise. And there she was, the reason he was up here hanging on so hard it hurt, like a baby monkey clutching its mother's fur. The girl who'd got him into this mess. Her slim, graceful body leaning back a bit in her own harness, dark almond-shaped eyes showing concern, the wide mouth smiling encouragingly. Encouragingly. At *him*.

"Just move your foot," she suggested again. "Don't make your arms do all the work."

Nate told his foot to move, but it refused to obey. In fact, he realized with disgust, he was frozen to this wall, terrified at the thought of the endless space beneath him. All because he'd seen a pretty girl and had had to follow her.

"Lean back in your harness like I am," she instructed now. "Take a rest. The rope will hold you, and your friend will too. You can't fall."

He obeyed the instruction, only because his hands were desperately slippery with sweat by now, his fingers cramping in their unaccustomed position, gripping the ridiculously tiny knobs.

"That's good," she said as he put all his weight on his harness. The relief was immense, and he had to force himself not to sigh with it.

"I'll stay with you," she said. "If you're ready to go down, or if you want to try climbing again."

"I'm good," he said brusquely. "You go on."

She glanced at him in surprise, then something in her expression shifted. She shrugged, grabbed for a handhold, and resumed her swarm up the wall like a…like a cat. If cats climbed walls. Her sleek, dark brown ponytail swayed against the crossed straps of her deep yellow tank top, and her bum looked every bit as choice framed by that harness as it had when he'd first seen it. When he'd followed it up this bloody thing like some kind of hormone-crazed teenager.

"Try something easier first," Mako had cautioned. But oh, no, Nate thought bitterly. He hadn't listened. Mako had been coming to the climbing gym for a month or so now, ever since they'd come back from the World Cup. Had kept talking about his lessons, until Nate had become curious to see what all the fuss was about.

"Mental fitness," Mako had called it when Nate had expressed his surprise. Climbing didn't seem like an obvious choice for his best mate. Mako didn't exactly possess the lean, streamlined body type that predominated in the gym. Not so much of a race-car, Mako. More of a tank.

But when Nate had seen the two women preparing to tackle the toughest-looking wall in the place, the sport had become a whole lot more attractive.

"That climb's dead hard," Mako had cautioned again as Nate clipped into the rope at the base. "I've only done it a couple times myself, and you've only just finished with the training ones. Try something easier first, mate."

"She's doing it," Nate had argued, jerking his chin toward the rope fixed next to them, where the brunette had already begun her graceful, startlingly rapid ascent, belayed by a truly spectacular blonde who hadn't looked at them, her eyes glued to her climbing partner, her hands moving steadily to keep the rope taut.

"She's good, though," Mako had attempted to explain.

"Right," he'd sighed in resignation at Nate's scowl, clipping into the rope himself. "Belay on."

Now, Nate got the point. This was a lot harder than it looked. He glanced down at Mako again, still patiently holding the rope, his broad brown face upturned, and could read the concern there.

"All right?" Mako called, his voice booming in order to be heard in the cavernous space. "Coming down?"

"Nah," Nate answered. "Climbing."

The brunette was already being lowered down as he progressed on with grim determination. Her slim legs were outstretched, the toes of her climbing shoes bouncing lightly off the wall as she passed him on her descent. She glanced across at him, and he tried to feel less like a sullen fool as he pinched his fingers around tiny protrusions, wedged his toes against bits of rock that were surely much too small to hold his weight. But she didn't say anything, which was good. Because Nate knew that he would only have snapped at her again.

♡

"I'm actually driving men away now," Ally told Kristen wryly. She clipped into the top rope with a few quick motions so her friend could attempt the challenging climb, then looked across the gym and saw the two men leaving. "I knew I was out of practice, but this is ridiculous."

"What happened?" Kristen asked. "I'm always so nervous about belaying you right, especially on something that high, I didn't realize what was going on."

"He froze," Ally said briefly. "Tried something too hard for him, got scared. And he's one of those guys who can't handle screwing up, or a woman making a suggestion."

"He was brave, though, to try this climb," Kristen said.

"Or just trying to impress you," Ally said with a smile, determined not to let one encounter with a jerk ruin her day. Too bad. He'd been pretty attractive until he'd opened his mouth and spoiled it. Not handsome, maybe, but he was working the tough, intense thing for all it was worth. And that was one terrific body he had there, muscular and hard. Not overly tall, six foot or so, but wow, was he fit. He'd tried to pull himself up by his arms, that was all. Like so many men, he was used to being able to rely on his upper-body strength, and hadn't followed through with his legs enough. And when you coupled sweaty, nervous hands with the strain of all your body weight hanging from your fingertips, a mind could get out of control fast. She'd seen it often enough.

"I'm not the one he was looking at," Kristen protested. "That was you, all the way."

"Really?" Ally couldn't help feeling a little cheered by that, until she remembered his scowl when she'd tried to help him. "He must not have seen you, then. That's a first. Put that one on your calendar."

"Don't say it like you're jealous," Kristen said. "It isn't really that much of a compliment."

"Right," Ally said dubiously. "Having guys walk into doors and fall down stairs because they're looking at you isn't a compliment."

"They don't want to know me," Kristen explained. "They don't think, gee, I'd sure like to talk to her, she looks so smart and interesting, like they probably do with you. They just want to have sex with me."

She finished clipping in, looked up at the wall assessingly. "I'm not sure I can make it all the way up this one," she said, reaching back for her chalk bag and rubbing her hands together. "But I'll give it a shot."

Ally smiled at her encouragingly. "As soon as you've had enough, just let me know and I'll lower you down," she promised.

"Right." Kristen took another deep breath, let it out with a *whoosh*. "Face the fear," she muttered. "The only failure is the failure to try."

"OK," she said with determination. "Climbing."

Printed in Great Britain
by Amazon

49339231R10232